HORIZON PROTOCOL

A JACKSON STONE THRILLER

BRANDON ELLIS
MAX WOLFE

FIBONACCI
BOOKS

PROLOGUE

The cold would kill them soon. Snow and frigid air stuck to Taylor's bare skin, burning him. If not for the small, crackling fire he and his friends had built in front of him, they would be dead. In the darkness, his breath came out like pillowed smoke. The wind rustled tall Douglas Firs that surrounded him and his friends. He shivered, rubbing his hands to stay warm.

He tilted his head back and winced at the moonlight piercing a cloud. Was the object back? Taylor shivered at the thought. What were those things in the sky? He shook his head. This time it was only the moon, thank God.

A chill breeze blew past, knifing through his underwear. What the hell was he doing with only these on? And one sock? It was soaked, and his toes stung and itched from the pernicious freeze. The snow continued melting by the fire. How could he be so stupid?

He bit his lower lip. What if the metallic spheres returned? He wasn't prepared for this. Who would be? If his phone had worked, he would have snuck a picture. But none of the phones worked since he and his friends spotted those things in the sky.

"Without clothes, we won't last," Taylor said. He narrowed his eyes as the clouds across the moon lit up the night sky and allowed him to see well off into the distance. In front of him, two pairs of bare footprints sank into the snow, leading away from them. His heart beat fast and he crossed his arms tight against his chest. "Where's Lance and Carl?" He scanned the forest. "Did they leave?"

Ken, one of the most experienced climbers in the group, blew into his hands. Shifting from foot to foot, he pulled his arms closer to his body. His blond dreadlocks hung like icicles. "They went to look for help. No boots, no jacket, no shell... They ain't going to make it, man. I told them we should stick together."

Next to him, three men and two women huddled by the flickering fire. In less than four hours, the sun would rise.

Taylor swallowed hard against his dry throat. "They're experienced. They have a chance."

"They'll die of hypothermia," Ken said. "I told them not to go. And you let them."

Taylor could only nod. "I didn't know. Do you think we should have stayed and gotten dressed with those things in the air? Huh? Man, slow your roll. Austin, give Samantha your socks."

About five inches taller than Taylor, Austin was by far the fittest in the group and the youngest at twenty years old. He held his socks over the fire. "I need these."

Taylor pointed a trembling finger at Samantha. "Look at her, will you? She needs them more than you do. Hand them over or I'll take them from you."

Crouched, Samantha ran her arms over her bra. Short, toned and an experienced hiker herself, her long brown hair swung back and forth. Her teeth chattered. "It's okay." She glanced at the sky. "Is that what I think it is? Oh my God. Do you see it? Look up there. I think I see it."

Her friend, Natalie, held her head in her hands. "I don't want to look." Her breaths came fast and choppy. "My mind. I-I can't think. The sound... It's making me nauseous."

Taylor looked where Natalie pointed. "There's nothing there. It's fine. We haven't heard the sound in a while. It's gone. We're going to make it."

Natalie pounded a fist against her leg. "Gone? You think it's gone? We're all going to die!"

Ken patted her on the back. "We're not going to die. We have a fire. We're safe for now. Stay calm."

"Don't you dare tell me to be calm! I should never have come along. Does anyone know how we got here?"

No one answered.

Taylor studied the tree behind him. "We have to get back to camp." He stepped away from the fire and surveyed the night sky. Was the disc-shaped craft still there? The thought of seeing the spheres drove a spike through his brain. The sphere's hum, a vibration unlike anything he'd felt before, caused goosebumps. He curled his fingers into fists, doing his best to stave off the rising anger. The cold ensnared him. "Peter, you think our camp is safe?"

Peter sat perched in a tree, surveying the forest. "Should be. I think we should..."

A crack whipped through the air. Everyone jerked back. Peter dropped from the tree, a broken branch coming down with him. He rubbed his bare legs, his voice weakened by the freeze. "My...back. They're... They're still there. Maybe three? I don't know. The blue lights are gone."

The ground vibrated. Snow drifted from the trees and coated the thicker snow cover below. Taylor stiffened.

Natalie panned around. "Watch out!"

Screams pierced the night.

A beam of light circled Taylor, and he gasped. His legs refused to move, and his body froze.

A wave of warmth spread through him like water veining through the soil.

Pop.

The light disappeared. Taylor lurched forward as if something pushed him. Another light surrounded him. He rose off the snow, his feet dangling, his body rigid. He tried throating a groan. His body rose higher and higher, encased in a glow, and he lifted from the ground as high as the roof of a house.

Everyone stood stunned, unable to move or help.

Then the light vanished. The force holding him let go. As he plummeted, his arms and legs flailed, and he landed on his side, his ribs crunching under his weight. The warmth inside him faded as the snow's freeze kicked in and clung to his skin. A light glared into his eyes. He twisted on his side.

The hum began again. Louder.

Taylor clenched his jaw, his palms over his ears. All at once, his perception shifted to forgotten memories—his mom and dad in the shadows, berating him, telling him they'd have a better life if he didn't exist. His dog bit his leg, him punching at the snarling beast. Throngs of skeletons pushing through the snow, their fingers like spikes.

He forced out a whisper. "This...isn't real."

The sapphire light brightened. A yell. Fear slithered through Taylor like a burrowing snake. A tingle veered down his spine, through his arms, and into his legs. He touched his throat, his scream now high-pitched. His throat ached, and he pushed off the ground, forcing himself to move and to stop the guttural cries from deep within.

The light shifted from blue to white. The snow crunched underfoot as Taylor ran. The hum intensified. Heart pounding, Taylor and three others dashed through the forest, too afraid to look behind him. Still, the light blanketed them, and the snow and rocks shined.

The three in front of him screamed. Austin picked up speed and disappeared behind a thick copse of trees.

"Where are you going?" Taylor asked, his voice only paper-thin.

Another screeching sound. *Too loud to think*, he thought. Taylor plugged his ears with his index fingers. "Stop! Stop!" A tsunami of terror washed over him. "Leave us...alone."

In front of him flashed images of war. Explosions thundered. Guns fired. Men and women twitched back and forth, filled with bullets. Blood spurted.

The city of Austin, Texas.

A nuclear fire.

Gone.

He blinked several times, and the images vanished. These couldn't be memories. He'd never been in a war. But they were as real as the snow beneath his feet.

Something blunt hit his shoulder, knocking him off his feet. He twirled and landed on his knees. Snow reached up to his mid-thigh.

Get away from us, he thought.

As if on command, the light shifted from him, but the hum intensified and pushed Taylor over. His face sunk into the snow, the white powder-like frozen thumbtacks sticking to his face. He shrieked, fighting against the noise, and stumbled forward.

The blue light returned and dowsed him, and through it, the snowflakes came down harder.

His friends? Where were they? The plan was for him to lead this hike, but he'd discovered a frozen hell. At this hour, they should be asleep, comfortable, snoring; excited for the next day. What a failure he'd been.

How did everything go wrong? How did this light, the odd hovering and darting spheres, and the hum, cause them to freak out like this? Even an internationally certified mountain leader, trained to operate in the most rugged terrain, had lost his mind.

Natalie zigzagged farther from him. The light surrounded her. She stopped and squeezed her blonde hair as if attempting to pull it out. A low scream slid past her lips and filled the forest. Her chin pointed at the light. Then she was silent. She fell to her knees and crumpled to the ground.

And so did he.

1

STONE

TWO DAYS LATER

Jackson Stone clicked his mouse and rested his elbow on the chair's armrest. Only the colored lights from his three screens and a keyboard lit the small, compact office. Empty file cabinets lined one wall. His pride and joy, a baseball bat with Jackie Robinson's autograph, sat enclosed in a glass case attached to his office wall across from the cabinets. To the side of it, Jackson kept his lone baseball with Robinson's signature in a clear plastic box underneath the bat with a letter of authenticity.

He lived and worked at Polaris, along with hundreds of other personnel and enough weapons to overthrow a small city. The agency did its work behind the scenes, and Jackson was part of that effort working as an analyst. Did aliens exist? Did ancient artifacts have unknown powers? No. But Jackson was there to make sure.

On three screens, he studied what appeared to be a "Grey", one of the many species of extraterrestrials people claimed to have seen. As a forensic analyst, Jackson's job was to verify videos like this one, though his training involved over a thousand hours of combat training.

In the 1080p video, the being appeared to be an actual alien. He'd used his arsenal of advanced AI and digital thumbprint analysis applications to scan for deepfakes, some of them stolen from the Department of Defense. Neither detected algorithms controlling movements nor body swaps superimposed on the creature.

The Grey stood in a room across from a person in a yellow hazmat suit. With large, almond-shaped black eyes, the creature's enlarged head was held on a thin, spindly neck the size of Jackson's wrist. Despite that, the creature's head remained stable. How did it not fall? If it were a suit, how could anyone's head fit through the small neck?

Long, thin arms hung at its sides, and Jackson counted three fingers and a thumb.

Sure looks good, this one, Jackson thought. His childhood was littered with pictures of extraterrestrial beings. He'd watched "Close Encounters of the Third Kind" dozens of times, and he spent his youth listening to Coast to Coast AM with Art Bell and later George Noory. Jackson read the likes of Whitley Strieber, Jacques Vallee, and many others in Ufology. Was there something out there? Either this was the biggest psychological operation in human history, or something so extraordinary was taking place that the governments of the world were colluding to keep it a secret.

Jackson rubbed his eyes and resumed work. The man in the hazmat suit sat on a chair almost too black to show in the dark video. The alien copied him, sitting on another chair, his movements like a dolphin diving into the ocean. Its ease, poise, and grace were distinct from a human.

This looks real. What am I missing?

The Grey turned its head. A tall flatscreen TV blinked

on behind it. Metallic glyphs formed on the screen's black background. At first, the symbols were hazy objects and became more clear as if emerging out of the water. Then they solidified.

Hieroglyphic symbols, similar to Sumerian and Egyptian hieroglyphs, appeared. A new language, one he'd not seen before.

He scrutinized the symbol's mathematical shapes and patterns. A programmer could create a language like this.

When the famous "Alien Autopsy" video leaked, he couldn't believe his eyes. Immediately, he saw it for what it was: a complex forgery. But he doubted himself. The motivation for making a video was obvious enough. The money must have been pretty good, a solid return on investment. But at what cost? No one would believe any such video again. They would think back and remind themselves to be vigilant and skeptical a second time. Was that the goal?

He knocked his knuckles against the mahogany leather desk, pinching his lips together in a straight line. A memory surfaced.

His father dressed in a purple robe and a silver sash hung at his waist. They stood in their unkempt front yard, and Dad pointed at the night sky. "Stay focused, Son. It's right above us."

Jackson was only nine years old. He smiled and played his part and said what his father wanted him to say. Deep down, he hid his real thoughts. There was nothing in the sky but stars, planets, and the occasional satellite. But every star could be something else, sometimes. And if he looked at them just right, he could swear he saw them move.

His parents claimed the earth's energy would attune him to the spiritual gifts associated with the "Third Eye". But he only had two eyes, and it never made sense to him. They promised he would see. See what? See what they saw? Sometimes he would draw little cartoons and pretend he was living with different parents.

One night, his father said to stay in a tent. It was cold, and his parents would only give him a thin sheet. When he went to bed, he wrapped himself like a burrito, tossing and turning, hoping he would pass whatever test they were giving him this time. When his eyes became heavy, the night went still, and an owl's screech pierced the night.

A branch cracked. Movement. He eyed the tent wall, his eyes widening. He sat up, his palms against the dirt. "Who's there?"

He gasped as a light blasted his tent. Lying down and curling into a ball, his eyes darted left and right. "Dad? Mom? " For a second, a silhouette appeared on one side of the tent. At the seam, someone had ripped a tiny gap. He peered out. Someone crept along wearing funny shoes and held two flashlights. The lights flicked off and then silence. He didn't sleep for the rest of the night.

The next morning, he walked into his house, groggy-eyed, and was absolutely convinced someone had come upon his tent last night by accident. He rubbed his eyes when he sat at the dining table.

His mom walked in from the living room with his dad by her side. A smile across her face and she wrapped her arm around him. "Did you see them, honey?"

Jackson shrugged.

She stiffened and stepped away. "Did you sleep?"

"No, Mom. It was too cold."

"Are you sure?"

"I'm sure."

She bit her lip. "I could have sworn I saw something last night from the window. It looked like...."

"What do you mean by that shrug? I saw two lights around your tent," his father said.

"I saw the lights." Jackson bit his tongue. He wanted to tell them the truth, but making Mom happy made him happy. She wasn't nice when she was angry. Neither was Dad.

A light blinked across the middle screen in front of him, bringing him back to the work at hand. "1:36. Play."

There it was. Less than a second. A flicker. In what should be a single stream image from a video camera, a signal interfered. A glitch. Running diagnostics, the system shot back several error codes. In one of them, he found frame filters disabled, which when enabled, showed where separate frames might merge into one. Normally undetectable, nothing was perfect, and the computer stations here at Polaris were a decade ahead of what the market offered.

He saved the file and restarted the application. The errors vanished, and when he checked the logs, the file was empty, all the logs missing or perhaps deleted.

What's that about?

After loading the file, he found his place and paused it. The alien was inches from sitting on a child-sized stool. He pinched the screen and zoomed in on the Grey's arm. "Lighten shade. Enhance contrast. Stop transition two, keep transition one. Play."

As the creature's right arm stood stationary in one frame, its right arm also drew back when the alien sat. Frame by frame, all appeared normal. All except for small, almost imperceptible details. The scene didn't flow right, its movements too smooth. Whoever made this video used high-end commercial software, normally reserved for movie studios.

Whoever wore the alien suit had to have been a child or a small person.

With his fingers around his mouse, he moved the cursor to the left monitor and brought up a secure browser. He searched for Hollywood special effects artists. Where was the pattern?

Thousands of images pulled up.

He scrolled down for similar prosthetics. Too many. He narrowed the search to horror and science fiction films.

Hundreds of names appeared, more than he imagined still existed in the age of digital special effects. Those people listed were all searching for employment. The era of practical special effects would soon be over once they perfected CGI and artificial intelligence caught up. Polaris had shown Jackson videos so realistic, he would have bet his life they were real.

The forged videos included people playing in cornfields. President Lincoln as Captain James T. Kirk. Fake newscasts about the clouds raining actual cats and dogs. Renderings of cartoon images transformed into real-looking objects. Videos so absurd, he couldn't stop laughing. But they all proved a point. Polaris could make hyper-realistic videos about anything they wanted and weaponize them.

Movie theaters had almost disappeared, and many studios vanished along the way unless they could land a gig on one of the many streaming services. But of those studios that survived, how many were in a dire financial crisis? More than he could count. But one studio struck his eye. The owner filed for bankruptcy when his film "Moonbeam" failed to elicit interest with Amazon or Netflix.

But good luck getting a Netflix deal. That's where the real actors were going now.

Jackson had never heard of "Moonbeam," and he liked

sci-fi movies—usually. But some Triple-A video games had better CGI than what Hollywood produced in their movie studios.

For a man employed by an intelligence agency, Jackson had seen the best. People marveled at the latest gimmick, but from what he saw, the real technology was five or six years ahead. Computer-generated faces were still cartoonish or rubbery. Still, it was hard not to love giant Steven Spielberg dinosaurs.

When he was small, his parents forbade him from watching movies. They owned a TV, one with two rabbit ear antennas on top. The knobs didn't work, and sometimes it would smell funny. They let him watch *Gilligan's Island* and *Leave It to Beaver* and the occasional Western. When Jackson went to bed, he'd listen as his parents watched the news and talked about the future.

And yet here he was, determining if this Grey was real or not. If the aliens existed, the government would never allow a video to be leaked. Would they?

He thought back to the alien autopsy video popularized in 1995 and seen by millions on Fox. In 2006, Ray Santilli and fellow producer Gary Schoefield finally admitted their film was a "reconstruction". The Grey in the video used the same type of body, and it matched the way Moonbeam's artist liked to create special effects.

He scrolled down the screen.

A woman. Hair cut short. Thin, manicured eyebrows. Thin nose. A little butch. What about her financial situation? Filed for Chapter 7 bankruptcy. Liquidation.

Her peers applauded her, but the details didn't add up. A few spoke about how they couldn't believe she hadn't been hired for blockbuster films. It's not what you know, but who you know.

Rebekah Shaner. Makeup artist. Prosthetics expert. Her credits included a handful of sci-fi B-movies. "Alien Dimension". "The Portal". The trailers on YouTube were the standard fare. Bad CGI and amateur acting by people who attended the gym regularly.

He leaned in as he surfed YouTube. Who else would make alien videos? Amateurs?

There. An unreleased movie trailer on YouTube. The name of the video was "Work in Progress" with a series of random characters at the end.

At the end of the trailer, the credits included Rebekah's name. The Grey in her movie, who sat across from the man in the hazmat suit, was nearly identical. The eye design looked a little less developed in this trailer than the one on the video.

He swallowed hard when he read the next article. Missing for the last two years, Rebekah was last seen on Highway 101, heading toward Northern California in her 2004 copper Chevy Cavalier. The alien video was dated two months after her disappearance.

Back to YouTube.

He pulled up her name and clicked on an image and a video documentary entitled "Behind the Scenes". The sword and sorcery film focused on the exploits of Genghis Khan, set in 1237. Another B-movie. Were those supposed to be mountain trolls attacking a village? The men wearing high-heeled boots and paper-plastic costumes roared and brandished clubs. Slobber rolled from their mouths like bulldogs, and their bodies were as real as any he'd ever seen. Not bad. In fact, better than not bad. Excellent.

And another Rebekah Shaner video, her name listed in the credits.

He downloaded all of her work, put it through AI match systems, and waited.

Whoever made the alien video must have made bank. At some point, a film this good would be picked up by some company and shown to the world without comment. Would anyone believe a real extraterrestrial video at this point? Maybe. And maybe that was the intent.

Her disappearance lined up with the video's release. Where was she? Who was she working for now, and why? He hunkered down and dug deeper.

A small white window appeared on the screen with a flashing phone. It was his handler, a man with a graying beard, hazel eyes, and wrinkles advertising his age. His hair receded up to the crown of his head. His name was Director Patrick Hill, and Jackson owed him his life.

"Find anything on the video, yet?" Director Hill asked.

"Yes, sir. I believe I did."

"Care to share?"

"Yes, sir. Open source intel leads me to believe a woman named Rebekah Shaner created the video with readily available software. She's in the movie business and neck-deep in debt. My guess is that someone hired her out for a quick buck. It's one of the best fakes I've seen, but I think internet sleuths would nail her down fast."

Director Hill waited. "What's your opinion on its intent?"

"If enough people see forgeries like this, it further distances the topic from normal conversation. As a Psyop, we've seen this done frequently in the past."

"Anything else?" he asked, hesitating.

He thought for a moment. "A program I used gave several errors, and when I checked the file history and logs, they were missing. Maybe someone loaded the video with some kind of hidden malware, but I don't understand why my computer wouldn't pick that up or why Polaris would allow anything like that inside its walls."

Director Hill's voice filled with joy. "Congratulations."

"I passed?"

"With flying colors. I'll expect your report within the...." The comm muted. "Stone, I need you in my office in five. Something's come up."

Jackson stood. "Yes, sir. On my way."

2

STONE

J ackson ran his hands through his hair as he turned the corner. Marching forward, he caught Maggie out of the corner of his eye typing a report, her blonde hair pulled back in a ponytail. In the lobby, the white walls made the room feel bigger. The wall sconces let off soft light to calm the area. More hallways branched off away from the lobby.

"Good afternoon, Mr. Stone. Coffee?" she asked.

He stopped in front of her desk. "No thanks. How's your sister?"

"Good. She should be leaving the hospital on Monday."

"I'm happy to hear that. Is Director Hill in his office?"

"Yes. I'll let him know you're here."

"Thank you."

Before he could sit, she buzzed Director Hill and sent Jackson on his way.

Up ahead, on both sides of a bulletproof glass door, two men stood ready. They wore suits without ties, and Jackson could make out an outline of Kevlar vests underneath their clothing. Former Navy SEALs or Delta, no doubt, patrolling the halls of Polaris and maintaining security.

They nodded to Jackson as he entered into a long corridor with doors on either side. Inside the main conference room, a United States flag stood in the corner, flanked by plaques and awards. Men and women worked at their laptops, but most of their attention remained transfixed on a massive screen displaying an infrared map. Next to it, members of Polaris' elite Scorpion commando team pointed at mountains and forests.

A lithe uniformed man in his late twenties said, "He's waiting for you."

Jackson knocked on Hill's door and his boss told him to enter. Director Hill's office was always immaculate and, other than an antique globe and a potted cactus, it was free of décor. His desk held two monitors, and as Jackson entered, he shut them off.

Director Hill was Jackson's handler, a man of many talents and as deadly as a viper. His eyes held years of hardship and violence, and his white hair and deep wrinkles verified him as a man who led a stressful life. Now sitting behind a desk, his days of adventure were behind him.

"Jackson, come in. Good to see you," Director Hill said with a slight Southern accent.

Jackson shook his hand. "Thank you, sir."

"How are you feeling?"

"Great, sir. Thank you for asking. Doctor Gonzalez said he's never seen an organ recipient have so few complications."

"Polaris knows more about the medical field than most countries. But by now, you're aware of our technological edge." Hill motioned to a coffee machine. A handful of generic mugs surrounded it. "Coffee?"

"My stomach is a little upset," Jackson said. "Thank you, though."

He sat and clasped his hands. "Take a seat." After Jackson sat, he said, "Tell me, how have you been sleeping?"

Jackson looked away for a moment. "I'm managing."

"You know, Doctor Gonzalez can prescribe something."

"I tried a few medications, but they left me feeling groggy."

"I understand. Don't take them myself, though I would love to get a good night's sleep for once. I need your opinion on something."

"Any way I can be of assistance, sir."

Hill opened a desk drawer and pulled out a USB stick. He inserted it into a slot on the laptop and turned the monitor. Now they could see the screen.

A satellite image appeared, chopped with static. The time and date were blurred. In the images, small dots ran across snowy terrain. The dots disappeared into a heavy tree line. Three bursts of searing white light hit in rhythmic succession, lighting the area, bright like helicopter searchlights. The static intensified. On the monitor, the trees turned into one bright line.

"Last night, one of our satellites picked up a strange burst of light between Frog Lake and Lower Twin Lake, thirty-four miles south of Mount Hood in Oregon."

Jackson squinted his eyes. "When was this taken?"

"Within the last 24 hours."

Polaris rarely gave full details, preferring to keep information on a need-to-know basis as every intelligence service does. Jackson had spent months training with firearms, martial arts, and the art of deception. But with missions under his belt, no doubt he'd learn more about what Polaris kept secret. What other clearances existed within the organization?

A burst of light, highlighted in the black and white image, showed long light trails like rippling water, which fanned outward above a hill populated with sparse trees. At an angle, the tree's shadows bent in a southwestern direction. A small tent sat in the snow. Upon closer inspection, Jackson recognized it as a tent. A light was positioned directly above it. Hill clicked a button, and Jackson watched screen captures of lights against the ground. The last image was black.

Jackson pinched his bottom lip, his brow furrowed. "Is there any more video, sir?"

"We only have these, and we lost a veteran agent acquiring them. He was a good man."

Working for Polaris was high risk. He'd already written his will, but after losing everything in a plane crash and working for Polaris, he didn't have much to give. "I'm sorry to hear that, sir." Jackson paused. "What happened to him?"

Without hesitating, Director Hill said, "He was sloppy."

Luckily, Jackson only worked in an office. "Sir, in the video with that much light output, I'm reminded of floodlights aiming down from a plane."

"FAA records indicate no flights took place during the event."

"These ripples.... Light projectors can be programmed to create graphically generated light ripples, mimicking water. Maybe a drone?"

Director Hill shook his head. "Look at the amount of light produced. A drone capable of producing that much light would be detected by radar. It would have been picked up."

"Where is this?" Jackson asked.

"Close to the town of Hood River, Oregon. And by Fort Hood Army base."

He blinked, his face tightening. "Radar would have definitely picked something up. What about weapons testing or military experiments? Do we have intel suggesting the military might have been conducting experiments that particular night?"

"Polaris has many military contacts. We ran it by them, but as far as we know, they were not. Again, radar would have picked up something."

"Stealth?" Jackson asked.

"Unlikely, but it can't be ruled out." Hill brought up an image on the screen; heavy light over a tent, light without a ripple. "Look closer."

Jackson leaned in. "I don't see the light source reflecting off the ice. The date and time are blurred. The moon is waning." He didn't take his eyes off the screen.

Hill poured himself a coffee and sat back down.

"That does smell good, sir."

"*Good?*" Director Hill laughed. "Stone, that coffee you will never taste anywhere else in the world. Do not let a small thing like an upset stomach deprive you of Columbia's *best*. Please, help yourself."

"Thank you, sir." As Jackson grabbed a cup, he asked, "What about light pillars?"

"Explain."

"An atmospheric optical phenomenon that creates a vertical beam of light above or below a light source. They are sometimes created by the light reflecting from ice crystals suspended in the atmosphere. What was the weather like?"

Hill grinned. "It was a cloudless evening."

He slunk back into his chair. "It's not meteors or bolides.

That bright and low, the forest would be devastated." He gave Hill a look.

"The forest is still intact, and from what we know, unharmed." He sat straighter, hands together in a steeple.

"No chemical plants nearby? Explosions from factories?"

"We checked. Nothing."

"Sir, it's not a lens flare. And I don't see how it could be a solar flare by chance reflecting off the International Space Station or a satellite, either. Anything mentioned on radio traffic?"

"Negative. We keep a close watch on communication channels near military bases."

"What about NORAD? Do we know if they picked up anything?"

"They did not." Hill slowly went through the pictures again, pausing at each one to give Jackson time to study them. "So after all that, give me your professional opinion on what you think it is."

"Okay." His eyes were like cold steel upon the monitor. "Iridium flares from satellites wouldn't give off that much light. Weapon fire, not an option. Nearby transformer pole explosions would brighten and cool down, lowering the light output. The light on the screen maintained its intensity." Jackson shook his head. "I'm sorry, sir, but I'm running out of theories."

"So are we."

"Maybe the question I should ask is do you know what we're looking at, sir?" Jackson asked. "I know we keep information compartmentalized, but is there something else I need to know?"

Hill locked eyes with him but didn't say a word.

The screen facing Jackson switched from an image to a conferencing window. The laptop camera showed Hill's face, but two other conferencing squares were blacked out. Hill pursed his lips. "Do you think he's ready?"

Jackson suspected others were listening and watching his responses, but he would have liked to have been told. He swallowed a tinge of anger.

One man said in a slight French accent, "I vote yes."

Another, her high-class American accent proper and flat, said, "He's not ready. He has not yet shown the committee standards we require. My vote is a strong no."

Director Hill sneered. "Noted."

The last person to speak was quiet at first, and everyone waited patiently.

The synthetic voice was modulated to sound like a machine. "Jackson Stone."

Jackson looked at Director Hill. *Was this a sir or a ma'am?* He received a shrug from his boss for an answer.

"Sir?"

The voice asked, "Do you remember the oath you took when you first joined us?"

Duty to Liberty. Duty to Secrecy. Duty to Polaris. "Yes, sir."

"My vote is yes," the mechanical voice said. "But the vote must be unanimous."

The woman asked, "Which do you enjoy more, caviar or bullets?"

Jackson sat up straight. What kind of question was that? "Caviar."

A pause. "Interesting," she said. "I vote in the affirmative."

Director Hill cleared his throat. "503656285. 541382551. 222999135." He squared his shoulders. "Stone, are you ready to be a field agent?"

He gripped the side of his chair. A field agent. This quickly? "Excuse me, sir?" He wasn't hired to be a field agent.

His training was relentless. Hard-won. Dangerous. But it was only training.

Polaris enlisted Jackson to do what he did best: investigate videos and audio recordings as he did in his previous life as an investigator—his real passion. A field agent? There was much more to learn.

Jackson's palms began to sweat. "I'm much more experienced at what I'm doing now, sir. Isn't there someone else better suited for the job?"

His boss leaned back and crossed his legs. "We selected you for a reason. Do not turn down this opportunity. Only fools think they're ready to be a field agent. Your skillset is exactly the reason I'm propositioning you for this job. Besides, you admitted yourself that you're feeling well after your heart transplant surgery."

Jackson's face hardened into a grimace. "When do I leave?"

Director Hill opened another drawer, pulled out a long envelope, and slapped it on the desk.

"What's this, sir?" Jackson asked.

"Your plane ticket. Your bags are already packed."

Jackson opened it and stared at the ticket, his stomach now a sack of bricks. "Is there anything else I should know?"

"You have a partner."

Dr. Alabama Wren looked at the clock. On most days, she stayed home. Polaris had purchased her a house in a secluded cul-de-sac. With cameras and sensors and alarms and her two Dobermans, she felt secure. At least, as secure as she could be in the civilian world. She left nothing to chance and bought her food over the web and never from the same place. Her mailing address was a PO Box under an assumed name. Paranoia wasn't a word used by her agency or by her. She preferred "prepared".

Alabama turned heads in public. Growing up, her friends called her *Blaze* for her red hair and cute smile. She could have had any man she wanted but chose only the best. So far, Polaris hadn't asked her to sleep with anyone for a mission, but if asked, she would.

Mission first, mission last.

She wore her makeup to accentuate her lips and plucked her eyebrows to match her eyes. What she wouldn't give for a nice manicure.

That morning, she received a call from Director Hill to

report for duty. Report could mean anything from wet work (a polite way to say assassinations) to robbery (borrowing something to better humanity). Her employment at Polaris included reading people's emotions and sensing the unseen. Working as an empath brought her accolades from her superiors but caused those around her to regard her with suspicion. She lived far from headquarters, but they protected her with snipers, guards, and cameras.

Before leaving in her tomato red Toyota RAV4, she placed a drop of essential oil beneath her tongue and told her dogs she'd be back soon.

When she was gone, a runner from Polaris would come by and check on her dogs twice a day. They also mowed her lawn and made sure no one was snooping around.

Another day at work. She imagined Director Hill would someday give her a few weeks off. Time to decompress and think about everyone she'd killed for justice and freedom. In war, people die. And the world was in an invisible struggle, the bad versus the not as bad, with America and Polaris stuck in the middle. How nice would it be if everyone let the truth out and laid down their arms? Someday.

Director Hill said to stay busy. Maybe he was right. Too much time to think.

Alabama arrived at the outskirts of Provo, Utah and entered a fenced-in warehouse. Once she passed security, a guard escorted her into an observation room and sat alone on the only chair available. She peered through a mirrored window.

In a bright room on the other side of the two-way mirror, an Asian man with black frazzled hair sat at a table, dark circles under his eyes. How long had they kept him awake? His loose tie was pulled to the side. He sported a fashion-wreck of an aqua blue suit. A gold Rolex decorated his left wrist.

A man with a black suit paced the floor. His short brown hair was combed back and glistened from gel, making his hair look polished. He pushed his jacket away and flashed an FBI badge hanging from his belt. He was Agent Tom Baker, and he didn't work for the FBI. But who questions someone flashing a badge?

Another man, Agent Lyles Herbert, looking fifteen years his senior, sat across from her subject. With silver hair combed to the side, the effect did little to hide his male pattern baldness. Freckles covered his face, and from his complexion, Alabama imagined he once held a full head of red hair like her own.

A stack of photos and paperwork faced the Asian man, and when Agent Herbert showed them to him, he folded his arms and turned his head.

Herbert cupped his hands. His blue jacket sleeves creased at the anterior elbows. "Mr. Chen, we have been at this for days, and frankly, we are ready to throw in the towel and send you to prison for a very, very long time."

"You can't do that. Your American justice system says I have rights," Chen said.

Agent Baker laughed. "Who told you that? Since September 11th, you'd be surprised what we can and can't do."

"I want to speak to a lawyer. You still haven't read me my rights."

Herbert shoved a series of photos in his face and flipped through them. Chen continued to look away. "Rights? You dare talk about rights? You don't seem to understand the gravity of your situation. It's time you cooperate. These files show you've helped funnel money to Hawala, a known LLC funded and operated by the CCP. We have traced your transactions to over forty bank accounts in various shell corporations."

Alabama focused on Chen's breathing, watching him take short, labored breaths. Although she wasn't told why she was here, Polaris had ordered her to use her empathic abilities before. Criminals lied better than politicians, but after honing her talents in Polaris, few could escape her gaze.

Baker pounded a fist on the table and shoved a finger into Chen's chest. "We have evidence under various names associated with your partner, Liu Wei, laundering over four billion dollars over three years." He poked him again and grabbed Chen's chin, staring deep into his eyes. "Just to be clear, we aren't *asking* you questions. We're letting you know how much trouble you're in."

Chen pulled back and spat on the floor. "Go to hell."

Herbert said, "Right now, you're facing a minimum of twenty years. You want to spend your life serving Tommy Beefcake his ramen soup and fighting the Aryan Brotherhood? I suggest you tell us everything you know about Wei's dealings in India and whether those link to corporations in Milan and Ukraine."

Alabama stood and inched toward the glass. She could feel Chen's heart, beating like a drum in a death metal band. For all his outward bravery, fear dwelt inside him.

Chen shook his head, his eyes on the mirror, judging those he couldn't see on the other side. Her eyes narrowed as she studied him like a test patient.

Herbert showed him files. "You see these? Look at them. You've also helped Wei funnel cash into the pockets of several senators. You think they're bought and paid for, don't you?"

"They are," Chen said with a half-grin.

Herbert grabbed his shirt, pulled him close, and punched him in the gut. Chen gasped.

"Listen here you little maggot!" Herbert shouted.

Baker raised a hand. "Easy. I'm sure he wants to cooperate."

Alabama winced. This wasn't the first instance of Herbert hitting someone. Each time, she could feel the blow herself. She coughed and bent over.

Chen sucked in air, his lower lip curling, his face reddening. "You will not get away with this. I demand an attorney!" He shouted in Mandarin until Herbert slapped him, leaving a red outline on his cheek.

Alabama touched her cheek and slowed her breathing. She kept her focus on Chen, studying him, reading him. Why didn't they waterboard him for information? It'd be faster.

"And you know where the funds lead to, don't you? Where Wei sent most of it, and why?"

Chen clenched his teeth. "My attorney...now."

Baker nodded. "Why did Wei fund a pathogenic lab, a BSL-4, in Shanghai? And why is he funding one that is being built in Ottawa, using a false name?"

Chen crossed his arms and leaned back.

Alabama straightened and tucked her red hair behind her ear. With her attention fixated on Chen, she studied his every movement, his every facial tick. She was building a profile. If this case involved bribery and money laundering, Chen would be turned over to the real FBI. If he presented an obvious danger, they'd fly him to Gitmo on a rendition flight and find out what they needed over international waters. Why bring her into this?

Baker put his hands on his hips and inched closer to

Chen, invading his personal space. "Where is Wei keeping the Ebola vials?"

After Baker mentioned the virus, Chen's eyes narrowed into hateful slits. "You can threaten me. You can torture me. I refuse to answer your questions."

Alabama stared between Chen's eyebrows. A deep breath. She held it in, pausing. Waves of truth flowed into her from someplace far away, as if she'd tapped into an esoteric stream. His emotions, impulses, and deep-seated concerns flashed before her like a stuttering film. In them, she sensed a hidden love, something he reserved for himself. What was he hiding?

She couldn't read minds, no one could. But behind his facade of toughness was a man of sadness and trepidation.

There was a woman in Chen's mind. His wife? No, not her. A lover? As if on command, Chen put a hand over his mouth.

Yes. A lover.

In the background, the two agents continued to berate and threaten him. She shut off the comm and only thought of Chen. There he was, sitting in fear, his pulse pounding like a greyhound sprinting on a race track.

She sensed embarrassment coated in sin. She reached under the window frame and called the front desk. "I need a copy of Chen's file. Pictures. Recordings. Anything you guys have."

Neither agent acknowledged her, but in seconds, a young woman delivered the request. She spent a few moments on each photo and file and moved on to the next until she landed on pictures of his wife. Alabama created separate stacks, those that gave her an emotional tug and those she called blanks: files and evidence that failed to elicit feelings in her. When she reached the end, she discovered two black and white surveillance photos in low res. In them, she made out an attractive woman with shiny black hair and a body most women would kill for. *Her.* She turned the pictures around, looking for a name to put to a face. But that's all she had.

She spent the next thirty minutes searching for her name in the files they provided. Polaris must have paid a fortune for these photos, she thought. What's her name? The CCP let powerful men like Chen break certain Chinese mores, but something seemed wrong. Holding her photo up and staring at Chen, she began gathering impressions, but nothing stuck. Was he sleeping with her without his wife's knowledge?

Who was his wife? Alabama's mouth fell open when she glimpsed at the woman's dossier. Mei Hua, daughter of General Li, a top member of the Chinese Communist Party. No one with Mei Hua's pedigree would tolerate infidelity. That's it.

Alabama turned on the comm. "Tell Chen his wife suspects."

Baker paused in mid-sentence and rolled up his sleeves, balling both fists. "Mei Hua suspects."

Crinkling his brow, Chen rubbed his temples. His lips tightened, and he grimaced so hard, Alabama thought his jaw would break.

Truth came into Alabama in a jolt of inspiration. Without thinking or second-guessing herself, she said, "He's having an affair with his housekeeper."

Baker dropped his voice to a thin whisper. "Does your wife know you've been having an affair with your housekeeper?"

Chen's face turned ashen. He recoiled, anger flashing across his eyes.

"His wife... She doesn't know." Alabama shivered as she sweated. Her pulse raced at the same rate as Chen's, and she closed her eyes.

Baker repeated what she said in his own words.

Fighting through her discomfort, she focused all her attention on Chen and continued. "Tell him the party won't look favorably on him cheating on General Li's daughter."

After saying that, Baker added, "General Li has a way to make his problems disappear. Right now, it looks like you're that problem. Oh, you thought you were irreplaceable? Lose the smug look, Chen. I can leave this room, pick up the phone, and make one call. We'll put you on a flight back to Beijing within two hours. I'm sure General Li would enjoy spending an evening with you."

Chen froze and glanced at the mirror again, this time in a different spot.

Alabama took a step from the window, her knees weak, her eyelids heavy. Drained, she flopped onto her seat and dabbed sweat with a handkerchief.

Her voice cracked. "I've done all I can, gentlemen. Good luck."

SUNLIGHT BLED through cracks in Alabama's curtains. Crossing her legs in a yoga lotus position, she rested on the back of her hands. Minute by minute, she tried separating herself from Chen, but it took time. With more intense and difficult subjects, it would often take days to recover. She'd made a private vow to die for the United States, though it wasn't her home. There was too much at risk if the U.S. collapsed, and it would make the fall of the Roman Empire look like a small town bar brawl.

Her two dogs whined next to her feet.

Tibetan prayer flags hung to her left, and a tapestry of a Yogi took up the wall on her right. Statues of Buddha and Quan Yin sat on a marble table her grandmother willed her before her passing. A raw food cookbook was open to a kale recipe on her couch.

She closed the book and walked to a runner rug in the hallway. Black geometric patterns of overlapping circles gave it a regal appearance. She flipped on the hallway light and rolled up the rug halfway. Alabama pushed her hands flat on the wood floor and six wood slats moved. Using a specially made hook, she lifted the slats and set them to the side. Underneath sat a safe with a panel full of numbers and a place for her thumbprint. She opened it, pulled out a picture book, and braced herself against the wall.

She flipped through it, knowing it by heart. How many times had she found herself drawn to it? Hundreds, if not more. Every glued photo reminded her of how lucky she was to be alive.

She paused on a photo of a wounded soldier, smoke billowing in the background. At the base of a coconut tree, a man held his stomach, his face scrunched in agony. A medic lurched toward him. At the top of the picture, "For Your Eyes Only" was stamped in red.

Unblinking, she turned the page. There, a picture of an Ethiopian general on the passenger side of a Russian armored personnel carrier. Two men in the back with rifles. A driver in military fatigues running in mid-stride, ready to open the door.

The photo meant everything to her, like it held the mysteries of the universe, like the winning lottery numbers to every lottery in the world. Her heart thundered faster, but her breath remained calm through her training and willpower. When she closed her eyes, she visualized the image, making sure her memory matched the photo with excruciating detail.

She flipped through the pages. Political figures. Celebrities. Lights in the sky. Then she halted on a page as if by instinct. Her stomach fluttered like the time she first kissed a boy. Fourth grade. James Richenbauer. What was he up to now?

A Missing Persons' label stretched across the top, and the person's headshot stared back at her. Half Asian, the woman was both beautiful and exotic. Somehow, she must have kept one of her parent's recessive genes because her eyes shined a bright blue, and her auburn hair was natural as far as she could tell.

Alabama lifted the picture from the page and read her short bio printed on the back in microprint. She'd spent years as a Hollywood makeup artist, working for the likes of Christopher Nolan and Ridley Scott and others.

A ring from her phone startled her, and she dug into her pocket. Patrick Hill showed on the Caller ID and she answered it. She waited for him to deliver a key phrase, which changed every few days.

"Are you in the market for house insurance?" Hill asked.

"I own two houses on the West Side."

"Are they painted?"

"Blue and green," she replied, giving the last code.

"Agent Wren, grab your bags. A driver will arrive in five minutes."

She nodded. "Yes, sir. I'll be ready."

"You'll be read in on the way to the landing strip. Good luck."

She shoved the book of photographs into the safe, locked it, and fit the wood slats in their places. Once she pushed the rug back, she hurried to her bedroom, grabbed a light carry-on, and made sure her automated dog feeder was full.

"I'll see you soon, boys. Don't tear up the house when I'm gone."

Pugsy, the bigger of the two, barked as if he understood her. Maybe he did.

At the doorway, she paused and swallowed hard. A mission. Just what she needed.

An eerie feeling rose. With certainty, she knew the man she helped interrogate was dead.

4

STONE

J ackson twisted a cap off an unlabeled pill bottle and spilled two cyan-colored tablets into his palm. Rejection prophylaxis. They helped reduce and hopefully prevent organ transplant rejections. He tossed the pills into his mouth and swallowed them with a handful of tap water. His keys remained where he always kept them; on the crown of his Himalayan granite hearth next to a picture of his dead wife and her wedding ring.

After a plane crash, where he lost his wife and he nearly died, Polaris granted him a new heart. When he woke up each morning, he still had trouble believing he'd survived. Lucky didn't cover it. Every day was a gift, though sometimes he had to remind himself.

At night, he'd close his eyes and hold a body pillow, pretending it was his wife, Nicki. How long would it take to let go of her and live his life? They said it took as long to get over someone as a couple had been together. No. In his heart, he didn't want to get over her. It would mean defeat. She was gone, perhaps waiting for him in some afterlife. Death wasn't the end. It couldn't be.

He remembered the blazing fire consuming her, her flesh bubbling under the licking flame, the pain, and acrid stench of it all. Him reaching his hand out to save her and then him pulling the skin from her flesh. People shrieking. Sirens blaring. Hell on Earth.

A gnarled plane's wing was ablaze and detached from the fuselage. He'd been thrown from a plane crash. His legs were broken along with a dozen ribs. Somehow, he'd managed to crawl to her, ignoring the pain.

Twice, he'd stared at his H&K 9mm held firmly in his hand. A quick squeeze of the trigger would end his misery. Send his consciousness into oblivion and go meet her. He refused to surrender life. She would want him to live on and thrive. Without Polaris, he envisioned himself on skid row, needle in arm, unaware of reality. And living that way wasn't an option; would never *be* an option.

There was only one Nicki Stone. Blue eyes, blonde hair, a perfect nose, and dimples. No one could ever replace her. His heart only had space for one love, and as corny as it sounded, he swore to never fall in love again. No matter what. He would trade both his arms and legs to spend one more hour in her presence, enough time to tell her how much he loved and needed her. They planned on having children. He shook his head. No wife. No kids. Now, only duty.

On the day of the crash, he blacked out after she died, subconsciously hoping to die along with her. What was life without her? Life happens, it is said. They most likely never watched their loved one burned alive.

Polaris helped him by giving him a reason to live. As much as he loved his country, he knew the Deep State, those embedded in the intelligence community weren't always allies. Like Polaris, they had own their agenda.

Outside, tires crunched on gravel. He glanced out his living room's bay window. A yellow taxi came to a stop in front of his driveway, sporting tinted windows. Rare for taxis, but a sign it belonged to Polaris. He nodded at the vehicle and pulled his bag toward the front door.

His Heckler Koch USP Compact 9mm was concealed in a holster on his hip. Jackson liked the weapon for the 9mm's manageable recoil. When the brass casings were ejected, the pistol remained flat.

Jackson locked the house and wheeled his suitcase down the drive, giving a silent "Farewell, I'll see you again" to three Jacquemontii maples surrounding a rock arrangement at the edge of his front yard. It brought an emptiness to his heart, a black hole where feelings of home and security once played a role. Planted by his wife the day they moved in, one tree was for him, one for her, and another for their future child. They would plant more for each child they brought into the world.

It wasn't to be.

The taxi driver popped the trunk open, and Jackson loaded the suitcase inside and slid onto the car's backseat. In front of him, a black divider kept the identity of the driver a secret. Though they could communicate through a speaker, they didn't.

The taxi drove onto a back road, avoiding freeways and traffic. He rubbed his stomach. Damn medication, always giving him a sense that something crawled in his gut.

He arrived at an airstrip a few hours later. An Embraer Phenom 300E private jet waited for him. Its twin engines and low position made the plane's swept wings look more striking. The open cabin door and airstair steps acted as an invitation. The roar of the twin turbine engines whined, ready to usher him to his unknown destination. Finally, he would be an agent. He laughed to himself. What a surreal experience. Fox Mulder from the *X-Files* didn't get this kind of treatment.

Then panic slapped him. A plane. He avoided them as if they were cancer. He gulped. Sweat dripped from his armpits. Recalling his wife, he gnashed his teeth together and wiped his palms on the seat. He stepped out of the taxi.

A man dressed in a black suit, wearing sunglasses and an earpiece, snagged Jackson's suitcase from the trunk and wheeled it toward the plane's luggage compartment. The man walked past Director Hill. An attractive woman dressed in a low skirt, flats, and business attire stood by Hill's side. Was this his partner? The smell of jet fuel blew his way.

A few yards from him, Hill motioned with a head nod at the woman. Blue eyes, maybe five-foot-seven, her long, dark red hair would make her stand out anywhere. Strikingly beautiful, like a runway model. He caught himself staring and looked away.

"Meet Dr. Alabama Wren. She's been read in," Hill said.

Jackson extended his hand. "Jackson Stone. Nice to meet you."

She accepted it and gave him a firm shake. "Same."

Hill gestured toward the steps. "Get going. I'll see you two when you get back." He cupped his hands at his waist.

Jackson and Alabama climbed inside. Fake cedar scent met his nose. Walking down the aisle, Jackson pulled on his tie and blew air down his chest. One first class leather seat per row. He sat at the mid-cabin and shut the window slat. He fanned himself like he was in Florida in July, suffering from the stifling summer. A drop of sweat trickled down his temple.

Stay calm. It's only a plane flight. Before you know it, you'll land and it will be over.

A woman stopped in stride in front of him. Her brown hair up in a bun, she couldn't be more than twenty-one years old, if that. She wore a navy blue blouse with a jacket and the same colored skirt.

Her brows rose in concern. "Can I get you anything, sir?"

He shook his head and then nodded. "I could use a drink. Where can I get one?"

"We have—"

"Scrap that. Water is fine. Ice if you have it."

She held up her index finger. "Just a moment, sir." She made her way towards the front.

He checked his watch. 08:38. In this jet, he'd get to their destination in a fraction of the time it took a commercial plane. At least he wouldn't be cooped up in this thing for very long.

"My brother always hated flying, too," a woman said.

Jackson looked across the aisle. There, with her red lips curled into a smile, sat Dr. Alabama Wren.

"I'm fine." He wiped the sweat from his face.

"Maybe we shouldn't start the mission with you lying to me?"

Before he could answer, the flight attendant handed him a bottle of water, condensation dripping down its sides.

Alabama arched a brow. "I was informed you worked as a paranormal debunker before being brought into Polaris. Welcome aboard. If you've made it past the training, Director Hill must have faith in you. Have you been briefed on Project Horizon?"

The plane rolled forward. He wanted to curl into a ball. "Project Horizon?"

"Our mission."

"Right," he said. *Project Horizon? It would be nice if they'd tell me these things.* "Somewhat. I wasn't a debunker. I was a

Paranormal Investigator. After training, Polaris assigned me to an office."

"Hmm. Haven't you debunked every paranormal event you've investigated?"

He cringed as the jet engines roared. "If I found something real, I wouldn't have to do that. What do you do, exactly?"

"I read people."

"Like a cop?" He squeezed the armrests, and his stomach tossed and turned. As the Embraer Phenom 300E lifted into the air, he pressed back into the seat from the g-force and forced in a breath.

"You could say that," she said. No one in Polaris was just a *someone*. They *were* someone.

Nausea rose. He raised his hand. "I'll be right back." He unbuckled and pushed out of the seat.

"Excuse me, sir," said the flight attendant. "You can't—"

"Sorry." He headed to the rear, using the seats to keep his balance. Saliva rushed into his mouth like a broken faucet.

In the bathroom, he kicked the door shut and threw open the toilet lid. His breakfast surged up his throat and into the toilet.

The plane jostled, and he heaved again. Out came the coffee, splashing. He placed a palm on the sidewall as the jet rose higher. Turbulence. Another shudder.

Dammit. Get it together. You're going to be fine. What happened in the past, happened in the past. Flying is safer than driving. Right?

He gasped. The memory of the plane crash, which killed Nicki and left Jackson broken, plunged into his mind. Here came the rollercoaster he relived day after day after day.

· · ·

JACKSON HELD his wife's hand, stroking her thumb with his. Nicki was ecstatic that day. She took a drink of orange juice from her small plastic cup. Their plane ride would take them from Philadelphia to Roanoke.

"What did you think of the town?" he asked.

She shot him a look like he was stoned. He winked, and she laughed in the best way.

"It wasn't that bad."

"It was worse than bad." She wrinkled her nose. "I'd rather stay where we are. We live in such a nice, small 'every-one-knows-you' town, and I'm happy to be away from the city. I don't want to—"

Bang!

An explosion ripped apart the stern. The plane bucked forward. The cabin vibrated and whined, straining to stay together. Jackson lurched forward, his head hitting the seat in front of him. Nicki squeezed his hand.

JACKSON SPIT into the toilet and flushed, the sound like an industrial-strength vacuum. He washed his face.

I'm not going to let Dr. Wren see me like this. I'm a mess. No. Stop saying that. I'm fine. I'm fine. Master this. It's going to be all right. Think about something else.

Back in his seat, the sound of the crash that took his wife and everyone else on the plane but him, faded, replaced by his conviction.

Whoever blew up that plane and killed his wife, nearly killed him, too. One day, the culprits would face bullet justice. Two to the chest, one to the head. If Polaris arrested him or took him out, at least he would know the transgressors would be dead and never hurt anyone again. Director

Hill had informed him the crash wasn't an accident, but he wouldn't go further than that.

He looked across the aisle at his new partner. She was fast asleep. But somehow, deep down, he was certain her name wasn't Dr. Alabama Wren.

T he crisp, frigid air caused Jackson's nose to drip. A deep bed of snow blanketed the terrain. Jackson and Alabama marched through the white powder, and beyond the massive tree line stood Mount Hood, its peak set in front of a blue sky. It loomed like a giant, offering its bounty of lush forests and clean lakes.

A few hours earlier, they had touched down at the Hillsboro, Oregon airport, otherwise known as HIO. Before exiting the plane, one of Director Hill's assistants provided them with FBI badges and IDs. Part of Jackson's training involved impersonating federal agents—their lingo, their walk, the way they looked at people.

He'd spent weeks learning law enforcement codes and filling in all manner of federal paperwork. He role-played as an FBI agent, a beat cop, a detective. For him, it came naturally. His investigator's background made it almost routine, and this time, he had a badge to go along with his fake identity.

Still, the idea of him presenting a badge to someone unnerved him. What if they called his ID in? Jackson's instructors told him not to worry about that. Act cool. Be the part. Become the person.

After a Polaris driver dressed as an FBI agent dropped them off in a black Chevy Malibu near the base of Mount Hood, they walked up an ascending trail toward their pickup point.

A cold breeze whipped across the snow, and the chill pierced his heavy coat. Jackson and Alabama stopped at a rock, and he snacked on a pack of peanut M&Ms.

Alabama wore a winter jacket, fur lining the jacket's hood, and waterproof ski pants she'd slipped over her khakis. A microphone was clasped around her lower neck. Its transponders were taped against her throat, and an acoustic coil ran up her neck, attached to an earphone secured in her ear. Jackson wore the same, though he kept the hood loose against his upper back.

"I don't think I've been given all the material about this case," he said, his mouth full of chocolate. He picked out the yellow ones and threw them in the M&M bag. "For example, what happens if we show our IDs to the FBI, and they realize they're forgeries?"

"Do you think Hill kept information from you?" Alabama asked, chomping down on a granola bar.

"I'm not sure. Just something I feel."

"Because you're a debunker..." she said, clearing her throat, "paranormal investigator. Likely, Director Hill didn't want to tell you everything. It might taint your judgment. You don't need to worry about our IDs. They're as real as they get."

Unsatisfied with her response, he waited for her to explain more. She didn't. "If they find out we're not in the FBI, what happens?"

She shrugged as a flurry of snowflakes fluttered past him. "Follow my lead, okay?"

"You didn't answer my question."

"Yes, I did." She took one last bite of her granola bar and tucked it away in her jacket.

When they came within sight of federal agents, his heart thumped faster. Why couldn't she at least give more information on what to do in case the situation soured? And why didn't these agents meet them at the airport? Was all this FBI protocol? After spotting them, the agents waved them over. An empty Ford Crown Victoria awaited next to them.

A man with cropped hair and sunglasses approached. "May I see your IDs?"

"Sure," Jackson said.

Jackson and Alabama pulled their cards out and showed them. The man looked them over, comparing the photos, and called for his associate. Once he arrived, he handed their IDs off, and the man walked back to an unmarked SUV.

"Agent Rhomberg," he said, introducing himself. "Any trouble getting here?"

Alabama gritted her teeth. "Is there a problem?"

"Not necessarily. Just need to check your IDs against our database. Won't take long. Stand by." Rhomberg's statement sounded rehearsed. A good sign they weren't the first people to be questioned.

Maybe undercover reporters could try to infiltrate their way inside the area?

Alabama looked over the agent's shoulder. "This is highly unusual. Is there something we should know about?"

Just then, a freezing breeze kicked up. Jackson and Alabama pointed their back to the wind, shivering.

"I'll let you know right after your identification checks out. Where are you guys from?"

Alabama's eyes turned serious. "We're both from Norfolk."

Jackson paced his breathing and recalled his backstory.

"Oh? Do you know Special Agent Harrington?"

Giving an authentic smile, Jackson nodded. "Six foot seven. Arms like steel beams? Played tight end for Ohio State? He's hard to miss."

The man in the car called out. "You two. Come over here a second."

Not good.

Jackson kicked the snow aside on their way to the SUV and stood on the other side. Alabama's eyes wandered the surrounding area, keeping her hand close to her pistol.

Jackson looked over his shoulder. Did she mean to kill them? He didn't see anyone else other than these two. Until the agent left his SUV, he would be behind ballistic glass, and his 9mm H&K didn't have the firepower to blast a hole in it. The other agent? He'd likely drop in the snow and disappear before emptying his mag into Jackson's back.

The man exited the car, their IDs in hand. "Where are you guys from?" he asked, repeating the first agent's question.

When he asked, the other agent spoke. "They're good."

They took their IDs back. So far, so good.

Alabama asked, "Read us in. What's going on?"

"Can't say much right now. Got word from DHS that something might be up. I can't say more than that. You guys be careful." He handed over the Crown Vic's keys. "Heater works great. It drifts slightly to the right. Needs alignment. Snow chains are on. Any questions?"

"No," Alabama said. "We've got a lot of work to do."

They slung their bags in the back. Jackson took the keys, and they piled in. She tapped Jackson's leg four times, a code meaning not to say a word or do anything suspicious. When they were out of sight from the two agents, she motioned for him to pull over. He popped the trunk, grabbed a cellphone-sized spectrum analyzer, and waved it inside the car. If someone bugged the car or installed a camera, the device would register it.

Nothing.

That makes life a lot easier. What the hell have I gotten myself into?

"Is this how most missions start?" he asked.

She showed him her pistol and then a circular scar on her forearm the size of a nickel. "Depends. Some start with a gunfight."

They drove to Sno-Park and parked close to half a dozen police cruisers and unmarked FBI SUVs.

Jackson brought along a Geiger counter. When investigating paranormal activity, this radiation device came in handy. UFO enthusiasts insisted Geiger counters often recorded abnormal radiation levels, but when he'd show up, he never detected anything. Why did they always lie?

"Stay calm around these guys. Remember you're an FBI agent," she said, reassuring Jackson.

"Do I look nervous?" he asked.

"A little. It's your first mission. It can be nerve-wracking."

"How many missions have you been on?"

She shrugged. "A few. Did you see the pictures?" Alabama's breath clouded shortly past her lips.

Jackson adjusted his gloves. "Yes. But I'm here to see what happened in person."

While onboard the Embraer Phenom, he'd brought up the mission files on his laptop. Pictures of corpses. Strange lights in the sky. Scorch marks on trees. Some frozen bodies were missing their eyes. Others had caved-in chests. Whoever murdered them did a real number. What kind of psycho would mutilate people like that? How did he or she manage to fight them all? According to the reports, none of them were shot or involved in a physical conflict. So, how did this happen?

As soon as this case was proven to be nothing more than a serial killer or a dispute gone wrong, he could return to Polaris and do what he did best; video forensics.

After a tense minute, the police waved them through. A deputy and two FBI agents traveled in front of them, their boots creating fresh tracks.

The deputy stopped and faced them. "You Californians not used to the snow, are you?" he asked, a smirk on his face.

Jackson shuffled his feet. "What makes you say that?"

"The way you're walking," the deputy said smugly.

Alabama chimed in. "Maybe you should concentrate on getting us to our destination rather than staring at us."

The deputy sighed, pivoted, and continued forward.

To Jackson, everything about the scene—Mount Hood, rows of Douglas fir trees, western hemlocks, ponderosa pines, the glint of sunlight off the packed snow—was all too familiar. He couldn't believe he was back in his home state of Oregon. He'd lived close to Mount Hood as a child, and it always seemed majestic and impossibly tall.

It took them just under twenty minutes to walk to the Pacific Crest Trail off of Forest Road 2610 and trek by Frog Lake. Water lapped gently on the shore. On their way, Jackson noticed no one had used these paths. Odd, considering the popularity of the park. Maybe the police and FBI cleared the area.

Jackson checked his watch. 11:32. When he saw poles

with yellow police tape stretched in a massive rectangle to the tree line, he picked up the pace. A few images he studied from the flash drive on his laptop flooded his mind, one after another.

A man, naked except for his underwear, chest glistening with snow, bore two large oval bruises on his chest. His eyes were closed. Charred and blistered skin ran up his right temple, and a portion of his hair was singed. Dried blood crusted over his mustache and extended to his swollen upper lip. The poor man's foot was burned to the bone. More oddly, a gray foam-like substance stuck on his cheeks. Did he suffer from pulmonary edema? Excess fluid in the lungs precipitated it. The fluid collected in the lung's numerous air sacs, making it difficult to breathe. In most cases, heart problems caused it. However, fluid could collect in the lungs for other reasons, including pneumonia, exposure to certain toxins and medications, trauma to the chest wall, and traveling to or exercising at high elevations.

Another man with dreadlocks died next to him. Both of his hands were burned, though not like his friend's foot. Bruised similarly on the chest, the tip of his long, wide nose was missing; gnawed off to the nasal bone. Blood had coagulated around his cheeks and lips. A hungry animal might be responsible for the missing tip of the nose, but an animal like a fox or coyote wouldn't stop there. The young man's body would've been fresh, a predatory animal's delight. So would the rest of his group.

Other than why these two were naked, why did one of them show signs of pulmonary edema? In that state, the man shouldn't have been hiking and most likely wouldn't have been. Edema would've had to come on fast. But the man was young, and the disease is extremely rare in the youth unless some sort of trauma suddenly hit him in the chest.

He walked closer to the warning tape and eyed a large, yellow and black tent, flattened out on the ground inside the perimeter. West of the trees and beyond the tape, a police helicopter sank in a snow-filled meadow. An FBI agent let them inside the scene.

Alabama rubbed her hands together. "How many hikers did you find?"

The deputy rested a hand on his hip and pointed northeast. "Three died on the way back to the campsite. We found four dead in a ravine seventy-five yards into the woods past the tree line over there. Two more died a short way away from the camp. We believe they were trying to get help. One of their tongues was missing."

Alabama cocked her head. "A tongue?"

"Probably an animal," Jackson said. "But running in all directions, that would rule out one serial killer."

It had to be more. Perhaps a gang of killers. Drug dealers? One man couldn't chase down each person, slay one, then rush to another, especially this spread apart. Plus, one against nine young men and women in tip-top shape wouldn't bode well for the assailant.

"Did you recover any brass? Any signs of a gunfight?" Jackson asked.

The deputy pushed out his bottom lip. "None."

Jackson crossed his arms, tasting the ice in the calm wind. This reminded him of the Sno Orkan Incident in Sweden. Nine campers died on a skiing trip from the cold elements ten years ago. Authorities solved that case and closed it quickly. In the report, officials mentioned flying lights from a few witnesses. "What's your theory on what happened?"

"Aren't you here to find out?" The deputy shot him a glare. "Look, I'll be honest with you. It's strange to see only the hiker's footprints. We were sure we'd discover more, but there are none in the area. We have all kinds of people come up in these forests. Some up to no good, if you get my meaning. I have no idea. Only one of them wore a shoe. Now, explain that to me."

Alabama raised an eyebrow. "One shoe? Did you find the other?"

The deputy shook his head. "We have a few K-9 units searching these woods, but we haven't found it yet. Haven't found their clothes either. A few kept their socks on. Damnedest thing I've seen since joining the department."

Scanning the area, Alabama squinted against the light ricocheting off the snow. "All of them only in their underwear?"

The deputy adjusted his gloves. "That's right."

Jackson itched his chin and wiped his nose. "Something must have scared the hell out of them."

"That's one way to put it."

A loud grunt echoed. An FBI agent was bent over at the edge of the tree line. Although his back was turned, Jackson could hear him dry heave. Then another FBI agent joined him. Had they seen something?

Walking forward, Jackson hurried like a horse in deep sand. Slow, but steady.

The agent who first vomited walked toward him, hands out, staggering as if drunk or dizzy. "I'd advise you to stay—"

Jackson called over his shoulder. "Medic!"

Alabama rushed to him. "What's wrong?"

"Sick. Can't think straight," the agent replied.

Jackson spotted a scorched tree, black on its west side, facing the giant snow meadow. Black streaks extended from the treetop to the branches and down the trunk. He counted seven trees on one side and eight on the other with the same markings.

Biological attack?

Jackson noticed a recently used fire pit made of rocks next to the tree. The hikers didn't have their clothes on, but they somehow managed to carry some of their firewood. Odd. If they were running from something, why would they carry wood to make a fire not too far from their tent site?

Alabama called out, "Check the Geiger counter."

He ran it over a darkened branch and gasped. 300,000 microSieverts. What would cause that?

He touched his throat mic. "Tell them to stay away from this tree line. It's hot." He read off the number on the device. "We can't stay here long either. From this point forward, we'll need lead-coated hazmat suits to continue the investigation."

Alabama came through his earpiece. "Get over to the campsite. I need you to take a look at this."

"Hold on. I'm going—"

"I need you here immediately."

"On my way." He hiked up a small incline toward the camp.

She inspected the tent with latex gloves, worry on her face. "A lot of fear," she said.

He stood next to her. "What do you mean?"

"The hikers didn't know what was going on. Their tracks move from side to side. Their lack of clothing, the way they left each other, all show signs of panic and confusion. See the tent? It's cut open." She measured the cut. "They must have cut their way out. That makes no sense. Why not unzip the tent to escape?"

"Maybe this cut is the work of the attacker or attackers,"

he said. "Do you see any prints leading to the tent?" Jackson crouched and studied the tent. The plastic tent fibers poked outward. Alabama was right, these cuts came from inside the tent.

Alabama shook her head. "No footprints at all. The FBI would have seen them. It's strange, to say the least. No evidence that any attackers came and left the scene."

"Has anyone mentioned this before? The knife cuts coming from inside the tent and not from the outside?"

She glanced behind her and whispered, "Keep your voice down. This wasn't in the file. They're either hiding something or...."

"Why would they keep this a secret?"

She picked up a handful of snow and let it drift from her hand. "You'd be surprised."

6

After leaving the scene, Jackson and Alabama arrived at their new base of operations, a small one-story bungalow on Thirty-Fifth Avenue in Portland's Hawthorne district. She set her suitcase in the entryway and peeped out the open doorway. Jackson had driven to the local grocery store to grab some food and supplies.

Clouds dulled the light outside, a much different tone than Frog Lake's blue sky. A drive-by rain shower had drenched the streets and sidewalks. Now, it sprinkled.

After pulling her suitcase into the living room, she searched the rest of the house for anything out of the ordinary. What a poor excuse for a home.

Was this the best you could do, Polaris? she thought.

Being assigned a nondescript house was one thing, but Director Hill could have spared some amenities. Like toilet paper.

Furniture check. Two desks, one in each corner of the living room. Beige couches. A shaker coffee table sat between the couches with straight legs, a dovetail drawer with a wood knob. File cabinets pressed against a wall, an impressionistic painting of a man and woman dancing in the rain above it.

Nothing here made her feel at home, but it didn't need to. Polaris knew what they had in this location: security. That's all that mattered. Their new base of operations was located around the corner from New Leaf, an organic, hippy food co-op. Probably a safe place to shop.

She pulled a green file from her suitcase and emptied the contents. Maps of the area around Frog Lake. Profile pictures from the dead hiker's social media pages. Still images from satellite photos capturing light bursts. Next, she opened a box of tacks.

With a handful of photos and maps, she tacked them above a rectangular desk, out of sight from prying eyes, which might see through the window. Technically, she shouldn't display any evidence from the case. If someone broke in, they'd discover everything. But breaking the rules is what she did. What Hill didn't know wouldn't hurt him.

While exploring the kitchen, she rifled through cabinets, patting them down to make sure nothing remained hidden. A red granite island with black stools sat in the middle.

Jackson opened the front door and hefted plastic bags on the bench in the entryway.

She brought them to the island as he continued to unload the car. "Did you go to New Leaf?"

"Too expensive. Went across the street to Outlet Grocers."

"You said you'd stop into New Leaf."

"I did. They're asking way too much for stuff in there."

She sighed, and when he wasn't looking, she made a face and threatened to sling a can of beans at him.

He walked to the living room. "File cabinets?" He took his eyes off the floor and smiled. Wrinkles formed on his cheeks. "It will be the first place anyone looks."

"Are you going to help unpack the groceries?"

"In a second. Bathroom," he said, disappearing.

There was something odd about Jackson's energy. On the plane, he'd been nervous and skittish. Now, cold and calculated. A typical Polaris agent.

He may yet prove useful.

Jackson left the bathroom, closed the door behind him, and folded his tie on his desk. "Have you been upstairs?"

"Not yet."

"You didn't have to wait on me."

"I wasn't." She opened another grocery bag filled with yogurt and grapes.

Jackson tilted his head at the maps and photos she tacked to the wall. He wrinkled his brow. "If someone were to come in here and see those, our cover would be blown, and so would our employment."

"I work best this way."

He folded his arms. "We're taking it down."

"How many cases have you been on since joining Polaris?"

"You know this is my first one."

"So, you don't have any instances where this was a problem."

His face reddened. "This isn't Hollywood. In the movies, they splash the walls with evidence. They're coming down."

She tightened her arms around her chest. "Listen, Stone, this is your first mission. They stay up."

He scoffed. "You're going to get us killed."

"Don't think because your instructor told you to do

something a certain way that it's done that way in the field. I need to see these while we work."

He glanced at the photos and back at her. "And if someone breaks in?"

"If you don't like them, don't look at them. Some of them aren't real anyway. We use disinformation on a regular basis."

He shook his head and took off his gloves.

"Now then." She zipped up her suitcase and pulled it into a bedroom. Inside was a bed with a wood frame without a headboard. No windows, a closet, a beige lamp on a bedside table, and a beat-up dresser. If this place were any more run down, it would be in a museum.

"Hey, check this out. There's a loose panel here," Jackson said.

"Don't touch that."

"Why not?"

Alabama walked into the hallway where he studied the wood floor. "Let me do that." She removed several boards, revealing a thumb scanner and a keypad, the same kind of safe she had in her house. "Remember the nine-digit code in the briefing?"

"Of course."

"That's the code. Put it in, hold your thumb there for five seconds, and this place explodes." She slid the wood boards back.

He stood straighter and turned toward the kitchen. "What do you mean?"

"In case something happens and we need to destroy the house, there's enough C-4 packed into the walls to shake buildings several blocks away." Alabama watched his face drain of color.

"How long is the timer?"

"I'm going to assume you're a good runner."

"Thanks for the nonanswer."

She tacked another picture to the wall. "You're welcome. I see we're going to get along just fine."

Back in her room, she stuffed her clothes into a drawer. A few minutes passed. The smell of coffee carried through the bungalow.

"Coffee?" Mugs clanked from inside the kitchen.

"No." She hesitated. *Might as well try to smooth things over.* "But, thank you." *He's got a sweet touch.* She left and grabbed a bottle of water.

"How long do you think we'll stay here?"

"That depends, but always be ready to relocate. Polaris has several bolt-holes, but Director Hill doesn't want us to move around unnecessarily. We'll stay for as long as possible."

"For some reason, I thought we'd be relocating more often." Jackson sat at his desk, his laptop open. "Do we have a basement?"

"This house doesn't. Why do you ask?"

He scrunched his lips. "I thought Polaris would provide computers and servers. But if there's no basement, anyone could break in and steal it."

She nodded. "We don't have anything like that here."

"So, we have a murder scene with high levels of radiation and no suspects."

He gets to work quickly. "Hold on." She hurried to her desk and tacked up more photos.

He sighed.

Oh, you'll be fine. "Let's talk about the lights in the sky." She shuffled through some papers and handed him the documents. "Have you seen these reports?"

"Let me see." He read a page and leaned back in his chair. "Actually, no. How did you get these?"

"Polaris gave them to me. You don't have them?"

He ran a search on his laptop. "No."

"That's strange. When this mission is over, you should talk to Director Hill about it. Anyway, these are eyewitness testimonies."

She'd read them on the flight to Portland. Three people not related and without knowledge of the others called in at 2:04 AM, 2:05 AM, and 2:08 AM on the night of the incident. "They're similar to the Phoenix Lights back in '97." She knew more about that than she could tell him.

"Similar detail to the Cowichan Valley Sighting images and the Lubbock Lights sightings, too." He blinked as if he'd recovered from a coma. "It could be an experimental aircraft, perhaps out of Nellis. Our government is decades ahead in advanced aeronautical research."

She glanced at the wall in thought. "Wouldn't they stay in Nevada? Why fly here and risk sightings across the country? The Air Force wouldn't allow a craft to leave the Nevada desert with radiation leakage. The craft could potentially be traced. They send up birds to detect radiation, bioterrorism, anything unusual in the sky. And if it was radiation, they would have to explain that to the public. Talk about a PR nightmare. It also doesn't explain the witnesses' description of the erratic movements."

Jackson held a document and read. "This one says she saw some of the lights drop from a thousand feet to just above the forest canopy in under a second. But she doesn't describe a sonic boom or noise of any kind. I don't think we have technology that can break the laws of physics, do we?"

She finished her water. "I like how you ask questions

that suggest I know everything. I'm as much in the dark about this as you are." Hill had warned her about this.

Secrecy was the elixir by which Polaris lived. When would Director Hill raise Jackson's clearance?

When she read Jackson's file, he had failed two polygraphs relating to UFOs. Director Hill brought him to the side and warned if he started poking around for answers about aliens, he'd find himself out of work. Which really meant six feet under. Maybe that was why they sent him with her.

She traced an *X* on the table and whistled the *X-Files* theme song. "Or?"

Jackson's eyes brightened. "A saucer?"

"It's not out of the question. You of all people should know there are things in the sky we can't explain."

"Under the water, too. Sure. Black budget military craft. If aliens existed, don't you think it would be impossible to hide?"

She sighed and threw away the bottle. After opening the refrigerator, she grabbed some grapes, washed them off, and put them in a bowl for them to share. "Ask your question again."

He did.

"They might not be hiding," she said. "People have been seeing them all over the world for some time."

"You believe that?" he asked. "Do you know how many have been investigated and found to be nothing more than stars? Or planes? Planets? I've hoped to find one legitimate UFO or UAP case since I was a kid and have spent thousands of hours on cases like this one. Director Hill assigned me to Project Horizon for a reason."

She smirked. "So what do *you* think the Phoenix Lights

were?" *Now to find his biases.* She made herself comfortable again and glanced at the photos.

As he spoke, his tone changed, and his emotions peeled back layer by layer. "I honestly don't know. They said all kinds of things from flares to planes out of Prescott as a practical joke."

"See? In that case, I—" She cut herself off when a photo of a woman's eyes caught her attention. She'd either missed this image when compiling them or didn't see the woman's face at all.

Maybe in her seventies, she wore gobs of makeup to hide her wrinkles. White, curly hair, cut short. Light brown eyes flashed like a woman with integrity. Her chin set. Her smile genuine. At the top of the photo was her name.

"Stone, we need Barbara Wakefield's address." She shuffled through documents. Her heart fluttered and pins and needles expanded outward from her chest. "This is urgent."

"How do you know it's urgent?" he asked.

"Experience."

He handed her a picture. "Her address."

She tapped her index finger on a mailbox with a legible street sign in the foreground.

He rose and grabbed the keys. "Ready to go?"

"Ready."

Jackson pointed at the wall. "Are you going to take those down before we go?"

She took them down and stuffed them in her bag. "There. Feel better?"

"Yes."

"Don't get too comfortable. Let's pay her a visit."

7

STONE

Windshield wipers squeaked back and forth, erasing the sprinkles dotting the glass. Jackson's fingers gripped the Crown Vic's steering wheel, his foot on the accelerator.

He remembered Oregon's rain too well.

It was mid-afternoon and Portland's rain had diminished to almost nothing the closer they came to the mountain. He drove up US 26. Mount Hood towered in the distance. The dense trees grew thick on both sides of the freeway. Above, the clouds thinned out with the baby blue sky pushing them aside. It was a day to ski or play in the snow.

Alabama rested her elbow on the passenger door's ledge where the glass met the door. She held up her head and massaged the top of her forehead.

Jackson remembered Nicki in a V-neck, her skin bronzed from their vacation down in Cabo. As they stood in wait for their bags to launch down from the luggage chute at the airport's carousel, her ruby pendant necklace sparkled. He drew her in for a kiss, ready to get back home.

It was years ago, but he could still smell Nicki. Her Dior Miss Dior Eau de Parfum priced at over a hundred dollars for a 1.7-ounce bottle. Damascus rose. Calabrian bergamot. Rosewood from French Guiana. Pink pepper from Reunion Island. Nothing else smelled like it, and it left a permanent mark on his heart. Thankfully, the perfume was rare, and no one wore it.

The road began its ascent toward the mountain. According to the GPS, they'd arrive at Barbara Wakefield's house in twenty-two minutes.

Alabama stared at him for a minute, unblinking. He frowned at her. Now would be a good time to turn on the radio and find an 80s channel. What was she looking at?

"Take a picture. It lasts longer," he said, rolling his shoulders.

She mimed snapping a photo. "What are you thinking about?"

"Putting the pieces of the case together."

"That's *not* what you're thinking about."

He tightened his lips. What did she mean when she said she could *read* people?

"You mind not staring? I'm driving, but you should keep your eyes peeled."

She turned away and tousled her red hair. "I'm doing both."

The trees opened up on the side of a Quik Stop convenience store. A beer sign advertised a Coors Light special on the inside window. An obese woman waddled, 48 oz. Diet Coke in one hand, a dozen scratch-off tickets in the other. Traces of snow covered the parking lot.

Jackson had walked this road as a kid many times, grocery bags from the same store in his hands, his boots slopping through the slush. Not a happy place for a child to learn the lessons of life. He'd learned to steal, how to find cigarette butts in ashtrays, and beg for money.

One day, he showed Nicki where he grew up—a community home where a commune of forty people convened for meetings. Shed-sized earthen domes surrounded it. Nicki once asked to go inside. Never again.

This town was a place he thought he left behind forever. Polaris knew his secrets. Was this a test to make him overcome his childhood trauma?

Alabama typed on her laptop. "Let's have a look. Barbara Wakefield. Date of birth, March 7, 1943. Not a young woman. She worked as a journalist for the Oregonian. Arrested once in her youth during the Civil Rights Movement while protesting against racial violence in Portland. That was 1964. She's lived in Oregon her entire life."

Was she one of the many reporters that wrote a story on his parent's community growing up?

"Three years ago, her husband died of a stroke." She scrolled down. "Looks like she's reported seeing the lights more than once."

He changed lanes. "You mind if I turn the heat down?"

"No, go ahead."

After he did, he asked, "Who did she report them to and when?"

"She filed police reports in both instances, the last one on June 20th, a year ago. That's funny. She saw discs in parks, both times around Mount Hood. No, revise that. According to our files, she's reported seeing them five other times. The other files somehow disappeared."

"A cover-up? Why would the police remove files unless someone told them to?"

She checked. "Unknown. She describes the object as a ring of aqua lights. Though, it's a little different from this case. She didn't report any white electric balls dropping from the sky and hovering over the trees."

If the light involved some kind of experimental military craft, drones maybe, then the base would send in people and make certain files disappear. Then it would come down to a person's word, and the military would deny everything. "Was there anyone else who reported seeing them at the same time?"

"For this sighting or her last sighting?"

"The last sighting."

"Unfortunately, no. It would have given her more credibility. She lives in the middle of nowhere. I don't think she's connected to the power grid. Poor woman. Hopefully, someone checks on her. We're lucky other witnesses came forward this time around."

"Nine people died, and you want to talk about luck?" he asked, a sharp bite in his tone.

She looked at him. "When nine people die and we have corroborating witnesses to stop more killing, that's a blessing."

Though Alabama was stunning, she rubbed him the wrong way, like petting a cat from back to front. Her attitude made her lose about ten points from the beauty scale.

Has she ever seen anything like this before? Better ask her later. "Many people think they're seeing unidentified aerial phenomena when in fact it's Mars or Venus. Sometimes Jupiter."

She pretended to yawn. "Yes, yes. Sometimes people see things that aren't planets. They aren't planes or satellites, either."

He turned a worried eye to the sky. "I want to believe we're not alone." He chortled. "I guess I sound a little like Fox Mulder."

"As long as you don't look like him," she said.

"You think he's ugly?"

"Hideous."

"You're in the minority. Anyway, mathematically, we're not. It doesn't mean aliens are visiting us. Most UAPs are explained away. The universe is a big place, though."

The GPS announced a turn up ahead.

"I've watched enough UFO shows to know the talking points, but without proof, it's all speculation. You know the guy with the funny hair on *Ancient Aliens*?" he asked.

"I wouldn't call it funny."

He scratched his head. "Then what would you call it?"

"A trademark."

"Good point. But you know the guy I'm talking about, right?"

She nodded.

"Don't let him fool you. He'll say anything to keep himself relevant."

She turned on the heater full blast.

He frowned.

"I dunno," she said. "I think he's said some interesting things. I don't judge a person by their hair."

"What do you judge them on?"

"Competence."

Fine, then. As they turned, Jackson glanced at the passenger mirror. A black SUV with tinted windows, changed lanes, keeping pace with him but staying two cars back. "Wren, check your mirror. SUV at six o'clock."

She checked while keeping her head straight. "They've been with us for a few miles. Don't change speeds. They might be FBI. Act normally." She casually tucked the laptop under the seat and unholstered her handgun.

"If they are, why are you taking out your pistol?" He

pulled his sidearm and set it next to him. "We're not going to start a shootout on the freeway, are we?" His stomach dropped like a roller coaster.

Through the tinted glass, he could see four men, all wearing sunglasses. The driver had arms the size of Thor's. The vehicle, a Mercedes-Benz GLS, sped up and stayed in the middle lane. It lacked a front license plate.

Jackson thumbed on the cruise control and braced the wheel with his knees. The Crown Vic drifted into another lane, almost smacking into an adjacent car.

"Easy. The alignment," she said. "If they come closer, speed up and put a car between us. Whatever you do, don't let them pull beside or in front of us."

He tensed his shoulders and lowered his voice. "Grab the wheel."

"What? Keep driving," she said. "Remain calm."

He swore. "I said grab the wheel!"

She scowled, steered with one hand, and tightened her grip on her pistol. "Don't do anything stupid."

Opening the middle console, he withdrew an electronic device the size of an old flip phone. It was an EOCU—Electronic Override Control Unit. When pointed at an engine, it hacked into its computer. He turned it on, found a menu of Mercedes-Benz, and scrolled until pressing on a GLS icon.

She huffed. "You use that thing and you could potentially blow our cover. It's not a good idea. Put it back."

The SUV began catching up to them. He pressed the pedal to the floor. The engine revved. "Getting into a shootout will blow our cover. They're speeding up." The EOCU's display blinked as white dots appeared on the screen.

Attempting to connect, it read.

"Stone."

"Come on, come on." His face flushed red, and he became more determined to avoid violence this early in the mission. A sense of déjà vu swept over him. Yes, he'd trained for this, but now it seemed eerily familiar as if he'd done this before a dozen times.

Her words dried, emotionless. "Pay attention."

He shook his head. Out the back window, the SUV closed in. Were they going to ram them?

"Speed up," she said, ducking slightly.

"Not yet."

"They're going to—"

The EOCU beeped. "We're connected." Jackson touched his chin against his chest as he looked over the EOCU's screen. The SUV's engine control unit, its ECU, appeared in black and white on the display.

"Hold this," he said, taking the wheel. He held his speed at eighty-five. He swooped around a Chevy coupe. The coupe's driver swerved and skidded, its back tires sending smoke in the air.

Someone is going to call the cops on us at this rate.

The device beeped.

"Steer!" Jackson said.

He took the EOCU and tapped on the screen. Another beep sounded as the display highlighted words: *Clear connection with the EOCU's 32-bit, and the 40-MHz processor.* Data streamed, attempting to control the SUV's system to bypass into its CPU.

"If that thing doesn't work, we go to Plan B." Alabama's eyes darted from her pistol to the rearview mirror and back to the freeway. A driver held his horn down when she nearly sideswiped him, and the driver slowed and flipped them the bird.

Crack!

Their Ford slammed into the car next to them, ripping its driver's side mirror off. Debris splattered as it bounced on the ground.

Jackson gritted his teeth. "Keep it straight!"

"You try to drive from the passenger's seat!"

He jerked his head up to see traffic moving away from them. *Not good. Not good.* "You mind not getting us killed?"

"Accelerate! You're only going eighty-five!"

"There's ice on the road."

"And I can't drive this thing and shoot out of the window. Let's go."

The Vic became a bullet, racing down the barrel of a rifle. Ninety. Ninety-five. She yanked the steering wheel, dodging a patch of black ice. The car's tires dug into the side of the road.

Hot anger burst from her lips. "If you don't hurry up!"

Dozens of pings. The device ran through millions of calculations, and the SUV's sensors blipped on the EOCU screen. It reset and powered off.

What the hell?

"Something is wrong. It just shut off." Jackson turned it back on, and it took seconds to re-establish a connection. "Almost there. I'm inside the engine." A second later, data appeared: Temperature, Pressure, Voltage, Acceleration.

His shoulder pressed hard against the door as Alabama cranked the wheel. He slammed on the breaks.

"Take the side street," she said.

The tires spun, and they headed down a street bordered by forest.

She glanced back. "Ready your weapon! They're behind us, coming in fast."

Their transmission hit something in the road. The

Crown Vic bounced, and the EOCU slid off the seat, down by his feet.

He tried reaching down but he couldn't grab it. "Pick it up," he said. He pushed her hand off and steered. Sweat trickled down the bridge of his nose.

Metal crunched. His head jerked back, pounding against the headrest.

"They're ramming us. Get ready to open fire."

Through the chaos, he managed, "I'm not going to shoot FBI agents!"

"They're not FBI!" She rolled down her window. Cold blasted inside, and her hair whipped around her face.

He sucked in a sharp breath. "Grab the damn EOCU and zero in on the SUV's spark timing."

Another crash. Their car fishtailed toward the edge of the road, splashing gravel into the woods. A hubcap flew as the back tires caught the asphalt and straightened out.

"Drive!" Before she could argue, he grabbed the device and set it in his lap. "It's not working!"

Why doesn't it work? What kind of crap device did Polaris give us?

Boom!

The SUV rammed them. Jackson took over the wheel and floored it. Ahead, a green light turned yellow.

Alabama stiffened. "We don't have time. Gun it."

The stoplight flashed red. Light traffic spilled forward.

She snatched the EOCU off his lap and put it in the middle compartment.

Just before he crossed the busy street, he leaned on the horn. Drivers looked over at him and made room.

The SUV shot through traffic, its windows down. Finally, confirmation of their intent—an MP5 submachine gun with a suppressor as long as Jackson's forearm.

Jackson swore and said, "According to Polaris, we can't engage until they do."

"Ramming us is engagement." She leaned out of the window and fired. The shot hit the SUV's window, but it didn't crack. Jackson's ears rang. She spoke, but the ringing drowned her voice. She unloaded her magazine. Brass casings plinked on concrete.

The SUV accelerated.

Crank!

The SUV's bumper slammed into them. Jackson braked. The car spun, and the back end lifted momentarily. As it crunched the pavement, another hubcap broke free and rolled into the snow.

"Hang on!" Alabama popped in a fresh mag.

"We can't outrun them."

Bullets raked their trunk and rear window. As the high-pitched whine in his ears subsided, a beep echoed. The EOCU. "It's working!" he exclaimed. He stole a glance. "Just a bit longer."

A silver Chevrolet Equinox pulled out from a side street. He swerved into the opposite lane and smashed against the door a second time. Horns blared as their vehicle swerved.

"Stone, you really need to—"

An intentional U-turn and he floored it, zipping past the SUV.

Alabama turned. "They're turning around and following us. Persistent bastards."

Jackson's heart skipped a beat when two men in the back of the pursuing car aimed at them.

Beep! Beep!

A stronger connection.

Finally! It's working! Now, don't die on me again.

He bit down on his bottom lip as data ran to the SUV's

ECU, sending information to the fuel injector's control valve. From the EOCU's screen, he could see the valve was operating quickly, opening and closing every few seconds.

He looked up and swerved around a car.

"Stone, pay attention!"

"Hold on. Almost got it." He peeled his eyes away from the street for a moment and to the EOCU.

The fuel supply to the engine is determined by the amount of time the fuel injector stays open; a pulse width. To halt the fuel to the car, turn off the pulse and kill it.

Words ran across the display: *Swipe downward to proceed.*

"Yes! Just do it!" He swiped down and with a new order to change the ECU's function, the EOCU's screen informed him it was shutting off the valve and closing the pulse.

"Wait," she said, glancing back and forth from the mirror to the road. "They're slowing down. No. They're stopping."

Jackson wiped off as much sweat as possible. He imagined he had a wet stain on the seat's backrest from perspiration. "Good."

She shot him a look as he turned onto the main street. "I haven't done that before. It worked."

"Sorry, I was slow. I won't do that again."

She shook her head. "Be sure you don't."

He ran a shaky hand through his hair, his shoulder muscles almost too exhausted to hold up his arm. "All right. We keep going. Any idea who that was?"

"Someone who doesn't want us here."

8

STONE

J ackson breathed a sigh of relief. The violence became a blur. At least that was out of the way. First time for everything. It was like losing his virginity, but with bullets. Above, the clouds had parted, and sun rays beamed from the blue sky, creating shadows from trees across the snow and gravel. A long road extended up a hill, bordered by snowmelt and slush and fir trees. What he wouldn't give for a bourbon.

The gunfight wasn't what he expected. He was trained in the arts of war, but there was nothing like the real thing. His trainers told him how he'd feel before and after a firefight.

All he felt was numbness.

"What's actually going on, Agent Wren?"

"With what?"

He slowed, keeping an eye out for other surprises. "We aren't the CIA or the KGB. Who shot at us?"

"Hard to say. If it's a disc or craft, and it operates off of new physics or antigravity, governments would want to get their hands on it. This type of technology will one day change the world. Besides, Polaris has enemies worldwide."

"I asked Director Hill about that. He wouldn't give me specifics. I'm not sure why he would want to keep our enemies a secret from his agents."

"Ask him."

"And they just happened to find us?"

She brushed her hair aside. "Do you know how easy it is to find someone these days? Our enemies can access any camera on a network. Every three letter agency can tap into house cameras, phone cameras, microphones, social media, email, you name it. It only takes one compromised person for information to leak to the right people."

"Then our enemies know what Polaris knows."

"The better ones. I don't know who shot at us," she said, "but they won't be the last."

Jackson's eyes hardened. "We're going to need another car. They'll be looking for the Vic, and we can't hide the bullet holes."

Flashing a quick smile, she let her lips drop in a straight line. "Easy to patch. I've got supplies in my bag. Pop the trunk."

After pulling over, he killed the engine. Immediately, the chill began invading the cab, and his nose began to run. "I'll take care of it. I need something to focus on. First time someone has tried to kill me."

After he spoke, he knew he'd lied. He'd been shot at before. Hmm. Shaking his head, in truth, he'd never been shot at. Not once. What was wrong with him?

He hopped out and opened her kit and then used a ball-peen hammer and flattened the holes. Using filler and hardener, he fixed the damage. She handed him an unmarked brush and honey-like paste.

"Smear this over the paint and your repairs. It acts like paint." She showed him how the paste blended the colors.

While she watched the road, he finished. Now that he'd seen what could happen on a mission, maybe she would trust him more. "Panic kills," his instructors had said.

He pointed to the bumper. "What about that?"

"Let's take it off. We're going to need a new car." She texted someone. "What happened back there? You were slow. Clumsy."

He removed the bumper with some effort, his cheeks red from the cold.

What did she want him to say? "We survived."

"Look at me a second."

He gave her a dubious look. "I'm fine, Wren."

"That's to be seen. You're shaking. Adrenaline dump. Your pupils are huge. You might get sleepy, but I need you to stay alert. I have a Five-Hour Energy Drink you can have. It's in my side pocket there."

"Not allowed to drink those."

He climbed back inside, but she snatched the keys and drove. Did he perform well at all? Would she tell Director Hill every last detail?

Jackson took the time to disengage and watch the white landscape remind him of his youth. "Thanks for driving."

"You're worried about what I'm going to say to Director Hill."

Was she a mind reader?

"Not at all," he said.

"Good."

The gravel road continued under a rusty, metallic archway. Arborvitae trees, twelve feet in height, grew on either side like a fence and through the arch, painted steps led to an oak porch.

She pulled to a stop under the archway. A midnight blue

Suburu Outback sat in the driveway. The Outback glinted. Not one speck of mud or rust anywhere on it.

A two-story red farmhouse with white siding and cedar shakes butted up to the drive. A brick chimney stuck out of the middle of the roof, and wood-framed windows lined the house. A large door with a bear's shadow greeted newcomers.

Before stepping out of the car, he holstered his weapon. Like her, he surveyed the area, looking for anything out of the ordinary. Nothing but snow.

"Stand ready," she said.

The forest ruffled in the wind. The swing under a tree hung from a branch and swayed.

They marched up a few steps to the porch. She paused midstep.

"What is it?" he whispered.

She pulled out her Sig Sauer P365 micro-compact pistol from her holster. "Ready your weapon. Something is wrong."

The curtains prevented him from getting a good look inside. Recently, someone had taken the time to melt the snow around the front of the house, and patches had remelted into ice.

Alabama knocked twice on the door. "Stone, ready your weapon." She knocked again.

He tilted his head, hand on his gun's grip, but he wasn't going to draw his weapon without a threat being identified.

Her face contorted, and she bent her back.

What was wrong with her? He waited for her to say something, but whatever it was, she shook off a moment later.

He rang the doorbell. "FBI! Open up!"

Determination rose in Alabama's eyes. "She's inside."

"How do you know?"

Alabama curled her gloved hand around the doorknob and twisted it.

Unlocked.

A slow creak.

Jackson walked in, gun pointed ahead and toward the floor.

Someone's been here.

"FBI," he yelled, announcing their presence. "Barbara Wakefield?"

Alabama came in behind him.

No response.

Beyond the entryway, a staircase led upstairs to the left, a hallway to the right. They stood in the living room. Wooden floors. A couch from the 80s, worn down. A muted flatscreen TV was mounted front and center across from it, turned to the QVC network.

Jackson held his breath. The smell of death flooded the house.

A glass door across from him was shattered, and glass shards littered the inside floor and outside back deck. Blood streaked from the living room through a doorless entry into the kitchen.

He aimed up the staircase, and they crept forward, using the walls as cover, their boots noiseless on the carpet. They swept their guns up and down in rhythmic fashion, clearing rooms.

Just like training.

Jackson rounded the counter inside the kitchen, and his heart sunk. His muscles tensed when he spotted a woman on the floor, face-up, eyes open. Her mouth ajar, she had short, gray curly hair, jeans, and a white blouse with purple flowers.

Barbara Wakefield.

Blood had poured from two rounds striking her in the chest and abdomen. Her forearm was severely injured, broken by another shot. Barbara probably struggled into the kitchen. From the bullet wound in the woman's forearm, she blocked the brunt of an attempted kill shot to the forehead.

Gore was splattered against the bottom of the oven next to her head.

"We're too late." Alabama walked past the kitchen sink to the hallway. "I'm going to clear the upstairs. Be sure not to touch anything."

"Could it be the same people who followed us?"

"Good question," she said.

Her steps creaked as she ascended the stairs. Outside the backdoor, he didn't see footprints in the snow. He searched the hallway, stopping diagonally to the bathroom.

Drugs?

The door was open and a medicine cabinet mirror stared back at him, and she didn't keep any medicine inside. Flowery scents from the potpourri basket on the toilet tank's lid filled the room. She was clean.

Back to the hallway, then toward a bedroom. "Bathroom clear," he said into his throat mic.

"Master bedroom and guest bedroom clear up here."

He nudged a half-open bedroom door. The bed's white antique frame sagged in the corner. A thread-bare black bedspread and two ivory pillows topped it. The room's desk and dresser were antique, too. Maybe 1940s. Windows, one on each wall, faced the side yard.

He rifled through the drawers. Clothes. Old Home and Garden magazines. A box of jewelry, untouched. No gun.

"Clear up top," she said.

"Clear." He lowered his weapon and walked back to the

living room. "This wasn't a robbery gone bad." Jackson checked the back door. "Shoe prints."

"Good eye."

Someone covered the prints beyond the porch, and when it snowed, they became almost invisible. Whoever the killer was had escaped into the forest.

"Let's go," Jackson said, leading the way. As his foot touched the cold earth, he glanced back at Alabama.

She pointed ahead. "Take point. If the killer is here, he'll be watching this place and likely try to come at us from behind."

"Understood."

A thick forest acted as the backyard's fence, and she followed him past the wood's edge. His hair caught a snow-covered branch, flicking it back and forth.

"You hear that?" he asked in a thin whisper. A branch cracked. "He's close."

They maneuvered toward a creek trickling up ahead, his eyes and ears open to danger.

Was that something up ahead?

"Down," Jackson whispered.

She kneeled and braced against a tree. "Movement. Eleven o'clock."

More cracking from broken branches and more clunks from feet clomping in the snow.

"He's near," he said, staring through the cracks in the branches. *There.* Jackson stood and aimed his weapon. "Hands up!"

Branches shook as someone ran for it. He tried getting a better look. Shoes slapped across the snow.

He fired, clipping a branch. The assassin bolted in the other direction. Alabama rose.

Through trees, the outline of Jackson's prey appeared. Brown fur. White spots. Tail.

"Ceasefire," she said.

He shook his head in disgust.

She rolled her eyes. "A deer."

"What about the tracks?"

He stepped over a leafless shrub and continued the search. So much snow. Where did the prints go?

"The tracks stopped," he said. "They're just...well...it's almost as if he vanished."

She reached him, her hands grasping her handgun. She eyed the last shoeprint and then the terrain. "He's covered his tracks."

"Either that, or he just floated away."

labama texted Polaris again and explained their need for another vehicle. They'd replied, "We'll arrange something." Whatever that meant. Maybe Director Hill would bring him a tank.

Jackson pushed the curtain aside and peered through the window down Hawthorne Avenue. A few cars drove past, splashing water onto the sidewalk. When would it stop raining? The overcast sky held the sun at bay, and today, Portland smelled clean, like a freshly cut apple.

A man walked up the steps to a church down the street. Jackson poked his tongue against his cheek, exhaling his frustration. As his eyes swept the horizon, he frowned when he saw the steeple, the white cross rising high in the air. He huffed and shook his head.

Was Nicki alongside God, strumming a harp? Was she able to look down on him? He liked to think so. She could be with him right now for all he knew.

He couldn't sleep last night. When the heater would kick on, he'd flinch and check the front and back doors. Rather than lying in bed, he cleaned his weapon and tried to keep his mind in the present.

Alabama woke up early, took a shower, and joined him.

He set his 9mm on the coffee table and leaned back against the couch. The soft cushion felt good against his back after the long day.

"Morning."

"Morning," she said, sitting at her desk. She opened her laptop. "Good news. One of the witnesses is safe under police protection."

"How can you be sure?"

"His record. The FBI keeps Witness Protection off the internet, so you look for other patterns. Would you mind making some orange juice while I work?"

Orange juice did sound good. He brought two glasses over and gave her one. "Regarding the laptop. The briefing said it's secure, but if you're on the web, how secure can it be?"

She took her drink. "Thanks. Back at HQ, we have former CIA, NSA, and IT specialists whose sole job is to find vulnerabilities and exploit them. White hat hackers." She tapped the edge of her computer. "Every system has vulnerabilities built into them. The Chinese have been known to insert malicious code into their software, and United States companies do the same. This laptop," she said with love, "is one of a kind. If anyone other than me tries to open it up, it explodes. If someone manages to get inside, the parts inside are all unique."

"I understand Polaris has a deep budget, but creating a unique computer is no easy feat. What do they do with the production machines?"

She pressed her hands together and flung her fingers out. "Boom."

"I see. So this is worth what?"

"I asked Hill one day about that. He wouldn't say." She turned the screen to him.

Was she using Windows? "It looks like you're using something from Microsoft."

"What did you expect it to look like?" She gave him an odd glare.

A young man pushed his child in a stroller down the sidewalk in front of their house, ducking a bit under a cherry tree's hanging leaves. A cartoon played on the kid's tablet. The little girl was mesmerized.

I'll never know what it means to be a father. He blinked and tapped his foot. *Stop thinking that way. You've got work to do.*

He twisted around. Between the kitchen and the dining room was a glass sliding door, no doubt with bulletproof glass. If things became spicy, they could run into one room or the other, slide the door shut, and make good their escape. A foundation stood outside where a shed once was. Good. They removed it. Better line of sight and no place for an enemy to hide.

Out of the corner of his eye, Alabama gazed through the back. He inspected every inch of her face. So beautiful. Strange that Polaris would allow a woman with such beauty to be an agent. Everyone would notice her.

She rubbed her eyes and stared at her hands for a moment.

He intertwined his fingers and glanced at her leg.

"Are you still thinking about the chase and firefight?" she asked.

"Actually, no. I don't know. I'm at ease, now. All except the murder. There's at least one assassin. Someone is covering this up, and I want to know who and why. I've been on plenty of UFO investigations, but no one ever kills a witness."

Alabama tacked up her pictures again. "Actually, they do. At a minimum, we are dealing with compartmentalized top secret technology. I doubt someone murdered a person after they saw a twinkle in the sky."

"Then why come alone? We only saw one set of prints."

She glanced over her shoulder. "It wouldn't surprise me if a person worked as a lookout. Before we left, I checked the front for tire tracks or other footprints in a different size."

"And?"

"Nothing, unfortunately."

Barbara's bloody face appeared in his mind. A nightmare, not like in movies or a show. Visceral and real.

Alabama paced and began to hum.

He cleared his throat. "What are you doing?"

"I'm humming."

"I can see that."

She stopped in the middle of the room. "Well, yesterday was a long day."

"So, you're humming?"

"Does it bother you?"

He immediately said no when he wanted to say yes. Of course, it bothered him. Now wasn't the time to hum away someone's death. "Aren't you concerned about who tried to kill us on the way to Barbara Wakefield's house?"

"I thought you said you weren't thinking about the chase and the gunfight." Before he could respond, she continued, her voice light and easy. "Of course, I'm concerned." She swiped her hair away from her eyes.

Why did Hill choose to torture him with this woman? This wasn't going to work.

Jackson hummed along mindlessly, accenting the lower bass-line in the song. *What am I doing?* He stopped.

She left for the bathroom and shut the door until the humming dulled and faded away.

He knew the words, though they were in French.

Tu oublieras / Les sourires, les regards / Qui parlaient d'ternit / You will forget / The smiles, the looks / That spoke of eternity.

Jackson continued to hum, then cupped his mouth.

I don't know French.

His nose wrinkled, and he shook off a shiver. The lyrics were foreign to him, the tune familiar, as if he'd sung it a thousand times in a language he didn't know.

She walked out of her room. "Tu sais ce Français?"

The language sounded so familiar, like the opening theme in Star Wars. Who can forget that? "Sorry, I don't speak French," he said half-heartedly.

"Are you a fan of French pop music?"

"I don't know any."

She studied him for a second and rubbed the back of her neck.

"I'm more of a classics guy."

"Like Led Zeppelin?" she asked.

He shook his head. "The 80s. Never a better time for music."

"What's your favorite song?"

"What year?"

She laughed. "Let's go with 1981."

"Oh, that's easy. 'Don't You Want Me Baby?'"

"That's The Human League, right?"

"Yeah."

"Ever hear their song, 'The Lebanon'?"

He smiled. "Wow. I'm impressed. I love that one. What

about you?" Alabama would have had to search for that track. "The Lebanon" wasn't played on the radio.

"It's a toss-up." She looked up at the ceiling. "Yeah, it's hard to say. I might get the year wrong. 'Our Lips are Sealed'."

Taking a moment, he studied her face. "You look a bit like Belinda Carlisle from that video."

"People used to call her fat."

"You're not fat." *Fell into that trap, didn't I?* "I didn't take you for a person who would like The Go-Go's."

"What kind of person did you take me for?"

Good question.

She pulled her hair behind her ear.

"I'm not sure," he said. "I'll get back to you on that."

An alert sounded from their laptop, and he clicked the bell icon. Opening the quantum encryption node, a pin camera scanned his eye and checked his capillaries. If he were dead or drugged, the computer would seize up until Alabama cleared it. A *Project Horizon* folder blipped on the screen.

A picture of an older man filled the display. His skin resembled boiled leather, and a few scraggly gray hairs circled his head. He stretched as best he could in a hospital bed, sheets covering him from the chest down. An IV was hooked up to his arm, and monitors surrounded him, showing his vitals. A bruise on the side of his temple accompanied his black eyes. No lacerations or casts or bandages. Who was he?

With iron blue eyes and a nose that had once been broken but didn't heal straight, he reminded him of Jackson's father.

Below the picture, the bio read: Owner and Operator of O'Malley's Trucking.

His injuries mirrored those of the hikers, and the image was taken on the same date. The man was sent to Providence Portland Medical Hospital.

"Wren, I've got something. Patrick O'Malley. Have a look."

She hurried to the couch and sat next to him. When the cushion sank, their hips touched. "See the timestamp? This was snapped seven minutes ago."

Jackson snagged the car keys and pointed to the pictures she'd tacked on the wall the night before. "Please tell me you'll take those down before we go."

But by that time, she'd left the house and stood by the car.

He snatched the laptop. *You're going to get us into trouble.*

A fter flashing their badges to the hospital registrar, they left toward Patrick O'Malley's room in the emergency wing. As Jackson breathed, he reminded himself to keep a low profile. Avoid eye contact. Walk with a purpose. How many cameras were inside this place?

He sucked on a breath mint, moving it between his teeth, a not-so-subtle gift from Alabama. He'd be sure to buy a roll of Life Savers on the way out. Must have been the coffee.

As they walked within sight of Patrick O'Malley's room, he tugged on Alabama's forearm and pulled her to the side. Two men wearing suits flanked the door. FBI. He almost missed their earbuds and the tiny cord tucked behind their collars.

Jackson leaned casually closer to her and pretended to check his phone. "Feds?"

"That's my guess, but we can't be sure."

He played with his phone. "If they're not Feds? We aren't

in the middle of nowhere this time. If things get spicy inside the hospital, then what?"

"You're Agent Timothy Simms, and I'm Agent Jenna Bailey. If anything happens, we have the law on our side, at least for a few minutes." She touched his phone. "Why do you think we spent so much time training? Don't freeze up on me now, Mulder." She smiled at a nurse walking across their path.

He finally let go of her arm after she pulled away. He pursed his lips, his eyes now fixed on a supply closet down another hallway. "Maybe we can get some mops and a bucket. Tell them the room needs cleaning."

She whispered, "How about we steal some doctor coats and pretend we're physicians?"

"What do you mean?"

"Oh, how I love working with the new ones," she said to herself.

"Now you're mocking me?"

"A little." She gave him another mint.

This one tasted like plastic strawberries. Who made these things? "What's next?"

"Trust the plan."

As they approached, a Hispanic man stepped forward, checked their badges, and grimaced. He'd seen better days and looked as if he was ready to fall over from exhaustion.

They introduced themselves as Agents Espinoza and Winters.

Espinoza looked up at a camera. "We weren't expecting any visitors. Where'd you come from?"

Ah, this line again. No problem. Jackson gave his story; Alabama her's.

Winters, a clean-shaven Caucasian man with a burn

mark on his neck, threw up his arm. "Step away from the door."

She nodded. "Sure." This time, she was the one tugging on Jackson's sleeve. The good news: if they were shot, at least they were in a hospital.

Looking the IDs up and down, the agents made small talk and handed the badges back to them.

"There's someone inside already," Espinoza said. "We weren't expecting anyone."

Alabama stared unblinking at Agent Winters.

"We're here on other orders." Jackson stepped between them. "Do you mind?"

She followed Jackson. "Thank you, gentlemen."

Inside, a man who sat close to the hospital bed massaged his elbow. He stood when they entered.

He wore the same black attire everyone who worked at the FBI wore. Did they buy them from the same store? It made them easy to spot.

Beeps from a heart monitor reverberated in the room. A blue curtain hung bunched near the head of the bed. O'Malley breathed calmly, sedated from the IV.

"Who are you?" the agent asked.

That voice. Where had Jackson heard it before? Polaris training? A movie? A show? Maybe he was imagining it.

"Special Agent Justin Carter." The man rose his chin high. His jawline, straight and strong—Eastern European? His haircut, shaved on the sides, flat on top. More the way a man in the military would cut his hair. If given the role for a psychopath in a slasher movie, he would have gotten it on his appearance alone. He could pass for mid to late thirties. Physically fit. Deep brown eyes.

And when he flicked his gaze to Jackson, and he didn't react, Carter gave the smallest smirk.

Jackson's hand formed a fist. He'd never been so repulsed by someone so quickly and for no logical reason. The FBI must have found this moron in their bottom bin of eligible agents, his file an inch from the garbage can.

At least they had someone protecting this witness.

"Badges?"

Alabama tilted her head, her brows low. "We just presented them to your men."

"We're on high alert. I need to double-check." Carter offered his palm. "Let's see them." If bad breath bothered her, this jackass had it in spades. The odor of menthol stuck to him.

Jackson waited until she gave up her ID. Then he did.

Carter studied them, paying particular attention to her's.

"So, you two are assigned to this case? I would expect..." He cut himself off as he ran his eyes from Alabama's feet to her chest. "Two *men*. But I have to say, I'm not disappointed. Here you go."

When he handed them back, Alabama clicked her tongue and kept her badge in hand.

Jackson edged closer to the unconscious man in the hospital bed; Patrick O'Malley.

Out the window, the sun reached for the horizon. Oak and maple trees, roofs, and street lamps stretched into the distance, green and lush.

"As you can see," Carter said, "O'Malley is unconscious. Why don't I get your numbers, and I'll make sure someone in my office calls you when he wakes up." Carter brought out his phone, and he threw a shoulder back, focusing on Alabama's chest. "Let's start with you."

Jackson wanted nothing more than to wipe Carter's smug expression off his face. With a hammer. "That's not why we're here."

"Either give me your numbers or you'll have to wait outside," Carter countered.

It was then that Alabama's jaw trembled with rage. "How about this? Cut the crap and quit acting like you're in charge of this investigation. We're here to get answers from this man. I'm sorry, but you're going to have to step out of the room while we conduct our interview. If you want our numbers, call the Portland field office."

Carter's shoulders went rigid. "Is there a problem?"

"Not yet," she said. "Wait outside while my partner and I conduct our interview."

Carter pointed at her. "We run a strict operation here, Agent Bailey. I did not get a call, text, or email from my supervisor. I have no idea what you're doing here, but clearly something fell apart in the chain of command."

Why does this man seem so familiar?

Alabama inched closer to him, frustration written on her lips. "Get. Out."

Carter pulled his arm back. "Have we met?" he asked her.

"No," she said.

"I could have sworn I've seen you before."

Something isn't right. But would she give him a signal if anything was wrong?

Carter said, "I'm not going to tell either of you again. O'Malley is a special case. Neither of you have been cleared to be here as far as I'm concerned, and we don't tolerate amateurish behavior in our city. If you don't leave, I'll have the two men outside escort you out of the building."

Jackson crossed his arms and tapped his index finger on his elbow. *Calm down. He's only baiting us. The question is— why? Did he want to get fired?*

The light from the window caught Carter's face, and one

of his eyes flashed green, not brown. Was he wearing contacts? Jackson changed his focus to the patient.

O'Malley's stitches ran across the bruise on his temple, and crusted blood edged each stitch. A blunt force trauma wound. The impact wasn't hard. He bent over to check his nose. Black eyes could be caused by a broken nasal bone.

Alabama raised an eyebrow and gave a glassy stare. "Feel free."

But Carter didn't call for the two men outside the room.

"I see," she said. "If you would have done your job, we wouldn't be here. There's a good reason we're here. Your department is incompetent. Get out or you'll be fired by this time tomorrow."

Carter's lip trembled, and he sized Jackson up.

"If you ever threaten either of us again, I'll make sure to plant enough evidence on you to send you to GITMO for life," Jackson said. "Am I making myself clear, Agent Carter?"

Carter nudged his chair to the side, the chair's legs causing a screeching sound across the floor. "In all my years, I've never encountered two more unprofessional special agents. I know for a fact neither of you should be here. This is a homicide case, and we here in Portland don't need Norfolk busybodies making our work more difficult than it already is."

Jackson straightened his back, both his hands prepped to strangle the life out of this pathetic jackass. "Unprofessional? Look here, the next time you stare at her chest, you're likely to find out..."

"That's enough," Alabama said, stuffing her ID away.

Carter pointed at the door. "Get out. I want both of you out! Now!"

There was that tone again. That anger. Where had he heard it before?

A memory flashed in his mind. The man before him—his facial expressions, his tone of voice, the way he carried himself—he'd certainly seen him somewhere. But something about his mannerisms struck him as awkward, and he couldn't put his finger on it.

What he wouldn't give to throttle him with hammer fists.

But why hate him? Who was he?

Jackson flexed and cleared his thoughts, confusion clouding his focus.

Alabama shoved herself between him and Carter. "We can take it from here, sir."

On the side of the bed, a blue nurse alert button stuck out a half-inch. Jackson pressed it repeatedly.

I've got to get this piece of trash as far from O'Malley as possible.

Jackson's mind slipped gears, and he said what he'd been thinking since he first laid eyes on him. "Your name isn't Carter."

The agent braced himself. "What was that?"

The world around Jackson shrunk into a pinpoint black hole. A memory manifested and blossomed.

A C-130 CARGO PLANE. A platoon of mercenaries. Body bags and spoils of war.

Hot weather. So hot, that day. Humid like crazy.

Spoken French. Sometimes English. The locals spoke Spanish.

Champagne. Vodka. Cocaine. A few side girls to make the afternoon interesting.

Three-story bungalow. South American style. Pink and soft brown. Beautiful.

So much money. So much fun. And all night long, whatever he wanted.

Hanging out with him, Agent Carter.

Not his real name.

BRUSHING his hand against his pistol, Jackson said, "Your name is..."

The door swung wide. A nurse in scrubs, hair pulled back in a ponytail, rushed in. "Is everything all right in here?" She swooped to O'Malley's side and clicked the button, turning it off.

Carter rushed the nurse and planted a palm into the nurse's chest. She screamed and flew into a tray, spilling coffee on the wall.

Alabama snatched Carter's jacket.

Carter chopped her in the neck, sending her flailing to the bed. Shoving Jackson aside, he tunneled through the maelstrom and sprinted out of the room.

"Don't pursue! Stand down!" Alabama said.

Defying her, his adrenaline pumping on overdrive, he rushed down the hall. Espinoza and Winters were both missing from their post.

Giving chase, Jackson ran after him, and the man dashed toward a stairwell side exit, turned, and fired his Glock. A glass window exploded.

Hospital employees shouted for help, and a woman shouted, "Someone call 911!"

Reaching to his hip, Jackson pulled his H&K 9mm. The man blasted again, and Jackson kept his head down. Doctors shouted for people to take cover. A nurse fell prone. Then the stairwell side exit door opened, and Carter disappeared.

Jackson's earpiece slipped out, and on the other end, Alabama yelled something. But her words were suffocated by his shoes slapping on the tiled floor.

You're not getting away, Hunter Flynn, you son of a bitch.

He flattened himself against the wall and opened the door, peeking through the slit. Someone hustled down the stairs.

Here goes nothing.

He leaped through and continued the chase.

The door opened from the landing below and slammed shut with a bang.

Grabbing the railing, he hopped to a descending staircase, ignoring the pain from his feet hitting the concrete, and crashed through the entrance leading back into the hospital.

A fist whipped by, grazing his chin. A lucky miss. He threw up an arm to block any more blows, but a jab landed neatly on his cheek. Stars appeared, and he took a step back.

"There's nothing I love more than playing with Feds like you," Flynn said, throwing a right cross, grazing Jackson's ear. He dodged a hook just in time to receive an elbow strike to his shoulder blade.

Flynn reached for Jackson's pistol, but Jackson landed a blind hammer fist, crashing it into Flynn's nose. His head bounced against the concrete wall.

He pushed Jackson away. "I like your style. Security!"

Every noise became amplified, and Jackson ground his teeth.

"FBI! Call 911! Get security!" Flynn laughed.

Patients and hospital staff fled into rooms.

Time to finish this fight.

Twisting on his back leg, Flynn landed a sidekick. Jackson gasped, the air rushing out of his lungs like a popped balloon. Fists flew at him faster and faster, his balance shaking. A fist caught him low, grazing his nose. Blood painted the floor.

"Having fun, yet?" Flynn asked, kneeing Jackson in the groin.

The reaction wasn't what he expected as his knee bone cracked against Jackson's metal cup Polaris insisted he wore.

Flynn cringed in pain.

"That must have hurt." Jackson raised his gun but was met by an uppercut. Stars. Black. More stars. He swung his H&K, hoping to pistol-whip him. When he gained his senses, he lay flat on his back, and Flynn barreled down the now-empty hall. No one worked the registrar's desk, but through a small window, a nurse spied on them.

A tiny voice carried through his earbud. Alabama. He pushed it in his ear.

"Stone, do you copy?"

She sounds like she's ready to rip my head off. "Go."

"Crown Vic. Two minutes or I'm leaving without you."

You're going to leave me to be arrested? "Understood."

Jackson leaped over the registrar counter. The computer screens flashed a login box. Pens and paper. A calendar. Water dispenser. Folders. Notebooks. Manuals. Didn't they have a map?

A heel slammed against the side of Jackson's head, hitting him squarely. He barreled into the wall. The world tilted. On instinct, his forefinger jerked back. But there wasn't a trigger. Or a pistol. His vision blurred, and he slunk on a copy machine.

"You don't know what you've gotten yourself into," Flynn said.

Thunk. Thunk.

Flynn thumbed rounds out from Jackson's handgun's

magazine, and they spilled out, bouncing harmlessly on the rug. "Heckler Koch USP Compact 9mm. Not your typical sidearm for a Special Agent in the Federal Bureau of Investigation, wouldn't you say?" He tore it apart, scattering the pieces behind him. "My, my. Such a waste. The next time we meet, you'll know to shoot first, won't you?"

Several of Jackson's teeth throbbed. He fished out molar fragments embedded in his cheek. Bloody saliva coated his fingers. "Who do you work for?"

Flynn pressed his Glock to Jackson's skull, his legs akimbo. "In this business, there are those who think they're the good guys and those who know better. Someday, you're going to have to decide which one you are."

"I'm the guy that's going to put a bullet in your head," Jackson said. "I've met you before."

Flynn shoved his pistol against Jackson's forehead until his face tilted up, and he studied Jackson's face. "If you had, you'd be dead."

Footsteps echoed toward them.

"Freeze!"

Two cops stood with their weapons drawn. Flynn swung his aim around. One of the police officers fired twice, sending sparks out of the copy machine. Flynn squeezed the trigger, hitting them both in the throat with single precise shots.

Seeing his chance, Jackson grabbed Flynn's legs and yanked, but they were like oak trees, and he easily slipped out.

Snickering, Flynn backhanded him and wore a sly expression.

It was over.

Jackson's duty was done. He would soon see his wife.

A bright flash.

Something heavy smacked him on the side of his head.

Spiral rifling from inside Flynn's Glock beckoned him like a tunnel into the underworld. "If I kill you now, I'll have little to look forward to in the next few days. By all means, keep investigating. But consider this your warning." Flynn kicked, smashing polished leather into Jackson's chin.

The world funneled into a speck of light and winked black.

11

I'm never working with another agent like Stone as long as I live, Alabama thought.

She squeezed her fingers together. *I should have known better than to listen to Director Hill. This is how I'm going to die someday.*

She could hear Jackson running down the hall after whoever hit her.

The nurse got to her feet, covered in coffee. "I'll call security."

As the nurse turned her back, Alabama threw her in a chokehold and put her to sleep. With only minutes to spare, she placed her in a chair and dragged her into the bathroom. She used her belt to tie her up and locked the door.

"Stone, do you copy?" she asked. Nothing. But she could hear him running. "Agent Stone, do you copy?" She bit her lip. "Put your damn earbud in, idiot!" Well, if he wasn't going to respond to that, he didn't hear her at all.

She yanked out her phone, set a timer, and aimed it at the witness. Then she shook the bed. "Patrick O'Malley?"

He stirred.

"O'Malley?"

He moaned and his eyes opened, then shut.

"Patrick? Wake up."

He touched his bruised temple and frowned. "Where? Where am I?" he groaned.

"You're in the hospital." Alabama showed him her badge. "I'm Special Agent Bailey, FBI."

He stared blankly at her, his head slightly off the pillow. "FBI?"

"Yes."

He gazed around the room. "What happened?" Wincing, he shut his eyes and sighed.

Focusing on her breathing, she rubbed her palms together. Rippling energy suffused her mind. Pinpricks of emotions spanned outward. A chill ran down her spine. The aura changed color. From blazing green to pine green. Over and over. His body was healing nicely.

"That's what I'm here to ask you," she said.

His mouth fell open. Rolling his shoulders backward, he moved a shaky hand to his chest, fingers splayed. "It was real? The thing I saw?" His eyes became fire. "Tell me it wasn't real."

She walked to him, doing her best to be slow and smooth. "We found you in the forest and brought you here."

He bent his knees and fidgeted. "You're going to think I'm crazy."

"No, sir. I'm here to learn the truth. Tell me what happened."

"It levitated me. And then..."

According to Polaris, she wasn't permitted to touch a witness. But in this case, she'd make an exception. She put her hand on his shoulder and nodded. "It's okay. You're safe now."

He took a deep breath. "I'm sorry. Makes me nervous to talk about it. It threw me."

"What threw you?"

"I don't know. I'm a God-fearing man. But what I saw ain't nothing like anything I'd seen before. God didn't have no part in it." Falling back on the pillow, his eyes met the ceiling. "Blue lights in the sky, spinning like a Ferris wheel, just like in the story in the book of Ezekiel." Terror clouded his words.

When did you see this?

"Highway 26. I didn't know what it was. Happened a few more times, so I pulled to the side of the road. That's when I saw them blue lights. It lit up Mount Hood, it was so bright."

"What happened after you pulled over?"

He rubbed his wound and glanced around. He lowered his voice like he'd been caught robbing a bank. "I got out." He shook his head. "I couldn't help it. I crossed the highway on foot and stepped into the forest. I took pictures with my phone. Where is it? Where's my stuff?"

"It's being kept safe for when you're released. Time is a factor, Mr. O'Malley. I need to know what happened."

Bang!

He shuddered. "What was that?"

Bang!

"Let me check." Those weren't the sounds of an H&K 9mm. That was a Glock.

She closed the curtains around Patrick and opened the bathroom door. Thankfully, the nurse was still unconscious, but she'd be awake soon.

She stepped into the bathroom and closed the door. "Stone, what the hell is going on?"

She received nothing in return.

"Stone?!" *Rookies!*

When she went to exit the bathroom, the nurse's eyes opened, but she couldn't keep them open.

Sorry about this. Alabama slid over to the nurse and said over her shoulder to O'Malley, "It was nothing. Keep talking." She used a chokehold and put the nurse back to sleep while he continued.

After closing the bathroom door, she opened the curtains and took a seat next to O'Malley.

He puffed up his cheeks and blew softly, his eyes cast to the side. "It beckoned me and, at the same time, scrambled my brain. It hummed. In my mind, the hum was more like laughing. Heckling me. Like a demon."

She shifted in her seat. "What happened next?"

"Well, the thing descended from the sky. Then I seen small balls of light flyin' at it. It sounded like steel grating across steel. That's when I heard the screams. People runnin'. I kept hurrying over to them." He paused. "Something bad was happenin' to them folks." He swallowed hard. "Almost like their skin was being slowly torn off."

"Did you see that?"

"No. But I felt it through and through." He tried folding his arms and winced.

His palpable fear filled her stomach, and his pain coursed through her veins.

What he described reminded her of Project Lightjump. Two years ago, a handful of monks witnessed balls of light falling toward their monastery and then ascended and descended. The fear stirring in one of the monk's eyes. She'd never forget.

"The lights made you *feel* those screaming people?" she asked.

"I... I don't know." He ran his hands up and down the top sheet. "But I run after 'em, pushing branches away. That's when the lights got brighter. The white lights grew brighter, too. Then the hum deepened." His breathing quickened. "I found myself at the edge of the trees. I could see plain as day what was goin' on. People were runnin', half-naked. That hum got even louder, and I covered my ears and crouched. I-I..."

Uncontrollable tears welled in his eyes.

She reached forward, hand on his forearm. "You're safe. Just a moment. I have some water for you."

An excuse to call Jackson. He wasn't answering. In case of capture, she would be forced to pull back and let Polaris handle it. She might never see him again. Polaris liked cleanliness.

"Stone, do you copy?" She checked her comm to make sure it functioned.

Over the hospital intercom, she heard two codes called out. Security. Lockdown.

"Stone, do you copy?"

"Go."

Well, about time you listened to me! I hate this man. "Crown Vic. Two minutes or I'm leaving without you."

"Understood."

She checked the timer on her phone. *If I'm not out of here in sixty seconds, I'm dead.* She opened the curtain.

O'Malley pulled away and grasped what little hair he had. "I thought I heard you talkin' to someone," he said.

"My partner. Continue." She tapped her foot.

"The people stopped yelling and marched in a straight line like in the Army. I did, too. Couldn't control myself." He looked at her phone. "Am I in trouble?"

Setting her jaw, she gave him a meaningful grimace. "Keep talking."

From his expression, he didn't like her tone, but her

scowl seemed to make him keep speaking. "The last thing I remember was being picked up off the ground maybe five feet or so, and a scream shaking me to the core, like nothin' I ever heard. Something possessed the forest that night. The blue lights lowered more." He laid his hand flat and whistled. "A saucer." He shrugged. "Saw a fog, too."

"A disc?"

"I think so."

Someone tested the door and knocked.

"Be right back," Alabama said.

"FBI, open the door," a man said on the other side.

Polaris taught her many things, but one thing she couldn't do was lower her voice enough to sound like a man. She wouldn't sound at all like Agent Carter or whatever his name was.

Think. "Mr. O'Malley is getting dressed."

"Where's Agent Carter?" he asked.

"CRT." Crime Response Team. And her? She was on the Emergency Response Team, right in time to protect O'Malley. "I'm part of the ERT. Witness secured."

"You good in there?" Less suspicion. More annoyance now.

"Help secure this floor," she said.

"On it," he said, leaving the scene.

"Am I in trouble?" O'Malley asked. "I ain't going back to the joint. I ain't seen a damn thing."

She pulled the curtain aside. "Now, you listen good, Mr. O'Malley. Violation of 18 U.S. Code 1001 could land you five years and a fine you'll never afford. Remember that one? That's the one about making false statements."

"Something don't seem right. Then again, never does." He sniffed. "I don't want to be in no violation. By the way, that coffee I smell? I could sure use a cup."

She watched the timer reach zero. *Beep.*

"You've been helpful." She stopped recording with her phone camera. Would he be safe by himself?

"That it? Ain't nothing else?" he asked. "What about my coffee?"

The door to the bathroom boomed as the nurse kicked at it relentlessly. Muffled words rumbled.

"Gotta run." Alabama threw open the door and smacked into a man's chest. Black suit. Buzz cut. Boring tie. Yup. FBI. Wonderful. Quickly shutting the door behind her, she looked up into his eyes, blinking rapidly and giving him a sexy smile.

Graying hair parted to the side, strong Navajo cheekbones, and a perfect chin. His appearance made her pause.

He flashed his badge. "Agent Marston. I was just looking for you." His crow's feet deepened with a smile. When her eyes lowered to his nose, he gazed at her breasts and cleared his throat.

She inhaled deeply and held it in. Everything about him, the intense stare, his monotone voice, and his charisma gave her chills. He felt wrong. Dangerous. Like he'd spent his life hunting serial killers.

He pointed toward the hallway. "Where are the two agents assigned here? Where's Carter?"

How am I going to get to the car in fifteen seconds with Duke Charming in my way? Time to change the subject and go on the offense. "We're in lockdown, sir. The witness is secure inside this room. If you'll excuse me, I'm going to find out what's going on. When I do, I'll report directly back to you immediately."

Towering over her, his eyes became slits. "Move out."

She hurried down the hall as if she could follow Jackson's inner warmth like the smell of chocolate chip cookies.

She rushed by a glass pane window separating doctors and nurses, who took refuge.

Her hands tingled. A wave of energy dove into her spine. The color red. Hostility. *Stone's in trouble. If I could only speak to him for a second.* Hopefully, he understood using their mics would get them caught.

Halting by a closet, she curled her body behind a door and closed her eyes. Where is he? Jackson Stone appeared in her mind, naked but obscured by a blanket of wild darkness. For a flicker, everything around her changed.

Became black.

Then a torrent of immense pain so deep in his heart, it would take a miracle to transform it into love.

Stone. She faced the side exit. *He went this way.* Dashing down the stairs, electricity stabbed into her fingers. His spirit tugged her.

Director Hill warned her not to use her abilities this way. "You're not ready," he'd said. "We have not been able to fully test you."

Alabama pressed her empathy, expanding it, pushing it outward into the infinite.

What's the harm in harnessing what the universe provides?

Alabama blasted through the side exit and her feet leaped from step to step, following Jackson's trail like a bee to nectar. Her legs were iron pistons, vaulting her to him.

When she reached the bottom of the staircase, Jackson felt closer. No, he *was* closer. Danger lay ahead. He was up to his neck in it. She shook her head.

Once through the door leading out from the staircase, she entered a nurses' station. A massive desk took center stage of the room, and hallways led in six different directions. Like a cat, she inched inside, her head swiveling this way and that, searching. Her breathing punctuated the quiet.

But someone else was close.

Groaning.

Behind a copy machine lay Jackson's body. Blood soaked his chest. Was he shot? When she followed the line of blood up to his chest, it led to his nose and mouth. She relaxed. He was alive. Something smelled like death, and when she observed the two dead cops with bullet holes in their necks, she covered her mouth.

She gathered up Jackson's disassembled pistol, the ammo, and checked him for injuries. He hadn't been shot anywhere, but he might have a concussion. She shook Jackson's shoulders. "Wake up! Wake up!"

His eyes fluttered, but he didn't move.

"Get up!"

Rummaging through drawers, she found an emergency medical kit and took the smelling salts. She ripped open the package and waved it under his nose. He shuddered and couldn't focus.

He grunted something and closed his eyes. The salts worked the second time, and she helped him to his wobbly feet. With two dead officers, the manhunt would be on in a big way. Stealing their pistols would only result in more investigators being assigned to the case.

Screw it.

She took one and stole a pair of rubber gloves next to a hand sanitizer.

As she put them on him, she said, "Here, hold this." Making sure he wouldn't drop the pistol or accidentally fire it, she flipped the safety on the police-issued Glock 19.

When she located an exit to the parking lot, the door

was locked. "Guard your face." She blew apart the lock and helped Jackson outside.

Pairs of hands grabbed her. Black suit. Military haircut. Bear strength.

FBI.

She kicked, but the agent blocked it with his knee. Her foot cried out in pain, and her big toe jammed. Arching her foot, she gritted her teeth and squirmed, fighting with every ounce of her will.

Jackson fell from her grip and banged his head on the rocks.

Her heart skipped. *I'm too late.*

Alabama put up her fists with no intention of throwing a punch. The agent adopted a defensive stance, and she feigned a left cross. He flinched, and she stuck her foot behind him and pushed, using his weight. He crashed into the brush outside the door.

She grabbed the Glock before he could stand.

He threw up his arms. "Don't shoot."

Throwing her full force to the side, she pistol-whipped him unconscious and pocketed the agent's phone.

Jackson began to gain his footing and then rolled his neck. "Is he dead?" His voice was nothing more than a squeak.

Keeping silent, she pointed to their Crown Vic, not more than twenty feet from them. He acknowledged her with a nod.

"Stone, look at me. Can you drive?"

He coughed and gave a thumb's up.

"Drive slow. If necessary, I'll blast us out of here."

"You'll what?"

He's not slurring.

She tossed him the keys. "Get your badge out."

The Vic fired up, and she helped Jackson buckle his seatbelt.

"We are leaving. Act normal." She opened her other pocket and pulled out the special agent's earpiece she'd snatched. "North Exit," she said to the Feds. "Be on the lookout for a black Mercedes E-Class sedan, license plate John William Nora dash Edward Lincoln ten, exiting the premises, over."

"Copy," the reply came.

She muted it.

"Good thinking," Jackson said.

"One of us has to."

"You're mad at me?"

"Furious."

"How long is that going to last?"

"I haven't decided, yet."

They showed their badges to the police blocking the exit, and he waved them through. She glanced behind her. A lone cop, blood decorating his uniform, smiled and waved goodbye.

12

STONE

Alabama made an emergency call to Hill using a modified burner phone and an internet connection. Before, this mission didn't feel real. The guns, the hand-to-hand combat. Jackson fought outside himself, muscle memory kicking in at the right moments. Or so he'd thought. Did Polaris expect him to fight people like this? They'd made a mistake putting him on this case. It was good Alabama called Director Hill. He'd probably bring a replacement agent. Jackson wasn't ready for this and everybody knew it, especially himself.

He undressed in the bathroom, singing The Smith's song, "How Soon Is Now?" and examined purple splotches covering his body like alien tattoos.

Did his head hurt more than his ribs? Thank God for Polaris making him wear a cup. That would have been the end of that.

Alabama moved close to the door. "Do you need anything?"

Her voice dripped sex every time she spoke and rated a ten when she tried to hide it. Like now. It'd been years since he'd had a woman. He buried that thought at Nicki's funeral.

And Polaris suggested he not find love. "When you are promoted to a field agent, you'll have as many women as you want," they'd said. "And you'll get paid to do it."

Pass on that idea.

But Alabama. It was hard to put a finger on it. She was interesting.

But it was only a thought. Nothing to stay focused on for any length of time.

"I'm good," he said.

She didn't leave. "Are you sure? I need you to stay awake for me. You might have a concussion. How about some coffee?"

What did she say? Something about a drink?

Why did his legs feel heavy?

The faucet ran.

Was that him in the mirror?

His knees bent, and he greeted the floor face first.

"Hey. Wake up. This is the fourth time now. Stay awake," Alabama said through the blur. Fingers snapped. "Agent Stone, are you with me? Look at my finger."

He sat on the couch, a towel wrapped around his waist. A quilt lay on top of his lap. Alabama's red hair drifted on her shoulders, strands of beautiful hair for him to admire.

Thoughts of Nicki pinged back and forth, and a mirage of her visage slipped over Alabama's face; the perfect mask. She was everything he ever wanted, and his body began to show it.

Closing his eyes, he leaned in. One last kiss with Nicki.

"What are you doing, nerd?"

"What?"

Crap.

She pursed her lips in disappointment and shook her head like a dismissive mother. "Rookies. I swear. One of these days, you will live long enough to be useful."

Ouch.

"I am so sorry, Dr. Wren. I was confused there. I would never..."

"Good. Well, you seem to be," she said, pausing and glancing at his groin, "ahem, awake enough to go finish your shower and have that cup of coffee."

He blushed. *God, why do you do this to me?* "Yes. That. I'll go do that now. Sorry."

Right when he opened the door, she said, "Cute butt."

13

Director Hill arrived on a sleek Black Hawk helicopter. Even flying military hardware, Polaris avoided scrutiny. A new midnight blue 2017 Ford F-150 truck stood parked at the gate leading to the airstrip. The front bumper wasn't stock. Other parts of the vehicle would be likely modified.

Why was Jackson alive? Flynn should have killed him. Why let him go? He had a million questions for his superior.

During training, Jackson's instructors told him not to ask too many questions. "The information will come," they'd said. "Data builds upon data."

As the chopper blades slowed, the gunner's door slid open, and Director Hill and a fire team consisting of four people in full tactical gear stepped out. They moved to secure the perimeter.

Director Hill waved to Alabama, and she went to speak with him inside the Black Hawk.

What would happen if they recalled an agent this late in an investigation? They would face a nightmare once they returned to Virginia and faced Polaris interrogators. All kinds of threats would be hurled like boulders from giants. Without access to lawyers or the Bill of Rights, those interrogations would get to the truth.

What did O'Malley tell Alabama when Jackson left the hospital room? That this investigation was a sham? That he wouldn't talk to the police or the FBI? If he was smart, he wouldn't. Lesson One: never speak to the authorities without a lawyer present. Well, that might be Lesson Four, but it was certainly in the top five.

Flynn might've gotten to O'Malley first and scared him into silence. If Flynn wanted to know what O'Malley saw the night of the strange lights, he would have been in a good position. Two guards outside the door—Flynn and the witness alone. What happened to them? If he could fool the FBI, who else could? Someone with resources.

Director Hill would need to start explaining a little more about Polaris.

Finally, they exited the helicopter, and Alabama sat inside the car. "Hill wants to talk to you."

Jackson's stomach tightened. "Okay." He unbuckled his seatbelt and rose his chin, meeting Alabama's eyes for a second too long.

"Good luck," she said, turning away.

The frigid air caught him by surprise. He'd lived far from the cold for too long.

Director Hill guided him inside the Black Hawk and closed the door, and they found their places next to each other on gray nylon seats.

"Agent Stone. You look terrible," Hill said.

"All in a day's work as a UFO debunker, sir."

"You seem upset. What appears to be the problem?"

Jackson's forehead wrinkled. "I find it difficult to be kept in the dark, sir."

He took his time, always taking the tone of someone in complete control. "I understand your concern. In the past, we fully briefed our agents, but for reasons I cannot mention at this time, we changed our policy. Everything now is on a need-to-know basis." He reached in his jacket and laid a pen on a series of papers. "I'm upping your clearance, Stone. Effective immediately. Sign on the dotted lines."

A promotion?

The car chase. Being shot at. Alabama Wren. Too much, too soon.

"Sir, I'm unprepared for this."

"You're the most qualified person we have, and from what Dr. Wren has told me, you've outperformed our best estimates."

"She said that?" Jackson asked.

During training, he'd been shot at, attacked, stabbed. Sometimes his trainers would feed him metallic-tasting orange gelatin and let him sleep eight hours. The next day, he felt rejuvenated.

Director Hill tapped the paper. "Sign."

Jackson didn't bother reading it.

Once Director Hill took the papers back, he picked up the pen and gestured with it. "I suspected you'd be a good fit for our organization, but not everyone agreed. They didn't think you were ready, but I assured them."

"Thank you, sir. It's an honor. In regard to this case, I believe it's more than simple lights," Jackson said. "I think a foreign agency is involved in acquiring some kind of military experiment."

Rubbing his chin in thought, Hill looked around him as if someone lurked behind him. "If the disc is from DARPA or some other engineering lab, we might have gotten word about it. If it were military, there's even a better chance one of our operatives would have picked up a rumor here or there and relayed it back to us. None of that happened."

"Dr. Wren hasn't told me what O'Malley said."

Hill furrowed his brow. "Religious talk. She suggested he believed the lights to be demons."

Demons. If he had a dollar for every time someone blamed demons for something, he'd have enough money to take a one-way trip to Mars on one of Elon Musk's rockets and leave this rock and all its crazy religious fanatics behind. Good riddance.

"You listening?" Hill asked.

"Yes, sir."

"You're pale." Hill waved a hand over Jackson's abdomen. "Did you get kicked anywhere here in this area?"

"Thank you, sir, but I feel fine."

"How's your heart? You've gone through quite a bit."

"I've been taking the medication."

"Your partner mentioned you've been acting strangely."

So Alabama *had* mentioned something wrong about him. "I'm not sure what she means."

"You knew the man's name inside the hospital. How did you know?"

His throat dried. "I'm not sure, sir."

"What is his name?"

"Hunter Flynn, sir."

Director Hill's eyes went wide. "What did he look like?"

Jackson gave him a physical description adding, "I want to hurt this man."

Hill tightened his lips. "Is Dr. Wren keeping her classified materials secure?"

"What do you mean?"

"Stone, you know better than to lie to me."

He nodded lamely. "We have a different opinion on that, sir."

"The blue F-150 is yours. If the right person calls your license plate in, it will register as an FBI vehicle. If a police officer runs your plates, he'll think you're a civilian, so drive smart. Play along and don't do anything that would attract attention. Before taking possession of the truck, I'll need you to check the turn signals, breaks, et cetera."

"Yes, sir."

"Any questions?"

It all seemed to be happening so fast. The promotion, the strange memories, the mission itself.

"Why did I know his name, sir?"

"I'm off to Virginia to find out. Good luck, Agent Stone."

Alabama smiled as a slice of moonlight peeked through clouds above them. Director Hill sent an emergency relocation message to Alabama. "You have the basement."

Finally, some access to decent equipment.

"Pack up," Alabama said, collecting her things.

"What's up?" Jackson asked, pulling out the kitchen garbage bag.

"We're compromised. Let's go."

He dropped the bag on the floor. "Do we have time to clean it?"

"A cleaner team will come and scrub it. I'll meet you out front."

Icicles and snow covered their new brick house, located in a destitute part of the city. She'd learned it was once called Criminal Row, but now it went by North Portland near 82nd Ave. The house was made in the mid-80s, and once she turned on the lights inside, she frowned.

Cracks and scratches marred the wooden floor. Only one of the bathrooms worked, where a dead mouse was rotting underneath the sink. The backyard was fenced in, and according to Hill, the adjacent houses were abandoned.

It would be daylight in less than an hour.

Jackson stood next to a faded orange couch, the cushions splitting with wear. "I was wondering," Jackson said, inspecting the rooms, "who was supposed to clean this place? I think they might have gone to the wrong house. It's unlivable in here."

"We won't be staying much in the house," she said. "Let me show you."

She led him outside and pointed at different parts of their new base of operations. Strategically placed debris littered the yard. Two barrels off to the right, filled with wet sand. A stack of tires was tied together and hammered into the ground. Several points of egress.

"The basement is over here." Outside, a set of thick metal doors flung outward when opened. Taking a few minutes, she checked to make sure the thin safety film still clung to the lock and door handles. Once she verified it, she unlocked the doors.

"We coat some surfaces with Veroxintine Gel," she said.

"You'll have to remind me."

"Smart gel. It detects DNA, gloves, anything that's not supposed to be there. If it finds anything unusual, it pings a 5G tower and transmits the anomaly to one of our offices."

A short concrete corridor led them to a set of stairs and to a stone wall. As she rubbed her hand against the wall, she uncovered a sealed micro USB port. After retrieving her USB stick, she stabbed a pin in her forefinger. A drop of blood pooled. She put her finger on a small sensor atop the device, and presented him with a small tack, wiping it clean with a wet alcohol swab. "Use this pin and prick your finger."

He did the same and gathered the blood into the USB stick.

"It uses our DNA?" he asked.

"Yes, but it also tests your bloodstream for anything unusual."

"Handy."

She inserted the USB stick into the slot, and the ground rumbled and cracked. A pair of metal doors hissed open.

She stepped into the darkness. "This is where we'll be living."

"Is this one of the bolt-holes Polaris talked about?"

"The same."

A reddish glow illuminated the way to the basement, and at the final door, she turned to him.

"Okay, new rules," Alabama said. "You've been promoted, and now Director Hill has allowed us to use some of their better equipment. If you don't know what something is, don't touch it. Any questions before we go inside?"

"Will we be sleeping down here?"

"No. As safe as it is down here, I prefer having multiple exits in case something happens. This house is rigged to explode, too, by the way."

"Okay, let's go in."

"Polaris doesn't take chances. Those micro USBs only work once and then meltdown." She pulled them out of an indentation in the wall that had opened up and pocketed them. "Do me a favor and touch the door handle."

He did and looked at the tips of his fingers. "I don't feel anything."

"The gel numbs nerve endings. You won't ever feel it. By now, the gel has identified both of us."

Oscillating ceramic space heaters hummed. The basement offered a simple wooden table, a lime green desk, a stinky refrigerator, uncomfortable chairs, and a bunk bed that was past the point of no return. Two computer Flexi screens sat on an oak table. Networked computers connected to racks of digital gear from Japan, the U.S., and Europe. A mishmash of top-of-the-line servers took up a nook.

"They sent us the good stuff," Jackson said. "Why doesn't Polaris put the gel on everything?"

She set her bag down on the table and unzipped it. "Cost. Some of our enemies have learned not to open doors with their hands." Her bag carried her files, the laptop, photos, and a can of bear mace.

Two Colt M4 carbine rifles hung from a rack on the cement wall, along with a Remington 700 and Glock 17s.

"No more private weapons while on the job," Director Hill had said to her. "Your sloppiness could have cost us the entire operation."

A footlocker housed frag, thermite, and smoke grenades. Rows of cash reached the lid. Dollars. Yuan. Euros.

Nothing beats cash.

The NSA attempted to hack into Bitcoin and all other cryptocurrencies months after their release, though they hid that information from the public for years. Did anyone seriously think the United States Federal Government was going to turn a blind eye to cryptocurrency in the 21st century?

Crates of ammunition were stacked high.

"It's bigger than I expected." Jackson found a seat at one of the computers and frowned. "Can't Polaris afford better chairs?"

"You're asking me?" She held her nose, stripped off the orange paisley cushion cover, and tossed it by the bunk beds. "By the end of this, I'm going to need a long shower." She hung her jacket on her chair.

"Thanks for speaking to Director Hill about me."

She raised a brow. "What are you talking about?"

"What you told the director. About how good I was performing."

"How *good*?" She rolled her eyes. "You believe I would lie to Director Hill? I wouldn't dare. He didn't ask me about you. He reads the final mission reports."

"So, you didn't say anything?"

"Nope."

He bit his thumb. "I can't tell if you're playing games with me or not."

Jackson was cute in his own way. Refreshing. Many of her other partners didn't live long for her to get to know them. Emotional distance was golden.

"You never served in the military," she said.

He frowned. "Is it that obvious?"

"I have nothing negative to say about your training. Sometimes you seem more relaxed and able than at other times. I'm not allowed to ask any real questions about you." She tore open a new bag of Gummi Bears. "What I said to Director Hill shouldn't matter."

"Can I get a few of those?"

She emptied some into his hand.

"Thanks," he said. "No, it shouldn't, but is he lying?"

"About what I said about you?"

"Yes."

"Stone, you're a hard man to figure out."

He gave her a startled look. "Me? I blame it on the orange gelatin I ate during training."

She froze and laughed. "It's a good thing Director Hill raised your security clearance. I shouldn't tell you this, but

Polaris training occasionally has side effects. They try different things with different people."

"What did the gelatin do?"

She shrugged. "How would I know? I can tell you this much—our turnover rate is pretty damn high. The faster Polaris can deploy trained personnel, the better. They have their ways. Always inventing new ideas. A year ago, you wouldn't have been considered for field duty. Today is a different story."

Alabama set a Faraday pouch next to her.

"What's this?" he asked.

"A phone I borrowed from the FBI agent outside the hospital. Polaris can crack them with the right equipment. These days, anyone can crack a normal phone, but the FBI ones are much more difficult."

They turned on their computers.

Nothing like breaking into phones. People's lives were on them. Their secrets and perversions and goals. Whoever thought up the idea to sell Orwell's "1984" as a product did a wonderful job and made her life a thousand times easier.

"You're decrypting the phone."

"You, Mr. Stone, have a talent for stating the obvious. I should have brought some food down here. I'm starving." She rocked her fingers back and forth for good luck.

The bag's zipper jammed, and she tugged the fabric away. She felt Jackson's gaze upon her.

"So..." she said.

"Sorry, was looking at the weapons."

Alabama pulled pictures out of her bag, all with lights in the sky, and half of them were stamped on the back.

The first half was composed of solved cases, camera lens flares, planes, and satellites. She set those to the side. Though the other photos didn't have writing on them, she knew their project names: Project Orb One, Project Pinnacle, Project Cloud Mountain.

"Put those down a second," Jackson said.

"We're working, Stone. Why don't you make yourself useful for once and familiarize yourself with your computer? It's slightly different from the ones you used in training."

He grabbed her photos, but she held them tight. "Excuse me? What the hell are you doing?"

This time, he pulled hard. She let go, sneering.

Jackson set his jaw. "You've had this passive-aggressive attitude since we started this mission, and if we're going to work together, it's got to end."

Oh, my. Someone's crabby. "If you acted more like an agent and less like a kamikaze pilot, I'd sure appreciate it. You could have gotten us both killed back in the hospital. You acted not only rash but stupid, and you're an embarrassment to Polaris."

He scoffed. "Oh really? An embarrassment? I saved us both."

"It was foolish to chase him in the hospital. You nearly got yourself killed." She turned away, whispering, "Or captured. And if I hadn't been there, who knows what might have happened."

"And *you* almost got yourself shot. I don't like working with *you* any more than *you* like working with *me*."

She squinted. "Whatever gave you the impression I don't like working with you?"

"Right. I'm going to go shower."

Jackson left, maybe to cool off. Hazing was part of Polaris' ritual, especially when an agent went off the rails and did what he did, acting like Rambo and leaving her alone with a witness. Sloppy didn't begin to cover it. And if an agent could be bullied, they wouldn't make it in this line of work.

Jackson returned a short while later, his hair slicked. He certainly smelled better now. Scowling, he nodded to the phone. "What do you hope to do with that?"

"The third witness. The FBI knows where he is. With help of this little guy," she said, pointing at the rack of gadgets, "we'll find his location easier."

He leaned back, arms folded, and locked against his chest. His breathing was shallow.

Leaning in, she asked, "Still hurting?"

"I'm fine." He bit his lip. "Actually, do you have some Advil or something in your bag?"

She told him she did and gave him a strong dose. "Do you want to hear a story about my last partner?" She cleaned dirt from her fingernail.

His face lit up. "Sure."

"Let's call her Linda. I knew her for two hours, just long enough to figure out she preferred to be called Belinda, not Linda. You make a mistake in this line of business, you don't lose a finger or an eye; you lose your life."

Rubbing his neck, he leered at the ceiling until returning his eyes to her. "I wasn't kidding about your passive-aggression."

She met him square, face to face. What beautiful eyes he had.

Jackson said, "It makes it impossible to work with you. If you keep suggesting I'm incompetent or not fit for this job..."

She threw a hand up. "You'll what? Call Hill and ask for a transfer? Call Hill and ask for *me* to be transferred?" Snorting, she wrestled a smile. "Until this mission is over, you'll have to put up with me."

This wasn't the man listed in the *Project Horizon* file as

her partner. This wasn't Jackson Stone. This version of Jackson Stone grew a pair. Maybe he needed to be confronted by a strong woman. That could come in useful.

He looked down at the photos. "Tell me about these while the decrypter is working."

She told him the story about an episode over Stephenville, Texas in 2008. That night, a half-mile-long cylinder appeared and was sighted over three counties in four hours. Witnessed by twenty-one people, only a few photographs out of the hundreds taken showed anything. According to the witnesses, the Air Force dispatched fighters to intercept it. The Air Force claimed they were training aircraft but later recanted their story.

None of it added up. And it was one of the few times Polaris couldn't gather more intel on what happened. Those involved simply disappeared into the military-industrial complex.

"A pilot, Steven Allen, saw the craft from the ground and described it as having flashing strobe lights. When the Air Force reached a certain distance, it flew away at over 2,600 knots."

3,000 MPH. Whatever was inside would be crushed by the inertia. That was always the problem with these stories —physics. Polaris didn't share much of what they knew about technology.

Maybe someday she'd step inside a disc and find the truth for herself.

Jackson said, "We have hypersonic military craft, but nothing that large."

"This is what Steven Allen had to say." She read from the file. "Quote, 'I don't know if it was a biblical experience or somebody from a different universe or whatever but it was definitely not from around these parts.'"

His ears perked up, puffing out air. "I know the story well enough. I helped work on it, and we found nothing."

"Oh, did you?" she asked.

"I worked the case for over two months."

She caught herself smiling in acknowledgment. "O'Malley thought the disc he saw was biblical, too. He spoke about the Book of Ezekiel."

"Of course he did. They all do." Jackson changed his voice, mocking the famous Biblical reference in the Bible. Then, without taking a breath, he perfectly quoted a dozen more, which some claimed spoke of UFOs and aliens.

As a researcher, would he take the time to memorize Bible passages? Perhaps. His prejudice might cause problems later in the investigation if he blinds himself to something he doesn't like. She'd keep an eye on that.

"The sighting in 2008 in Stephenville, Texas is almost a perfect match with the Frog Lake lights here."

She told him of another incident: a clear match between Frog Lake's lights and another recent UAP light encounter with the military—the Harbour Mille Incident in Canada.

During the event, two Canadian fighter pilots thought someone had launched three missiles at them. The main target remained unidentified. Out their cockpit windows, they witnessed something different. Three balls of lights. Several witnesses on the ground and near the harbor used their phones to capture some images. Only one came out well. But it matched.

"I admit, I don't work much outside the United States," he said. "I've been to Canada a few times and investigated a sighting an hour from Mexico City. Both times, nothing."

"Polaris goes everywhere."

Going through the photos again, she stopped when she reached the scene of the disappearance. What kind of object would cause psychosis in a person? If these were extraterrestrial craft and willingly attacked United States citizens, it changed the game quite a bit. As it stood, Unidentified Aerial Phenomena were still the biggest, most well-kept secret in the world. Everyone played along.

"Can I get another gummy from you?" he asked.

She complied and took one for herself. Cherry. "What's your favorite kind?"

He paused. How could he not know his favorite? "The gummy ones," he said. "I like the ones you buy for three bucks at the gas station. The worms."

"Those cheapo things? They'll give you cancer."

He gave her a knowing glance. "Probably."

She checked the screen. The decryption stayed in the upper green zone, but a series of errors knocked several minutes off its timed counter. 35:55 blinked ominously. The timer should read 39:08.

"Check your screen," she said, opening the list of processes threading through the decryption software. "I've shared a window. See all these applications running on the decrypter?"

"There must be over a million of them." He checked and then counted the number of devices. "How are these small racks and PCs able to handle this much stress?"

"Polaris keeps a lid on many of its technologies. If anyone were to find this technology, it would endanger our entire security apparatus." She opened a second window and shared limited admin privileges with him. "These red lines of text next to these lock codes show slight adjustments our rootkit worm is making to crack the phone."

He carefully examined it without touching it. "Looks like a normal phone, but it's a bit thicker."

"Since the new administration, certain government

phones have upgraded with RHg-Tops hardware. FBI. CIA. NSA. Secret Service. Every member of Congress. They received a lot of pushbacks to make the change. The NSA director wasn't thrilled about it."

The counter skipped another few seconds.

"It diffuses decryption protocols. Each mistake helps to build an opposite database. It then uses it to spoof our software, tunnels into our hardware, and hijacks it. It's a tug of war in there."

When she said the word "hijack", he peered at his hands. A trigger word. Jackson was a patriot. Did he lose someone on September 11th? Why couldn't he remember?

"I was thinking, are we investigating murders or the object?" he asked.

"Project Horizon involves all of it. If we can save lives, discover an enemy government is operating near our military base at Fort Hood by the mountain, or this turns into an honest to God alien craft, Polaris needs to know."

He searched through her files, comparing them. "The craft left residual radiation. If the object still exists, it could be leaking radiation, too. While you were talking, I checked airports, National Guard units, and FEMA for any unusual activity. Nothing." Jackson tapped his fingertips together. "My gut tells me this is likely an experimental military drone using a new kind of propulsion. The government is attempting to cover it up, no doubt. The lawsuits would be devastating."

She checked the timer. It lost a few more seconds.

Now is a good time to find out who this Jackson Stone really is. "How did you know the man's name inside the hospital?" she asked, catching him off-guard.

"What?"

His eyes rose to the ceiling. Good. He's searching for a memory.

"Hill asked me not to talk about it."

"Well, normally that would be the right thing to do. Keep to official standards. But I think I should know. If you and he know each other, he can get close to me, and I don't get close with anyone."

A secret tugged at the edge of his mouth. "I'm sorry."

Not as sorry as you'll be if I'm tagged and found to be a Polaris agent. Facial surgery hurts.

If Director Hill said he couldn't speak about it, she'd have to let it go.

Jackson held up his index finger. "What's wrong with the decrypter?"

Whatever kind of phone the FBI carried was more advanced than anything she'd seen before. Algorithms formed into battle lines, charging through computer gates and firewalls the FBI's tech department had created. The elegant frontal attack pierced through the phone's defenses. But it was taking a lot longer than expected.

Something was wrong, but she made sure to wear a calm face. "It still has plenty of time left. Don't worry."

"I can see my life spinning before me now. You know, you're never supposed to say that." Using air quotes, he mocked her. "Don't worry."

"Okay, worry then." She snatched a thermite grenade from the footlocker and placed it carefully on the desk.

"Thermite?"

"You never know."

"What's that supposed to mean?" he said, cringing.

"If our safe house is discovered, the mission is off. In case something goes wrong, we have thermite to melt the servers.

Anything able to resist our probes will trace us back here, and that can't happen."

"Why can't we remove the servers and get rid of them normally?"

"Because our enemies will assume that's what we'll do, and sometimes, they'll use police to pull our agents over and search their cars before they can dump them. We have had several problems in the past."

He made a face at the grenade. "If we set that off inside here, we won't be able to use the basement again."

"Correct."

A beep from the computer interrupted her train of thought. A message from Director Hill. Someone found a lead. She scrunched her eyebrows together as she read.

"This just came through," she said.

Jackson looked over her shoulder. "These images are from a different angle from the ones we had before at Frog Lake. These images of the lake just appeared?"

"Unknown. Look. These were taken a minute apart. This picture was taken from inside a truck."

Jackson smiled. "We have another witness."

The new witness took two pictures of the scene. Previously, from Frog Lake, the lights highlighted the mountain behind it. The left side was covered in a glacier, and the ridge line was higher than Hood's right side, which slanted lower and had a sharper decline.

In the new photos, they were taken from the other side of Mount Hood.

Alabama scanned the image into geospatial software for the Polaris Photogrammetry program. In seconds, the picture zoomed out. In its place, a topographical map of Mount Hood and the surrounding countryside popped on the screen.

She pressed the touchscreen near Parkdale, Oregon on Highway 281 and ran searches for trucks, then filtered those by dates, then by time, then weather.

The screen zoomed in on a white semi-truck pulling a trailer full of cars.

"Neat."

"The basement always gives access to the good stuff," she said.

"Do we know where that truck was delivering to that night?" Jackson asked.

"Not yet. That's next." She smiled an exacerbated grin. "Got the recipient. This new witness messaged these pics to O'Malley while O'Malley was being admitted into the hospital."

"They knew each other?" he asked.

"It's a small world. Portland is a large city, but the UFO community isn't what it used to be. They've probably known each other for a long time. And if this new witness is a trucker, they may have worked with each other before."

"When you spoke to O'Malley, did you get the feeling he might have known more than he let on? Do you think the government visited him first and warned him to be quiet?"

"Not at all," Alabama said. "He seemed more frightened of going back to prison than anything. While the decrypter is working, let's minimize the photos, and pull up the photogrammetry program."

He nodded.

"Next step," she said, "sourcing the image to find out who texted O'Malley the photo."

"With what information? Director Hill only sent you the photo without further information."

Polaris used some of the most advanced software applications to siphon data on the internet. But with AI, hackers, and governments always on high alert, Polaris was limited in how often they could employ their tools. If patterns were discovered, it would set off alarms.

The NSA stored all internet data at the Utah Data Center or UDC. Supposedly, the UDC's goal was to support the Comprehensive National Cybersecurity Initiative, but one thing could be said about Top Secret programs—they always had ulterior motivations.

Alabama had badgered Director Hill to tell her the UDC's actual purpose. When he said he didn't know, it was the first time she'd caught him lying to her. He showed her hundreds of other binary siphons, which mirrored their data to other collection sites. Anyone with enough money could have any information transmitted over the internet.

How much does Stone know? "The United States has been collecting everything sent over the internet for a long time. The data is funneled to massive server farms."

He watched her screen. "Well, of course. They use it against our adversaries and to prevent terrorism. I'm glad they do that."

Is that really what he thought? "Next step. Triangulate where these pictures were taken."

Alabama found and matched it to the phone records and confirmed his name: Fernando Lopez. Failed to meet Marine qualifications for entry. Psychological reasons. Prescribed a litany of anti-anxiety meds, which failed to help. And the DMV gave him a Commercial Driver's License?

"Fernando Lopez," she said. "Hispanic male fifty-six. Married. A few children but no other known relatives. No criminal history. Looks like Lopez was headed to a Hood River dealership and disappeared. There's an APB out for him. I wouldn't be surprised if they bring in three times as many FBI agents and lock Portland down."

"It won't be just the FBI." Jackson pinched the screen, zooming in on a list of errors as long as the Mississippi River. "What the hell was that just now?"

On her monitor, bright red errors multiplied like organic cells. "The main firewall inside the phone. We'll be through sooner than I expected. I can only guess what we'll discover once we get access to the FBI's special case files. We'll stay ahead of them at every step."

He drew a line from the phone to the rack and reached for the power cord.

She slapped his hand. "What are you doing?" She tensed. "Don't do that again."

"Look at the list of errors again!" he said. "Some of those aren't errors."

She maximized the window. Her heart stopped. *What in the...* "Someone is remotely hacking us."

"We need to unplug it," Jackson said.

"No! If we disconnect the phone, not only do we destroy it, the errors will generate a worm and hijack the primary, secondary, and tertiary security nodes. Then our system would ping ConUS J-Net on *every* 5G network. They'll trace us right to this location." She snapped her fingers. "Quick, grab everything! Oh, and grab that grenade."

"The thermite?" he asked reluctantly.

"Yes, the thermite!" Rolling the racks over, she pulled servers and devices and stacked them. "Hill is going to kill me," she mumbled.

"What are we doing? These things melt tanks."

She gave him an empty pillowcase to hold open, and she stuffed the electronics inside.

"The grenade, Stone!"

He picked it up. "What am I supposed to do with this?"

"You're going to go find a place and blow this stuff up without being caught."

"How much time do I have?"

"Less than three minutes."

"If someone sees me?"

"Make sure they don't. Keep an eye on the decrypter counter. Once it hits zero, those racks you're carrying will explode."

J ackson slung the pack over his shoulder and zipped out onto the street. With every step, an edge from one of the machines poked his back like a sharp screwdriver. The sun shined in his eyes, reflecting off the sporadic snow. Ice coated the streets in all the wrong places. Too bad he couldn't simply drive the truck, but with GPS and cameras, he couldn't risk being discovered.

Three minutes.

That's all the time she gave for him to find a place to set off a thermite grenade.

Thermite.

Was this part of his promotion? The street was devoid of traffic, but a woman running her Rottweiler darted toward him. She wore pink, with Apple earbuds stuffed in her ears.

"Good morning," he said to her. She paid no attention to him.

Going full tilt, his breathing rang loud in his ears. His feet pounded against the asphalt as he frantically squinted left and right, down streets, behind houses. Anywhere safe enough to blow the phone and the racks up safely. No witnesses. No proof. No one hurt. And no problems.

A man and woman in the opposite direction waved and smiled.

Oh, happy day. Yes. Whatever.

Another light flashed on the decrypter. What did that mean?

Bolting down a hill, he spied a chain-link fence situated behind train tracks. What looked like abandoned industrial buildings were butted up next to each other and sat behind the fence. A half a dozen street lights lined the buildings. All the buildings were red brick. A few with broken glass windows and gang graffiti.

Over the tracks and through a broken portion of the fence, he hurried between two buildings, his foot splashing into a freezing puddle. The last button on the decrypter blinked yellow repeatedly. He wasn't far enough from their safe house. He bit his tongue. The metal edges slammed into his back.

He swung it behind his other shoulder blade and instantly regretted it as the sharp steel dug in. Of course, Dr. Wren wanted *him* to get rid of these stupid things. Rookie, rookie, rookie.

He'd get revenge for this.

Behind a building in the tiny necropolis, cement steps lead into an open warehouse, empty and abandoned. Trees and shrubs had grown around it, and at any minute, a strong wind might blow it over. A thick blanket of snow formed part of its rusted roof. He entered, his heart pounding against his chest.

Beep. Beep.

Vestiges of beer bottles, fast food containers, and

needles lined the cement floor. Carefully setting down the bag, he prepped the thermite grenade and dropped it.

Why couldn't they have used a hammer and BleachBit?

Running like Flash, he raced for the entrance, counting down the seconds before it would detonate and rain down fire. It exploded behind him. His body vibrated with the ground. Hot air sizzled. The blast burnt the air and vaporized the ground below it.

His foot found an oddly placed brick, and he tripped and tumbled. His hands slid across the pavement, scuffing his palms. He kept moving. No one had seen him. Or if they had, they weren't here now.

That wasn't so bad.

He pushed off the ground, his palms like sandpaper from the fall. Next time, he'd wear gloves for this sort of thing. The phone, decrypter, servers, and devices were no more.

When a woman in rags, wearing nothing but Goodwill blankets, emerged from the shadows, a knot formed in his throat.

Dirt and grime tried to conceal her wrinkled cheeks. She dragged her feet as she walked in his direction.

The woman's once sad expression turned grim. "You don't belong here. You going around here, making fires. Who do you think you are? You trying to get drugs up here? Well, there ain't none, and now you burnin' down the place."

He fished for his wallet to present his badge. "FBI. Please vacate the area."

"Oh, no you're not. I don't think so. Not after what you did to that warehouse over there. Look at it. It's melting."

"Look at the badge, please."

"FBI or not. I don't care. You can't tell me where to go. And who is going to put out that fire?"

"The cold."

"That's not going to work and I haven't smelled rain in the air all day. I'm going call the police." She pulled out a phone.

She was right. The cold wouldn't stop the fire, and neither would the snow. It would burn out soon, but that left her as a witness. It would be easy to steal her phone, but the police would track the phone's GPS. That would be evidence and lead to an investigation. More problems.

I can't believe I'm going to do this.

"Give me that phone," he said.

She folded her arms. "No."

He swiped at it. She pulled away and twisted around. She ran for the train tracks.

"No, you don't."

She screamed. "Help! Police!"

He dove for her and wrapped his arms around the back of her waist. As feeble as she looked, she dragged him a step and then sank to the dirt and gravel like a well-muscled running back. The woman's will gave her extra strength.

She shoved at him and attempted to stand. Jackson found himself on his back and wrapped his legs around her neck. She caught her breath and hit chest-first on the ground. Jackson squeezed both legs together. She coughed and gurgled. Seven seconds later, she was unconscious.

He stood and pressed his palm over his mouth. He had to do it, but couldn't believe he did. To an old lady? What was he becoming? "Mission First, Mission Last" flashed in his mind, a motto from Polaris training.

He checked her pulse and breathed a sigh of relief. He didn't try to kill her and only wanted to knock her unconscious. When her pulse came back strong, he snagged her phone and rushed to the thermite burn.

He used his shirt to cover his nose and mouth and tossed the phone on the flames. He backed away as it burst and melted.

Before he left the scene, he checked all directions. Nothing stirred except the dying fire, but sirens blared from afar. He shoved five twenty-dollar bills in the woman's bag and hurried over the tracks as a train's horn blared, and a single light shone from the locomotive's nose in the distance.

Maybe today Alabama might compliment him for managing to save their location from the hacker. But he figured he'd sooner become the head of Polaris or the president of the United States before that happened.

labama balanced on the basement toilet, pushing up on a cement switch. The ceiling split, revealing a cache of replacement equipment. After setting up a secure Yo-I radio and sending a coded signal, she dialed Director Hill.

"Texas has yellow grass and green salad," she said into a mic. "Eight, six, niner, two, two, one."

"Verified. Good to hear from you, Agent Wren. O'Malley, the witness you interviewed, is dead. Just a moment. I'm going to put you on speaker."

Click.

Director Hill sounded farther away. "You're here with Vice Admiral Johnson, Director Baker, Director McDermont, Dr. Albert Hughes from the Toronto Noetic Institute, Cardinal Hue, and General Thomas. We'd like to hear your thoughts about Project Horizon."

Her throat dried. She's been on important conference calls, but small ones. Both Director Hill and Director Baker on the same call? At the same time? Incoming fireworks.

When speaking with Polaris officially, Alabama changed

her tone. It was something everyone did. "It is an honor to speak to all of you, today," she said. "I—"

Cardinal Hue interrupted her. "Agent Wren. It's been a long time, hasn't it?"

Was that sarcasm? Cardinal Hue reported directly to the Pope. The Church wanted data on whether extraterrestrials existed, and they'd made plans to discuss Christ with them. Too bad it was impossible to know what the supreme pontiff would say.

"Yes, Cardinal."

"I would like to ask you about the disc if I may," he said.

She told him what she knew, and the line went quiet.

"What is your opinion?" Cardinal Hue asked. "Are we being visited?"

"Your Eminence, I do not have enough evidence to make a claim."

"I understand, but what do you believe?"

She waited. Would one of the directors help answer the question or interrupt? Please?

Seconds ticked, each longer than the last. Answering him truthfully would result in leaking secrets she'd sworn to protect. But these conference calls were about discovering the truth in a system of disinformation and diversion.

No one came to her aid.

She bit her lip. "I feel something." Crossing her legs, she tapped her foot, stood, and took a few steps. "I don't know what it is. I have a feeling a horrible event is going to happen."

Director Baker, a woman the other directors feared like the Antichrist, said, "Agent Wren, your progress is slow and time is of the essence."

Listening to her speak was like driving nails into her eyes.

"Yes, ma'am. We are proceeding as fast as possible."

"If you feel you are unable to fulfill your duties to Polaris, let us know. I would be happy to secure a replacement."

Director Baker wanted revenge for all the times her special operators failed to bring results. Blame Alabama Wren. Baker had once said, "She didn't follow the rules, and that's why my team failed." Other times she'd cursed Wren's name and zeroed in on her accomplishments. She'd attempted to uncover why Alabama was able to perform so much better than the others.

Alabama sighed. "Ma'am, normally for a case this size, Polaris would provide an independent Scorpion team, a dedicated IT staff, and support personnel. We will complete the mission as ordered."

"Why would we provide you with resources when you have not yet produced results?"

"Let it go, Director Baker," Director Hill said.

It'd been a long time since Hill stood up for Alabama, and it warmed her heart.

"Perhaps Agent Wren is seeking to retire from our organization?"

Director Hill fist slammed a table. "That's enough!"

Director Baker steeled her voice. "We are at war. Project Horizon is one avenue of attack, and we have never seen this amount of enemy activity. I need you, Director Hill, to lean into your agents and get them to perform or all of us are dead."

In all her years, Alabama had never heard directors publicly admonish each other. Who could she rely on if not Director Hill? Was Director Baker in charge now?

"Director Hill," Alabama said, "I believe we should raise the threat level."

Vice Admiral Johnson, a kind man once she got past his unwavering glare and aggressive posturing, said, "Agent Wren, we're operating on a tight schedule, but I will assist you where I can."

Dr. Hughes cut in. "If I may address something? Dr. Wren, before this mission, you were tasked with performing an empathy read on one of our targets, and our readings show several anomalies. Have you noticed anything unusual about your empathic abilities?"

There were so many things she could have said. The plaguing nightmares. The feelings of emptiness and abnormal lucidity. Where to begin? She hadn't told the doctors about them, and the lab technicians would want to study her and keep her locked away.

"No, Dr. Hughes," Alabama said. "However, something happened at the hospital regarding Agent Stone, but it's hard to put into words. It was as if I could track him by a psychic smell. The more I think about it, the harder it is for me to describe."

The speaker muted, and she waited. After a minute, Director Hill said, "Dr. Wren, I'll be in touch." The call ended.

Too bad there wasn't time to ask more about Stone. With that many people on the line, why would the call end so quickly? Unless something big was happening behind the scenes. China? No, something bigger.

Part of what made Polaris different from other three letter agencies was their commitment to the human condition. Liberty, equality, fraternity, the battle cry of the French Revolution, lived at the core of Polaris' philosophy alongside their desire to uncover humanity's darkest secrets.

Once Alabama replaced the electronics, she took her place at her computer, zeroed in on the second image taken by the trucker, and called up the map. Parkdale, the nearest city to the picture, appeared. If Fernando, the third witness, stopped at Parkdale, it would be easy to locate him, especially in a truck pulling new cars on a trailer.

But a witness not wanting to be found wouldn't be out in the open. Highway 281 intersected Highway 35.

She interfaced with Polaris' database and marked the day's date. Next, she zoomed in on the city of Parkdale and traced Highway 35 north, where Fernando would likely continue on his route.

Panning out, she measured roads and distances and began accounting for road conditions that night. From the trucker's location, and a trailer full of cars, he would have gone east of Hood River to Pinegrove. GPS blips marked busses, cars, and semi-trucks on the roadside. None matched his vehicle.

After several minutes of searching north up Highway 35 on the glowing terrain map, she followed Powerdale Road going west toward Cedar Creek bordering Hood River. He would have been scared. If he were as religious as O'Malley, and with psychological issues, he might have experienced a kind of psychosis. Who knows? If he were still alive and not nabbed by the FBI or police, he would be waiting for the Men in Black to be coming for him. Alabama and Jackson matched the profile, minus the sunglasses.

Fernando Lopez could be dangerous.

In a small opening off what must have been a gravel road just before Penstock Flume Trailhead, half of Fernando's semi-truck appeared to be parked under trees. It was a brilliant location to hunker down for a week, maybe longer. Full access to creek water, and Hood River, and a large city beyond Cedar Creek for food.

Jackson would be back soon, and she expected more out

of him. Which man was he? The analyst-assassin or the assassin-analyst? He didn't know himself.

The door opened. Jackson carried himself down the steps and fell into his chair, his face an expression of mingling dismay and amusement. "Done."

"Good. Any witnesses?"

"No witnesses."

"Are you sure?" she asked.

"Positive. I'm glad to be back."

"Took you long enough."

He held a long blink. "I don't know if you're joking or practicing to be the Queen of Bitchville."

"A little of both." *I hate that word. Bitch. Demeaning. Worthless. Lazy. If I could wipe it off the planet with a punch, Jackson would have a black eye right now.*

He pointed at the map. "You found him? The third witness?"

"That's our man. Fernando Lopez." She printed off an expanded picture of his driver's license. "Let's lock the basement down and go see him." She took the two Glocks and three magazines for each.

He stared at the car keys on the desk before picking them up.

Alabama said, "Oh, by the way, I received a message from Director Hill. O'Malley was pronounced dead."

"What?"

"Yes. And you're driving."

17

As their F-150 bounced, splashing through potholes full of water, Jackson focused on the road. Trees leaned violently to the side, the gusts of wind manically toying with their limbs. The truck handled well, and Jackson appreciated its size. Nothing beats American trucks.

Alabama explained their next witness. Fernando Lopez was the guy in college who swallowed too many red pills, discovered the Matrix, and flew off the deep end. Jackson could handle crazy. In the past, Jackson's work brought him near conspiracy theorists. Now, being this close to the field of Unidentified Aerial Phenomena, maybe they weren't so crazy after all. He'd find out soon.

A handful of cars lined part of the road. Two black Audi Q5s, two silver Lexus ISs, and two red Porsche Panameras. Nice rides, but why buy two of each?

Jackson steered left into the bend, and the road opened into a wide elongated circle covered in dirt and sporadic gravel. Shadowed trees made an edge around a portion of the circle, and under the shadows and snow, the semitrailer stood unhitched. The front of the Semi's headlights reflected the F-150's light beams.

He lined up the truck, aiming its lights across from the Semi, and killed the engine.

Alabama stepped out, pistol at her side. "I bet he was about to leave."

Jackson did the same. The Glock's grip differed from his Heckler and Koch, and his gloved fingers still felt the biting freeze.

They stood behind the F-150's doors.

Jackson announced, "Fernando Lopez, FBI! Come out! We're here to help!" And waited. He repeated himself, and after not hearing a response, approached the Semi while Alabama covered him.

He rounded the Semi's fender to the driver's side and stole a peek. Empty. He checked the door. Unlocked. He swung inside, leaning on the middle armrest. An old bag with a half-eaten cheese burrito sat on the passenger's seat. The cab smelled like Taco Bell the moment he opened the door.

"He's close," he said into his comm. The surrounding woods strained against the wind. "Mr. Lopez. We're here to ask you some questions."

A rifle bolt slid into place behind him. "Don't you move, scumbag," a man threatened.

Jackson froze. "Easy now. Put that down. We're with the FBI."

"I see him," Alabama said to Jackson through his earpiece.

"Turn around," Fernando said. When Jackson did, Fernando stepped from the forest and into the light, his rifle firm in his shoulder. A deep crease drove a wedge above the ridge of his nose and between his eyes. He'd been away from a razor long enough to grow a five o'clock shadow and wore a flannel shirt under an Army-issued parka. Mud covered his cowboy boots.

Alabama appeared behind Fernando, aiming her Glock at his chest. "Easy, Mr. Lopez. Lower your rifle. That's it. Nice and slow."

Fernando set the weapon down and put his hands in the air.

Jackson showed him his badge. "FBI. Mr. Lopez, pointing an AR-15 at a law enforcement officer will land you in prison for a very long time. How about we start this over?"

Fernando's eyes darted back and forth. "I didn't do it."

"Clear the weapon," she said to Jackson.

With remarkable grace, he took the rifle, cleared it, pulled the mag, and leaned it against a car. All the while, her aim never changed, and Fernando stared at the stars.

Jackson tapped a set of handcuffs secured on his belt. Alabama shook her head.

"For your safety and ours, I'd like you to empty your pockets and allow us to search you," Jackson said.

Fernando waited. "I've got nothing to say. I don't know anything."

"Do you consent to a search?"

He nodded, and Alabama patted him down, asking him if there was anything in his pockets that would cut, stab, or poke her. He was clean. She stayed behind him while Jackson tried every trick in the book to put him at ease. Promise him they were there to help him. That he wasn't in any kind of trouble. Fernando would only grunt and fold his arms. And that's how he stood now.

"Would you happen to know a Patrick O'Malley?" Jackson asked.

Fernando shrugged. "I don't know who you're talking about."

"You sent a man named Patrick O'Malley two pictures of strange lights," Jackson said, showing him copies. "Lying to federal agents, too?" He showed his teeth. "Mr. Lopez, we are here to help."

"I learned early growing up in Venezuela not to talk to cops. Still true when I became a citizen of this country."

With obvious interest, Alabama said, "I'm sorry you've had bad experiences with the police in your past." She walked to Jackson's side. "Mr. Lopez, your life might be at risk. We would like to take you into protective custody and ask you some questions about what you saw that night."

"Protective custody is a fancy way of saying disappear. I don't think so. If I ask for a lawyer, what happens then?"

"If you haven't done anything wrong," she said, "there's no reason to get a lawyer."

His expression turned to cynical amusement. "I've heard that one before, too."

"Do you know a woman named Barbara Wakefield?" Jackson asked.

"Should I?"

Jackson scowled. "Quit lying to us. Ms. Wakefield is dead. The FBI is holding O'Malley in federal protection until further notice. We have come to offer federal protection, but we can't force you to go with us."

"I'm not going anywhere, especially with you two."

Alabama smirked. "Then would you mind answering some questions for us?"

"I can't promise anything," Fernando said.

She offered Fernando a breath mint. Without hesitation, he took one. She smiled. "You don't mind if we record our interview, do you?"

"I can't stop you."

They sought shelter inside a tall shed shortly beyond the tree line, keeping the doors open for illumination. Jackson brought the rifle along.

She tested the mic and checked the screen. "Let's talk about what you saw."

Fernando inhaled sharply. "Okay. They came from Mount Hood and headed southeast toward Twin Lakes and Frog Lake. I followed them."

Jackson held up his fingers. "How many lights?"

"I'm not sure."

She checked the phone's screen and brought it closer to Fernando. "Did the lights exhibit any kind of color?"

"Blue or green, or a mix of the two. I thought it was a group of helicopters at first, but I didn't hear the helicopter blades, and helicopters don't drop from the sky like that. Nothing moves that quickly. If it did, you'd hear a sonic boom. I didn't hear anything."

Jackson rubbed his chin. So far, Fernando appeared rational, but the way he spoke and his mannerisms made him wonder if he'd told this story before. Maybe Alabama put him at ease. She had that effect.

Fernando huffed and ran his hand down his legs. "As I followed the lights, I felt a hum. I couldn't quite hear it from my vantage point, but that's what I recall. I became agitated, and I damn near cried and tore my hair out. I almost lost control of the truck and drove off a bridge." He held his breath.

"It must have been awful," she said.

"Worst thing of my life."

"Then the balls of white light appeared?"

Fernando tried to pace, but she told him to remain still. He drummed his fingers on the sidewall of the shed and shifted his weight every few seconds. "Oh, God. This better not get me and my family killed."

How would Polaris protect him? Would they pass him to someone capable of protecting him? "Our offer of protection stands," Jackson said.

Fernando closed his eyes and stroked the back of his neck. "I had a vision then of our future. Those things," he said, pointing up, "are not our friends. I don't know. Maybe they are. But I don't think so. Someday, all of this will just disappear."

She turned off the recording.

Jackson gave her a look. "What do you mean by that?"

"The world. All of it. Reduced to nothing."

Jackson furrowed his brow. "And you heard this as a voice in your head?"

"I didn't hear the words. I felt them."

When Jackson glanced at Alabama, she did little to hide her concern. Why? So far, Fernando hadn't provided anything of value. No tangible proof. Two pictures? Maybe it was better to keep him in the wild and let the FBI pick him up.

They exited the shed and caught a massive headwind.

She pressed in a code on her phone and said, "Well, I'd like to thank you for your cooperation, Mr. Lopez. You've been a great help to us, and we appreciate your honesty."

Thunk.

A dart struck Fernando's neck through missing wood slats in the shed's side wall. As he fell, Alabama grabbed him and guided him to the ground. A team in tactical gear appeared behind rocks and trees.

"We'll take it from here," one of them said to her.

Scorpion.

She wiped her gloves together and stepped out of the doorless shed. "Make sure he doesn't remember anything."

Once inside the truck, Jackson put the keys in the ignition and paused. "What happens to him?"

"Scorpion takes him someplace safe and away from all this."

Jackson turned the keys, and the engine roared to life. "Is that our form of Witness Protection?"

She welcomed the heater with a grin. "Not exactly."

18

STONE

"What time is it?" Jackson walked into the kitchen, hair disheveled. He rested against the counter, palms on the countertop. Everything hurt. He stretched and rubbed ointment over his bruised face.

They'd stayed up, cleaning, scrubbing, making the house livable as best they could. He used the hours to think and rejoiced when he crashed shortly before sunrise.

"You slept in." Alabama poured a green drink from a blender. In gray sweats and a black sports bra, her eyes seemed brighter than yesterday. She sipped something from her cup.

"What is that?" he asked.

"Spirulina. It's a type of cyanobacteria; a family of blue-green algae. It doesn't sound good, I know, but it is. I've got some frozen bananas, chia seeds, berries, and coconut water I can throw in for you."

"Will it help these bruises heal faster?"

She began taking out the ingredients for him. "It can't hurt."

The blender roared. Nicki never used one.

It wasn't bad, but he couldn't see himself drinking more than once a week. "Thanks."

"You're welcome."

He set the empty glass in the sink and made his way to the refrigerator. He held up the sauce. "A real breakfast of eggs and Picante sauce coming up."

"Picante. You'll need to work on your Spanish."

"And you, your manners," he replied in German.

Pouting, she moved out of the kitchen, giving him space. "I have perfect manners," she replied in French.

When he tried to answer in French, he met an invisible wall. He didn't know the language. How could he understand her?

She continued, and nothing she said made any sense. But moments ago, he understood her? How? Staring at his arms, his mind blanked.

"I don't speak French."

"Seems like you understood me. No problem."

He cooked his food in peace and let himself travel back in time to his childhood. Back then, things made less sense than they did now.

His mother and father stood over him. His birthday party was the next day. He'd be turning a whopping eight years old, and it couldn't come fast enough. This year, Mom promised to buy him a new bed, one which wouldn't make his skin itch or his back hurt. He asked her in private if he could get a bed without number one and number two stains on it, but she didn't make any promises. He prayed night after night, hoping a new bed would appear. Please. No more bugs.

He sat at their dining room table. Through the window across the room, his sister played tag with young friends in the community. Sweat dotted his face, but his parents sweated more in the midday heat. This time of the year was when everyone smelled bad and the mice left little droppings around the kitchen. Jackson learned to make a tent, so the roaches and mice wouldn't crawl over him while he slept.

A few of his parent's friends came over that night. Members of the commune. They didn't have any kids, and they shouted when they spoke.

His dad crossed his arms at his chest, ruffling his Hawaiian shirt, scribbling shapes on a newspaper. "These scientists don't know left from right."

Buck was shaped like a pear, and Dad made him sit on a special stool he'd made for him. He was never without a two-liter bottle of Diet Pepsi. "Preach it."

For Jackson's birthday, Buck gave Jackson a book about the Solar System written decades ago. It was filled with blurry black and white pictures and complex maps. Two of the pages were missing, and when he asked Buck about them, he said they weren't good pages and didn't belong with the rest.

Asteroids were beyond cool.

But not cooler than a new bed.

Buck burped. "The ancient Martians destroyed the Maldekian homeworld. And our scientists are forced to lie by our government. If the truth got out that the asteroid belt was actually a blown-to-bits planet, it would change the paradigm."

"What's a paradigm?" Jackson asked.

Buck adjusted in his stool and put a fist on his hip. "The way people see things. We here at the commune have a different paradigm than the outside world. One day, when we can tell the truth to the world, well that's when things will change."

Dad wiped his forehead with his sweaty arm. A strange smell wafted through the room. "Son, the people at the top, they're not going to allow the real truth to get out. But one day, someone will."

ALABAMA STOOD and stretched her arms. "What do you think of what Fernando said?"

He served his food and stood across from her. "What was that?"

"Fernando."

"Right. He didn't say anything of note."

She watched him. "Do you discount the voices he heard in his head?"

"I'm not sure what to make of that." He burst an egg yolk and soaked his toast. "Our search for witnesses has led to nothing significant." He held his breath, his mind recalling the smell of gunpowder and cordite. He needed coffee for this discussion. "I don't see a path forward. None of the witnesses provided any evidence."

"Both witnesses corroborate each other's stories."

Definitely coffee. He added an extra scoop to the pot before brewing. Hopefully, it would be strong. "They were in contact with each other and knew each other well enough to have each other's phone number. Hell, I wouldn't be surprised if they had the same drug dealer." She didn't laugh. "You think it's a weapon."

"It fits."

The coffee began percolating. There was nothing better than the smell of coffee and Nicki's perfume.

"If it's extraterrestrial..." Jackson turned to her. "Would you say so?"

She avoided his gaze. "I don't know."

"Am I cleared to know?"

"I don't know." She walked to the bathroom and stopped at the door, keeping her back to him. "If it were extraterrestrial, what would you do?"

Time froze as his tongue caught in his throat. "Whatever Polaris told me to do."

"Good answer."

When she went inside, he closed his eyes. No more leads. What had they missed? Polaris would search Fernando's house, and if they found anything, he would know. Fernando mentioned the blue lights' quick descent. If the lights broke the sound barrier, people would notice.

Fort Hood would never allow psychological operations to be held so close to the base.

He set his empty plate in the sink and poured himself a coffee. She exited the bathroom, and he brought the steaming drink to his lips. Then a thought.

"We need Hazmat suits," he said. "I need to see something at the crime scene."

19

S huffling through the snow in yellow hazmat suits, Jackson panted. His heavy steps sank as Alabama and Jackson crossed the police tape and walked toward the trees up ahead. They were headed for a ravine seventy-five yards past the wood's edge. Snow glistened on the Douglas Firs. Last night's snowfall added six inches.

Jackson made a fist and raised his arm. She stopped, standing aside a log.

"Here." He waved the Geiger counter's wand, and the meter rose. Sticks stuck out of freshly fallen snow where the campfire at the forest's edge had once been. "Everything else can be explained except the radiation."

She pursed her lips and scanned the terrain behind them and off to their flanks. "An experimental vehicle might have left radiation, but the military tests those in the desert, not here. Too many people." She pointed to the treetops. "Burn marks. See them? All on this side of the trees, from top to bottom."

Facing different directions, Jackson studied the Geiger Counter and made mental notes. "Incredible. The residual radiation registers almost a mile wide." He aimed it at the horizon. That couldn't be right. He reset the device and ran another scan. "During my briefing, Director Hill said the forest wasn't damaged."

Lingering worry filled her eyes. "He might not have known. Did you say almost a mile? We don't have anything that size."

They helped each other navigate the snow. Wearing a giant yellow suit makes for an easy target, but he wasn't going to die from cancer.

"If you wanted to create a weapon of mass destruction, you could fly something like that over a city or farms and dump toxic materials onto a population. Why isn't the government out here investigating? Why isn't the military cordoning off the area?"

"Someone has ordered them not to," she said.

Another sweep with the device. Radiation remained the same. If she was right, then someone had infiltrated the military. Perhaps. But at this level?

Alabama broke the silence. "Any thoughts on why the kids stripped down?"

"Panic or delirium." Jackson recalled Alabama's full transcript of the interview with O'Malley. "Did O'Malley say anything about taking off his clothes?"

"No."

Jackson's lips trembled, and he pursed them and ground mud from his soles. When he raised his chin, they met each other's eyes until she turned away from him.

His thighs burned as they hiked up steep paths. Climbing these mountains and hills was easier when he was a boy. It was a wonder his parents let him explore this far away from the commune.

Alabama made it look effortless. The Hazmat suits made

the trek difficult. One slip and they might rip or damage the suit.

He grabbed a rock and braced himself on frozen dirt. "What would it take for an aircraft to penetrate United States airspace?"

"A miracle."

"No, really."

She glanced behind her and looked at him. "We're too close to Fort Hood. Our satellites would pick up anything in space, and NORAD would detect anything in the atmosphere. Space Force is massive. The scope is hard for me to imagine."

"Do you think Space Force has something to do with UAPs?" The answer seemed obvious to him.

"It's a question I've been asking myself. Hill won't talk about it, and I can't get answers. But I can say for certain that if China or Russia tried to invade our airspace with something that large, the DEFCON would be lowered, and the Department of Defense would be out in force like they were after September 11th."

A rabbit peeked out from under a fallen branch and scurried back inside. Poor guy. When Jackson grew up and would go hiking, he'd bring any scraps of food he could and feed the animals. He used to wonder if he could run away and live off the land. One day, he told his friend about it, and a day later, the whole commune knew. That was one of the worst months of his life.

"Do you think the military has been working on... how would you call them? Mental weapons?" he asked.

"No doubt, but not on this scale. The military works closely with DARPA and other corporations, all under the radar. You know those prosthetics that work when the user uses their mind to make them work?"

He made a mental note. "I've heard of them."

"The United States has evolved this technology much further. When wired, pilots can fly several fighters with just their minds. That's what's admitted publicly."

My God. He swallowed.

A craft, a disc. Hovering over the city of New York. It unleashes its payload and sends mental commands across Manhattan. It's caught live on Fox News and CNN. The screen goes black and then a seal of the United States appears. The voice of the President announces New York City no longer exists.

"Wren, very little of this case makes sense. Is this the first time you have encountered something like this?"

They passed a ravine, and while they hiked, she remained silent. Too silent.

"Dr. Wren?" he asked.

"No. But this is the first time I'm genuinely afraid."

A crow swooped, landing on a tree. His beak was aimed squarely at Jackson as if pointing to a student. Then more came, a sea of black feathers and beady eyes. Every branch held a crow, and all remained still.

Clouds swept their way under the sun, and the ice became dark.

Alabama froze.

The crows cawed.

How long would it be until the animals acquired enough RADs to kill them? Not long.

She pointed a shaky finger. "What's—" Her legs wobbled, and she took a step back, grabbing onto Jackson's arm.

"Are you okay?" He reached out to grab her.

She stumbled but remained on her feet. "My head is spinning."

Then his skin itched. He leaned against a tree. His head swam in a pool of confusion. His body weighed a ton, and his eyes wouldn't stay open. The ground spun. White crystals. Snow. The center sparkled under the light. Ice. Faster. Faster.

Motion stopped, and he hugged a tree to stay on his feet. *What the hell is going on?*

His vision doubled, and butterflies filled his stomach.

Alabama dusted herself off, her red hair catching a dash of sunlight from the ice. She slurred slightly, saying, "Give me a second." Putting her hands on her sides, she leaned over and gagged, her face pale.

His senses returned when he blinked, and the experience began to fade as if he'd awoken from a dream. The last minute was a haze. Alabama checked a color-coded radiation badge on her suit.

"Radiation sickness?" he asked.

She shook her head. "Check your suit for leaks."

He wasn't a doctor. Out here, who could get to them in time in case something happened?

A glint of metal caught his eye from a smooth, round, stone-like ball at his feet. He punched holes in the wife fluff around it and dug carefully, not to damage his personal protective equipment.

"I see something. There. Buried in the snow."

"What is it?"

He scanned it with the Geiger counter. "It's not picking up any radiation."

"Show me."

Giving her the device, he bent over the sphere, tucked his hands underneath, and lifted it out. It was a thing of perfection, but it didn't belong out here. They need to call Director Hill and have it moved back to Virginia for study.

Wait.

What happened a second ago?

She eyed the sphere. "It's beautiful."

He spun it. "Something's here beneath the dirt. A symbol?"

She wiped the sphere clean and traced her hand over the symbol's etching. "Sixty-four overlapping tetrahedrons. They connect. See it?"

"What is it?"

"Evidence."

20

STONE

J ackson rolled the sphere into her hands. "Hold this a moment."

She held it out for him to see from all sides.

He studied its geometric pattern. "Polaris is going to want to analyze this. What happens next?"

"Once we leave this area, we remove our PPE. I'll contact Director Hill, and they'll send in Scorpion teams."

As he studied the sphere, he placed his gloves on it. "Did you feel something a second ago?"

"Yes. I feel light-headed. We need to get back."

A brown cloth poked out of the snow next to Jackson's foot. Pulling it out, he shook the dirt and snow away. It was the last thing he expected—a habit. Did a Catholic monk visit here? That seemed as unlikely as anything else.

"How did the police miss that?" she asked.

"Or that?" Jackson eyed the sphere in her hands and examined the cassock. "Why would a monk be here?"

"Let's head back to where we parked."

She took point as they climbed an icy hill.

Once they'd left the scene and made it safely enough

away, they stuffed their hazmat suits into a hazmat bag Alabama had brought and tucked the round etched stone into a case.

She shivered. "It's freezing out here."

"I used to love this weather."

She handed him the case and held onto the bag. It would slow them down, but they couldn't leave them here. There were almost at the edge of the forest when Alabama halted. They drew their pistols.

Engines sounded in the meadow and snow spit into the air like a speeding boat parting water.

Jackson's face slackened. "Are we expecting someone?"

"Remember when I said Polaris has enemies?"

Men dressed in white, wearing Kevlar helmets, snow goggles, and rifles slung over their backs, surged forward on snowmobiles.

He narrowed his eyes. "I remember."

"Run!" Alabama spun and dashed in the other direction toward the middle of the forest and gulley.

Jackson's footsteps cracked. Behind him, snowmobiles crashed through mounds of snow, their engines growling like dogs of war. At least Jackson and Wren had one advantage—trees.

The snowmobiles stopped at the forest's berm. Unstrapping their M4s and slipping snowshoes on their feet, more of them hurried their way.

"Keep going." Alabama's short breaths quickened. She rushed around a tree. "Unknown threats. Do not engage."

Jackson caught up to her and pressed her forward with a gentle nudge. "Circle the ravine, lose them, and head back to our car."

In the distance, another set of engines approached.

More snowmobiles came into view and the riders leaped off their vehicles and raced toward them.

A voice boomed through the forest. "Federal agents! Hands up! Freeze!"

As the enemy closed in, the lead man pulled off his helmet. A fresh gash ran across his cheek, along with several bruises. An old scar snaked up his throat to his chin.

Jackson almost dropped the sphere case. The man he fought in the hospital stood before him: Hunter Flynn.

Alabama and Jackson raised their weapons.

"Department of Homeland Security. You're surrounded. Lower your guns."

They did.

Flynn focused on Jackson. "You look familiar." He balled his fist and punched Jackson in the stomach, doubling him over.

The sphere case clanked on the ground at Flynn's feet. Smiling, he picked it up. Where was Alabama's bag?

"Thank you." Flynn waved at his men, and they dispersed, heading back to their snowmobiles. "And your government thanks you." He gave a nod, his expression confident. "I'm enjoying our little game. It's been a while since I've seen someone so tenacious. Thanks for the sphere and keep up the good work."

No one approached them with cuffs or zip ties.

Is Flynn going to let us go? No. He's going to order his men to shoot.

Flynn stepped closer and then stood a hair's length away from Jackson.

"This is your second warning," Flynn whispered. "I am allowing you to live because you've helped me. The next time I see either of you, I will not kill you. I will force you to watch as I take out my frustrations on your partner. Are we clear?"

Jackson narrowed his eyes, his heart pounding. *Kill him now while you can.*

"Goodbye, Agent Stone."

Flynn spun on a heel and rode off. When the last snowmobile crested the horizon, Jackson inhaled. His stomach ached.

Jackson scanned the immediate area. "Where's your bag?"

"I dropped it back there. We should be dead. When Hill hears about this, he's likely to replace us."

"We should hurry to the monastery before we're followed."

"You know where one is nearby?"

"Yes." He looked off to where the snowmobiles had left. "Whoever those people are, if they get what they want, they're going to change the world."

"If they get what they want, they're going to start World War Three."

21

Western hemlocks and Douglas Firs obscured Mount Hood Abbey. Places of honest worship calmed Alabama. Buddhists. Christians. Muslims. Hindus. The power of prayer and the manifestation of Divine energy healed her pain for a time.

Jackson led her through the abbey parking lot. The monks in the abbey had cleared the snow, most likely with shovels and hot water. He smiled. "Had my friends and I not snuck here at night to drink box wine and smoke cheap cigarettes, I wouldn't have a clue this place existed."

Nodding, Alabama walked alongside him, always vigilant to an ambush. They needed to be far more careful. How on earth was she going to explain to Hill they'd lost the only reasonable evidence they'd found? Once spotted, they had little hope of holding onto it.

What exactly was that sphere?

A strange feeling, one she couldn't put her finger on, stuck her. Did something happen back there? She'd lost her balance, but an event had transpired, one she knew lay buried in the recesses of her mind. When she returned to Polaris, they'd find the memory during hypnosis.

She chose to wear black and looked every bit the part of a federal employee. She needed black shades. Her long, red hair cascaded over her shoulders and bounced in stride as she carried the cassock.

Jackson let his jacket fall over his gun, hiding it. His black and white attire helped him fall into his role as an FBI agent. For both of them, anything was better than the Hazmat suit. Well, almost anything.

She nodded toward three adobe-like buildings side by side. A large mosaic of the angel Gabriel and Virgin Mary graced the entrance, the words *AVE MARIA* on the left side and *GRATIA PLENA* on the right.

"An Annunciation house," Jackson said. "The monks should be inside."

The house was locked, so they walked a path leading toward the center of the monastery. Where she imagined grass normally grew in Spring and Summer, thick snow reached her knees. Several asphalt paths cut through the snow, and a statue of Jesus, arms wide, hugging the world, stood in the ground's center. Trees dotted the area.

Alabama noticed Jackson's scowl as he kept his eyes on the Romanesque-style Abbey church at the end of the grounds. Painted in white, a tower in the same color stood on one side. Six large, cement steps led to the two-door entrance; the doors as wide as they were tall.

Warmth soaked her face as they walked through the church's doors. Rows of pews. Large ornate columns. Antique glass windows of angels. Virgin Mary and Jesus. They made up the inside architecture. Religious art emerged from the soul. Timeless.

At the front of the church, several monks gathered

around a statue of Mary with baby Jesus in her arms. They faced their new guests.

A man sitting at an organ lifted his fingers off the keys and gently pushed his bench back, raising a hand to silence his monks. Shuffling her way, Alabama fished inside her pocket and pulled out her badge.

The monk smiled. "I'm sorry, but—"

"FBI," Alabama said, showing him her badge. "We'd like to ask you some questions."

The monk's short, pudgy nose held up his glasses. His small mouth and thin lips dropped into a straight line, and his bald head held the sunlight bleeding in through the windows. "This way, please." He took them into a small room and closed the door. Icons of the Virgin Mary and crosses lent the room a medieval feel. "I am the abbot. How can we help you, today?"

"We have something of yours." Alabama cocked her head at the cassock she held.

He studied it. "A few days ago, Brother Malakai came back from his nightly walk, but without his clothes on. We don't know where he went or why he came back this way." He ran his finger on the cassock. "May I ask where you found this?"

"We aren't at liberty to say at this time, I'm afraid."

"I understand," the abbot said. "His usual path takes him around the abbot, but we found no evidence of him taking his usual path. It snowed all night, and when he returned, we attended to him. We were not able to find his tracks."

"Did you call the police?" Alabama asked.

"Our brother came back to us by the grace of God. We felt no reason to call them as no crime had been committed."

"May we get your name, please?" Jackson asked.

The abbot blinked. "Nikolas Calbert."

"We would like to have a word with Brother Malakai," Jackson said.

Abbot Nikolas contorted his lips. "I don't think that's appropriate."

Jackson waited for him to explain, but all he did was stare at the ground.

"What seems to be the problem?" Alabama asked.

Abbot Nikolas reached for the door. "We should not be having this conversation. If you'll excuse me."

She slammed her fist against the door and held it shut. "I'm sorry, but this is a matter of national security."

Abbott Nicolas looked back and forth between them. "Do you believe in God?"

"Yes," she said.

They stared at one another, neither of them blinking, neither of them moving. Two statues. She sensed his fear, like an avalanche ready to bring it all down. What Christianity and nations and humanity itself. Ripping apart and entering into a stage where evil finally reigned. He hid it all behind his eyes. What did he know?

"Stone," she said. "Please wait outside. I need to speak to Abbot Nikolas alone."

He protested on the way out.

She muted her throat mic. "What is it you wanted to tell me?"

"May I please see your badge?" When he looked it over, he gave it back. "We have received threatening calls and messages on our phones." He rubbed his hands together. "My sister lost her baby an hour ago due to a freak accident at the hospital, and Brother John has lost his ability to speak. The Adversary is always present, but I feel this time, he is making a move."

How many times had Director Hill warned her not to fully open up her mind and exploit her empathic discipline? Too many.

But evil lay beneath the surface here. Why?

She opened her heart, her soul, and read his emotions. A cold reptilian shiver made her skin crawl. The back of her neck burned, and she held the wall for support. Her head pounding, she cleared her throat.

What was that? Director Hill was right. I need to be careful.

"I think you should be leaving," Nikolas said.

Through the door, Jackson said, "Brother Malakai wants to speak to us."

"No, don't..." the abbot said.

But she'd already opened the door. Jackson pointed down the hall.

Nikolas turned and faced a man on a pew far from the rest of the congregated monks. Elderly and alone, he had short, silver hair, and his head was bowed in prayer. He wore a brown habit similar to the one Alabama held.

"He is not himself," Abbot Nikolas whispered.

As if Brother Malakai had heard the conversation, he turned on his pew and rested one arm on the top of the backrest. There, he watched Jackson and Alabama approach. At several points, his eyes darted around the room.

Brother Malakai stood. "How may I be of service?"

She gave him the clothing they'd found by the sphere. "Good morning. We have something of yours."

Malakai set it down. "Thank you. Did I overhear correctly that you're from the FBI?" He grinned, excitement boiling in him.

Abbot Nikolas led them back to a private room and left, closing the wooden doors behind him.

She leaned forward. "We found your habit several miles from here."

Jackson shuffled his feet and set his arms to his side. "What exactly did you see, Brother Malakai?"

His chin lifted to the wooden roof, and he landed his gaze upon a Virgin Mary statue. "I don't know."

"Lights?" Alabama asked.

He licked his lips. "More than lights." He turned to Jackson. "Who are you really?"

"We're from the FBI."

"The FBI would not send federal agents to bring me my habit. All of us are ready to enter into the Lord's embrace."

Alabama straightened her posture. "We're also here to ask you some questions. That night, several died right where we found your habit."

"No one died."

She raised an eyebrow. "Many died."

"Nine young men and women, to be precise," Jackson added.

"You must leave."

Taking a step toward the door, she lowered her shoulders. "We are not here to hurt you. We are here to ask a few questions. You have nothing to be afraid of."

Tension saturated the air like dense humidity amid the jungle. Nothing she could say would help. And something else. When she'd tried to open herself to his emotions, something interrupted her. A voice.

Brother Malakai grabbed a rosary. "I know why you're here."

"Oh?" Jackson asked.

"The experience expanded me. I could see through my hands. I heard a voice say, 'We are here. We've been here before humanity.' And it sent a warning. I don't know." His voice became lost as he fed prayer beads through his fingers. "God, grant us mercy."

There comes a time when a person cannot be reasoned with. Jealous boyfriends. Drunk people. Brother Malakai's state of mind didn't allow for further discussion. She had what she needed.

A monk helped them to the exit. Once out of the church and down the steps, the wind kicked up snow as they walked the path to their car. Instead of taking a left, Alabama took a right on another path.

Jackson stopped. "Where are you going?"

She faced him. "To his room," she said, showing him a key.

J ackson pushed his hands in his pockets, the air biting cold against his skin. "Why?"

"We need to see inside his room. I have a funny feeling."

They jogged toward a two-story building made of brick and clay. As they rounded the corner, it spanned two city blocks long, by far the largest structure on the property. Trees covered in white ran up a hill behind the building. Finally, they entered inside a small lobby with bare walls and worn benches. Three archways led out of the lobby. One led to the stairs, the others to opposing hallways lined with doors; the monks sleeping quarters.

Someone approached down the stairs. At the bottom where the last stair met the lobby, a monk set a mop down and stopped cleaning. "Can I help you?"

Alabama held up her badge. "FBI. We're wondering if we can take a look at Brother Malakai's room."

The young man pointed out the door, his brown hair cut like a bowl, his innocent blue eyes like bright headlights. "He's not here at the moment."

"It's an emergency."

He straightened. "My, my. Would you like me to escort you?"

"If you don't mind, explain where it is and we'll find our way," she said.

The monk raised his index finger at the stairs. "Upstairs, second door on your left. God bless you."

Jackson didn't wait for the lobby doors to close before he began ascending the staircase. The rays from the sun streamed through several arched windows built on the staircase walls and sparkled on the steps. At the top, he walked past the first door and down a hallway.

"What are we expecting to find?" Jackson whispered.

"Brother Malakai might have a sphere."

"What?!"

"Shh. Keep your voice down."

Brother Malakai's name was painted on a slab of wood hanging on the second door. Alabama walked into the room and inspected a lone table set against a wall underneath a window. A lamp lit the room, and she stopped and closed her eyes, massaging her temple.

She took an awkward step back and bumped into Jackson. "I'm dizzy."

Jackson held her up. "Sit down."

She waved him away. "Search the room."

Jackson checked the small bed; white sheets with a purple wool blanket over top. He lifted the pillow. Nothing there, but what about the headboard? Nothing behind it nor the sheet beneath.

He dropped to his knees and checked under the bed. The wood floor was clean and bare. Standing, he focused on the bookshelf. Bibles. Theology tomes. Nothing out of the ordinary.

Alabama hurried through several drawers in the dresser and rifled through clothes. Her hand fell onto something, and she pulled out a long, thick book with a black cover. The word *UFO* stretched across the top.

He moved closer to her. "What's that?"

She sat in the lotus position and set the book on the ground. "Hard to read. The world is spinning."

As she flipped pages, Jackson loomed over her shoulder. Several passages were highlighted in yellow.

Alabama sighed and put the book back in its place. "He's interested in the subject." Her eyes stopped and locked onto something. "The nausea is getting worse." She pointed at a corner wall. "Maybe over there?"

Jackson saw it the moment she pointed. In the corner, a red sweater lay bunched up and covered something round. Jackson tossed the sweater to the side.

Another sphere.

The etched pattern matched the sphere they found at the crime scene.

"Unreal."

"Grab it. Let's go," Alabama said.

When he picked it up, a zap tingled his hands, ending at the top of his head. His feet bolted to the floor.

We're watching.

He blinked several times and willed himself to move.

"What's wrong?" she asked.

Jackson dipped his head. "Did you hear that?"

"Hear what?"

"Nothing." He hurried toward the door when something caught his attention. A paper with chalk scribbling and mathematical symbols hid against the floorboard and door jamb. He tucked it into his pocket.

They walked out of the room as a loud crack whipped across the air. Jackson froze. "A gunshot."

"They're here."

"Who?"

Unholstering her weapon, she crept slowly down the stairs and crouched when she was in a position to see through the windows on the entrance door.

Jackson moved beside her, the sphere in one hand, his 9mm in the other. "I hope we didn't lead those bastards here."

"Don't lose the sphere."

Through a window, he made out a young monk motionless in the snow. Crimson blood splattered the snow around him. A statue of Gabriel, hands toward the heavens, wings outstretched, stood over him.

Several armed men in white camouflage advanced toward the church.

Jackson's mouth widened. "Wren..."

"They're after the sphere."

Not this time.

Alabama was by his side when he reached the lobby floor. The cool chill swept across his face as they hurried outside. Two men maneuvered from an SUV onto the grounds, two others toward the chapel.

"What about the monks?" he asked.

Her silence spoke volumes.

Her expression turned grim. "We're engaging."

"Here?"

"No choice. Get behind the trees."

Jackson aimed, poked his finger through the trigger guard, and squeezed. An enemy flung forward, his arms flailing. The man's weapon flew out of his hands, disappearing into the snow along with him.

Alabama dashed in the church's direction toward a patch of Douglas Firs, Jackson tailing behind her. Bullets pelted apart the frozen earth, sending snow into the air.

Taking cover behind a wide tree, Jackson pressed his back against the freezing bark. "Two behind Gabriel, the other behind Jesus."

"Great. We're going to piss off the Big Guy."

A bullet whizzed by, and another round took a chunk of bark out of a tree.

Jackson rested his shoulder against the tree. One of the men next to Gabriel extended his pistol in Jackson's direction, and Jackson fired, his bullets splitting the bottom of Gabriel's wing. The man jumped away and hid behind the statue. A cloud formed. Stone fragments slung into the snow.

Tucking the sphere close to him, he stiffened as a zap drove down his spine. His mind fogged in a whirlwind of ideas and images. An entangled web of future possibilities blinked like scenes in a movie trailer. The world slowed, his mind trying to decipher the mirage.

The sphere pulsed.

Lights in every direction. Stars. Worlds beyond measure, some created artificially. Warnings wrapped in emotions. The essence of reality crystalizing like snowflakes.

Is someone there?

Something is here.

"Get it together!" Alabama spun around and took more shots only to split one of Gabriel's arms off.

A round whizzed past Jackson's ear, and he flinched. The sphere slipped away. In a swift motion, he caught it before it hit the ground.

The church doors opened. Abbot Nikolas held Brother

Malakai around his waist, doing his best to pull the old man inside.

"Stop!" Nikolas shouted above the battle.

Malakai pushed Nikolas away, and the abbot lost his balance and fell onto his side.

"Don't!" Nikolas pleaded.

The door shut on Nikolas's leg. Malakai rushed forward, eyes narrowed, mouth open in a yell. He made it down the steps with his fist in the air, speaking Latin, and charged like a Marine storming the beaches of Iwo Jima.

The man behind Jesus fired, hitting the earth inches from Malakai's feet.

Alabama put her hand up. "Brother Malakai, stop!"

An instant later, two bullets blasted Malakai, jerking him back and forth. Blood spurted out his back and shoulder, and his screams resounded off the surrounding buildings.

An attacker stepped too far from Gabriel's cover, and a light flashed from his weapon's muzzle. Malakai's head lurched back. Like a rag doll, he went limp to the ground.

Jackson returned fire, his mind whirling. Three well-aimed shots blew his target to pieces. Alabama hustled around a line of boxwood brush bordering one of the paths. Jackson followed. Two flashes erupted from Alabama's weapon. A loud grunt. The man behind Gabriel flipped off his feet, his eyes closed.

She dashed to Malakai, dropped to a knee, and checked his pulse. She shook her head. "He's gone."

Cursing, Jackson gnashed his teeth together. *Flynn, you're going to pay for this.*

She stood and rested her back against the side of Gabriel and what was left of his wing.

Footsteps slapped on a path. A man ran to the church, his long hair tied in the back. Reinforcements?

Jackson took a shot, missing wide. A glass window pane of Virgin Mary praying shattered. The long-haired man reached the top of the church's stairs and pushed through one of the doors.

"Target inside the chapel." Jackson raced across the snow, the church in his sights.

"I'll go around the back," she said.

"Go!"

She curled around the corner of the church and out of view.

Time to go.

As his heart thrummed in his throat, he nudged the entrance door open.

A shot cracked.

Jackson ducked and rolled toward a pew, the sphere uncomfortably pushing into his ribcage.

Where is he hiding?

The long-haired man shuffled in front of him. When Jackson stole a peek to find him, he didn't see him.

There should still be one more outside. He could come through any minute.

Through the cracked window, he heard Wren's 9mm Glock dispensing death.

"Target down," she said. "Flanking new target inside the chapel. Watch for my entrance on the west side."

Zap!

Jackson grunted. For a moment, his body went rigid with electrical sensations spreading like veins through his limbs. A voice, something distant and true, whispered to him. Something beyond language. A separate distinct entity spoke.

Do you hear us?

Gunfire erupted from inside the chapel, splintering the door like shards of ice. Jackson caught sight of the assassin using the organ as cover.

As Jackson dove behind the pews, incoming fire peppered the wood. When Jackson fired back, organ keys buckled and fractured. Wood split.

"I'm inside," she said through her mic.

Jackson could see her outline in the hallway next to him, both hands on her weapon. She took a shot. Wood cracked. After she missed, the long-haired man hit the ground and rolled.

Now!

Jackson leaped over pews, his barrel aimed where the man should be.

As the man threw his arm in Jackson's direction, Jackson fired wildly. The shot clipped the man's neck. Blood gurgled from his throat and coated his teeth.

"You will never stop us." In the man's last gasp, a blast flashed from his muzzle.

The sphere under Jackson's arm exploded. Rock-like shrapnel pelted against his ribs and into a nearby pew. Jackson fell to his back. A swirling dust cloud grew, and as the pieces hit the ground, they vanished into nothing, as if erased from reality itself.

Alabama dashed toward Jackson and rested her palms on his chest. "Are you hit?"

He patted himself down. No blood, only a bump the size of an orange.

"I'm good."

She rose. "Where's the sphere?"

"I don't know." Jackson bent and touched the ground.

"It's gone?"

"It was hit and disintegrated."

Stunned, her eyes searched the ground, and she touched where the sphere had exploded. "Stay put. Going to do a perimeter sweep."

His heart fell. The church. The statues. The bullets. The dire cacophony of violence stilled. And now the sphere. How did it disappear? What was it made of? If only he could have put it under a microscope.

Should I tell Wren about what happened? Was the sphere trying to communicate? Was it mind manipulation technology? Impossible. That kind of thing doesn't exist.

As he stood, he dusted himself off.

When Alabama returned, she collected the brass casings littering the chapel. "Can't freakin' believe this. The sphere vanished just like that?"

"I don't understand it, either." He fished the paper he'd found in Malakai's room out of his pocket. "Maybe this will tell us something?"

She tilted her head at the dead man lying next to the organ. "I'll call a cleaner. They'll probably burn this place down."

He took in one last look. His heart hurt.

No. I'm not going to pray. God, if you can hear me, I don't know what to feel. I don't feel anything at all. I'm empty. If this is part of your plan, you'll have to explain it to me sometime. Because right now, I need to feel something.

"Come on," Alabama said. "Let's go before the police arrive."

On their way home, Alabama's post-combat jitters vanished. Her stomach growled. Food. She located a vegan burger joint called Jando's a few blocks from a Super Wal-Mart. About twenty blocks north sat an extinct volcanic vent known as Mount Tabor. After buying half the menu, they headed up the long drive to the top of Tabor, where they'd notice anyone approaching them.

Once they drove to the mountain's highest point, the majority of Portland sprawled out before them. Downtown Portland glowed on the west side of the Willamette River, where skyscrapers reached for the clouds. The sun was setting and lit the sky with pinks and lavenders. They remained in the car.

Alabama took a bite of a beet burger. As she chewed, Thousand Island dressing oozed down her lower lip. She ran her tongue over her lip to savor the sauce. Food was exactly what she needed.

She reached into the bag and pulled out a handful of tater tots, plopping a few tots in her mouth.

"I choose our takeout place next time." Jackson sucked

an organic strawberry milkshake through a paper straw. "Where do you find dives like this?"

"Don't whine." She gazed at a forest that lined the hills west of downtown, the sun sinking behind the vast trees. She closed her eyes; the first unwind she'd had since the start of this investigation. "Try your black bean burger. It's got all the protein you need."

"I'm not a machine. If all I needed was protein, I'd eat that way. I eat what I like because I don't live in the Matrix."

"Red pill, blue pill." She shrugged. "And you know how they treat animals...."

"I do, but I'm not an activist. Besides, isn't there a study about how plants communicate telepathically? Are you going to stop eating them because you hurt their feelings?"

"We aren't plants."

"We aren't cows or chickens, either," he said. "This is the last time I'm listening to you about where we eat. This stuff tastes like cardboard."

She made a face. "Suit yourself." *At least he's starting to show some backbone.*

"What do you think of Malakai?" he asked.

"I think he's dead."

"You don't care that he's dead?"

She took a drink. "We all die. I didn't know him."

He finished his potatoes and crinkled the wrapper. "Has anyone ever asked you why you care more about animals than people?"

"Yes," she said, munching the last of her meal.

"And?"

"Plants don't have souls. It's part of the Earth's spirit, with which she freely gives to us."

"But you don't know."

"You can look into an animal and see its soul. They communicate. They're aware."

"Plants warn each other when there's a fire."

"But they don't have souls," she said.

"I think you harbor hatred for plants and that's why you're a vegan. I'm going to put that in my report." Jackson smiled and laughed.

He grabbed another burger. By the look on his face, he didn't like the mushroom Chao Cheese, either. His loss.

She blasted the heater and pulled out a proximity jammer and a white noise amplifier. "In case someone is listening."

"Thanks."

The screen showed lines of green; blips for cell towers. No other signals.

She set the devices down on the dash. "Okay, looks good. What do you think we've discovered?"

"Not sure. I'll admit I'm part of the group that has biases about extraterrestrials. The subject is poison."

"Stone, I think you're trying to convince *yourself* rather than me. Your job is to keep an open mind."

He dunked a handful of sweet potato fries into ketchup and showed her Malakai's piece of paper. "What do you think these symbols mean?"

"The five platonic solids. Tetrahedron, hexahedron, octahedron, dodecahedron, and icosahedron."

"The same ones on the sphere," he said.

Alabama lifted her shoulders and let them fall. "Ancient cultures believed them to represent fire, earth, air, water, and spirit."

"It seems odd a priest would draw something like that, especially considering how much they work during the day and how little personal time they have." Jackson hovered his finger below the symbols over words written in orange chalk. "Angel alpha mates together. Devil buttons abduction's certain blunt atheistic Catholic union."

She shook her head. "Cryptic. Something he doesn't want the church to know."

"Abductions barbaric attempts unrepenting arrow commits ablative backhand. Abbey's magical consort swarms bluebook's house."

She rested her palm on her chin. "He didn't use scripture for code."

"True. Why? Too easy to crack?"

"The Bible is too well-known to be used as a code. Cryptography machines are loaded with religious texts because they are so often used to pass messages."

Jackson lowered the heat. "It's blowing right in my face."

"Do you mind? It's freezing in here."

"Turn the vents."

She sighed.

"Okay, okay." He turned it back up.

She rubbed her hands together. "Better. Malakai also said no one died. His body language indicated deception and stress."

"Perhaps he had his own experience." He clawed his neck and sipped his milkshake. "From the radiation and the burn marks on the trees, the disc, as you call it, must have been huge. It doesn't make sense something that large would be created to target a small group."

She wiped her mouth and packed up the trash. "The radiation could be from its propulsion. It might be damaged. Brother Malakai wasn't targeted by whatever happened to the hikers. He ended up safe and sound."

"Targeted?"

"Keep your mind open because in this line of work,

nothing is certain. He said he heard a voice saying, 'We are here. We've been here before humanity.' What does that sound like to you?"

He started to say something and stopped. "I honestly don't know what to make of it without further information. I believe he thought he heard it, but that doesn't make it true." He pointed at her using a French fry and set it down. "I haven't had time to process what happened."

She grabbed his fry and ate it. He grimaced, and she grabbed a handful of them and put them in front of her.

"You're welcome," he said.

She smiled. "Process what?"

He stared off into space. "All of it. Losing the first sphere. Then the second."

"You said it disappeared?"

"Like popping an air bubble." He used a napkin and wiped his hands clean. "I thought I'd feel something after killing someone, but I don't. I'm numb."

"That's normal. At some point, your mind will want to think about it but compartmentalize it. You'll have plenty of opportunities to process it after the mission."

Her chest tightened. She still thought about the time she'd first killed. She was twelve, living on the streets of Chicago. No place to go. No money. She'd done things she tried to forget, and over time, they'd become foggy play-backs. The man she'd killed still burned hot in her memory, a seething, lisping meth dealer who enjoyed harassing girls thirty years his junior. *Harass.* Too weak a word for some-thing so disgusting. She borrowed a snub nose .38 and put three into his chest and ran with the wind.

Jackson steepled his fingers. "How long did it take us to drive from Frog Lake to Mount Hood Abbey? About fifteen minutes? If Malakai walked fast and cut through the forest, it would take him seventy to ninety minutes to reach the location where we found the sphere and his clothing." He started the car and drove down the long, winding road.

She noted the distance from the abbey. "He would have to know the lights were there first. If he were in the abbey and looked out of his window, he would not have had the time to make it there. The event would have ended. He must've known about it beforehand."

Jackson tightened his lips. They swapped seats, and he drove out of Mount Tabor's entrance and merged with traffic. "You know, something strange happened to me when I held the sphere."

Alabama leaned in, taking another bite. "Do tell."

"I can't be certain, but I could have sworn I heard a voice, too, but it's hard to explain. I felt something like electricity shoot through me."

She arched a brow. "You're telling me this now?"

"Well, it doesn't do much good now."

She stopped blinking. "You said you heard a voice?"

"Not like that. I shouldn't have said anything. It's not a voice. Sometimes I think I'm visiting a memory. Never mind."

Subconscious training. Polaris didn't waste a second. A person can be driven insane if they think their thoughts aren't their own. Always better lie to them, especially when they're your partner.

"But something led you to believe you heard a voice?"

He brought his gaze away from her and fixated on the silver BMW in front of them. "Either way, the sphere is destroyed."

She studied him for signs of deception. Eyes looking directly at a person. The *believe me* look. Too many details.

Not with Stone. Here was one man she couldn't read. Either that or he couldn't resist being honest.

"It might have been created with nanites," she said. "Tiny machines housed inside, which could've transformed the sphere into smaller particles on a molecular scale."

"Do we have something like that in our inventory?"

"Yes, but they're costly." She took Malakai's paper and studied it, and her eyes narrowed.

"So, it could have been man-made."

"Or woman-made. You really should have said something about the voices you heard. It validates what the witnesses said."

"I didn't know if I was hearing things or not."

She shook her head, frustrated. "You need to let me know what's going on, Stone."

"I don't know what to say. Okay, I will. My mistake."

Not bad. Not exactly an "I'm sorry" but better than she expected. "Malakai probably wondered the same thing." She took the note. "The letters touch the bottom of the geometric symbols."

"And?"

"Interesting." She wadded up the wrapper that held the beet burger and threw it in the bag.

Jackson took a right down 74th Avenue. "What do you see?"

"A code. The words don't mean anything."

"Some people believe in something called Sacred geometry."

"I'm familiar with the idea. Natural geometric forms are said to be some kind of proof of the Divine. Honeycombs. The Fibonacci Sequence. Nautilus shells. It's an interesting theory. Malakai believed in it," she said. "Remember the patterns on the sphere? Let me see." She touched the page.

It couldn't be that easy, but it was. The first letter of each word spelled out the meaning. "Last location. Disc. Camp Withycombe." She shot Jackson a look. "Know where that is?"

"Clackamas County, less than twenty minutes away."

They had parked a mile down the road past Camp Withycombe and ascended a forested bluff bordering the camp's chain-link fence. The damp soil and vegetation from the Oregon rains made for a quiet hike.

An image of her old partner popped into her mind. A warm feeling from a long time ago she wished she could relive forever.

Dubois Lavigne.

The love of her life.

At first glance, he was a stunning man, who could walk in a room and command attention, the kind of man who other men listened to without thinking about it. His brown eyes and stern jawline magnetized her. Broad shoulders. Muscular arms and chest; muscles that saved her a hundred times.

.   .   .

AN EMPTY RACE TRACK. Yellowed grass. Far away from the city. Dubois and Alabama and a modified bright lemon Alfa Romeo GTV took the stage.

Dubois smiled. "Pass this test, and we move on to stage eight. Ready?"

Alabama dipped her head. "Ready."

"Go!" Dubois reclined in the passenger seat, the back of the backrest touching the rear seat.

With her fingers curled on the driver's wheel, Alabama slammed on the accelerator. The wind rushed to her face and through her hair as the GTV raced down the track. Metal silhouettes of terrorists and hostages popped up around the track.

She slammed the brake and turned the wheel, while simultaneously pulling out her weapon. White smoke from the rubber skidding on the track clouded the rear window. She extended her arm toward the open passenger side window. She shot. A clank bonged from the bullet's impact. The target went down.

In a flash, she switched the gun to her other hand. Turning the wheel and pressing the accelerator to the floor, she fired. Two more targets slapped to the ground.

She pulled a U-turn and smoke plumed from the tires as she headed toward more targets. Changing hands, eight others down.

Slamming the brakes, she fishtailed to a stop and threw a fist in the air. "Yes!"

Dubois lifted from his reclined seat, wrapped both hands around her temples, and touched his lips against hers. They kissed long and hard. His white teeth shined past his smile. The last few months of kissing him only garnered the want for more, and she pulled him in.

"You did it," he said, mid-kiss. "I've never met anyone like you."

She pulled away and laughed. "There's no one else like me." She leaned and arched her back, contorting to the tiny space inside the car. Her breasts pushed up against him. "There's no one else like you either."

He bit his bottom lip, something she knew meant he wanted to keep a secret but couldn't hold it in. "I'll talk to Hill about what happens next, but never tell him about us. You can't."

"I won't."

"And you're sure you can pass the polygraphs?"

She caressed him the right way. He closed his eyes, moaning in pleasure. She sat in his lap, whispering in his ear, "I already have."

THE SUN HAD SUNK below the horizon and twilight descended.

Alabama gazed through binoculars, and she activated the infrared imagery. Soldiers patrolled around the perimeter, armed with M4 rifles. Around fifty or so buildings made up the base and more than a dozen massive hangers.

One warehouse, on the northeast side of the base, dwarfed the rest. Trailers surrounded it with men in hazmat suits. She zoomed in on the roof. Twisting the lens, digital numbers appeared on either side of the inner lenses; the zoom rate and image enhancement quality. Housed on the roof facing her, steel lattice and two main transverse beams were powered by electric motors.

Alabama crouched and leaned her shoulder against a tree, grasping the backpack straps around her shoulders. Her abdomen muscles stabilized her as she balanced on one leg while using her other foot to lower a fern in front of her for a better view.

Jackson crouched next to her. "See anything?"

"A retractable roof. If I were a betting woman, I'd bet that's where the disc is being kept." She lifted her leg slowly. The fern elongated to its original position with little to no sound. With both feet planted firmly on the ground, she clipped the binoculars to her utility belt. She frowned, her focus on her view of the base. "I count thirty soldiers along the fence in front of us."

Jackson tapped the GoPro clipped to his belt. "That's quite a few. When we get inside the warehouse, I'll record what I can and exfiltrate."

She leaned more weight against the tree and pointed to the southeastern section of the base. "We move in that direction. Military vehicles parked along the gate will give us cover after we cut our way in."

"Alarms?" he asked.

"Be wary. Using our goggles, we'll be able to see L beams. They'll glow bright red and be as thick as a pencil. If you see them, those act as tripwires. But that," she said, pointing to a sensor cable attached along the middle of the fence, "is physical security."

At a fence corner, ten feet inside the boundary, a black security alarm box stood chest-high off the base of a pole. She reached into her bag and assembled her Wire Puppy, a long-slide pistol fitted with a smart system and an electro suite. Because of the pistol's special rounds, it could reroute electronic signals inside a security system. She pulled out a silencer and tightened it in place.

"Won't that alert everyone?"

"No. To them, it will still appear as though it's working."

She took aim, and fired, hitting dead center. When the round hit, a purple halo formed around the box.

"Nice shot."

Winking, she grinned and said, "Why thank you."

"If the disc is here, it's not secured." Jackson motioned ahead. "The southeast corner is clear. This way."

They hiked until they reached the edge of a forest. Dozens of parked vehicles sat near the fence and beyond.

Alabama took off her backpack and set it on the ground, the night concealing them well.

She pulled a wire cutter and began cutting through the gate. "Fold the wires up and away, so we don't cut ourselves."

They crawled through and found themselves between two Humvees. She exhaled and then stiffened as footsteps ran in her direction.

"Over there," a soldier yelled.

"There goes that idea," she said.

B ending his knees, Jackson laid his hand on a Humvee's tire as the footsteps grew louder. Boots splashed a puddle fifteen feet away.

"We have a breach," a man in camo said into his radio. He sprinted by the line of Humvees, and several soldiers followed him in military precision.

Are they looking for us?

Alabama jimmied underneath the Humvee, dragging her bag. Jackson did the same. The wet pavement soaked through his shirt and dampened his chest and stomach as he pushed himself under the thin space. He held his breath.

More soldiers dashed by, boots shimmering against the lights from the buildings. Lamp posts lit inside the perimeter. As they maneuvered, he noted their coordinated tactics.

"What's your status?" a guard asked.

A gunshot cracked across the night. He flinched. Bright flashes and sparks illuminated the area. Then like fireworks, gunfire rang out.

A soldier went prone no more than five yards from Jackson, aiming at something in the distance.

Bullets rained from every direction. The impacts cracked asphalt and thumped when they hit the soldier, splitting holes into the back of his fatigues. Troops advanced behind buildings and vehicle cover, exchanging fire with the attackers.

"We're not alone," she said.

"M4 rifles. 5.56. Locals."

CIA? PLA? KGB? Flynn? All would have known about this place, too. Who else would be brave enough to stage an assault this brazen? SWAT teams and other police would arrive. The attackers didn't stand a chance. And now, Jackson and Alabama would lose theirs.

"Go to night vision," she said.

The world became green, bright flashes in white.

A squad dashed to his right and dove behind a long, brick building. Others took up positions, protecting their flanks.

"Who the hell are they?" one of them asked, his voice wavering.

"We're screwed," came a reply. "We're getting shut down."

The shortest one popped off bursts and reloaded. "Who's shutting us down?"

Alabama threw an index finger at the building with the retractable roof.

Jackson acknowledged her. It was a way inside without getting perforated with bullets. There would be snipers on top. Sensors. Cameras. The military would want to keep the high ground.

She slid out from under the Humvee, and soldiers advanced.

How in the hell were they going to reach the warehouse without being gunned down? It would be suicide.

Scanning the roof, she said, "There's got to be a ladder."

More gunfire. A cry for help. Someone else had been hit.

Jackson's chest dripped with sweat. In the green hue of their night vision, the firefight became the Fourth of July.

Alabama backpedaled. Waving her free hand, she motioned to the gate they snuck through. "That way, between the vehicles and the gate."

"Who's attacking? Flynn?"

"Flynn."

They high crawled, their elbows mashing into the snow, and reached the rear bumpers of a line of Humvees. A two-and-a-half-ton truck sat parked a hundred yards away, its tarp removed. More shots riddled the air. A windshield shattered.

Warning signs marked radiation hazards and noted trespassers would be shot. No kidding.

Alarms blared, their wails drowning out the firefight.

Up ahead, a commissary building with overly large windows stared back at Jackson. No one occupied it unless they remained hidden. "Could be clear there."

Massive clouds of smoke appeared, flowing from smoke grenades. Flashbangs added to the confusion. The entire base mobilized, but none of the soldiers mounted their vehicles. Any moment, Black Hawks would be inbound.

Jackson dashed across a patch of wet grass and reached the commissary. Rounding it, he threw his shoulder against the wall.

Alabama accompanied him, her breaths choppy. "See the warehouse?"

"I think so. Smoke clouds." Jackson dipped his head, catching his breath. "A hundred yards to our northwest, behind the line. Sounds like an army out there."

She grimaced. "Flynn."

He motioned to a radiation sign.

"We only have one shot at this," she said. "If our hair falls out, we'll get over it. Do one thing for me?"

"Sure," Jackson said.

"Run between the bullets with me."

She nudged him to go, and Jackson burst across the asphalt toward the towering warehouse, its roof hovering above an office and the barracks.

His feet smacked concrete. Run. Run. Run.

I'm not going to die. I'm not going to die. Don't shoot me. Don't shoot.

An explosion shook the ground.

The world slowed, and a high-pitched tone drowned out the cacophony of battle. A bright white light accompanied a hefty, hot wind. Jackson lost his footing. When he landed, he grunted and rolled across the wet pavement. So did Alabama.

She pushed to her feet. Yellow flames dazzled against her pupils.

Attackers advanced toward the warehouse. Jackson's pulse raced. "Go, go! They're going to get there first."

No one shot at him or Alabama. They would make it. They were halfway there. Closing fast. His feet running on air.

Whack!

Jackson's knees buckled, and he braced his fall. Sharp pains erupted in his wrists. A pair of gloves grabbed him.

The man who kicked him stood a head taller than he did and weighed a good 230-235 pounds. His teeth shined white against his dark tan skin. In the smoke, Jackson could see him bring up the barrel of his rifle.

Bullets buzzed around them.

"Don't shoot!" Jackson shouted.

Alabama landed an open-palmed knife strike to the trooper's throat. The man gagged and fired, but his rounds perforated a few of the Humvees. She sidestepped and snatched the rifle. Jackson grabbed the soldier's legs, pulling him down. A blank look washed over Alabama, and she put two rounds into the man.

"Warehouse. Let's go," she said as cold as the Arctic wind.

She was a killer. An iron shiver ran down Jackson's neck. The man she'd killed wasn't one of Flynn's toy thugs. He was a soldier, one of the men and women who'd sworn an oath to protect and defend the Constitution from all enemies, foreign and domestic. And she'd killed him without blinking.

No time to think about it. She'd done her duty.

Soldiers would form a perimeter around the warehouse, but cover would remain scarce.

The commissary remained hidden by massive smoke clouds.

A breeze wafted from the east, and the upper portion of the warehouse came into view. The open roof extended on the sides, which would mean the ladder would have to be on the front, back, or inside the warehouse.

She pointed ahead. "Hear that?"

Jackson listened, but his new heart thumped, bullets ricocheted, and men shouted at one another through the chaos. Though the smoke made it impossible to see, he counted a dozen shooters on each side of the warehouse, exchanging fire with an equal number.

Pop. Pop. Pop.

Flynn's army wasn't advancing from their direction.

"Won't the camp's troops be waiting at the front door?" he asked.

"Not if they know Flynn's here."

The commissary exploded in a ball of orange fire, flinging concrete and glass, like cannon shells. Chunks bounced behind him as Jackson and Alabama jetted toward the warehouse.

In the shadows, Flynn's kill teams went to work. When an RPG hit one of the Humvees, it exploded, sending flame and burning wreckage into a squad of soldiers. Fire engulfed them, and they cried out, hitting the ground and rolling to put it out. Flynn's men decimated them and sent another RPG into an awaiting fire team, manning a light machine gun. The impact turned the soldiers into red mist, blending in with the smoke.

If Jackson opened fire, he'd reveal his position to Flynn and the Army.

They slowed, sweeping in their frontal arcs. A pair of soldiers guarded the door behind concrete slabs. Before Jackson could utter a remark, she gunned them down.

This wasn't right. They were only performing their duty. He fought back vomit after seeing what remained of them.

She reached the front and stood next to a security console. Jackson searched for a ladder, but he wouldn't be able to see a Boeing 747 through the smoke, let alone a ladder.

Alabama pulled the panel open and thrust a spike in its side. A wire was attached to the end of the spike that threaded into her unzipped backpack. She pressed several buttons, and the warehouse door jostled and moved upward. "We'll exfiltrate from the roof."

"Look out!" Jackson said.

Rocket-propelled grenades slammed into the side of the warehouse. Fires licked the sidewall and acrid smoke saturated the air from the explosion. Somehow, the building remained intact. The roar of an MWRAP armored vehicle filled his ear, its machine gun rattling. Nothing either Jackson or Alabama had could shoot through its thick plated armor. Its speed caused the smoke to whirl around it.

"Flynn," she said.

Designed to withstand mines, MWRAPs were tough to breach. Window slits gave the vehicle 360-degree vision, and they often carried troops to the battlefield. Its color blended with the night sky. A battering ram protruded from the front.

Crash!

It slammed into the warehouse's sidewall.

The building shook. A portion of the wall crumbled onto the warehouse floor. As chunks of rubble and plasterboard splattered, the dust and smoke swirled together.

Jackson reached Alabama, slid onto the smooth warehouse floor, and hid behind stacks of olive-colored ammo crates. The open roof reached up four stories tall, and a security terminal with a conveyor belt and an X-ray scanner blinked red. A gunner atop the MWRAP peppered the inner warehouse with his fifty-caliber machine gun.

Sergeants barked out orders to men, dying seconds later.

All this killing. The blood. Jackson's heart throbbed, and he held his chest, wincing.

"You good?"

He nodded.

She scooped up a pair of grenades from the dead soldiers.

"Here," Alabama said, handing him a frag grenade. She held one in her other hand. "On three," she said, counting down. After the count, they lobbed them at the turret. Meat and bones showered the vehicle, and the machine gun blew apart.

Seeing an opening, Jackson launched himself further inside the warehouse. The MWRAP was to his left, soldiers to his right. He coughed, tasting the cordite and blood-soaked air.

Moonlight through the open roof.

Noise faded into the background.

Jackson froze.

There it was.

A large hubcap-shaped craft on three landing sleds sat in the middle of the building. Silver in color, the ship took up the entirety of the warehouse. It had portholes for windows, and it peaked at the top like the apex of a pyramid. A muddy haze surrounded it, making it difficult to see. A ramp went up the center and into its belly, large enough for an elephant to walk inside.

"It's real...." Jackson said.

"Get inside!" Alabama cried, running toward it.

"Get inside?"

"The disc!" Alabama pushed him and fired off a burst.

The MWRAP thundered inside the warehouse, slaughtering all that stood against it. On instinct, Jackson sent bullets its way, giving him nothing but sparks in return. The armored personnel carrier disappeared into the darkness of the ship's hull.

"Go!" She flung herself up the ramp and at her third step, lead cracked at her feet. She lurched back, lost her footing, and slid to the concrete.

Pop! Hiss.

The ramp retracted until it clicked in place. A blue glow washed over the craft, and it lifted a few feet off the ground and hovered in place.

He couldn't move. Couldn't believe his eyes.

The ship hummed and rose through the open roof and shot into the sky. In an instant, it merged with the stars and disappeared.

Jackson blinked several times, head tilted toward the night sky. Gunshots slowed to a trickle, and the soldier's voices carried long and far. Flynn's men were scattered about the warehouse, but the smoke still kept Jackson and Alabama concealed.

"We need to go," she whispered.

She cried out as a wire from a Taser hit her in the neck.

Then an electrical shock.

Jackson flopped helplessly. Seconds later, his hands

were bound with plastic zip ties, and soldiers patted them down and stuffed their heads inside bags.

"We have them, sir," a voice said.

"Sir," another said. "Check the badge. They're Feds."

"You have got to be kidding...."

Portland's Federal Bureau of Investigation building stood four stories high, its exterior the color of fresh bark dust. It sat on perfectly manicured green grounds on 9109 Northeast Cascades Parkway. A large metal gate surrounded the property like a prison.

This was the last place Jackson wanted to be.

He rested his hands on a table in a second-floor interrogation room, fingers intertwined. The tabletop softly vibrated from a plane coming in for a landing; the building too close to the Portland International Airport for Jackson's liking.

Alabama sat in the chair next to him, her hair disheveled. A few red strands scrawled down her face, stuck by sweat. With her arms crossed, she slumped back in a chair.

Both of them smelled like death, and the stank clung to everything inside the interrogation room.

An agent named Carl Alvarez, six-foot-eight inches tall, blue eyes, and built like a lumberjack, leaned over the table.

Another man sat in a chair closer to the door. Forearms

on a chair's backrest, the agent had turned the chair around. His name was Barney Boyle, a senior in the agency. Sandy blond crew cut. Brown eyes. Cleft chin.

The base notified Portland's FBI field office, where Jackson and Alabama now sat for over an hour. They had a lot of explaining to do and lacked explanations. If they did any type of forensics, they'd soon discover she was the one who killed three soldiers. And then what?

Alvarez pushed off the table and stood tall. "Agent Simms," he said to Jackson, "and you're Agent Bailey." He stared at their badges.

Alabama shifted in her seat.

Alvarez squished his lips together. "Both of you are in the FBI files and database, but I find it odd we weren't given notice you'd be here in Oregon. Your IDs check out, but neither of you strikes me as FBI agents. You especially." He pointed to Jackson.

"We're working in conjunction with DHS," Alabama said. "Call them."

"We did call DHS, and they won't speak to us. Why were you at the base? That area is labeled special access. Do you know what you've done? You poked the Department of Defense, and I suspect you'll soon be hearing from the DOJ and brought up on some serious charges."

Jackson leaned in. "Agent Alvarez, the mere fact we're in here talking to you means you're the one who's going to be in trouble, not us."

"Spare me," Alvarez said. "Do you know what a storm you've caused? Both of you will be flown to GITMO. Let them deal with your sorry asses."

The last time Jackson was interrogated, he'd underperformed on the test. Polaris made their exams hard and realistic. He'd endured waterboarding, sensory deprivation, and worse while being flown over International Waters. When Director Hill received his poor torture exam results, he gave Jackson a pass. Maybe he shouldn't have.

Alvarez scratched something on a piece of paper. "You mentioned homicide."

"Part of our investigation," Alabama said, "involves approaching potential informants and building a profile for our case. Do not interfere with our work. We're not at liberty to say much more. Call DHS again and give them our names. Talk to a woman named Mary Blankenship."

Boyle poured himself more coffee, loosened his tie, and sat. "It sounds like you're trying to make us call your friend, who will bail you out."

Jackson sighed. "I suspect the FBI Director is going to call you into his office, make you sign a few sworn statements, and threaten to pull your pension after this discussion. Every minute you delay us is another minute we can't operate in the field."

"I know the FBI Director quite well, Agent Simms," Agent Alvarez said. "He would want to know why two of his agents are refusing to answer some basic questions and why they keep insisting I call DHS."

A click pierced the room. The door opened. A man too handsome to be an agent strode inside. Sharp, sapphire blue eyes, perfect nose, chiseled jaw—the man could be a model. "Sorry to interrupt." He handed a file to Alvarez and exited the room.

Alvarez opened the file and skimmed it. He wrinkled his brow in confusion. "It looks like you two are being shipped off."

"What do you mean, *shipped off*?" Alabama reached for the file.

He closed it. "That's all."

Jackson stood. "What the hell is this?"

Alvarez strode to the door. "Message from the Associate Deputy Director. You're to come with us. Come on. Let's go."

Jackson exchanged glances with Alabama. They could be going anywhere. Who was to say Agent Boyle and Agent Alvarez legitimately worked for the FBI? That was always the problem with law enforcement. Now that Jackson had joined Polaris, he'd learned anyone could be anyone, and he could only trust those in the organization.

The two FBI agents took Jackson and Alabama out of the interrogation room and led them down a wide hall. Jackson narrowed his eyes, doing his best to hold back a gasp. The place smelled like coffee and hard work. Agents met by a water cooler, and men and women typed reports and studied analytics.

A man stood at the end of the hallway, his arms folded. Two women flanked him.

Hunter Flynn.

He wore a red power tie, a fake mustache, and glasses. His hair was dyed blond.

Being handed over to Flynn sounded like a bad idea.

Jackson nodded at Flynn, and he tipped his head back, mouth open. It faded into a grimace.

"Thank you, Agent Alvarez." Flynn held up a folder. "I'll take them from here."

F lynn grabbed Jackson's arm, squeezing it tight. "You'll like your new living arrangements, but I don't promise you'll get a lot of rest."

The two women accompanying him wore sunglasses and kept their brunette hair wrapped underneath FBI hats. They could have been twins.

"We're not going with you," Alabama said.

Flynn turned his gaze on her. "Yes, you are. I hope you've said your goodbyes."

The sea of agents parted.

"Make a hole," someone said.

Director Patrick Hill marched down the hall from the other side. Leather notebook under his arm, he wore beige slacks and a dark jacket. He held an equally grim, hard look. He raised his badge high. "Mo Murray, Assistant Director, DHS Internal Threat Office, Norfolk." He stopped between Jackson and the FBI agents, a fist on his hip. "Uncuff my agents."

Flynn and Hill exchanged knowing glances. Agents

around the room both stared at the two men, now glaring at each other like dogs of war.

"Release them," Director Hill said.

Flynn waved two fingers at one of his detail, and she unlocked their handcuffs.

Jackson rubbed his wrists. When he looked up, Flynn had disappeared. Alvarez bit at his lip, Hill's false badge still facing him.

Good time for Polaris to come through.

Director Hill squared his shoulders. "As my agents have no doubt explained, they're currently on a case involving national security. You have not seen us." Hill shoved his badge into his pocket and led Alabama and Jackson to the elevator.

Jackson pressed his shoulder against the elevator's side-wall. "Sir...."

"Later," Hill said.

Once out of the elevator, they walked past the FBI emblem mounted on a wall behind a long wooden desk in the lobby.

Armed guards waved them through, and they left out into the chilly Portland weather. Once they reached a Chevrolet Suburban, Hill's driver opened the door for them, and Jackson and Alabama climbed in the back seat while Hill sat in the passenger seat.

"What in God's name were you two thinking?" Director Hill asked as they drove into traffic. Cars sped over an over-pass, and concrete buildings lined the street. Streetlights at the road's edge gave off a dim glow. "Your job is to keep a low profile and not be spotted. For me to come down here personally is dangerous."

Checking the rear window, Jackson said, "Flynn was

ready to take us from there. How? Who are we dealing with, sir?"

Director Hill lowered his head and raised his eyes at him. "The organization has many names and many leaders, but its informal name is Eclipse." He pressed his upper teeth over his bottom lip.

After finding a secluded road, the driver pulled the SUV onto a patch of gravel with long, dead weeds and grasses. A wall hid the freeway from view. The driver killed the engine.

"Why didn't you mention them before?" Jackson asked.

"Because if you're caught, you would talk. The less you know the better. Most of our agents know we are fighting rogue intelligence agencies and organized crime. You assumed as much yourself."

Alabama rubbed her hands together. "Same thing."

"I don't make all the rules, Agent Stone," Director Hill said. "I have probably told you too soon. In the past, we told our agents about them, and they suspected all of our enemies worked for them. A great many people died due to misunderstandings and paranoia. I feel better telling you because you're assigned with Agent Wren. She's able to sniff them out most of the time."

Director Hill and Alabama smiled at each other.

"They don't like her very much," Hill said. "Update me on Project Horizon."

Jackson and Alabama took turns explaining the abbey and the craft. He didn't tell his boss about how she'd killed the soldiers, and she didn't mention it, either. Would she write it in her report? Should he?

Director Hill reached between the middle console and his seat. "Here. More information on the spheres." He laid a green folder on the console and opened it like a book. Pictures, some black and white, others colored, were displayed before them. "Intelligence indicates Eclipse unearthed them, but we are still cross-referencing to determine what the spheres are."

As best they could, Jackson and Alabama explained how they'd both been affected by them. Hill listened thoughtfully but said nothing.

"How large is Eclipse, sir?" Jackson asked.

Hill tilted his chin up and set his jaw. "Membership extends all over the world, in every government and major corporation. They do not wear uniforms, and they are next to impossible to trace."

Alabama didn't ask questions about them. How much did she know and when did she know it? She knew about Flynn, but why didn't she recognize him at the hospital? Plastic surgery? At the very least, she should've told him about how dangerous he was.

Director Hill stared intently at Jackson. "The man we're facing goes by Hunter Flynn. That's one reason you've been picked, Agent Stone."

"Me, sir?"

"Agent Wren, would you mind stepping out for a moment?"

She exited and guarded the road.

"Agent Stone, Hunter Flynn is one of the most dangerous men in the world, but he's only a cog. He's managed to co-opt and circumvent governmental agencies around the world, and unfortunately, his motives are unknown to us at this time."

Jackson pinched his lip. "Sir, he let me live."

Gazing out of the window, he said, "I'm aware."

"Why?"

Hill put his hand under his chin. "Because he thinks

you're weak, and he'll want to use you to get to us. That's what he does."

"If he's so dangerous, why don't you send Scorpion to eliminate him?"

"Do you remember Operation Desert Storm?"

"No, sir, but I've read about it."

"Many factors contributed to the decision to topple Saddam Hussein's regime. But the Americans made a mistake. The CIA knew Hussein well enough to predict his movements, and he kept the warring factions in check. When he died, pandemonium spread over the region."

Jackson nodded. "I understand, sir. What happens if we are given the opportunity to kill him?"

"You won't be given that chance." Hill tapped on the glass, and Alabama climbed back in.

"Continue with the mission," Hill said. Before Jackson could ask anything else, Hill placed a satellite image on the middle console. Clouds surrounded one side of a half-blown volcano, the upper half of the mountain jigsawed out into a jagged bowl. Raised above the land, a large cliff face edged the mountain as if pushed up by gods of the underworld. To one side, a jungle reached upward like bushels of broccoli and eased up against the cliffs.

Jackson said, "That's Turrialba Volcano in Costa Rica."

"Correct." Hill placed a photo on Jackson's lap of a cobblestone road that led to several stone foundations with a flat mound of grass atop each. "Agent Stone, have you seen this before?"

Jackson's mind poured over the thousands of Costa Rican pictures he'd reviewed over the years. "Guayabo is a national monument at the shadow of Turrialba Volcano."

"What do you know about it?" Hill asked.

"It was a Stone-Age society. They've been mentioned on

the History Channel a few times." When Hill and Alabama glared at him, Jackson shrugged and continued. "Anyway, they built roads and pathways that stretch into the surrounding forest for miles. There was something about aqueducts that were lined with especially small stones to filter drinking water. There are tombs and petroglyphs everywhere."

Hill smiled. Alabama studied Jackson, her arms folded.

"One of our sources believes the spheres might originate there, but we don't have enough information," Hill said. "They're located at Guayabo or nearer to the volcano. It might be a dead-end, but if true, we need to be there before Flynn arrives. We can't afford to lose another sphere."

Alabama took the picture, drawing her finger along the side. "The spheres are designed with precision-cut geometric symbols. How sure are we about their origin?"

Hill pulled out an image of a sphere in an excavator's hands. "We intercepted this." The man holding the sphere stood on a thick rock, yet the hole he dug was in heavy clay and soil next to his feet. In the hole, several more round-shaped stones with etched symbols lied half-buried in mud. Hill poised himself like a general. "We need the spheres in *our* labs."

Jackson took the picture back. "These are made of rock?"

"Unknown," Hill said.

Alabama took the photo back, and her face glazed over.

Hill gave her a moment. "Last picture." He picked up an image of a large stone near a flattened mound, no doubt in the mysterious Guayabo City. A carving of a being with two tails and what looked like tubes at the top of its head was carved on the face of the rock. An extraterrestrial with enlarged eyes and a wide mouth.

Had beings visited there before? No. It couldn't be.

"Where did you get this?" Jackson asked.

"Deeper in the forest, well off the beaten path. It's a wonder anyone found it. Heavy rains turned the ground to mud."

Jackson held the picture up and flipped it upside down. "Not a lizard. Not an alien. It's a man with a mustache and a ceremonial hat." He set it down so they could get a good look at it. "In this region, the inhabitants used to call him the wisest of men. Quetzalcoatl. The god of wind and air."

Hill wrinkled his brow. "If I didn't know you better, I'd say you're a Central American scholar."

"I'm no scholar, but thank you. Guayabo was the location where the tribe received and guarded information, languages, and treasures from their gods." He lifted his hand, palm toward Hill and Alabama. "Who knows? They may well have guarded those spheres for their," he said, making air quotes with his fingers, "gods."

Hill pushed out his lower lip. "Our tech team analyzed the picture of the excavation site and found two places that match similar soil density, exact color, and clay to soil depth. Guayabo and Volcano Turrialba."

Alabama gave a pleased look. "Next stop?"

"When I drop you off, pack your bags. You both leave on a plane tomorrow morning."

Jackson went rigid. They'd just made it to Portland and even though he didn't like the idea of being back in his home state, they were making headway on the investigation. "We're going to Costa Rica?"

"Tomorrow morning. Sleep well. You'll need it."

J ackson woke, adrenaline soaring through him. His nerves tingled from his fingertips to his toes. A dream? He shifted his head. For a moment, he thought he heard a sound, like a chair sliding an inch over the wooden floor. This place had mice, probably rats.

He touched where he slept, the fabric hard and rough, though soft enough for a semblance of comfort. What a day. He replayed the events in his mind. He and Alabama packed. Before he knew it, the clock read 19:30, and he closed his eyes for a brief doze.

Eclipse. A rogue international clique and who knows what else. Jackson always suspected something like that existed. Most people did to some degree. When was Polaris created? Before or after Eclipse? Was one the counterpart to the other?

The thought of Alabama and him inside the FBI building left him cold. Normally, they'd be dead one way or another. Polaris didn't guarantee an agent's safety if they'd been compromised. In that way, they were like every other intelligence agency. They say torture doesn't work, that the answers prisoners give are not reliable. They're wrong.

He closed his eyes and imagined Nicki close to him. Would she agree with what he was doing? How he missed her.

Growing up, his father said he didn't need to find love.

In a faded memory, his father wore a torn flannel shirt and finished reading him a story before lights off. Another tale about the ones who lived on other planets and how the government was keeping it a secret. The stories rarely repeated the same information except for the basics, and even those changed over time. A UFO. A weather balloon. No, an experimental weather balloon to monitor radiation and the Soviets. A craft over Florida. No, a toy craft found in the photographer's basement built and painted to convince people in a photo. The Greys. The Pleiadians. And a weird Christopher Walken movie based on Whitley Streiber's "Communion".

Jackson just wanted a good blanket that didn't make him itch.

"Love is one of many emotions, and it's no more important than hate or jealousy. You end up falling in love, you're bound to get hurt. Skip it. Find you a girl who's smart enough to cook and clean and hold a decent conversation. The rest will sort itself out, Son."

Creak.

What was that noise?

His eyes burst wide when a hand slapped down on his mouth. He jerked away and threw his arms up, his yelp muffled behind someone's palm. A man pressed a knee on Jackson's chest and leaned his body weight on him. Glinting in the light, a syringe was a hair's length away from his throat.

Jackson managed to shift his head for an instant against the man's strength. Two other men crept down the hallway, both with something in their hands. Guns? He wrapped his arms around the man's leg and twisted. The attack pushed the man back. His foe removed his hand off Jackson's mouth and pressed cold steel against Jackson's temple. A gun? The syringe dropped and rolled under a table. "Don't move or I hurt you."

The voice was low. Gruff. A heavy, Slavic accent. Ukrainian or from Central Moscow.

Inching his hand toward the back of the man's hand holding the gun, Jackson turned his head toward the window. In one quick motion, he thrust a fist at the man's anterior wrist.

"Red Raven!" he shouted to Alabama, using a code phrase.

Crack!

Jackson struck. The impact relaxed the fingers around the man's grip, and he dropped his pistol. But not before a loud pop from a gunshot vibrated the air. A vase shattered near the couch's armrest.

The weapon bounced off the floor, skidding to the side. Jackson slammed his palm into the man's chin, and his head flung back. As the man fell, Jackson grabbed his shirt, pulled him back in his direction, and drove his elbow into the man's nose. Blood splattered onto Jackson's face and over his forearm. He threw jabs, punching wildly in the dark.

Crack.

Bones broke.

Thump.

The man dropped to the floor just as a door opened in the hallway. Jackson's stomach sank.

Wren!

Jackson picked up the syringe and plunged it into the man's shoulder.

Tearing down the hallway toward her room, a kick caught him in the side and slammed him against the wall. His chest seized. His lungs wouldn't take in air. As his legs buckled, he held his chest, close to his transplanted heart.

The attacker went to his knees with a knife in his hand, slashing downward.

Crossing his forearms, Jackson caught the man's wrist holding the knife mere inches from his artery. His attacker pushed against Jackson's forearms. Jackson brought his arms together, pinning both sides of the blade between his inner wrists.

Twisting to the side, Jackson ripped the knife free, but it slipped point first and stuck in the floor. Jackson waited, and the assassin bent down to rip it free. He brought his knee into the man's face and snagged the knife by the hilt.

Jackson jumped to his feet and lunged, lowering his shoulder, and connected at the man's hip. Hands reached for the knife. Jackson swung one leg behind the man's ankles, and they tumbled to the floor. Plopping to his knees, Jackson pinned him, using his knees on the man's upper arms just beneath his shoulders.

A plea came from the man's eyes.

With the butt of the dagger's handle, Jackson pounded it across the intruder's temple, and his eyes closed.

Jackson got up and charged into Alabama's room. In front of him, a man pinned her to the floor beside her bed, fingers gripped over her throat, and a syringe close to her vein. She squinted against the light's glare as the man went for his 9mm tucked into his waistband. Her eyes bulged as she attempted to push him off.

Target the man's heart. Upper back. Between the spine and shoulder blade.

Jackson brought down the knife, sliced through the man's ribs, and buried the blade deep into flesh. The man bowed his chest toward Alabama and let out a blood-curdling cry as he fell on top of her, blood squirting.

She pushed him off and gasped for air, her hands over her throat. Her face reddening, she lay on her side and huffed for air between coughs. Her eyelids fluttered.

"We're clear," Jackson said.

After a few minutes, the color of her face returned to normal, and he helped her to her feet. She shook. Wobbled. With her arms around him, she used him as a crutch. She buried her head into his chest.

Jackson brought her closer and their eyes met for a second too long.

"Let me go," she said, pushing off him.

"We have to get out of here."

She coughed. "Grab the laptop and our files." She hurried past him into the hallway and paused when she saw a man unconscious in the hallway and another on the floor in the living room. She gave a quick nod and went to her knees and pushed the hallway runner to the side. "We have to blow this place."

"Understood." He helped her lift the wood boards from the floor. The thumb scanner and keypad came into view. They both looked at each other. "You ready?"

"Ready," Jackson said. He punched in the code. The digital timer counted down.

They hustled to the driveway and threw the suitcases in the back. Jackson jumped into the driver's seat and blazed down the road. In seconds, a blast shook the street. Car alarms screeched. Bright oranges and reds lit up the rearview mirror. Fire licked from out of the house's roof and windows.

He hooked a left, found the main road, and stopped at a light. His stomach hit the floor. "The computers in the basement...most of our weapons. All gone."

She let out a short, breathy laugh. "Better to be alive, wouldn't you say?" She winked and made a call on her phone and then put it on speaker.

Director Hill's voice cracked when he answered, soft and lethargic. "Go."

"Sir, yellow tree road blanket adapt," she said.

"Oscar Tango Tango Juliet."

A click sounded through the speaker.

"Connection secure. Agent Wren, I can't fly you out of there until tomorrow at 08:30."

"Sir, we also need a cleaner team," Jackson said.

Hill's fury came swift. "Go dark. Drop the car off at Sam's Pick and Pull at 05:30. Wren?"

"Sir?" she asked.

"You and I are going to talk when you return."

Cumulus clouds like white, fluffy cotton balls whooshed above her, the wind ushering them along beneath the blue sky. Alabama's face was close to the plane's window as she drank the last drops of her apple juice and set it on the tray table in front of her. The plane reached its top altitude, and thanks to Director Hill, they lifted soon after their headquarters went up in flames.

She massaged her neck. *If it weren't for Stone, I'd be dead.*

Jackson sat across from Alabama, twisted off a cap from a pill bottle, and dropped two tablets in his hand. She'd seen him take those before, and they weren't for air sickness.

"What are those?" she asked.

"Something for air sickness."

Right.

In some ways, he was an awful lot like her ex in his stoicism and secrecy. She expected nothing less from a Polaris agent. Yet, it enticed her in ways she'd nearly forgotten. A kind of lush freshness, rooted deep, where she kept her secrets close to her heart. A flickering warmth, which threatened to be extinguished every time she killed someone. Someday, that light might truly die out. What then?

Sweat had formed on Jackson's brow. He wiped it off with a shaky wrist and lifted his knees to his chest. After several deep breaths, he closed his eyes and then opened them.

As if her gaze beamed a hot hole in his head, he swiveled and faced her. Another swipe to clear his perspiration, and he grew still.

"You know, flying is part of your job description."

He leaned on his armrest. "Don't remind me. I'll either get used to it or carry around a barf bag everywhere I go. I've been meaning to ask how many missions you've been on."

She frowned. "That's not something I can talk about."

"An estimate?"

"More than one but less than a thousand."

"You're so helpful."

Smirking, she sipped her apple juice. "Thanks."

Jackson brought up a map of Costa Rica on his laptop. "Juan Santamaría International Airport is here. Director Hill booked us a hotel close to Turrialba Volcano National Park, near the Guayabo excavation site. Casa Turire hotel. Take a look." He showed her a picture of a white-painted, large adobe two-story Victorian-style mansion. Now a hotel, extravagance beamed from its very pores.

"We're sharing the suite." Alabama shifted in her seat. "Hmm. The room comes with a queen-size bed."

"I'll take the couch."

She shrugged. "Suit yourself."

The hotel image showed a bathtub full of water full of soap bubbles beneath two rectangular wood-framed windows, a shower with its own room, rose-colored tiles on the floor and walls, a bed with propped-up pillows, white sheets, and a pink, red, and white plaid comforter. At the foot of the bed stood a wood chest, which doubled for a seat and storage.

He pulled up a map of Costa Rica's Central Valley and rounded the cursor around Guayabo National Monument. "We're going through Guayabo. If we don't find the spheres there, we can camp at the site and continue to the volcano in the morning. We should fill our water packs at Guayabo. Best water there. I don't want to get sick." He twirled his index finger. "Safe to talk in here?"

"Of course."

"We should talk about the sphere and this mission."

She reached over and closed the laptop. "You're still thinking about what happened in the abbey?"

"I failed to secure it. It's one of the strangest events in my life."

At that moment, a reassuring touch would have helped him. But Stone needed to understand what he'd signed up for. Everyone in Polaris went through a mental crisis. If society only knew the mysteries lurking under the surface of reality, people might think twice about wasting their time on trivialities.

"Don't obsess on your failures. If Director Hill is right, we'll find more in Costa Rica."

"Why would Polaris give any credence to the idea that tribal people could make something so perfect?"

"I can't answer that. But what I can say is Polaris has identified hundreds of anomalies throughout the world. We don't have enough agents to investigate them all."

He turned toward the window. "Someone found our safehouse."

"Did you talk to anyone?"

Folding his arms, he shook his head.

"Well?" she asked.

"She was already there when I detonated the phone by the train tracks."

"Who? So, someone did see you?"

"Yes."

Now to see if he remembers her name. "Did you get any details about him?"

Jackson bit his lip. "Her."

What was he holding back? "Did you take care of it?"

"As best as I could."

"Did you kill her?"

"No."

"Good. The moment we start killing people on the street is the moment we lose the confidence of those who assist us, like the police. You should get some sleep," she said.

"What about you?"

"I'm going to use the laptop. Seriously, catch sleep while you can in this line of work."

He grabbed a pillow from overhead, leaned his chair back, and closed his eyes.

The spheres.

Her cursor moved from the city to the volcano. Cobblestone roads. And they led right to Quetzalcoatl petroglyphs. Onto Kongbu Fen server, whose FTP servers were brilliant works of art. File Transfer Protocol, or FTP, is a communication protocol that transfers computer files from a server to a client on a computer network.

The dark web had many places like Kongbu Fen, but few so sophisticated. Dark web layers went deeper. Here, a person could rent a Spetnaz team for twenty million dollars, make payments to judges, and blackmail American senators. Illegal 3D blueprints, child abuse videos, and drugs. Of course.

People often confused the dark web and the deep web. The deep web consisted of non-indexed websites. Throw a search term into Google or DuckDuckGo, and nothing would be found. To find those sites, people needed an exact address or an embedded link.

Alabama scrolled through the Kongbu Fen forums in Chinese, English, Russian, and Japanese, reading the subject lines. Turrialba, the name of the Costa Rican extinct volcano, caught her attention.

The Marine Corps had tested security drones in 2012 at Quantico and the Naval Amphibious Base in Little Creek in 2014. Were the spheres experimental drones? If so, why would the military make etchings on them?

The rest of the message dealt with a radiological dispersion device in a specific location. But the message had nothing to do with a device or spheres, and the timestamps didn't match.

Instead, it had everything to do with a suicide.

Did the CCP design a device able to penetrate United States airspace to contaminate the country with radioactivity?

CollusionBlue199 posted a week ago. The subject line read, "Gao Li."

The plane jostled up and down, and Jackson threw his hand against the side of the cabin. He leaned back, his head in his hands, his breaths erratic.

Keeping his eyes closed, he said, "Did you slip me something to sleep?"

"Something minor. Doctor's orders."

Jackson loosened his seatbelt and rolled over.

Highlighting CollusionBlue119 and copying it to the computer's clipboard, Alabama brought up *Ahmia*, a dark web search engine, and pasted in CollusionBlue119 and Gao

Li. Forum messages scrolled down the page. She tapped the screen. 2476 Ed Bluestein Boulevard, where they found Bojing Pang buried deep in illegal activity. But General Li's daughter committed suicide?

She didn't commit suicide. No way. The CCP covered up the death and made it appear that Bojing Pang did the killing.

Pang was involved in Liu Wei's laundering, scamming, and forgeries. Wei also bribed local governments to lie about certain archeological findings.

Interesting. Who did Wei sell to?

Message boards popped up. She clicked on the first one, and information in Mandarin appeared, with a link to the author: Liu Wei. She brought up the terminal, typed in *SUDO* commands, also known as *superuser do*, to access restricted programs on the server. A moment later, she entered through its backdoor, and she typed in *IP Decode*, pushed enter, and closed the terminal, and waited.

On the window, an *IP Decode* application blinked on the screen. Opening the app, it looked identical to the terminal. She pinged the message board, inserted *Waox* malware, and gathered Wei's IP address.

In seconds, she gained control of Wei's computer using remote access. Clicking on *Devices*, she opened his computer's hard drive and selected Wei as the user. A myriad of files blasted on the monitor. Under *Search*, she typed in Ed Bluestein Boulevard; an Austin, Texas street where several banks operated.

One blue icon file matched the *ICB National Bank,* the bank where Polaris, acting as FBI, followed Pang and arrested him in the middle of an illegal transaction.

More files. Checks. Bonds. Dividends.

So much data. But this is how she solved crimes,

through random data points, put together, mapped, and annotated. And here. A picture of Bojing Pang. Now deceased. Back behind a hole, Jackson saw a floating hubcap-shaped ship about half the size as the one at Camp Withycombe.

Boom. Found ya.

Below the image, the date—2003. Abusir Archaeological Dig, Egypt, Africa. Material of unknown origin. Estimated year of construction, 19th century BCE, dated more than twenty-thousand years ago.

How could that be?

The screen went black and the computer's power light blinked off. Alabama jerked away.

"Excuse me." The copilot, a woman in her mid-fifties, single-breasted jacket, navy blue suit with a starched white shirt, stood at the head of the aisle. "We'll be landing in a few minutes. If you wouldn't mind, keep the computer powered down."

The hotel was all Jackson expected and more. A red camelback couch with a mahogany frame with detached cushions and was a welcome sight. He'd couch surfed before in his late teenage years, and he would have killed to have something like this.

After sweeping the room for electronic listening devices, they put their phones in Faraday pouches, which blocked electronic signals.

The cool air tasted sweet. He opened a window and stared up at the clear sky. Never in his life did he expect to be so close to the equator. He made a mental snapshot, something to reminisce about many years into the future. So this was what it meant to be in an international spy organization. Not bad. Not bad at all.

His khaki polo shirt matched his cargo shorts. Dressing like a tourist was another new experience.

His suitcase butted against a dresser, next to Alabama's, and a silver suitcase sat in the middle of a round rug between the dresser and the bed. Alabama rolled the suitcase's passcode in place and opened it, revealing the tools of the trade.

Jackson rubbed over his lips. "Do we need all of that?"

Alabama swept away her hair. "We might."

"What about money? They accept dollars?"

She closed the suitcase. "Yes."

"What's our budget?"

"Ten grand. More than that and we'll attract too much attention. Some of this money is for bribes. The cops here will look the other way for a few hundred bucks as long as drugs or violence isn't involved."

Across the room, two French glass doors led to a balcony where a line of coconut and palm trees peeked through. A mountain range poked behind the trees.

She tested the bed. "If the ancient inhabitants of Guayabo created or guarded those spheres, they might have a map."

"Where would they get paper?"

"They wouldn't need paper. They could've used stone similar to the Norse rune stones."

"Remember what appeared to be those snake petroglyphs that were on the edge of the cobblestone roads? They could mean something."

She looked up. "In just about every culture, snakes lead to some kind of subterranean world."

"I'm not sure I'm following you." He opened a small refrigerator and grabbed a beer.

"Don't," she said, shaking her head.

He laughed. "Do you want to check my ID?"

"We don't know what's in the beer."

It hit him like a freight train. Would his life always be like this? If Eclipse discovered Alabama was a vegan, she would make for an easy target. How many people ordered vegan and how many would shop at certain places for food? It would be easy to nail down those spots and watch for her if they wanted. As to the beer, Eclipse might figure out where they were staying ahead of time and poison them. Was that it? Then what was the point of being here at all? He put it back.

"About the snakes, you think they lead somewhere?"

"Let me check something." She opened her laptop, activated her VPN, and opened a Tor browser. "If someone dug them up, petroglyphs or the spheres, they would need heavy equipment. Backhoes. Caterpillars. Tractors. And the ability to transport them without notice."

"Can we get satellite images or feeds?"

"The jungle would hide a lot of activity. If the dig is ongoing, they wouldn't want anyone around. Plus it would be nearby the Guayabo site. It's doubtful anyone would have flown over and seen it."

He paced. "Call the Guayabo National Monument."

She fetched her phone. "Calling."

Like Jackson, she paced, the phone against her ear. "Hola, estás abierta hoy," she said in Spanish. She stopped pacing. "Entiendo. Si, si. Cuando vas a abrir? Okay, espere." She covered the phone as a small grin grew on her face. "They've been closed for a year now. Repairs and excavation. No one allowed in."

"Ask them when in their history was the last time they closed."

She did and her eyes narrowed. "Gracias." She hung up the phone. "It's never happened since he's been working there."

"How long has he worked there?"

"Eleven years."

S pikes pointed upward from the giant lizard's neck down to its tail. A four-foot-long iguana crouched on a downed tree on the side of a plant-infested trail. When Jackson whacked at a wild sugar cane with a machete, the iguana darted under a pink ginger plant.

Sloths hung from cecropia trees, some studying the new strangers making their way through the jungle.

"Hold on," Alabama said through her throat mic, a streak of mud on her cheek. "Look."

Posted on a tree on the trail's edge, a white and red "No Trespassing" sign cautioned them. Another sign was nailed below, all white with black lettering.

"What's it say?" Jackson asked, the muggy atmosphere like slime on his vocal cords. Two-piece earphones stuck in both ears—annoying. With the turn of a small dial on a dongle near the acoustic tube's clip, he turned up the external sound.

"It says it's dangerous to proceed. Ecological work in progress. Trespassers will be prosecuted."

"Good. We're on the right trail."

They proceeded onward. Jackson swung the machete to clear the path. A snake slithered away, its color more light green than he'd like. He inched back.

"Not all snakes are venomous," Alabama said. "Most aren't."

"I'm aware, but emphasis on the *most*. Don't want to accidentally tangle with the *few*. Don't think getting bit by a snake would feel good, poisonous or not."

Earlier, they'd rented an SUV, drove less than an hour from their hotel, and parked on the outskirts of the jungle. They'd found the best location on a satellite map to slip inside Guayabo in a round-about way and figured investigating the surrounding area would be their best bet.

When they stepped out of the vehicle, Jackson stripped off his tourist clothes to camo pants, a short-sleeve shirt, and boots. He strapped on his backpack and buckled his utility belt.

He bent down and tied his boots. Alabama stood a few feet from him. His eyes lingered on her like she was made of the finest. She was toned like an aerobics instructor. Not only was her face beautiful, but her body was also impeccable.

For a moment, she turned and faced him, her head cocked. She slipped her shirt on and grabbed the global positioning system device off of their vehicle's dashboard and shoved it in her pocket. Minutes later, they entered the jungle on an old, makeshift trail.

"You know, it's not polite to stare," she said.

"I wasn't staring."

"You're the worst liar, Stone."

Pushing his back foot off a rock, he lowered his eyes and bit the inside of his cheek as his face flushed red. Of course, it wasn't polite. If there was anything good to say about his mother, it was that she raised him to respect women. But he was human. Jackson kept his mouth shut and came down hard with the machete on a teardrop leaf that blocked the trail.

"Stone, another sign. According to this, people have died from flash floods."

He stopped, his breath heavy. Sweat stained his shirt from his armpits to his back. "The next sign will probably say dinosaurs roam the area. Turn around or risk being eaten by a pack of velociraptors." He hacked at a plant and stepped over roots that bulged out from the soil. "Did you like the *Jurassic Park* movies?"

"The first one," she said.

"What do you mean the first one? They're all good."

"The last one? They drove around in a bubble."

"That was the best part."

After twenty minutes of hiking under the dense forest canopy, the sun trickled in through the gaps in the leaves. Jackson put his arm out as he came to a slow halt. Small chunks of dirt tumbled down a rock cliff face that went five hundred feet down, maybe more. "I guess they weren't kidding, but this isn't a flash flood."

At the base of the cliff, trees huddled in masses. He slung his backpack off and grabbed his binoculars. From here, he had a good view of the area.

Yellow Elder trees with long droopy branches grew wide on the jungle below, and monarch butterflies dazzled the tall bush's golden blossoms. Soncoya trees reached high. The Elders towered over them, their hairy leaves and green, ball-like fruits with hook-like projections hung from its branches.

A small opening in the jungle led to a cobblestone road,

old and worn. Guayabo extended this far, perhaps farther. But what about the spheres?

He saw another opening in the jungle. There. His heart skipped a beat. Tractor tires left a path. "Earth-moving tractors. They would have had buckets in the back for digging and big shovels in the front."

"You see one?"

"Only their tire tracks. They've been here."

After roaming and clearing the area, Alabama pointed down a cliff. "Let's get climbing."

The jagged rocks with their difficult-to-reach foot and handholds bit his hands as if the cliff face was made of teeth. Wherever he grabbed, the rock found its way into his skin. His boots scraped along the side, and he rested one foot on a jut in the cliff and descended to another foothold. He'd climbed before—with ropes. Fear thumped heavily inside his throat.

Alabama's boot slid across a piece of rock, and she took a step down to the next hold. "Take your time. It's a long fall." She moved another few feet lower on the cliff face.

"We should have brought rope and rappelled instead of climbing down."

"Where's the fun of that?"

He gripped his fingers on a rock. One foot on a slab of stone, the other dragged across the cliff. When his foot landed, a loud click sounded and pressure grabbed hold of his boot's toe box. He went rigid, and his nerves rushed through his veins like pinpricks. He kicked out wide.

"What is it?" she asked.

One hand slipped, and he sucked in air as he brought it up to another rock and held firm. Small chunks of rock cracked and dropped on him and then cascaded down the cliff. The clamp on his shoe didn't loosen.

In a reflex, he kicked against the cliff. Something snapped and ripped into the sole of his boot and fell far to the treetops below. "Monofilament wire. Watch your fingers." He paused and puffed out his cheeks and exhaled deeply.

"Putting them up here must have been quite a feat."

Click.

Alabama cursed. Her hands slipped. "Ahh...." She threw her hand up and grabbed hold again. She tossed something to the side. "They're all over the cliff." She descended and kicked at another trap, shoving it off a crag.

Crack.

Jackson gasped.

Rocks tumbled as his weight broke his foothold. Dangling his legs, he flexed his fingers with all his strength on a small crease in the stone wall. Nerves hit his feet and tingled like wasps trapped in a glass jar. As he swung his foot up and found a tiny nook to hold, he steadied himself. A drop of sweat tickled the tip of his nose. "Where's an elevator when you need one?"

Nearly fifty feet on the face below him, Alabama stopped. "Check for tripwires, too. Anything out of the ordinary."

"If not rope, then a parachute," he said, under his breath. "I'm going to find whoever put these traps up here and give them a piece of my mind."

She continued her descent. "I would hope you'd give them more than that."

Jackson nudged a trap and pushed it over the edge of a protruding rock. Little by little, he climbed down. He planted his leg on a knot in the stone and rested his hand in a divot.

Slipping, he reached for anything to break his fall. His gloves found nothing.

"Stone!"

He reached. His boots hit a small ledge and bent, and he fell further. A branch grew out of the stone. Coming up fast. Only one shot to grab it.

Got it.

Jackson held on and balanced himself. It wasn't time to meet Nicki. Not today. One more inch and he'd break his back from the fall.

I'm not going to be afraid of climbing. Get a grip. Ease down and don't die.

Forty-five minutes later, his feet touched the ground. And there Alabama sat, picking at her teeth.

"Ready?" he asked.

"Take a second for yourself. Drink some water."

Jackson lifted the bottom of his shirt and swiped it across his face to wipe the perspiration.

The jungle stretched out for miles, perhaps hundreds. Cobblestone pathways crossed his view as well, made beautifully, and carved through dense trees and brush.

Weeds poked through the compact paths.

Alabama grasped her backpack's straps and hiked forward. He walked after her, passing a snake petroglyph carved into a boulder.

Petroglyph after petroglyph, most with snakes, some with double tails, lined the pathway. A jaguar, spots carved into the animal's side, spread out onto a boulder that sunk into a dirt mound.

"Amazing they carved this," he said.

She studied a stone while he kept watch.

"You see something?"

To think this place hadn't been demolished or turned into a theme park.

Dusting the stone, she traced the glyph. "Not good. We should go," she said.

"What's up?"

"Come on. Hurry."

Why did Alabama act like she was holding back something? She navigated through the jungle like it was her backyard. Had she been here before?

Curling a clutch of trees, Alabama put her fist up. "Vehicles up ahead."

Industrial tractors with crane booms to stack and pull, along with earth-movers, and small utility tractors for plowing and digging, were parked in clusters. A dozen black trucks of all sizes with roof racks and LED light bars sat next to them.

A dozen single-wide manufactured homes were built across from the vehicles on a large lot of cleared land. A warehouse stood at the far side.

Over the cleared land, camouflage netting hung from tree to tree. Birds chirped. Wind rippled the leaves, and they walked softly off the path.

"It's like a ghost town here," Jackson whispered.

"Stay frosty."

Jackson didn't spot movement on the other side of a trailer's window and decided to turn the knob. It opened quietly. He stepped inside, and Alabama occupied the doorway behind him. Half a dozen desks mingled with computers. When he checked them, their insides were gutted. No offices. No bathrooms. No kitchen. Dried mud caked the floor, all in the shape of shoe prints. Yet, the place had been recently visited. Lamps sat on each desk. He flicked one on. Nothing.

"Power is out."

"Anything of value in here?" Alabama asked.

No papers on desks. The whiteboard was erased. No tools. "They've cleaned everything."

"Looks like an evacuation."

Once outside, the trees rattled in the breeze.

Metal dropped on metal, and it rang across the jungle.

Alabama put her finger to her lips. She pointed in the direction of the sound and whispered, "You hear that? Did you trip a security wire?"

Jackson peered through another trailer's window. "Absolutely not. Perhaps they're waiting for us to leave?"

Up ahead, he spotted a new warehouse, its exterior camouflaged by tarps and nets. Alabama propped open the door. Jackson aimed his weapon, sweeping it up and down. A putrid smell blasted his nostrils worse than a mix of rotten eggs and sewage.

And something else.

He gagged and backpedaled. "Oh my God."

Men and women lay on the floor; dead, thirteen bodies in total. Flies and insects swarmed the swollen bodies. Coagulated blood had pooled around the corpses. Bruises riddled their faces.

Covering his nose and mouth, Jackson ran his hand over the blood on a man's ripped shirt. Dipping his toe onto the shirt, he pulled the shirt away from where the blood had seeped. A rib poked through the skin.

"This one too," Alabama said. She tugged the shirt. Two ribs stuck out. Jackson crossed his arms and let out a slow breath. The stench returned. He stifled a gag and walked around a body.

Computers lined the walls. A row of servers, stacked in threes, pressed up against one wall. A handful of desks were either pushed to the side or tossed over. Computer pieces and monitors lay broken on the floor. Spare tractor parts, chains, load binders, wheel bearings, extra tractor shovels, and diggers lay scattered in piles.

The corpses slouched on their sides, backs, and stomachs, some with mouths open, others clutching their chests.

Death has a way of making the ugly, peaceful. Not here. Along with facial bruises, burns had bubbled on their skin.

Alabama waved her hand around the dead. "Reminds me of how the hikers died. If we checked their organs, I would guess we'd see ruptures and internal bleeding."

Jackson circled an overturned desk and pointed at the east portion of the warehouse where a few men and women slumped over tractor supplies. "Whatever killed them caused chaos first."

"Over here." Alabama inspected a metal shelving full of servers. "Some of these are blown."

Jackson made his way to her and studied them. The server towers were melted. He grabbed a flashlight from his utility belt and shined it through a burnt hole in one of the machines. The hard drive, the power supply, and the motherboard were warped and partially disintegrated. "Looks like a pulse devastated these parts. Something extremely powerful. The plastic is melted from the heat. See it?"

"EMPs don't have this much power."

"Not even close. Some type of rogue current of electricity moved through the towers' circuits and hammered them. That's why I couldn't power anything in the trailer. Nothing in the warehouse will work either."

A low hum vibrated the air. Alabama gripped her gun tighter.

"Did you feel that?" he asked.

A scream penetrated the jungle. Alabama darted for the door and fell to her knees in the doorway. The hum surged in intensity, vibrating the windows and walls.

Like an unending adrenaline shock, Jackson's transplanted heart began beating faster, set to explode. A stream of anxiety-like electricity rippled through his veins. Crumpling to his knees, he adjusted his earpiece dial and lowered all outside sound to the lowest position. "Sound! Lower your sound!"

Alabama rose to one knee, her eyes slits. She pressed her hands against her head.

"Dr. Wren!"

The hum stopped.

"Dr. Wren," Jackson repeated.

Alabama shook her head, adjusted her earbud, and stumbled outside, her palm blocking the sun. "Stone, get out here. Quick."

A sonic attack? It came from everywhere, like being at the center point of the biggest rock concert in history, where the speakers forced their sound into his ears.

His hands shook, and he fought the urge to urinate. When he swallowed, he caught himself holding his breath.

What the hell was that?

In the distant reaches of his mind, the drums of war beat steady. Cannons blasted. Artillery fired for effect into the trenches of Verdun. Biplanes turned to Messerschmitts and Spitfires, morphing into MiG fighter jets with snub noses and loyal Soviet pilots. The MiGs became bombers, dropping their ordnance on hapless civilians.

Soviet T-34 tanks assaulted helpless Romanians on the Eastern Front.

Napalm death dropped on the Viet Cong.

IED explosions in the desert.

AC-130 gunships circled the air, pummeling terrorists from on high.

Such joy. Such pleasure. Watching the little people die like the filthy rats they were. Ridding the planet of people. There were too many humans. Remove them forever.

Jackson clenched his fists and cracked his neck.

Blissful violence. That's what he wanted. To kill. To laugh.

To murder. To break someone's head open and drink the insides. Rip out his enemy's lungs and watch them suffocate.

He could kill Dr. Wren right now without her knowing what hit her. A shot in the back.

Why do I feel this way? Something is wrong with me.

"Stone, come quick," Alabama said.

His mind cleared, and his stomach ached. He doubled over, holding his belly, a hum shaking his bones and cartilage apart.

What was he thinking about?

Something about war?

What's wrong with my mind?

Then those thoughts melted away. Alabama waved him forward. He bolted after her.

The hum blared from the sky like the trumpets from Jericho. His earbuds dulled the sound.

A shadow blocked the sun.

There it was—the disc.

The craft hovered over the jungle, metallic and shimmering under the sunlight.

What was I thinking about? Something isn't right with me.

The disc remained partially obscured through the gaps in the trees.

Dad, I wish you could see this.

Beyond a path in the distance, a group of construction workers screamed. A few pulled at their hair, agony contorting their faces. Others dropped to the jungle forest and rolled in the long patches of grasses and ferns.

Alabama dashed across the path. A man cried out as he jogged in place. At the same time, he held onto a woman's shirt and pulled her in close. The man reared back and threw a haymaker. It went high and wide, almost like he swung at an apparition above her. The woman held her abdomen and screamed.

Alabama reached the man and shoved him away. His eyes rolled back, and he tripped over a stump. As he fell, he grabbed Alabama, and they slammed hard onto the soil. The man's arm twisted at his elbow, and his knee popped out of socket. Eyes wild and mouth open, the man cringed in pain when his chest caved, breaking in several places. Alabama pushed to her feet, her hands up as if in surrender, her eyes like saucers.

The construction workers tore off their hardhats and attacked each other, a brawl to the death. The melee grew in size, bodies swarming around one another, and soon, Jackson was inside the eye of the storm, and the hum's power made Jackson's bones quake.

Jackson ducked an awkward kick from a tanned man, his pupils the size of quarters. He wrapped the man's arms under his own. "Can you hear me?"

The man's tongue poked past his lips and blood dripped down his chin. He uttered something hideous and went limp in Jackson's arms. Jackson dragged him toward the path, blood oozing from his eyes, nose, and mouth.

Jackson's hands were now crimson gloves. "We have to get these people as far from that sound as possible. It's affecting their minds." *And maybe mine.*

Alabama pulled a woman along, the woman's steps erratic as if drunk. "Our earbuds can't cancel this hum out for much longer. The batteries are draining."

Over the cobblestone road, Jackson found himself behind the last trailer which dampened the hum to a small degree. Huffing, he set the man down and checked his pulse. Slow and unsteady. "He's still with us."

"This one too." Alabama laid the woman she dragged with her on her side.

"We can save more of them."

She shook her head. "Stay back here. The hum is too powerful. I know what you're feeling but let it go, Stone."

As Alabama tended to them, the hum broke glass windows. Birds detoured around the massive disc hovering in the sky.

Jackson's gums hurt. He went to put his finger in his mouth to check his teeth, but his hands were still sticky with blood.

"I'm saving the rest of them," he said.

"Damnit, Stone. No!"

Jackson sprinted toward the chaos, and she followed, cursing like a character from a Quentin Tarantino movie. He sidestepped a dead woman, blood seeping out of the sides of her eyes and down her temples. Her chest pressed inward, her neck and face bruised. More than a dozen men and women scurried around the trees, yelling to the sky.

A gun blast echoed across the jungle. Jackson dove, crashing into ferns and hibiscus. Alabama flopped next to him.

"You have got to be kidding me," Jackson said.

"Would you keep your head down? Listen."

Boom!

A woman twisted as blood splattered from her shoulder. A second shot impacted, and she curled forward, her hands to her stomach. Like a punching bag cut from its rope, she dropped to the jungle floor.

"Three o'clock!" Alabama yelled.

Jackson bit his tongue as rage boiled through him. He crawled backward, 9mm in hand. "Where's Scorpion when you need them?"

L ike sawblades, gunfire shredded the leafy jungle. Blood spurted from a worker, his body now in pieces. Tufts of soil and rock clouded around Jackson as the bullets continued in a continual stream around him and at the other men and women.

Jackson jumped away from the cobblestone path and instinctively pushed Alabama with him. "Fall back to the offices."

The hum ceased.

Men in Russian camouflage lumbered from the deep jungle north of the warehouse. Cigarettes hung from their mouths and smiles graced their lips. They took their time, cackling, shooting the workers one by one, using as many rounds as sadistically possible to do the job.

"Keep going, men. They don't see us," a man said with a baritone voice. He licked his lips, sighted a worker with gray whiskers and a missing tooth, and peppered him from stomach to forehead.

"This is like the time when we went hunting in Los Angeles."

Both men spoke with a Minnesota accent.

"Good times," another replied.

Alabama aimed her weapon. "We're engaging." She pulled the trigger. A soldier grabbed his neck and tumbled on his side, his legs flipping upward as he rolled over a bush with tear-shaped leaves.

Jackson shot twice, sending one of them to Hell.

"Everyone down!" came a voice.

As a few troopers changed their target's direction, Jackson's breath caught in his throat. Jackson and Alabama went flat to the ground. Bright lights flickered from rifle muzzles. Bullets zipped overhead.

Hot lead met the ground and sent dirt flying, splattering against Jackson's cheek and shoulder. He pushed off with the ball of his foot and dashed, landing next to Alabama, and they crawled and reached the last office trailer. His elbows were raw, bloody stubs and stung angrily. Rounds hit the office like hail on a tin roof. Sparks flew against the office trailer's wall.

"Other side." Jackson reached the other end of the structure and took the corner.

Alabama's boots thumped behind him. "It's Flynn!"

Jackson peeked around the corner and choked on his tongue. A soldier stood inches from his face, a black knife aimed for Jackson's heart. Jackson snatched the man's hand and turned the blade toward his enemy, then rammed it into the trooper's solar plexus. He didn't die until Jackson yanked the blade out and rammed it into his heart. Another nightmare that would forever haunt Jackson's sleep.

Fresh blood coated Jackson's hand, overlapping the dried, cracked blood from before.

Alabama glanced at the body. "Good kill," she said.

Jackson held in vomit and collected the man's M4, his

ammo, and patted him down. Nothing else, but the M4 would serve well.

Tree branches cracked above from bullet impacts.

Jackson and Alabama counted down and emerged from each side of the trailer, shooting anything in camo. The jungle was too thick. Too many trees and bushes.

Was that a head? Jackson fired at it four times and still wasn't sure. Then a body crumbled forward and rolled down a hill.

Alabama switched to her rifle. "Incoming!"

More shots rattled the air. Jackson's stomach dropped at the screams of dying workers, their cries reverberating.

Men in camouflaged body armor charged from the bush, while others laid down cover fire. Jackson risked a shot, killing the man in the lead. Alabama lifted her rifle, and without aiming, cut a swathe through the enemy, killing two. The last man fled back into the jungle.

"Can't stay pinned down," Jackson said.

Alabama slapped his shoulder. "Go!"

In front of them, a line of office trailers stretched ten yards from each other. And then the glorious, safe warehouse. Here, there would be plenty of places to hide. Hidden from Jackson's view and on the other side of the warehouse, Flynn's thugs sent hot hate into the workers.

Jackson dashed to Alabama and rapped the side of his head with his palm.

What happened to me? My mind. If that happens again....

Alabama checked their six and nine o'clock.

Flynn's men stopped shooting at the workers. They'd be looking for them now.

Jackson paused at the edge of a trailer and peered around the corner. Two soldiers stood in the open, their focus on the incredible disc breaking all laws of physics.

They moved fast and low, rifle butts against their shoulders, heading for Jackson's last location.

He held up two fingers and pointed west when his partner arrived. She nodded and risked a look.

"One more trailer and we're at the warehouse," Alabama said. "Then we open fire."

"What about the workers?"

"They're dead already." She motioned to a hill overgrown with roots and shrubs twenty yards away. "Get to high ground."

Pop. Pop. Pop.

As they burst for the hill, rounds pelted the dirt, and he jimmied up the steep incline. He caught Alabama's hand and helped her up. As she pushed off, a round grazed her camo pants.

They dropped prone at a tree where the hill smoothed to level ground. From here, he could see the bloodbath in all its sickening glory.

He held in vomit. All the killing. All the death. His bloodied hands shook. *This will be over soon. Be strong. Remember your training.*

A soldier planted himself next to a tree at the jungle's edge and emptied a magazine, ruthlessly gunning down a man who tore at his skin.

Flynn's assassins. His thugs. Worthless scum. When he got his hands around Flynn's neck, he'd squeeze until he turned purple and lifeless.

The soldiers shifted their attention to the hill and covered each other on the way toward him. Alabama and Jackson crawled backward until the soldiers stormed out of view. Like a stampede, boots headed their way.

She motioned by her. "Over here."

For an instant, he paused. In zig-zag rows, stone foundations with a dozen flat dirt tops lined the hill's apex. A few were dug out, and mounds of dirt were piled beside the foundations. Trees gave a canopy of cover and shade.

Alabama jumped over the lip of an excavated foundation and landed on the other side. Jackson ran toward her. Flying lead shattered a tree. As men crested the hill, Alabama provided covering fire, sweeping the landscape with her M4. He leaped over the foundation and to the other side where Alabama stood.

Flynn had an army out here. Where did he get his men?

A tingle rushed into Jackson, like drawing four aces in an opening poker hand.

What was that?

Focused electric bolts shot from his pinky to his wrist, twirling, then guided its way along his forearm and deep into his soul. He remembered the sensation back at the chapel.

Time slowed.

The stone formation captured his gaze.

His vision closed into a tunnel.

Heart pounding, his mind hazed.

What's happening to me?

An image of the Milky Way appeared in his mind—a swirl of lights amidst the expansive darkness. It zoomed in at a phenomenal speed and then splintered into a million pieces of rainbow colors, revealing two almond-shaped eyes behind it. Violet irises and black pupils.

Mathematical principles raced in sporadic bursts, each luminous and energetic. Those became twinkling beams trapped in a cloud, like marbles trapped in a void. Those shrank and more spinning clouds appeared, each full of billions of lights.

Love. Abundant love. That was all there was and ever will be.

Stars. Galaxies.

Eyes leered behind them.

Deep. Knowing.

Alien.

He shook his head, backpedaled, and skidded to a tree. Two half-buried spheres sat in the ground at the corner of the foundation where he first fell. The same pattern was etched in them.

"Wren...."

"What are you doing?"

"Found them! Look! Look! Hurry. Quick."

Alabama reloaded her last mag. She didn't take her eyes off of the oncoming men, and she unholstered her spare pistol. "Take it," she said, slinging it to him. "Use it when you're out of ammo."

"I found two spheres," he said. "Over there."

"We are leaving!"

Ammo was running short. Shooting blindly into the jungle, he killed, reloaded, and slaughtered more, all the while feeling outside his body.

Enemies continued on their path, laying down suppressive fire. A handful took cover behind petroglyphs. When Jackson tried shooting back, they opened up on him, and he ducked. Across from him, Alabama lit up one side of the hill with gunfire. But there were too many, and the enemy howled in victory.

Out of the corner of his eye, Jackson caught sight of soldiers on his left. "They're flanking us!"

Alabama picked off those she could.

Jackson narrowed his eyes and sent a bullet into a man's

thigh as he ran from tree to tree. Then five more shots. The bolt snapped back in place.

Last magazine for the M4.

He patted the area where he kept his ammunition and then pulled the magazine out of his weapon. That *was* his last magazine.

"Changing weapons." He pulled out the other and brained a man leaping for cover.

"I'm out," Alabama said, unsheathing her knife.

The muzzle of a gun pressed against his head. "Freeze! One move and I blow your head clean off."

A match flame illuminated Flynn's face, the scar on his neck like an extra frown. He sucked in his cheeks as he lit his cigarette. After he tossed the match inside the foundation where Jackson and Alabama stood, he blew smoke past his teeth. A smile crossed his lips.

This piece of trash just ordered his maniacs to slaughter the workers. Jackson shook with rage, his teeth gnashing so hard, they might shatter.

Three of Flynn's men stood by Jackson's side carrying aluminum batons, their arms bowed outward as if in wait to pounce. A fourth held a sawed-off twelve-gauge shotgun.

Flynn pulled the cigarette out of his mouth and studied it. "Here I come upon two people trying to kill my men, and to my surprise, it's both of you." He stepped closer over brass casings.

The soldier with the shotgun moved aside for Flynn.

Jackson set his gun on the ground and raised his hands. Alabama's rifle fell onto the dirt.

Fury and anger burning in his blood, Jackson pulled back for a right cross. "You son of a...."

Flynn caught it and with his other arm, backhanded Jackson and broke one of his teeth.

"Don't ever raise a hand to me again or I'll take it off," Flynn said.

Jackson's face landed in the dirt.

"There is a saying we have: Chaos is profitable." He motioned to his dead men and laughed. "Men! It looks like we have some openings."

Disjointed chuckles filled the air. Psychopaths.

Flexing, Jackson stood. When he did, Flynn's men grabbed his arms. He tried breaking free, and the blunt end of a baton rammed into his chest. He coughed out a piece of his molar.

Flynn put out his cigarette on Jackson's neck and flicked it into his face. "Take your self-righteous behavior back to Polaris. I'm not interested in your version of morality. We live in the modern era. I am, however, interested in both of you."

Jackson sized up Flynn's men. "Covering your trail? Killing off your workers just in case one or two talks?" He balled his fingers into fists, wondering why they didn't put a bullet in them and dump them in a ditch.

"What difference does it make now?" Flynn said. "I assume both of you understand what's at stake. The Dove Sequence is in its initial phase and will start soon."

Flynn pulled out his phone and opened an image of the world with its cities glowing in orange.

"Do you have any idea what the Middle East would do if they witnessed a disc hovering over Jerusalem or Mecca? I'd hate to think about what might happen. What a terrible shame it would be." Flynn gazed up at the disc. "All those legends about demons and the Book of Revelations. Someone would get hurt, don't you think?"

"Don't," Jackson said as if pleading with him would make any difference.

"Watch me."

Alabama moved her eyes, examining the men facing them down. She switched back to Flynn and glared in anger. "Nice scar."

He touched it, a grin creeping on his mouth. An exchange of recognition beamed between them. "Yes." He waved a finger, and his men patted them down and bound them with zip ties. "You coming here was a mistake. Holding you hostage would slow me down."

Emotional gouts of flame surged in Jackson's veins. Hot and fierce. His pulse quickened.

Alabama winced and bent her knees. In a deft movement, she gathered a chunk of mud below her feet and kicked it at Flynn. He dodged too late, and it slammed him in the face. At that moment, none of Flynn's men moved.

The king had lost his crown.

And if the king's guards were caught off-guard, now was the time to act.

Jackson flung himself at Flynn, landing a hard shoulder against Flynn's stomach, and she wrapped both feet around Flynn's legs.

Flynn grunted when his side pressed hard into the soil. None of his men came to his aid. Flynn threw a hammer fist against Alabama's thigh and as she stumbled, he popped Jackson in the nose twice and landed a solid uppercut.

"Enough nonsense," Flynn said. "Now."

The three men with batons reacted. One attempted to slam his baton on Jackson's head, but he only clipped his ear. Alabama lowered herself and kicked sideways, crippling a knee with a crunch.

Jackson bull-rushed the two standing closest to him. A

man on the ground thrashed and grasped his leg. Jackson stomped on the man's chest with his boot and kicked under his chin.

An elbow met Jackson across the jaw, and he flinched from the blow. A baton slammed between his shoulder blades. A sharp pain.

Breathe. Breathe.

Flynn gripped Jackson's hair and pulled him closer until they stood nose to nose. "I shouldn't enjoy this, but I do." He plowed a fist into Jackson's face. "Look at all that blood." He brought a finger alongside Jackson's upper lip and wiped blood on it. Flynn licked his finger. "O Positive. Universal donor."

Alabama threw a wheel kick at Flynn, but he tucked his arms and delivered a front kick, smashing her in the abdomen. She fell into the mud, gasping.

Flynn smiled, his face covered in mud. "You're good. But I expected better."

She dashed alongside Jackson, and something sharp poked his wrist. He felt his zip tie jerk up and down, loosening.

A knife cutting me free?

"What's in store for you, Stone, won't be pretty. It will hurt more than you've ever hurt, and you will remember this conversation for as long as you live. Getting information from you will be child's play."

All at once, Jackson felt a small razor in his palm. *Nice, Wren. Next time, tell me how to hide a razor.* As he cut himself free, Alabama rose and threw rabbit punches at Flynn.

He casually blocked them, grabbed her wrists, and leaned close to her. "Your pain will be even worse." Flynn headbutted her, and Jackson could feel the hit from where he stood.

A few hefty steps and Jackson put the razor to one of the men's throats, taking him hostage. "Go!" Droplets of sweat dripped from Jackson's brow, and his wet clothes stuck to his skin.

Flynn smiled. "I don't negotiate with terrorists." He grabbed one of his men's shotguns, closed one eye, and aimed at Jackson's hostage.

Jackson pushed as hard as he could, throwing the man into Flynn. The impact pushed Flynn back. By that time, Jackson and Alabama sprinted down the hill and toward the warehouse.

She disappeared around the warehouse, and he was right behind her, just a few steps to catch up.

Something metallic cracked Jackson's skull, and his face kissed the ground. Stars and black covered his vision. When it cleared, he stared through a tunnel outlined in stars. A kick caught him across the nose, and like a faucet, blood showered his clothing.

Dizzy, he crawled as fast as he could. Laughter sounded, echoing in his ears. His arm weakened.

Flynn and three of his thugs approached, roughed up and spent, but ready to kill. Jackson stood, backed up, and waited.

"Kill me then! Do it!" Jackson shouted, taking another backward step.

The enemy stopped. "Don't move."

A gust of wind. Chirping birds.

He stepped back again.

"Freeze!" they said.

His feet met air.

Arms windmilling, the ground beneath his feet disappeared out from under him.

A cliff.

The jungle rushed from below. *This is going to hurt.* A canopy of leaves gave way, breaking his fall. As he collided with a branch, he grunted, toppled over, and slammed his stomach against another tree limb. A sharp stab smacked his arm, turned him, and his leg crashed through another branch.

Thud.

Unable to breathe, he found himself on the ground and at the base of an anthill. His body raged with pain. His eyelids fluttered. Darkness consumed him.

F ollowing her instinct, Alabama followed his trail, though not a physical one. She sensed him, hurt, his mind confused. *Mission first, mission last. You better not die on me.*

Following an intuitive route, she concentrated, focusing on an invisible, energetic cord tugging her to this spot. Fifteen minutes before, she'd hid low in brambles and bushes. Flynn's men scattered around, searching for her. They disappeared into the jungle, their voices dying the farther they searched.

Jackson's white energy blossomed and folded in on itself. A subtle hint guided her through the foliage, a call, a whisper, the lines from a French song. His subtle gestures and words and the same natural French accent when he spoke it. Why had Director Hill insisted upon using Stone? Was this why? Because of how much he sometimes reminded her of Dubois?

If God was making a joke, she didn't like God's sense of humor.

She found him crawling with ants. "Stone, can you hear me?" she whispered.

He slumped to the ground until his chest became motionless.

She heaved in and out as her heart pounded. She crept toward Jackson with her mouth agape and touched his back. He breathed. Her shoulders relaxed. "Jackson?"

He moaned.

"Let's go." She wiped the mud off him.

He murmured something incoherent.

"Stay with me."

Jackson grasped at a stick puncturing his upper thigh. Blood oozed and soaked his pants. She pushed his hands away.

"If you pull it free, you're going to bleed out. I'm getting you to someplace safe."

His head lolled back, his eyelids fluttering.

Broken branches rested on the jungle floor around him. Limbs hung by a thread. It must have hurt, breaking the fall this way.

At least he wasn't dead.

Not yet.

Scratches lined his forehead and cheeks. A golf ball lump grew on his temple and large welts decorated above both eyes. She checked his nose and ran her hands down the nasal ridge and then pinched both sides. It wasn't broken.

His shirt was ripped to shreds, and she tore the rest off in a few long pieces and wrapped a tourniquet above his stick stab wound. She shoved the rest of her shirt into her pockets and checked his collar bone, ribs, and sternum. All intact.

The guy's a tank. How could nothing be broken?

His eyes opened, but before he could say anything, he grumbled and closed them.

Strangely, his pulse beat strong and healthy, although too fast for her liking. But the bleeding would continue unless she acted.

Fast.

Before Flynn finds her, and then him.

His stomach was bruised, but not soft to the touch. Blood hadn't pooled. No lacerated spleen or liver. *You lucky devil.*

Like a bag of cement, Jackson was a heavy beast. She moaned as she lifted him in a fireman's carry and shifted her weight. Her legs shook as she walked toward the line of offices. Sweat dripped to the ground, dropping from her every pore. Ten minutes later, her legs were like pudding. Up past a hill, she saw parked camouflage trucks. Behind them stood an office building, whose door was blasted open by an explosive.

When she reached the first truck, she set him down. He gurgled, and she turned him on his side. "Stay here." She checked all the trucks. Locked.

The office building reeked of cordite and smoke. The desks were full of pens, pencils, lined paper, sticky notes. Cabinets lined a wall. Was there nothing here at all?

She'd seen death come sooner than later on many occasions, even from smaller wounds.

If she admitted him to a hospital, Eclipse would find him. She'd have to rely on herself and find some way to stop the bleeding without causing an infection.

She searched the next cabinet and clapped her hands. Keys hung on hooks, all with emblems on the key chains. She shoved them in her pockets and bolted out of the office.

One set of keys fit the truck. After she opened the door,

she threw the rest of the keys on the floorboard. The truck's extra-long cabin and split-bench seats in the back would give him plenty of room to lie down. She leaned the passenger seat back as far as possible and dragged him inside.

The cut in his leg widened. Blood oozed.

"You there, Stone?" she asked, firing up the truck.

He grunted.

The truck jostled as she drove over uneven terrain and onto a cobblestone road. When she thought she saw one of Flynn's men poke through the jungle, she floored it. The crack of bullets faded the longer she pressed the accelerator to the floorboard.

"Stay with me." She rested her palm on his cheek. His cold, clammy face concerned her. Without him, the mission couldn't be successful. What would she say to Hill? That another agent died on her watch? That she'd failed again? Not this time.

After she turned down an asphalt road, she searched for ambulance services on the truck's GPS.

Ambulancias Privadas EMS blinked on the screen along with a map to the building.

An hour's drive to San Jose.

He didn't have an hour.

Perspiration dotted Jackson's face. Alabama touched his cheek. Cold. His shaking wasn't bad. Yet. She pressed on his wrist, checking his pulse. His heart rate came quick.

The empty two-lane highway lay before her with few vehicles in the way, but she avoided major roads until turning on the freeway after a few miles. Flynn could be watching the main thoroughfares.

Dusk changed to twilight. The truck's bright lights beamed over the black asphalt and the white lines dividing the highway. Shadowed hills bordered the road, and thick grasses met the jungle, sweeping up the many hills dotting the countryside.

Up ahead, empty buildings came into view like echoes from decades ago. Five minutes later, the hills leveled out and sporadic adobe buildings lined the road. The GPS signaled to take an off-ramp, and she curved around where it merged onto a bridge crossing the highway. Traffic blitzed by on the other side.

Beyond the bridge, a rectangular one-story building

spanned a block. She pulled into the driveway and stopped beside it, her bumper in front of a metal wire fence.

A dozen vehicles marked *Ambulancia* were parked behind the fence on a gravel parkway. Barbed wire strung the fence's apex, and a hefty lock held the gate secure.

Jackson moaned and turned. He reached for his wound, his lips in a straight line, his brows crinkled.

"I'm here, Stone. We'll get you fixed up."

He drifted in and out of consciousness. He probably couldn't hear, but maybe his subconscious would.

She typed in the *American Consulate* on the GPS and memorized it with a glance. Her dirt-stained clothes, patched with blood, made a mess of her pants and shirt. Her arms were scratched as if an angry cat had clawed her. Not the best look to present herself to anyone, especially strangers.

She slowed her breathing as she walked to the ambulance station's main entrance.

Calm and confident.

A woman sat at a desk and raised her eyes, greeting her. Near the same age as her, the woman's black hair, tan skin, and thick brows lent her an exotic look.

"Puedo ayudarte?" The woman pushed her curls behind her ear.

"I'm with the American Consulate, United States Embassy. Vía 104, C. 98, San José." She breathed quick and shallow to appear hurried.

"Hablas español?"

"Sí, pero soy mejor en inglés. Eso está bien?" Alabama asked.

The woman nodded. "Yes, I speak some English okay. How can me help?"

Alabama leaned on the counter and frowned. "We have

an emergency at the consulate. They told me to come here to grab the supplies we need."

"Why you no go to hospital? We have little supply here."

"Una emergencia." She motioned at her clothes, touching a spot of blood. "And you were closer than the hospital. We don't have much time." Her chin quivered as she deepened her frown.

"Bad danger?"

"Yes. We have our best doctor waiting for the supplies."

"What supply you need?"

"Quite a few." She drooped her shoulders. "It's a bad wound. We need a needle driver, tissue forceps, scissors, sterilized needle, and thread."

The woman wrote it down. "We—"

Alabama raised her index finger. "He's losing blood, too. Saline solution to decrease osmotic pressure. Tubing, clamp, and a port."

"To embassy, yes?"

"Yes."

"I'll send person with the supply now." She rested her hand on the phone.

Alabama gave her a piercing stare and glanced at the phone. "I'm here to pick them up *now*. It's okay. You can hand them to me."

"I sorry, we cannot do." She picked up the phone. "Hold on. We—"

Alabama shoved her pistol in the woman's face. "Put the phone down or I will take off the back of your head."

The woman froze. The skin on her throat rolled with a swallow.

"Get me those supplies." Alabama motioned with her gun toward a side exit. "Now."

"I sorry. I don't know where—"

"That's why I'm going to follow you." She tilted her head in the direction she wanted the woman to move.

The lady raised her hands in surrender. "Okay."

With the muzzle of the gun on the small of the woman's back, Alabama led her into the ambulance yard. "Move!" The crunch of gravel under shoes dulled as they passed between a row of emergency vehicles. "There you go." She shoved the lady toward an ambulance at the back of the lot. "Open the hatch."

The woman unclipped a keyring with a dozen keys attached to her belt. She fumbled with them, her hands shaky. "I sorry."

Still behind the woman, Alabama wrapped her forearm around the woman's neck. The crook of her arm pressed hard against her throat, and she gagged and struggled as Alabama lowered her to the ground. Her flailing arms went limp when she fell unconscious. Alabama released her hold, and the woman's eyes fluttered in rhythm with her twitching legs.

Alabama snagged the right key to the ambulance's back door.

Jump kits and medication bags were strapped on shelving, along with a spinal board. A stretcher sat in the middle of the ambulance and an electrocardiograph monitor with a defibrillator rested on the side of the stretcher.

Grabbing the jump kit in one hand and the medication bag in the other, she smiled. Perfect. Two saline drip bags sat on a shelf near the exit. She placed them in the jump kit.

She started to leave and then halted. Paramedic clothes were neatly placed on a chair attached to the wall, so she pulled off her clothes and shoved them in the medication bag. After slipping the EMT outfit on to look the part just in case, she hopped down to the gravel with a bag in each hand.

"Perdóneme."

She went rigid. A paramedic walked out from behind an adjacent van, and she followed his gaze, which landed on the unconscious woman lying on the gravel.

He bent down to check the lady. "Que esta pasando? Por que es—"

Before he could finish, Alabama sent a knee into the side of his head. His arms flew upward in a late attempt to block her. He rolled onto the ground with a grunt. He tried standing, but Alabama grabbed the back of his hair and pulled him forward, contacting her other knee with his forehead.

The paramedic sunk to the gravel.

Once out of the ambulance yard, she hurried out the front entryway and tossed the bags in the bed of the truck.

Jackson trembled as she sat in the driver's seat, his arm colder to the touch now.

"You still with me, tough guy?"

He didn't respond.

"You better not die on me."

A light flashed into the truck's cabin and swept across her lap. Someone tapped on the driver's side window. Her chest tightened.

A police officer stood outside, his face close to the glass.

" I 'm here to be of assistance," she said in Spanish.

The officer raised the flashlight to her eyes. "Passport?"

With one hand up, she fished five hundred dollars out of her pocket and stuffed it inside her passport.

After he took the money, he gave the ID back. "What is your business here?"

She nodded toward Jackson. "I need to help him."

"I ask again. What is your business here?"

"One moment." She handed him another thousand dollars. He looked over his shoulder, and he strode around the building and disappeared.

You're welcome.

She drove out of the parking lot and down a side street. Lamp posts reflected water on the sidewalks and illuminated the poro trees, their greenish-brown bark, orange flowers, and green leaves towering in front of homes and buildings.

Finding a safe place, she parked under a streetlight behind a hotel. Two glass doors formed the entrance. A large, blue accent awning displayed the words *El Lugar Para Ser* printed in white. She threw her jacket over Jackson's chest and studied his leg.

This is quite a nasty wound you have, Agent Stone.

Hooking the saline bag on the roof rack, she inserted the needle into his arm, bevel upwards at thirty degrees, and advanced the needle until a flashback of blood was in the hub at the back of the cannula. After she attached IV tubes, she let the saline drip and then tied the tourniquet tighter. Her gaze drifted from Jackson's pale face to the injury. His arms and hands trembled, and his lips quivered.

After pouring hydrogen peroxide onto his wound, she squeezed her fingers around the sharp stick half deep in his leg and pulled slowly.

He lunged forward, gasping, his eyes bulging.

"Relax." She held his arm. "Lay down."

Jackson moaned as he laid back.

"What's the matter? Don't like my outfit?"

She dropped the stick on the truck-bed, and a minute later, she poured more hydrogen peroxide into the wound. The fizz died down. He didn't move while she stitched him up.

Part of his pocket had torn, and inside the rip, she caught sight of a white pill bottle cap. When she pulled it out, it held several unmarked blue cyan pills. Why did he hide them?

The tablet's octagon shape caught her attention, and tiny golden flakes were caked inside the pills. She'd seen these before, but not in a long time. They were something Dubois would take, and he also kept them hidden. These pills were smaller.

Jackson carried twenty pills. Written in pen on the

bottom of the bottle: *Twenty pills, two a day*. Enough for ten days, and their window of operation lasted eight more days.

Dubois also took two a day.

Dubois refused to tell her about the pills when she confronted him. She'd discovered them in his slacks one evening in Vienna. "It's not of your business," he'd said in a fit of rage, unlike anything he'd ever done before. He'd smashed her favorite jewelry box, scattering her treasure across the glossy wooden floor. He'd apologized; his first and only time he'd said sorry. She'd forgiven him but never forgot.

He wouldn't explain either, not even a little. Polaris allowed their agents to take drugs if the situation warranted, illegal or otherwise. Mission first, mission last. Drugs were often required when dealing with technocrats, bankers, celebrities, and the noteworthy. To fit into their corrupt world. Get in with the movers and shakers.

Then there was Cabo San Lucas two years ago at the Waldorf Astoria hotel.

DUBOIS GRABBED takeout at The Golden Dragon, a greasy MSG-fueled restaurant. The breeze carried in through their deck's open doorway, and soft, white curtains blew into the room. His desk faced the ocean. Hard waves crashed outside. She'd give her thumb to go for a swim. Today just wasn't the day.

Before he returned, she found the same pill bottle, this time hidden so well, it took her twenty minutes to find it in their hotel. Before he brought back food, she searched for anything else which would help her understand him, a clue he might have forgotten about.

The door creaked open, and Dubois stood behind her clutching a paper bag. "Sorry. Big line to get the food."

She held up the pill bottle. "What are these for?"

"Put that down and grab some plates while the food is still hot."

"Please don't dodge the question."

He smiled his fake smile. "It's not something I can talk about."

"Are you dying?"

"No." He reached for the bottle. "Give it here."

"Not until you tell me what's inside."

"Would you rather me lie to you? If I could tell you, I would. You know well enough how our organization works. It's why we meet in secret."

She held up a pill. "What happens if I take one?"

His eyes flared. "I wouldn't do that."

"Oh? Why not?"

"Don't. They aren't for you."

"What do they do?"

He ran his fingers through his thick, graying hair, and sighed. "My love, there are more things in Heaven and Earth than are dreamt of in your philosophy. Polaris is what it is. I can't change that."

"You've changed."

"We all change."

THE WEEK BEFORE DUBOIS DISAPPEARED, she'd contacted doctors, pharmaceutical reps, and browsed the internet for information, but all she found were ads and their side effects warnings.

She lifted Jackson's shirt. Near the sternum, a light scar touched his skin. About five inches long, it stretched faintly in a straight line through a myriad of brown hairs. That was surgery and he had healed well.

Jackson stirred, and she lowered his shirt. With her palm on his forehead, she brushed his hair from his eyes. "When you wake up, we need to talk."

In the vortex of the jungle, the Casa Turire hotel was a paradise. Away from San José, Jackson and Alabama were confident of their safety, far from the major urban centers. Out here, not all police worked for drug cartels and human smugglers.

Jackson cringed. "What about the spheres? Were you able to find anything?" Instinctively, he went to touch his bandaged thigh, but he let his hands rest on the bed and scooted against the headboard.

On the red camelback and mahogany framed couch, Alabama kept her eyes on her laptop, her fingers tapping away. "I didn't see a sphere."

"How could you have missed them? They were underneath my feet."

She shrugged. "I didn't sense them, and if they were there, I would have. Why didn't you point them out?"

"When people are shooting at me?!" Thinking about it for a minute, Jackson could've sworn he pointed them out.

"One must overcome obstacles," she said as if quoting from some manual. "Now we have nothing."

"And Flynn?"

"You tell me. You're the one who seems to know him."

He gave her a puzzling frown. "I don't."

"But you do."

Jackson thrust his hands out.

She looked away, her gaze drawn to the upper-right corner of the room.

"You have an idea what the spheres are?" he asked.

"Maybe."

He grinned. "Care to share?"

She interlaced her fingers and sighed. "I read something on the plane on the way here. They're...old. Eclipse has found a method to control them, and they create some kind of mental link. What they are is anyone's guess."

Jackson bit his tongue. For the last two days, as he healed and gained his strength, Alabama had been more quiet than usual, sometimes answering with only a glance or a nod. Was this the reason?

"So the spheres use...telepathy?"

She snapped. "Listen, Stone, I don't know."

"The workers heard the hum. Our earbuds blocked the sound a good amount, thankfully. Now we know the disc's hum is a sonic weapon."

She pulled the stem out of the fruit and returned to her keyboard. "We're 0 for 3. Flynn has one. One was destroyed in the abbey. And now you say you saw two of them, but we don't have them."

He sat up and moved his sore leg. "I did my best."

"We both did." She tossed the apple core away. "That's the sad part."

This morning he was able to walk, though with a slight limp. He'd been eating meat since they arrived, taking in massive amounts of calories and protein, and drinking pitchers of chilled water.

When he tried to make small talk, she brushed him aside and left the room.

What the hell is her problem?

He found her outside, her hair shiny in the sun. When he shut the door behind him, she turned and started to walk back inside. He threw up an arm. "There's something wrong. What is it? You're not acting normal."

"You don't know how I normally act."

This couldn't have been about him.

She folded her arms. "There are secrets and then there are *secrets*."

"What does that mean? I don't understand why you're upset. The mission...."

"It has nothing to do with the bloody mission, Stone."

"Oh, *Stone,* is it? You don't need to use my name when I'm the only one here."

She balked. "Call it a wall I'm building around you."

Jackson sang a verse from a Sting song.

She gave him a strange look. "I'm not building a fortress around your heart. But speaking of your heart." She pointed to his chest.

He ran his fingers down his scar. "My surgery?" He shrugged. "Broke my sternum and ribs. They cut me open and fixed me up, using metal plates to set my bones. After they healed and another surgery, doctors removed the metal plates."

She folded her arms.

"Why?" He straightened his lips to stop frowning.

She threw a dismissive hand. "Nothing."

"What is it? We discussed this in the basement, and I assumed we'd sorted our differences out."

"Let me through. We need to uncover more information about the spheres."

He stepped aside. She tried closing the door behind her, shutting him out, but he put his foot in the door.

"Oh, sorry. I thought you went outside for a reason," she said.

"I did." He walked back inside and made himself a bologna sandwich. "Want to make a deal?"

She opened her laptop. "What is it?"

"Tell me what you know about the spheres, and I'll tell you about my scar."

Without looking at him, she typed and busied herself. "We don't need to know each other's details, and you're not in a position to bargain. I shouldn't have mentioned it in the first place."

"So, that's it?"

Alabama pursed her lips.

He waited a moment and gathered his thoughts. There was so much to say. "You're incredibly frustrating. I'm on a mission with you, and you won't tell me what's going on."

"How about we start here? I find it odd you saw two spheres, but I didn't. I believe you *think* you saw them. Maybe you wanted to see them."

"Damn it, Wren, I did see the spheres."

"When we were at the abbey, did you feel something?"

The abbey. Yes, something happened there. Something strange. Would she understand? How to codify it into language?

When he didn't answer, she left the room for a few minutes. When she returned, her poise relaxed.

He took a deep breath. "The spheres were the same as the ones we found in the States. I think these were metallic as well, but I don't know why you didn't feel them. Combat stress? Proximity?"

She laughed. "Maybe. I like how you say the States like you're a seasoned veteran or an expatriate."

"Oh, excuse me, Ms. CIA Director, Queen of Polaris and all things spy."

She hovered a finger over her mouth. "Thank you for the promotion."

"You're welcome." Even when she exuded arrogance, a bit of charm leaked from her. Feistiness. He both enjoyed and hated it. "Those spheres talked to me or affected me somehow."

"You still haven't told me what was said."

Jackson fidgeted with his hands. "I don't know if I can explain it."

"You can't explain it? If Flynn does what he said he's going to do, nukes will fly in the Middle East, and the Christian world will think Revelations has begun. If you hadn't been injured, our mission would be complete. We've lost the initiative. What did the spheres say? Please try to remember."

He rubbed the back of his neck. "It wasn't in a language. I.... I'm not sure what to think. While I want to say I definitely saw...something, I'm at a loss to explain it."

"Saw something?"

"A mental projection."

"And you can't describe it?"

"I wish I could. How do you describe a color you've never seen before?"

She adopted a wolfish grin. "Welcome to Polaris." Grabbing the TV's remote, she flipped it to CNN. "If something happens with Flynn, CNN will report on it."

"You trust CNN to report the news?"

"As much as any other news outlet," she said, changing channels. "They're all propaganda."

"What about Alex Jones?"

She busted out laughing. "Don't get me started on Alex." When she relaxed more, she continued, "Either the disc and spheres are experimental devices from the military, or we're about to discover something greater than either of us can explain. I've been doing this for a while. Probably too long. My guess is the spheres are psychological warfare devices. We already know what the disc can do—it causes mass hysteria and incapacitates enemies. If I were Flynn, I'd fly one over Washington D.C. and watch the world burn."

He reached for the remote, but she pulled it back. "You sound like the Joker."

"To get power in this world, it takes a certain kind of person. Many of them are sociopaths, some are psychopaths. A few others want to help other people."

She was right. He folded his legs. "We need something to detect frequencies."

"It's doubtful we would be able to detect them. If we could, others could as well. DARPA has been busy with all kinds of technology they don't share, some of which is so dangerous, I often wonder why they're not shut down."

Did Polaris work with DARPA, too? It would make sense if they did.

An advertisement for soap came on the screen. "How do you know we're the good guys?"

She laughed. "Because we count on operators like you to do the right thing."

"And you?"

"Me? Define what a good guy is, and I'll tell you."

The news showed the usual. Crime and looting. Corruption. Having gone through mock FBI training and listening to Polaris, what the media force-fed people was a stage show and a bad one at that.

"By the way, are you hungry?" she asked.

"My stomach is still upset."

She went to the kitchen and made a salad. He checked the time and left to get his utility belt on the bedside table. The pouch was empty. He took a few minutes, searching under the bed and in his other pockets, but they were missing.

"Hey, Wren, where are my pills?"

"Good question. Why do you take them?" she asked, her mouth full. "They weren't mentioned in your med file."

"Personal reasons."

"*Personal reasons*," she repeated. Her voice lowered. "If you have a medical condition that might cost us the mission, you're obligated to report it. Does Hill know?"

"Of course. You know how many medical examinations we get."

"So...." she said, leaving a space for him to answer.

"Director Hill told me not to mention the pills. That's all I can say." He brought his handgun to the living room, set it down, and removed the magazine.

She set her fork on the side of the bowl and rolled her fingers on the counter where she stood. "See? We all have our secrets."

Jackson field stripped his weapon more times than he could count, and as he disassembled his pistol, he remembered his training. Polaris taught him to use several weapons. AKs, M4s and their variants, bullpups, revolvers, shotguns, grenades, and everything else under the sun. The training lasted over six months from predawn to midnight. But this felt different. He pulled the slide from the frame and removed the barrel. With the rag, he wiped carbon remnants from the slide. It felt natural to him like his blood burned bright with a soldier's memory.

One day, the strangest thing happened. When the instructor brought in a MAC 50, a French 9mm pistol, he outshot everyone at the range. Second nature, he'd said to everyone's astonishment. To his own astonishment as well.

Director Hill asked him to not mention it to anyone. Though Jackson didn't question Hill, he could tell the director knew something Jackson didn't.

What's happening to me?

Alabama typed. "Message from Hill. We're leaving."

"To where?"

"Flynn will suspect Polaris or American Special Operations teams to deploy to Guayabo. Because of that, the disc won't be there. Flynn would have moved it."

"If I were to hide a disc, I'd want to avoid satellite images and radar. I wouldn't want to be seen by the Navy, either. I'd pick something out of the way. Like Iceland."

"Or a less known island."

J ackson sat in the passenger seat of a Hyundai Elantra; white paint, black trim; the fanciest car rental Costa Rica had to offer. He adjusted in his seat, and although his leg ached, he didn't let it bother him. After Alabama rented the car and stopped at the hotel, they loaded their supplies and headed out. On Highway 39—a two-lane, unkempt road—she drove the speed limit, her hands fixed at ten and two o'clock.

The worst part about Costa Rica? Their music. Where was an 80s channel when you needed one?

A security sensor with a readout at the top rested on Jackson's lap. "We'll be there in twenty minutes. Are you sure this is a good idea?" Jackson asked.

"Ask me in an hour."

"I hope you're right about this plan. Sneaking into a classroom filled with computers so you can get a decent internet connection sounds like a bad idea."

"Fastest way we'll be able to find the island we're looking for. Sometimes the internet goes out here, and the hotel manager couldn't give me a time he thought it'd be fixed. This will be safer. I hope."

Jackson rolled down the window and stuck his arm out. "I love this fresh air."

"It's better than the air in a Costa Rican prison cell. Trust me. Don't mess this up," she said.

Alabama took a slight right onto Highway 27. The shadow of jungle trees lined the road and thinned out as more buildings cropped up. In the darkness, and with a lack of street lights, the buildings resembled black boxes with curved and flat roofs; concrete blockhouses, and businesses. As Alabama took an off-ramp into San Jose, the buildings grew in size. So did the lights.

Passersby stared in bewilderment at Alabama and glared with jealousy at Jackson. Her red hair stood out, and as far as he could see, they were the only two *gringos* driving on this side of town.

Pre-Columbian-like houses flowed down Calle 56 Street. She drove past Gasolinera Tres and Ferretería, a failing hardware store swarmed by mangy dogs and feral cats.

They pulled into an empty parking lot.

"It's up ahead. They have the fastest internet around here, and we'll find out exactly what we need," she said.

"It's startling to know how reliant we are on the internet."

The muddy brown Inxacom building and its mirrored windows made it impossible to see inside. A wide path led from the parking lot to a storage building, where a row of dumpsters stood.

She drove down by the dumpsters and looked around. "There's a concrete path that leads to that fence. That's the back of the school."

"I see it. So, the plan is to cut through the fence and go through the back door?"

"It's the best way in. They have cameras, but most of them are aimed at the front. The gate protects the back entrance." She checked her watch. "It's half past midnight. Use the wand."

He fished out a small black cylinder with a keypad on the side. The "wand" was an automated hacker, radio scanner, and jammer with decent range. Polaris quickly learned not to use them too often because they left a distinct electronic fingerprint.

The wand's keys were split diagonally, one side orange and one side blue, and abbreviations snaked around both sides of a key. It made the whole keyboard a giant glowing crossword puzzle.

"How do you turn it on?" she asked.

"Like this." Jackson held down the P, T, and Q buttons, tapped the tilde key three times with his pinky while holding down Backspace and End for two seconds and mashed the spacebar as fast as he could.

The device turned on.

"You think I'd forget something like that? Greenblatt made me do it a hundred times one day because I'd pressed Delete, not End."

She rolled up her sleeve. "See this burn mark? I sneezed during one of Dr. Greenblatt's lectures on poisons. He used a 1995 Cuban cigar he'd been saving to give to his father on his 75th birthday."

"He burned you?"

"No, but I wanted to see your face."

Jackson rolled his eyes and pointed the wand at Inxacom, beyond the fence. Two systems appeared; a door alarm and a camera.

"Okay, found two. I'll shut the bubble camera down first."

It took a few clicks to disable it.

Many alarm companies carried a one-code-fits-all approach to disarm an alarm system. If someone forgot their code and couldn't turn off their alarm, they'd need to call the security company and receive a code that turned their alarm off.

He pointed it at the building and pressed a button on the side. Red digits spun on the sensor's clear screen, scanning for an alarm. *Alarm detected* blinked on the screen. The alarm company's name appeared in abbreviated letters: *ABD*. Less than a minute later, *4895* was displayed on the device.

He raised the sensor. "Easy."

"Don't jinx us." She handed him their tool bag. "Let's go."

Trees grew, and their leaves hovered over Inxacom's roof, giving extra shade. A wire fence with two rows of concertina wire surrounded the back, keeping Inxacom secure from that end. They cut through it and crept to a small set of concrete stairs leading to a reinforced metal backdoor.

"All this for a decent Internet connection," he said.

She pouted. "Hill said Polaris couldn't exfiltrate us right now. In the field, we make do with what we can. It's not my fault this part of Costa Rica offers 1999 level Internet speeds."

"You'd think we could use a satellite."

Waving a hand, she shrugged "Not out here."

He touched the door. "Looks formidable."

"Think you can fit through the window above it?"

He looked up and noticed what she was talking about. She'd have to hoist him up through the window, and in his state, he wasn't sure it was a good idea. "How can we get through the glass?"

She opened the bag and displayed a glass cutter, two

suction cups, and a rope. "Don't leave your hotel without them. I'll lift you."

"I'm a little heavy."

"I'm aware. You nearly broke my back when I pulled you from the jungle."

He held the bag, and she helped him lean against the door. He didn't see signs of an alarm on the window, but the inside was pitch black. "Looks clean."

"There might be a motion detector inside. The alarm could be a good distance from the door, and it will be hard to find in the dark."

He adjusted his weight. "Did you bring a flashlight?"

Reaching in the bag, she handed him one. "Here. If anyone passes by and sees a light from the front entrance, they'll call the police. Be careful."

He positioned the suction cups where he could tease the glass out and then used the rope to connect them, so he could lower it to her. He scored the glass, making a quick and erratic spider web-like pattern. Jackson slid a few layers of tape over each score on the glass and pulled the glass free.

Beep! Beep! Beep!

Jackson's heart jumped a gear.

Crap!

Thirty seconds to punch in the code or the outside alarms would blare. Then the police would arrive. He lifted himself and went headfirst through the hole. But his shoulders wouldn't fit.

"Tuck your damn arms in."

"I'm trying. Quick, you go in."

She pushed his feet up. "On-the-job training. This is your gig. Make it work."

No matter how much he tried, he couldn't climb in. The

alarm continued wailing. Only one way to get inside. He drew his handgun, nearly losing his footing, and smashed the rest of the glass.

She swore. "Now climb in there!"

As he crawled inside, he dragged his wrist over a shard of glass, drawing a trickle of blood. Wincing, he climbed in further, falling inside a supply room on the other side.

He beamed his flashlight across reams of papers stacked on a table, along with printer cartridges, pens, and staplers.

He darted down a hallway. Where was it? The keypad should be right around here.

Fifteen seconds until the alarm sounded the police.

He hurried past several classrooms strewn with computer stations and into the lobby. Chairs lined the entrance wall. A lobby desk sat behind him, shadows of cacti in pots on top.

Ten seconds.

Wren, I'm going to kill you for this.

He swept the flashlight over the bare wall next to the door.

Seven seconds.

"It should be here, but it's not." His heart plummeted. "The alarm panel isn't in here!"

"Keep looking!" Alabama's voice burst in his earbud.

He turned and ran the way he came. "We have to get out of here."

In minutes, siren lights from police cars would bounce off the building; red and blue, red and blue.

B ut then the alarm shut off as someone punched in the code. Jackson halted mid-stride. His chest heaved in and out. A person in a shadow stood at the end of the hall. He drew his pistol, took cover behind a desk, his fingers clenched like a vice grip around the flashlight's grip.

"Put that thing away before you hurt someone," Alabama said. She stood next to an alarm panel with a keypad at shoulder level.

"How did you find it?" he asked.

"Deduction. I searched the rear. First shift enters through the back and turns off the alarm."

"Why didn't the stupid wand discover this?"

She shrugged. "Polaris stopped making them, hence no more upgrades."

"That's it?"

"Pretty much."

Jackson bent over and rested a hand on his knee. "No high-speed chase away from the *policia*?"

"Maybe later." She motioned toward a classroom filled with computer stations, two computers per desk.

Alabama sat at a desk and brought out her computer.

"Won't they see activity coming from your laptop to their servers?"

"They're going to see only what I allow them to see."

Jackson sat by her side. His foot nudged the large desktop under the desk as he rested his elbows on the table. "You really are the Queen of Polaris, the CIA, and all things spy."

"You forgot the KGB, MI6, and Mossad. Oh, and I even sit in on CCP meetings with the Chairman. He's quite something." She winked and connected to a server in Los Angeles. Several new icons were displayed in the system tray. "Much better. Good job on getting the window, by the way."

"Sarcasm is your bread and butter."

"I was being serious. Sometimes, good old brute force is the best option." She opened applications displaying internet commands and typed in a series of codes. "I'm in. We need to find a privately owned island." Her eyes lit up, and she tossed her hair back. "Some tycoon billionaires like Bobby Savior have attempted to set up their own nations. He wanted to build some silly Libertarian city-state in the Virgin Islands. It didn't go well."

"What happened?"

"Libertarians."

"I see."

"Let's check something." She typed names and scanned. "Indonesia archipelagos contain 17,000 islands. That might be the most of any territory, and it's practically on the equator."

She checked the network and brought up a map of

Indonesia. Amazing how fast she worked. Was she part of a hacking crew before joining Polaris?

"You're good at this," he said.

"The network isn't secure. One second. Let's see." She chewed on her bottom lip. "Let me set up a few macros and let the computer do the heavy lifting. Checking Polaris. They use several inane websites that store bits of top secret data from the FBI, CIA, NSA, and other United States agencies."

Jackson pointed to a spider icon. "What's that?"

"A PROP web crawler. It gathers composite images, renders the background pixel noise out, and sends them as passwords to Polaris' database. Let's see if the CIA tracked shipping routes in Indonesia recently."

"What's your take on the CIA?"

Her eyes rolled across the screen. "Mine? It doesn't matter what mine is. All that matters is what Polaris tells us to do."

"In my briefing, I was only provided cursory information on our policy. They're Americans, so...."

"Don't be naïve."

"You shot those Americans back at the hanger without thinking. Boom, boom, boom, three U.S. servicemen dead."

"Now isn't the time or place."

True. But she still needed to explain.

After a few minutes of uncomfortable silence, she tapped the screen. "Here. A route from Hong Kong, China to Indonesia. It doesn't mention the island's name. Doesn't have a number, either. No identification. Hong Kong is a huge port. You'll have to see it one day."

"I'm not sure I want to visit China."

"We don't choose where we go. The CIA usually keeps

their attention on this route until world affairs forces them to redeploy their assets to other regions. CIA intelligence is obsolete at best, sometimes. However, cargo ships can be traced around the Philippines and then west through the Halmahera Sea." She pointed to the map. "The route runs south between Buru and Seram Island, dead center in the Banda Sea."

Jackson traced a line. "Might have been going to Australia. How many shipping companies?"

"Checking. Looks like one. Bantam, out of Ukraine."

"Bantam. Odd name for a Ukrainian company. Who's their supplier and why are they coming from Hong Kong?"

After a few minutes, Alabama rapped her knuckles on the desk. "Not sure. But it appears as if Bantam specializes in underwater construction."

"Interesting. Who's their CEO?"

"Maria Hycha. CFO is Danilo Andreiko. Glib Vasiv, the founder." She perused the database. "The company disbanded a year ago." She typed in Danilo's name, and information streamed across the screen. "Father of three kids. Divorced. Worked in oil before he became the CFO of Bantam."

"Check the CEO again."

"Mother of two. Husband works in nanotech. Looks like much of her file is missing." She paused as more data filled the monitor. Pages of data popped up. "Their founder has a bit of criminal history. Mr. Vasiv has been a busy man. Racketeering. Extortion." She reached the bottom of a page. "How about that? He's in a Russian prison. Vasiv owns several patents, and his company built an underwater test facility in Lake Ilmen, Russia."

"You ever see what Russian prisons look like?" he asked.

"Up close and personal, I'm afraid." After she said it, her eyes flared for a second. "You didn't hear that."

He nodded. "Hear what?"

"Thanks." She continued scrolling. "Another underwater construction project in Lake Ladoga, again in Russia. It doesn't say what the construction was. Maybe he and Putin got along once. If he's in a Russian prison, something happened." She clicked past more data. "This isn't good. He was going to plea bargain using information related to a secret construction. Turns out, prosecutors weren't interested. Oh. Here's an update. The cameras happened to turn off moments before he hung himself in prison. No investigation was launched into his death."

Jackson frowned. "Sounds like I've heard that one before." He mocked a silly accent. "No soup for you."

"I didn't take you for a person to watch Seinfeld," she said.

"I couldn't stand it. I just like the Soup Nazi. He made the show."

"Kramer made the show."

"Kramer? The guy with the crazy hair?"

"Never mind."

Jackson sat back. "Vasiv might be our man. He knew about the construction, and someone took him out to prevent him from talking."

"Let's see where the shipping route led. It didn't just stop in the middle of the Banda Sea unless it capsized, and there's no mention of that." She checked Polaris' satellite maps of any islands where the route ended. "Just ocean."

"It looks scrubbed." Jackson moved closer to the screen, his nose a few inches from it.

"It's an old file. Hasn't been updated since 2016. Let me

check Google Maps." She switched and found the map location. Her shoulders drooped. "Scrubbed."

"Check the Wayback Machine."

"It doesn't work like that. Agencies wipe those. Anyone can ask for those to be removed if you pay the right people enough money. Corporations do it all the time."

"Is there a map in the Polaris database?"

"Checking."

After several clicks, she found a Sir Charles Warwick map, a World War II admiral in the British Royal Navy. Though he most likely didn't create the map, he was there when it was created. It dated to an expedition to help with war plans, which included ship routes away from the Japanese navy.

"This might be all we have to work with," she said.

The Indonesian map showed the surrounding islands. Warwick labeled one island *Jungle London Point*, where Bantam's shipping route ended. Though not a name that would stick, the name didn't matter. The location did.

"Where would you hide a building on an island?" he asked.

"It's almost impossible to hide anything from the world. Satellites can read your phone from space."

She brought up treaties and jurisdictions in that area. Nothing with those names popped on the screen. No country owned it. Whoever took claim of it had kept it in the shadows.

Jackson bit his cheek. "That's out there. How do we get there?"

She pulled out her phone and dialed. "Scorpion Team." She paused and waited. "Dr. Alabama Wren." She nodded a few times as a grin grew across her lips. "I need relocation assets assigned to my location. Priority one." She hung up and set the phone on the desk, her index and middle finger tapping on the wood top. "Have you ever visited the Costa Rican coast?"

"I thought you said Polaris couldn't exfiltrate us."

She rubbed her nose. "Did I say that?"

The ocean pounded the Polaris' *latest acquisition*—an M80 Stiletto designed for special operations. Used in counter-terrorism missions and drug interdiction, the boat crewed three and carried fifteen special operators, usually SEALs. Polaris worked in cooperation with the Department of Defense on occasion, using Scorpion as an outlet for missions the DoD couldn't officially be involved in. Polaris' elite military component swore oaths to never surrender and to defend Polaris at all times. And they'd proven themselves through remarkable feats of valor and discipline. To be in their presence was to be protected by men and women who were ready to give their life at any moment. They made Jackson sweat and Alabama smile.

Their boat measured only 88 feet long and an unusually wide 40 feet. Due to its unique construction, it sported superior maneuverability. A helipad marked the aft section.

It slammed amidst the crashing waters, the crew ready for any engagement. Next-generation electronic warfare equipment kept them hidden from the enemy, and the boat almost glided over the water.

She sat by a window with a glass of wine with Jackson across from her. The small room was one of the few not attributed to war. Here, at least, she could settle in for the ride.

The Captain gifted her a bottle of white wine—2011 Domaine Weinbach Gewürztraminer. He remembered.

Rain pelted sideways against the windows. "The Captain said the storm would be getting worse." Alabama sipped her drink.

Their route would bring them north to Belize as soon as the helicopter arrived. But they had time to relax for once.

Jackson swirled the wine and sniffed. "Sometimes, I wish we could see these places without being shot at." The skin under Jackson's eyelids sagged. When he blinked, his eyelids held a millisecond longer than the last.

"I need you to stay awake for a bit. You should get some caffeine." She pointed to the coffee machine.

"Maybe you're right. Can barely keep my eyes open."

She kicked his shin just as the ship dipped, speeding along at forty-five knots. She squeezed her finger and thumb against the bridge of her nose and swallowed her nausea. A wave slammed on the deck. Seawater slipped off the boat's stealth hull. The waves were getting worse. Jackson seemed completely at ease. Lucky bastard.

Jackson's eyes had a sense of compassion to them. "We should be passing through the storm shortly."

"Let's hope."

"I'm suspicious of planes, and you don't do the ocean," he said.

She gripped the table. "Didn't your father almost die in a plane crash?"

"He did. It happened in the invasion of Grenada. He wouldn't give me specifics. Back then, information was easier to control, and people kept secrets to themselves. He ejected and landed in the sea. Waited for three days before anyone picked him up. By that time, he was starving, thirsty, and hallucinating. I'm not a fan of the ocean, either, but I can't think of a better place to be right now."

"Is there another reason why you're scared of planes?"

He paused and looked at his feet. "Not at all."

The wind picked up. The craft slowed and voices shouted from another room. She pressed her palm hard against the window.

He wasn't telling her the truth. That was okay. Eventually, he'd tell her the reason he feared planes. It had to be more than air sickness.

"The storm's grabbing hold now," Jackson said.

Alabama froze, her fingers splayed outward. Maybe a direct approach would work. "So, why are you scared of flying?"

"That's for me."

She scooted to the side of the chair as waves clobbered the deck and slashed against the window. The ship jostled.

He massaged his leg. "Do you want to talk about what happened at Camp Withycombe now?"

"You're still upset I killed a few soldiers?" she asked.

"I don't know how I should feel about it. I understand why. My problem is that you didn't seem to be bothered by it."

Who did he think he worked for? Polaris wasn't some shining beacon on the horizon, though it tried to be. It held fast to the old values of liberty and freedom, a losing battle against the tide of Big Tech data harvesting and governmental overreach.

According to the shrinks at Polaris, she let killing bother her in Chicago when she was growing up. Before missions, psychologists gave her routine tests, and she'd always been approved for duty. Director Hill didn't want safe and sound. He needed killers to counter Eclipse. Dead men tell no tales and all that good stuff.

But how could she be mad at Stone for mentioning her coldness? She remembered when fieldwork was new to her, and how the constant slaughter affected her. Then she found the switch to turn it off, a simple conscious act of choosing not to care. Life here wasn't the end of existence, and perhaps it was only the beginning.

"You okay?" Jackson's eyes softened.

She finished the glass and grabbed another. Director Hill would kill her if he found her drinking, especially here and now. But rules were made to be broken, and a bottle of wine went a long way to help remedy her discomfort. "My dad took me fishing once." She held her index finger up. "Once." She smiled.

"I can't remember what movie that's from."

"Was it from a movie? My older brother used to say it all the time."

He remained quiet.

"You're not going to ask me about my older brother?" she asked.

"Nope."

She grinned. "Now you're learning."

Someone rapped on the door. "Dr. Wren, Cormac is here."

"Thank you. We'll be right out."

"Who's Cormac?"

"Oh, you'll love him." Lights filtered through the window

behind her. She stood and gripped the chair's backrest to keep balance. "Let's go."

Once through the door, the chatter stopped, and members of Scorpion sized Jackson up. They weren't impressed.

A Sikorsky UH-60 Black Hawk helicopter sat on the helipad in the rear of the boat, the chopper's spinning rotors adding to the wind slapping the rain against her face. She pushed her hair out of her eyes.

Cormac, a longtime friend, waved them forward. From what she could discern, he hadn't aged more than a day.

Alabama pulled herself into the Black Hawk's cabin, and Jackson scrunched in next to her. The boat didn't slow, and waves came up over the deck.

Alabama and Jackson grabbed helmets off the rail. The earmuff-like padding fit snugly around her ears, drowning the ocean's crashing waves and the helicopter's roar. She adjusted the helmet mic and brought it closer to her lips.

"Grab the emergency locators behind you." Cormac sounded through her helmet as if he'd smoked since he crawled out of the womb. His voice carried the gravity of a man who'd seen the darkest side of war and death. "When you're ready for exfiltration, use them."

"We're going to the island now?" Jackson asked, adjusting his helmet mic.

Cormac threw a thumb by his ear and pointed at Jackson. "Get a load of this guy."

"Don't be too hard on him. He's made it more than a week."

Chuckling, Cormac took the flight stick. "Impressive."

The exfiltration locators were small EKG stickers, and she glued one underneath her bra, near her heart.

"They're smaller than last time," she said.

"Upgraded. We're hoping to eventually use dental implants, but they still show up in X-rays. The ones we have can't be electronically jammed, but once you use them, they'll run for a few hours and die. Use them wisely. When you're ready, press down on them, and I'll fly to your location."

The rotor's speed increased. Cormac pulled the collective upward, the helicopter lightened on the skids, and it lifted off the helipad. Amid the heavy wind and rain, he had no trouble navigating through the storm. The cockpit aimed toward Belize.

Rain scattered across the window, almost blinding their view even more than the night. "We're heading to Hector Silva Airstrip in Belmopan where you'll board a plane. Any questions? I know it's not much of a briefing, but Hill wouldn't tell me much more."

As Jackson started to speak, she elbowed him in the shoulder and wagged her finger at him. He remained quiet.

Why did people always assume they were entitled to know the details of an operation? True, Cormac could be counted as a friend, but seriously. No. He was a pilot, and that was it.

"Between you and me," she said, "we weren't told a lot, either."

"Roger that."

She pointed to the pilot and smiled. *Watch this,* she mouthed. "What do you think about Iran?"

When her friend heard Iran, he wouldn't shut up. He waxed poetically before realizing no one was listening. That was her gift; making people think they were smarter than they were. A useful skill in her trade.

"I have Director Hill on Security Channel Three. Says he wants to speak with both of you."

She clicked her comm. "Put him through."

"Can you both hear me?" Director Hill asked.

"Yes, sir," Alabama and Jackson said.

"China has lost contact with the islands in the South China Sea."

Jackson's mouth fell open.

War?

Alabama's voice rose with concern. "What's going on, sir?"

"They claimed to have seen a large disc over the area. It caused disruption. Lots of disruption. The CCP is blaming the United States through back channels, and the president has called an emergency meeting with the chiefs of staff. A New York Times reporter has gone missing. Both of you better be right. If the disc isn't at that island, there won't be a world to return to."

My God. Flynn has already started using it.

"Understood, sir. May we call upon Scorpion assets?" she asked.

"Negative. They're putting out political fires across the world. This is getting out of control. Are you able to handle this mission?"

Jackson balled his fist. "Yes, sir. You can count on us."

She cleared her throat. "Cormac, where are the parachutes?"

After the flight, they boarded a C-20 Gulfstream, a United States military variant of a Gulfstream III and IV aircraft. The jet was a thing of beauty with both engines mounted in the tail section and long wings. After heaving whatever food he had left, Alabama offered him mints. Delightful.

At this rate, Jackson would need a new set of teeth from vomiting every few days.

As the plane lifted from the runway, he asked himself when he'd be over his fear of flying. He held his breath.

Cormac had mentioned signal jamming the closer he flew to the island. Without the ability to use radar or other electronic measures, it would be hard to find if a structure existed below the water.

The crescent moon provided only the slimmest light.

Calm. Take slow, steady breaths. Focus on the breath. Focus.

The tingling in his limbs faded after several breaths. His mind sharpened, his vision cleared, and he placed his hands on the seat's backrest in front of him.

"You feel that?" Alabama asked.

He looked around. *Where's a good glass of water when you need one?* "Feel what? My stomach is in my throat? Don't tell me I'm going to get used to it after a while."

She studied him. "You'll get used to it after a while." She tossed a backpack and a parachute pack on the seat next to him.

The plane dropped, throwing him to the side. His stomach lurched, and he held his mouth. His knuckles were white. He closed his eyes. Like a punch to his heart, a shock of nerves blasted outward and down his arms and legs.

Nicki squeezing his hand after a loud sound that cracked the plane's cabin apart.

Her death, always hovering in his thoughts.

The plane shook, and as fast as it started, it ended.

They stood and grabbed the heavy backpacks. Supplies, and probably more than they needed, were tucked inside. She checked her gear and helped him strap his parachute on his back.

They checked each other over.

"You ready?"

"Ready."

"Testing throat mic."

"Check."

Cormac's gravelly voice ground like metal against cement. "Wren, come up here a moment, will ya?"

She moved toward the front of the plane. They spoke for a while, and he gave her a phone. "We're over the island now. On my mark," Cormac said.

Stuffing it into her pack, Alabama touched Cormac's shoulder. "You going to take your lady here for a holiday?"

The pilot snickered. "Which one?"

"You have more than one?"

The plane banked left and pitched down. "I have one for every day of the week."

Alabama rolled her eyes. "Since when have you found more than one woman who can put up with you?"

"Not all of them speak English. Don't forget what I gave you."

Lurching, the plane dropped, and Jackson held onto a seat with both hands.

Cormac turned around and pointed his finger to the window. "Stone, do me a favor and look through there."

Why did he sound so strange?

The ocean blurred—endless blue waves for as far as he could see.

But through a reflection, Jackson watched Cormac give a small box to Alabama along with a card. Her bright smile lit up the cockpit, and she gave Cormac a mock hug.

Cormac came over the comm. "Sixty seconds."

She took a step toward the door. "Moving."

Jackson's first combat drop. He'd learned the hard way how to jump out of a perfectly good airplane. He'd practiced numerous jumps in every condition for the real thing.

"Thirty seconds," Cormac said. "We'll be on standby."

Jackson swallowed. "That was a fast thirty seconds."

She grasped the plug door's handle. "At the door."

"Ten seconds."

She gave a nod, and he half-grinned and crouched beside her. Anything to get out of this plane.

"Go!"

She pulled on the handle. The door hissed and unlatched.

A freezing wind buffeted his face and smashed his clothes against his body. She jumped, and twisted, facing his direction as she fell toward the earth.

Jackson grasped the edge of the doorway. The wind attempted to pull him out like a vacuum. He jumped. The cool, fresh air became colder.

For an instant, his stomach felt the lurch of free fall, as if he was on a roller coaster at full speed at a ninety-degree descent.

Then the sensation of floating, like every time he'd skydived. The sound of wind roared like a jet engine. The heavy wind pressed his body.

Below, azure waves pummeled white sand beaches. A maze of trees as thick as the Costa Rican jungle rose toward him at an incredible speed. The island was half the size of Maui.

No buildings lined the beach, or at the edge, or deep in the jungle.

His helmet beeped; the altimeter indicating he'd reached forty-five hundred feet.

He pulled the ripcord, and lurched upward, torn from the rush. Everything quieted. His legs swung as he steadied himself, and he grasped the control lines to slow his descent. Heat and humidity took over.

Alabama had deployed her chute a few seconds beforehand and rode the canopy about twenty yards above. "Aim for the beach."

As they approached the sand, Jackson kept his arms up to keep the speed and the parachute stable. Just above the ground, he yanked the hand toggles, leveled his descent, and he slowed abruptly. A foot-and-a-half above the sand, he leaned forward, lifted his legs, and gradually pushed lower on the toggles.

His feet slid across the beach until he touched down in a run, his knees buckling on impact. As he rolled a few times, the parachute fell behind him and tugged.

He spat out sand, rose, and wiped his hands on his thighs. Thankful to be standing, he pulled the chute off and dropped it onto the sand. The heat warmed him. Waves crashed, and birds took into the air.

Beside him, Alabama had already unstrapped her chute, slipped off her backpack, and slid out her MP5 submachine gun. She twisted on a silencer.

Jackson bent and grabbed the backpack's zipper when a roar echoed from the jungle. He froze. "Did you hear that?"

"Uh...turn around."

He did and sucked in a sharp breath. Instinct made him pull his weapon out from his backpack. Another growl vibrated him to his core.

"Stone, do not move."

Anoxious urine smell stirred in the air. Alabama backed away slowly. "Don't shoot."

The shoulders of a black-and-orange striped tiger flexed as it walked down to where the jungle ended in a cliff and onto the sand. A paw stretched in their direction and then another.

It crept low, hunting. About twenty yards from her, it leaped a few feet, its paws thrusting outward. Baring its fangs, it throated a growl.

"Don't shoot? It'll kill us!" Jackson twisted on the silencer.

Alabama's gut clenched. "Stone. Do. Not. Fire."

The tiger lurched forward in a pounce and then halted as sand sprayed between its front claws.

"It's hungry," he said. "And I'm not going to be today's entrée."

"Don't look in her eyes. Don't turn your back to her. Stay calm." Alabama held her backpack and MP5 and continued backward. Sweat dripped down her spine. "Do what I do. No sudden, fast movements."

"How do you know it's a her?"

She sighed.

"Well, just shoot the damn thing." Jackson aimed at the tiger's eyes.

"Make yourself big." She sucked in a breath and pushed her chest outward. "Act confident. Let her know you're not helpless prey."

The tiger bared her fangs, pouncing again and lowering her head when her paws met dirt. She planted her rear legs. Alabama retreated. The tiger swiveled her head in Jackson's direction.

"Stone...."

"I didn't come here to be eaten."

"Smell the urine. Its—"

Another tiger called with a low growl. A few plants at the jungle's edge jostled, and a larger cat planted his paws on the sand. He growled a second time, his pace slow and strong.

Alabama motioned with her head toward the other tiger. "Mating season. Our friend is in heat. There's no need to kill them, yet. Stay easy."

"Easy for you to say."

"They might be known to people on the island. If they go missing, they'll know something happened."

The female tiger halted in stride, turned, and rested on its haunches, lowering and rolling on the ground, its tail swiping the sand.

The male approached the female, and Alabama hastened her pace as both tigers circled one another. "Keep walking away. More distance, Stone."

"Let's get behind the rocks."

Once they shuffled a hundred yards from the beasts, they retreated and watched as the female sat on her hind legs and caressed the male with her snout.

What beautiful animals. Thankfully, he listened this time. She'd put that in her report.

She rounded a handful of tall, wide volcanic boulders on the beach that melded together at some point hundreds of years prior.

They dropped to the sand when the tigers were out of view, their faces dripping with perspiration.

He rested his head in his hands, his breathing fast. "You're crazy."

"For not killing the tigers?"

"For a lot of things."

"They were only defending their territory."

His eyes met hers with intense fascination. "You care more about animals than people."

Was he right? Maybe. It was something she'd never admit to anyone, not even to herself. But she wouldn't answer questions meant to entice her. Others had asked her the same thing. Losing Dubois hurt more than losing her mother, her father, her brothers, and her son, all the same.

Since then, love was a fantasy.

She looked out at the ocean, steadying her heart rate. Waves broke and tumbled, advancing as it calmed and only to retreat again. The sun rose, shining like gold off the water. She fanned herself, the heat all-consuming.

"You a tiger enthusiast?" he asked.

"I'm a survival enthusiast."

She grabbed a handful of sand and let it slip through her fingers. "When Glib Ivasiv came and built the project for Bantam, the equipment would have made makeshift roads or left evidence somehow. They might have placed security cameras. What's your EMF reader say?"

After checking his device, he shook his head. "We're

being jammed." He tucked it away and scanned the horizon. "You think Eclipse owns Bantam as a shell corporation?"

"What do you think?"

He fished out his canteen and drank. "I'm sure they own many corporations."

Wiping sweat from her brow, she said, "It's hard to tell. That's part of the problem."

Walking on the sand and over a sandy embankment, they trekked through the jungle, keeping low.

The spheres. What were they? And the disc. The United States owned something so advanced, it dwarfed any known technology. Now it was in Eclipse's hands. One disc was bad enough, but if Polaris could seize it and reverse engineer it, with the little she witnessed from the disc, they'd dominate the world. As it stood, war looked inevitable. China blaming the United States and vise versa. A disc and spheres used against both. The world's economy would soon crash. Chaos.

Exactly what that bastard Flynn wanted. He'd ratchet up the situation soon.

She halted outside a small clearing. "This could take a while, and we don't have a lot of time. I suspected we'd see tracks or evidence by now, but there's no sign of construction. There should be something here. We haven't seen *any* tracks."

"The structure is under the water and there has to be a way down from the island to whatever they built below it. If not, they would get there by...."

They both spoke. "Submarine."

Jackson pointed east. "Back to the beach."

She took point, making sure to avoid obvious paths where troops might look.

He excused himself to pee, and she drank water and ate a handful of peanuts.

Once they reached the beach, it looked perfect for landings and for setting up encampments.

If I were in charge of this island, I'd make it appear uninhabited and dangerous. And I would station my jamming equipment here. "Grab your EMF again. See if it works."

He shook his head.

"Nothing?" she asked, facing away and keeping their flanks and rear secure while he used binoculars to survey.

"Don't see anything. Seaweed. Seashells. Tracks. Wait. Found something. Boat tracks."

"Let me take a look. Watch our six." She took the binoculars. "I see them. Two F470 CRRC tracks. Inflatable rafts."

"They must have left recently. The tide would wash away the sand." Jackson pointed out where the island extended in a sharp triangular jut further into the ocean. A cluster of coconut trees grew close to a hill. "They could have gone around the bend."

Farther down the beach, humps of sand stuck above the earth. She furrowed her brow and squinted.

"What are they?" he asked.

"By their size, I'd say buried barrels. It's common for Eclipse to store their supplies this way and hide them."

"And a few more in that direction. Five more near the bluff. Is it clear?"

She handed him the binoculars. "Here. Cover me."

They bounded toward the mounds, scanning for enemies.

She stopped ahead of him. "Wait. Look."

Dead birds littered the ground. The air was still.

"Check your Geiger counter," she said.

When he did, he quickly turned it off. "Reading is point

one. Could be uranium. If so, one barrel is leaking. We can't stay here."

She checked her submachine gun. "I have something to help with that." She handed him iodine tablets to prevent radiation from collecting in their thyroids. "Follow me."

"If my future babies have green skin, I'm blaming you."

They pushed aside banana leaves half the size of their bodies as they left the beach and entered the jungle. Shadows from the jungle's canopy covered them, and their view encompassed the ocean and the barrels.

Jackson shifted to the side and away from a line of red ants.

She gestured toward the sea. "Look."

From the water, what appeared to be an upright tube, emerged from the depths. In the dim light, it soon became clear it wasn't that at all.

"Submarine."

J ackson scooted forward. "Perfect. Now we just need to convince them to pilot us underneath the water and take us where they came from. Should be easy."

"Somehow, I don't think they're going to be too keen on that idea," she said. "It's a DSV-6 Turtle. I'm familiar with its sister sub." The DSV-2 Alvin class deep-submergence vehicle was years ahead of its time and was part of a secret rollout for the DEA for interdiction.

The submarine's bridge bubbled out of the water. Attached to it, silver antennas stuck upward like thin spikes. The submersible's outer hull surfaced a moment later.

The bridge's hatch opened. Men in black wetsuits climbed out. In seconds, the commandos deployed a raft and floated a series of steel cages to the island with the help of heavy-duty inflatable floaties. Once on the beach, they hurried to the barrels, dug them from the sand, and secured them, carefully dragging them into the ocean. Did they know about the radiation leak?

"That's enough uranium to create a serious dirty bomb. Can we afford to let them take it to the sub?" he asked.

"Not part of our mission."

"You've said that before."

She sighed.

Jackson quoted from his training. "To help maintain international stability, it will become necessary for an agent to act outside mission parameters."

The men in wetsuits carried around a barrel and set it inside a cage.

"This isn't a normal mission."

"We saved your tiger. We're doing this. If you insist, tell Director Hill I made a bad call." Jackson aimed.

She wiped a bead of sweat from her eye. *Okay, I guess we are going to kill people.* Positioning herself on one knee, she targeted the farthest man. "I'll take the two on the left. You, the two on the right."

Lining up the sights, she executed a commando. Shifting her aim, she sent a shot, dropping another. Jackson dropped the rest. The ambush lasted seconds. All four men lay lifeless on the beach.

They hustled to the dead.

The submarine sat still in the water.

Gore was splattered across the sand, and she searched the corpses down for intelligence and stacked their weapons. The radiation would be leaking into the ocean by now, and it wouldn't be long until someone caught wind of it.

Counting the bodies, she glanced at the sub. The DSV-6 Turtle carried a crew of four, but it could squeeze five.

He stared through the binoculars. "I don't think anyone is inside it."

"We have to hurry, then. I'm sure it has a radio, and someone will contact it if it's late. This is going to be a huge headache, but you were right. If someone gets all this uranium, Director Hill will *not* be happy. I need to call Cormac and request an evac. Scorpion should take care of this. We'll use your evac pad when we're set to leave."

Jackson touched his lips. "I have an idea. I know how to get in touch with the CIA."

"Since when do you know anyone in American intelligence? At any rate, we can't contact them. We're being jammed."

His face stared off into the distance like a man who'd seen too much. "Did you bring any kind of radio?"

"A burner phone." She fished it out of her pack. With an extended range and encryption, it would normally link to a satellite. Because the signal would be traced, it could only be used once and then destroyed.

He inspected the phone, his eyes a million miles away. "Cormac gave that to you?"

"He did. A backup."

"I have an idea."

"What are you doing?"

Unblinking, he robotically disassembled the phone, removed a chip, and rigged it to the EM reader. In under a minute, he was ready to send a coded dispatch.

"It's rigged to send a one-time message to the CIA," he said.

What would it mean for him to call them? How many operatives would they send, or would they contact the Navy? Hill mentioned the deteriorating conditions between China and the United States. Would this exacerbate it?

They could ultimately be used as cannon fodder.

And how in the hell did Stone know someone in the CIA?

"How well do you know your contact?"

"Well. I'll make the call."

He sent a coded dispatch, and it fried both the phone and the device. "Sending both signals overloaded it." He buried them under the sand.

The pungent smell of burned electronics made her hold her breath. "How confident are you the message was relayed?"

"I'm certain."

"You'll have to show me how to do that sometime."

After stripping down the men on the beach, they slipped on their wetsuits and waded into the ocean. Like bathwater, the sea was warm.

Salt dripped into her mouth. As she ducked under a wave, she spat and rolled, righting herself and kicking. Gasping for air, she wheezed in and out and took in a deep breath, duck-diving under the surface.

Back down until she saw the submarine's hull. She glided her hand up the side as she came out of the water, Jackson behind her. Her fingers found the handholds to the bridge, and she climbed in headfirst and dropped her bag down the hatch. He scurried down after her.

She stepped between oxygen tanks on racks, fins next to them, and sat on one of the two seats that made up the cockpit.

Jackson glowered at the controls. "You know how to pilot one of these?"

"Basically." She grabbed the control stick on the middle console. The sub bobbed up and down on the ocean's surface.

"There's a black site not far from here," she said. "I suspect the Americans will send a sizable force. They aren't keen on uranium sitting around."

"Aren't you an American?"

She shrugged. "Sometimes." Polaris and the CIA weren't

allies, and she was hard-pressed to think of any intel agency she could trust. People, yes. Organizations, no. The agents themselves—she'd dealt with the gregarious good and the beastly bad. Some people so crooked, she wondered if some dark force controlled them from behind the scenes.

Instruments, dials, and gauges glowed in abundance. Switches covered the walls and ceiling. Two computer screens faced her, but only one of them worked. The other bled colored lines into the image like purple, yellow, and green icicles. This submarine differed from the one she'd been trained to operate. But a sub was a sub, right?

She closed the hatch, pressurized the ship, and engaged the submerge lever, steering it under the water. Bubbles foamed and drifted upward as they descended.

Compared to the one she'd piloted with Dubois, this boat reacted slowly to her commands, like a lenses teenager. Interesting that they weren't using a Chinese or Russian submarine.

She turned to Jackson. "A little rusty. Nothing to worry about."

"Me worried?"

The sub's light pierced the darkness of the ocean, and the hull dragged across another bed of coral, cracking it to shreds. They lurched forward, and Jackson planted his head in the bubble window in front of him.

She frowned. "Believe it or not, I do know what I'm doing. I think." They continued their descent, her heart jumping to her throat. "There it is."

Between two rocks, what appeared to be a massive cavern bore deep into the island. Metal beams grew wider the closer they came to the ocean floor, and they held up a long, expansive black and silver facility. Tinted windows made up the front, and although it was a few football fields wide, the true dimensions were embedded inside the rock.

Underwater walkway tubes reached from the large main structure to smaller domes, and from the submarine's light beaming through the ocean, she could see tunnels connecting each dome.

Someone had been very busy.

She pushed hard left on the control stick. Holding her breath, she gasped as the sub surged upward from another impact. A cavern wall appeared.

Jackson leaned away from the window. "Should we don our scuba gear?"

The stick wouldn't move. The engine coughed, and she smelled smoke coming from the aft.

Alarms blinked on the console.

"It's unresponsive." Somehow, she'd killed it.

He got up from his seat and turned his head. "I'm going to fix the engine."

"Hang on!"

The submarine impacted rock, and they jerked forward on impact. Plumes of blinding debris clouds burst outward.

A ping clanked against the outer hull.

"What was that?" he asked.

A handful of commandos in scuba gear swam and attached themselves to the hull with heavy magnets. One of them turned and drew his Pii pistol.

She winced. "Looks like someone wants their sub back."

A s a slapping sound hit the sub's hull, it dipped abruptly. Jackson lifted off his seat an inch.

"They're attaching something." Alabama stood with her hands on the front bubbled glass shield. She craned her neck, doing her best to get a good look. "They're fastening hooks to the rocks. I bet the prop is tied or broken. We aren't going anywhere."

"Let's put on scuba gear and prep to pop the hatch."

Flynn appeared on a screen mounted in the center console. He wore a tailored suit and a red power tie that would make a billionaire blush. A cigar burned between his fingers. "CIA, how may I direct your call?"

Jackson's stomach hardened. Flynn. He'd intercepted the transmission. He covered his image, and cut the video and double-checked to make sure their mic was muted.

"Keep him busy," she said. "It'll give us time."

"For what?"

She shrugged. "Still working on that."

Jackson unmuted himself. "Hunter Flynn." Even his name made his veins burn with unnatural hate. "So once you're done causing the world to panic, what do you intend to do? Walk down the disc ramp and declare yourself Jesus Christ?"

Flynn roared with laughter. "I like the way you think, Stone. No, nothing so small. Without you, I might have failed, but as you probably know by now, China and the United States will soon be at war."

If Flynn continued his actions, that may damn well be true. Jackson stared at the comm. A red light blinked.

Jumping over the small barrier between the cockpit and the sub's cargo bay, Alabama pointed to the radio. *Keep him talking,* she mouthed.

He heard Flynn relight his cigar, and the sound of him twirling a lighter's flame around it. "Have you ever wondered why movie villains always explain their plans to the protagonist?"

"Because they feel the need to justify their evil?" Jackson asked.

"Because they hope to be understood. We both desire the truth, don't we? And there's so much to know. The Dove Sequence is coming, and to whose benefit? Do you want to see it occur?"

"When I find you, I'm going to kill you, Flynn." He cut the audio feed.

"Oxygen tanks." Alabama smiled at him as she strapped on a tank and grabbed another off the rack for Jackson.

He made his way to her side and put the tank on his back. She opened his valve. Thin, cold oxygen pulled nicely through his mouth and down his throat through his mouthpiece.

As they pulled their fins on, Alabama tilted her head toward a set of revolving firearms with five barrels hanging on a rack.

She gave him one. "HK PII. Five darts. It's hard to hit anything while you're swimming, so don't fire too far from your target. We don't want to carry too much weight. They have a few Glocks in their armory. Put this ammo belt on. Here." She handed him a quick reload for the dart gun. "We're outnumbered, and it's been good working with you."

As he buckled the belt and slung a bandolier across his chest, he couldn't help but watch Alabama. What if this was it, his last day of his life? Right now, he could drop all his emotional baggage about Nicki and tell Alabama how beautiful she was.

What a strange urge. His hand shook.

Would it be unprofessional?

As stupid as it sounded, the urge burned so hotly, the thoughts became all-consuming.

Your name isn't Alabama Wren.

A commando knocked on the cockpit window, hammered the hull, and planted an explosive the size of a computer speaker.

Boom!

Glass flew past them. The rush of incoming water lifted him off his feet, and his tank clanked against the ceiling.

The sub dropped. He felt a vice crushing his eyes and ears, and he pressed his nostrils together with his fingers and blew outward, so his ears didn't rupture.

Alabama tugged on him, and he followed her out of the shattered window. Thousands of bubbles camouflaged their escape.

Rising higher, they kicked their fins. Off in the distance, the commandos swam closer.

A dart burst from a soldier's dart gun zipped between them, sticking into the cave wall. Jackson pushed himself down, dodging more darts coming his way.

Jackson targeted a soldier closing in on him. Aiming through the cloud of dirt, he fired. In the dim light from the sub, he watched the enemy's gun drift into the abyss. The enemy reached up to his neck and yanked out the large steel dart stuck in his flesh. Blood seeped from his wetsuit. He swam up for a moment and fell limp.

Clear the pressure. Relax. Don't panic. Jackson squeezed his nostrils and blew out.

Another man headed for Alabama. Her shot punctured his breastbone, piercing the heart.

A dart rocketed past Jackson's face. As he flung himself left, another one caught him on the side, skimming his wetsuit and ripping it. A trickle of blood streamed toward the surface.

He fired back, but swimming made aiming nearly impossible, and the shot missed wide.

A dart plinked the white rock inches above Jackson's head. He inhaled deep and pushed off, lining up the sights of his HK P11. The enemy swam backward, retrieving a reload for his pistol.

Gaining distance, Jackson became a spear and squeezed the trigger, never more sure of a direct hit in his life.

But the dart missed low.

A pair of goggles suddenly appeared in front of him. Bearing down on Jackson, the commando grappled him by the shoulders and pulled him in. Jackson grabbed the enemy's fingers and tried to pry them free, but his grip was iron.

The man slammed his knee into Jackson's lower rib. A sharp pain ran up his side as his mouthpiece was knocked free. Saltwater rushed in his mouth, and he fought the urge to inhale.

Air. Can't breathe....

Jackson swiped the man's head and yanked off the attacker's goggles and mouthpiece.

Panic rose in the man's eyes. Jackson reached back with his arm, felt the tube at his inner elbow, and fished it upward.

Jackson shoved his mouthpiece back in, cleared the water, and breathed in a huge gulp of the tank's air.

With his feet, Jackson pushed off, his fist clutching the man's air tank tube. Using all his strength, he yanked. The tube snapped, and the man kicked and flailed until unstrapping his scuba gear and bolting toward the surface.

Alabama gave Jackson a signal. Out of ammo. Then she pointed at a nearby dome.

He saw it. A hole the size of a small, round pool. He propelled himself onward. On the way, he reloaded.

Once they reached the opening, Alabama placed her palm straight and raised her head. Artificial light bled through the water, and he could see a chamber inside the cavern.

A pressurized cave? By using this as an entrance, the architect could use its trapped air.

He poked his head up. A well-lit domed room, along with small submersibles on tracks, stared back at him.

My God. This place is massive.

He removed his goggles and tossed them on the floor, past the edge of the pool and at the base of a midget sub. Alabama emerged, her red hair darkened from the water.

"No one here?" she asked.

"Not at the moment." Jackson pushed himself out of the water and set the HK P11 aside and pulled out his Glock.

Alarms blared, and the lights dimmed.

He twirled his finger. "That's not good."

She sat on the edge, taking off her fins. "Looks like the cavalry has arrived."

"What do you mean? Flynn intercepted the message."

"Either Cormac retransmitted the signal or ocean sensors detected the radioactivity."

"We might make it through this after all."

The dome's lights dimmed in rhythm with the siren's blare. Jackson raced to pull his scuba gear and dropped it next to hers. They sprinted, stopping behind a mini-sub, and crouched.

Three more mini-subs sat in rows beside them. Connecting into the rock, the dome's metallic wall continued on the other side and met with the enclosed walkway tube leading to the main underwater complex.

Jackson glanced at a round mirror-like ball in the corner and pointed it out. There were few places to hide from the concealed bubble camera.

"Wish we had another wand," he said, pointing it out.

"Shoot it."

He aimed. *Pop*! It shattered, camera pieces bouncing on the floor.

Boots tapped on the metallic floor in front of the subs. Shooting the camera this early exposed them. Great.

"On me!" Smart replies came in order. They were running to the other side, unconcerned about the subs or them. Was something else happening inside the base more important than him blowing out a camera less than fifty yards away from them?

"Chen, how many Americans?" a man asked with a thick, Slavic accent.

Jackson focused his hearing. How many boots?

Ten to twelve men, not including the Russian or Chen. Make it fourteen. Probably armored in Kevlar. Assume two shots for a kill at this range. Fifteen rounds in the Glock's mag. Factor in Alabama. We'll kill half before they react if we're lucky.

Let them go and face them on their terms?

Not today.

They exchanged glances and nodded in understanding.

Jackson peeked. Fifteen men. Some of them in a shirts and ties. Six armed with a mix of A-545s, a rifle used by the Spetsnaz and other Russian Special Forces, and short-stock M4s.

The men dressed as civilians carried MP-443 Grach pistols. Eighteen shots in each.

Jackson let rip, clipping a rifleman's jaw, and he dropped.

Thud.

Center mass.

Thud.

Head shot.

Splat.

Three more dead. Five. Six down. Seven down. Blood pooled.

He continued rolling and took cover as gunfire lit the room. Pangs. Ricochets. Jackson rounded the sub away from the gunshots and looked.

Two riflemen retreated toward the tube, a point man guarding the tube's entrance. Jackson pointed his weapon around the sub's bow, leveled his aim, and squeezed the trigger. The commando's rifle blasted auto-fire as he died. Alabama positioned herself behind them and picked off the rest. There would be no quarter given.

Jackson picked up an M4 and three magazines.

Saltwater and some type of cleanser flavored the air, like an ocean of Lysol. A red stripe was painted along the side of the wall.

Would someone turn off that damn alarm?

Once they crossed the tube and reached the main facility, they skidded to a halt.

Orders echoed throughout. Metallic walls glinted off LED lights. Beams ran just below the low ceiling. With the help of the metal supports, Jackson and Hill snuck into a room with armored rectangular shells sitting middle.

The shells touched the ceiling, measuring the length of a bread truck. Wires weaved in and out like Christmas lights. Two large water tanks stood on either side.

"We blow that, this place floods," she said.

But without an air tank, they'd be swept away by the water and drown.

Jackson motioned toward a corridor which connected to the control room. "This way."

A moment later, a deep-voiced woman silenced the cacophony of confusion. The men stopped speaking. "I want all of you to go down that tube and guard the entrance. Jerry, you take Vlad and eight others and search the sub docks."

Jackson turned to Alabama. *Same plan?* he asked with his eyes.

One small nod from her.

The clap of feet became louder.

Here goes nothing.

Jackson emerged from a shell and blazed through an

entire magazine. After the first burst, she joined in the mayhem, gunning them down without a thought. He slammed in a fresh mag.

Muzzle flashes and splattering blood.

Everyone lay still.

"Watch the halls," Alabama said, retrieving a Russian pistol next to a corpse.

The lights pulsed red, and their piercing wail drove spikes into his ears. A few of the bodies carried large Bowie knives, and she gave one to Jackson.

He discovered an M4, and he took and pilfered a few mags.

Then a woman's voice next to him. "It's you," she said.

Jackson lurched back.

Alabama hadn't reached the woman yet, but she'd be dead without immediate medical attention.

Her hair had partially grayed, and she bore scars on her face and hands. A bullet had found her abdomen.

Alabama bent down, grabbed her navy blue blouse, and pulled her in. Blood dripped from the woman's lips.

"I never thought I'd see you again," the woman said, giving a fake smile. She hacked up blood, and it dribbled out of her mouth.

"Where's the disc?" Alabama asked, pointing the gun under the woman's chin.

She coughed, harder this time, and began to lose consciousness.

"Tell me and I'll make sure your family is protected."

The woman turned her gaze to Jackson. "Don't." Blood seeped. "Don't let Polaris have it." Her eyes remained open, but she stopped blinking.

Then, from every corridor, voices.

"In the control room. Charge!"

Jackson and Alabama sprinted down the northern tube, hip shooting in stride. As soldiers unleashed hell behind them, Jackson flung himself prone and aimed south, protecting their six. Alabama sprinted ahead.

Voices coming closer. Closer.

"Is that him?" someone asked. "I only see one."

A few troopers looked down the corridor.

"Hey you!" a man called out to Alabama.

Boom!

Kill shot.

Crack!

Pop. Pop. Pop.

"We're pinned down! Send reinforcements!"

The world was a blur of colors and sweat.

"Motorpool, up ahead," Alabama said.

I was trained for this.

The next chamber contained light tactical vehicles known as MRAPS, Humvees, and an elevator that rose through the rock and would likely take it to the island above. Other tubes led off in different directions. How big *was* this place?

Compressed air tanks sat next to a gas pump connected to an olive drab fuel cylinder.

Alabama found cover behind an MRAP.

"I feel like we're lost," he said.

"Ammo check."

"Two extra mags for this." Jackson held his rifle and pointed to his spare pistol magazines.

A loud blast reverberated. The base shuttered.

He pulled her down. "Look out!"

A blinding fireball exploded, and the world turned midnight.

J ackson's body smashed against the wall, the whiplash causing his head to bang violently. The world spun and spun; a twist of colors. A water tank crashed onto the ground, and gunshots popped from every direction, echoing against the walls. Bullets tagged metal.

"Check behind the vehicles!" a man with a Russian accent shouted.

His head pounded with fury, but Alabamas recovery spurred him on and he collected his senses. The bump rising on top of his head would have to wait.

Jackson gritted his teeth and drilled three-round bursts into advancing troopers wearing Russian camo. Every burst hit its target, and the enemy dropped, sliding to a halt. His breaths came fast.

Alabama slowly turned her head. Her brows crinkled, and she wiped the sweat off her face. "Get their ammo."

"The explosion was a breach."

As he searched them, she kept her aim down the tubes,

switching from one to the next while keeping her back pressed to the wall.

Jackson slid in a new magazine.

"Hide," Alabama said.

In slow motion, he caught sight of United States Special Forces closing in their position, their movements coordinated and precise. Eyes landed on him, and he froze.

One of the men stood out from the rest, an older black man who wore his uniform with staunch pride. Jackson had never met him before, but he knew his name, where he lived, where he grew up, and recalled spending time on the range with him. He could've sworn they'd been neighbors once.

David Dennis Davis, the man who always caught flak for his name. His friends called him Trip D, but mostly DD, sometimes Daredevil.

The more Jackson looked at him, the stranger he felt. Had they met once before? Polaris training?

Jackson set his M4 down and raised his hands. "DD, it's me."

DD pulled out two sets of zip ties. "Come out! On the ground!"

Alabama emerged from hiding. Her expression switched from anger to indignation to fury.

"I'm the one who called you," Jackson said. Then, a thought manifested and rose to his lips. His transplanted heart thumped in his throat, his mind on autopilot. "Bravo Tango Alpha Zulu Eight Six."

DD narrowed his eyes. "Charlie Delta Leema Five One Six. I haven't seen you before. You going with us?"

CDL516. The code rang hollow, but he'd spoken the right words, meaning—Independent operators from the Pentagon.

"No, sir. Tell Maggie I said hello."

DD disappeared with his team, advancing toward their mutual enemy.

Alabama could only stare. "How did you?..."

The telltale sound of grenades thundered down hallways. Flashbangs exploded. Gunfire erupted from all directions. Bursts of light. Lightning in smoke clouds. How many were there?

Jackson touched his chest.

"Down here!" the enemy shouted.

They ran down what looked like a newly drilled tunnel leading further into the rock. Half the lights worked, but much of the tunnel was veiled in shadow. Wall-mounted ventilation fans dispersed the smoke.

A man dressed in a black suit dashed down the hall carrying a Chinese Type 95 rifle. As he raised it, Jackson squeezed off a burst, hitting the wall behind the man.

The man in the suit yelled bloody murder in Chinese and struggled to flip the safety off.

Alabama peeled off bursts behind them.

Jackson's next round impacted the same wall. The man shot.

Crack!

A sharp pain in his hand.

The sights aligned and Jackson squeezed the trigger. Another down.

His finger burned like lava.

Crimson gushed.

Pain.

Alabama gasped. "You're hit!"

"**G**razed." Jackson held up a mangled finger. The bullet had clipped the side of his ring finger, tearing half of it away. It flopped backward against his hand, and his teeth clacked tight. The bone was shattered, the tendons shredded. Somehow, through the agony, he kept his composure.

Alabama leaned in to get a better look.

Well, that looks painful.

She patted him on the shoulder. "It will hurt when you least expect it, but push through the pain."

Down the other end of the tunnel, muzzles flashed. A commando tumbled to the ground. Her pulse raced like quicksilver as Jackson's blood pooled down his arm. Today, Jackson had proved his valor.

What a mess. "Give me your finger." She went over the person who'd shot him, tore off a piece of his clothing, and used it to dress Jackson's wound. *You're going to lose this.* "Ignore the pain." She grabbed his shoulders.

He shook and drew his Glock. "The disc."

Running would increase his heart rate and blood loss. If

she cauterized it, he'd never be able to regrow it. Polaris' technology worked miracles, but it had limits.

"Double-time walk," she said. "Don't run. If you feel light-headed, tell me."

"My finger?"

"Yes. Try to relax. I know it hurts."

The tunnel ended in a small chamber with plants growing in rectangular stone pots. But like the other rooms, it functioned as a wheel hub with tunnel spokes leading to different parts of the base. They cleared room after room.

Almost there.

But it wasn't the disc she was here to find.

Something far more important to her.

"Stone, I'm going to need a favor from you."

"What?"

Then around a corner, she found an office corridor, five doors on each side of the hallway. The blue walls were shut, each of them with a DNA sniffer next to them. An elegant glass desk stood in front of the hallway.

Jackson winced. "The disc isn't down there."

She faced an office door and met Stone's eyes. "There's something I have to do."

"I don't understand."

Alabama stopped at the fourth door on her left. This one. Surely, it had to be. Jackson wouldn't understand, but he should trust her and listen to her.

She'd done her best and now she needed him to do one simple thing. Just one thing.

"Guard the door," she said.

"You can't be serious. We're after a disc."

She checked his finger. The bandage was soaked.

"Are you able to fight?"

"Yes. The pain comes in and out."

"Did I question you about the Americans who didn't kill us?"

He shook his head.

"Trust me, Stone."

A DNA card reader and an eye scanner glowed next to the door.

The card. She'd stuck it in the box containing a pair of special contact lens. Director Hill came through once again. After putting in the contact lenses, she blinked away the slight burn and let the eye scanner operate.

The door clicked. She entered and flipped on the lights. A computer screen. An old wooden desk. A picture was taped on the desk bureau. Nice Italian leather chair.

This *was* the right office. Dubois had told her the truth. Though she wished he would have said it was under the sea.

She locked herself in. "Stone?"

Panic framed his words. "Forty-five seconds."

"Go find the disc. When you do, destroy it. Mission first, mission last. Remember the code phrase for exfiltration?"

He pounded on the door. "Open up. Let's go. I'm not leaving you here."

She faced him and put her hand on the door. Taking deep, rapid breaths, she closed her eyes.

Who was Jackson Stone?

It was time to find out.

None of her training had prepared her for this.

Her heart expanded into beams of white energy. Love, pure, sensing through reality.

As she pushed her empathic abilities, a buzz sounded in her ears and geometric patterns began to appear on every surface.

More. I must know.

Her mind branched out, finding the truth hidden behind Stone's facade.

An outline of him behind the door.

Emotions.

A tinge of fear. Eagerness. Surprising focus.

"Wren, open the door."

Pain. Frustrations. His soul burned and collapsed and rose like a phoenix.

This would likely be the last time she saw him. She'd taught him enough to survive. It would be up to him, now. There was something special about him; Director Hill was right. Like seeing a four-leaf clover or his soul. There, in whites and blues and reds and purples. Swishing.

A second ticked.

Slow.

The clock moved at a hundredth of normal speed.

Jackson humming in French.

Tu oublieras / Les sourires, les regards / Qui parlaient d'éternité

You will forget / The smiles, the looks / That spoke of eternity.

Jackson's subtle smiles. His powerful eyes that locked her in place.

Jackson's reaction inside the submarine.

Jackson's favorite pistol.

Jackson's music.

She shook her head.

I trust you now and for reasons I shouldn't, and I care about you for reasons I can't explain. I know you'll do the right thing where others have failed.

"Mission first, mission last," she said to him.

He paused. "There's something I want to...." Bullets zapped down the hallway. Automatic weapons came in hot. "I'll... I'll come back. Wait here."

I know you will.

Now alone, she stepped toward the picture. She couldn't believe her eyes. Hunter Flynn standing next to Dubois, right there in color. All smiles and cheer. In front of them, mailbags stuffed with stacks of hard-fought American cash. Behind them, rows of soldiers in various uniforms boarded a C-130.

Director Hill's orders repeated in her head.

"Gather intel to stop Flynn and destroy the disc. If necessary, Polaris will ensure the disc is destroyed if you cannot. I know neither you nor Stone have what it takes to defeat Flynn, but bring back any information to assist our analyst teams."

But this wasn't about what *Hill* wanted. It was what she wanted. The truth.

Pulling the box insert out, she found a USB card, pushed it into the computer, and used it to boot to a new operating system. The card installed a JU-8 password adjudicator, and when the computer shut itself down, she withdrew the USB stick and waited for the computer to POST. At the login screen, she typed "1234" for the username and "password" for the password. Always the classics.

The JU-8 worked behind the scenes, taking her information and logging her in. When the desktop background appeared, she recoiled.

What was on his screen?

A picture of *her*?

It was taken when she was with Dubois, during the good times. When he still loved her or at least she believed he did. Summertime, right there on the border of Ecuador. She'd worn a skimpy top, mini shorts, and huge glitter sunglasses that made everyone stare at her.

In the upper corner of the screen, she noticed a black circle icon. A network connection.

Before clicking it, she pondered again and began cloning files.

A faint cigar smell loomed in the background.

As she copied the files, an emerging flood of errors appeared.

Smart. Someone had thought ahead. She wouldn't be able to transfer them this way.

The screen blinked between the login screen and the desktop background.

ERROR

ERROR

ERROR

The blinking then strobed, flashing faster and faster and faster.

Which way to get it inside the system?

The screen froze.

LOGIN

It worked.

Alabama typed in commands, uploading a Batch-Z-0 worm. It replicated, injecting invisible code into the system's security, destroying and overriding permissions, and mutating files.

A virus, indeed.

Then batches of programs flooded into the system, hacking their way through vulnerabilities like the Visigoths sacking Rome. All those months programming for this one event.

Please work.

Then, the computer screen turned an off-yellow and pulsed.

Partial success with limited time. As the yellow faded to

black, Alabama delved deep into the computer's files, blasting through encryption and state-of-the-art firewalls.

Bilderberg Group? She scrunched her lips. *Where is the craft?*

Is this it?

The Dove Sequence.
Diminish populations to sustainable levels.
Nano-Cloud Disbursement. *See Weather Modification.
Genetically Modified Food Systems.
IMF Administration Protocols.
Elections.
Vaccine Graft Sequence.
U.N. Military Operations.
Real ID and Shadowing.
Cloning.
DNA Auditing and Tracking.
Cryptocurrency Manipulation.
Softcore Data Correction.
Human-Animal Genetic Splicing.
Consciousness Configuration Security.
Cure Suppressions.
Blue Zone Eradications.
Planetary Ecosystem Synthesis.
Red Print EYE.
Trans-Dimensional Echo Location.
TORC.
Project Horizon.

My God, what is Flynn doing? Gunshots cracked like fire-crackers behind the office door. *Hurry. Hurry.*

Personality Replication.
J-Test.
Dubois Lavigne.

There it is. Finally.

Organ Tissue Recovered.
Cellular memory/nano YTIT-ATAT.
Gain of function memory transfer.
Enhancement Feature Tracking/Skill Acquire.
Biological adhesive.

What the hell?

She held her breath. Dubois was buried in a casket near Normandy, where one of her great-grandfathers died on Omaha Beach. Could they transfer memories from one person to another? Did Flynn dig up Dubois' bones and use his DNA?

Words glowed on the monitor. "OP9.DLL. Tunnelfish.exe. Trident Overload. MALWARE FOUND."

Malware? She didn't load those files.

She ran a redundancy kit, hoping to find the problem.

Who loaded malware onto her USB?

The screen darkened and the computer shut down. "Great."

Boom!

The door blasted open.

"It's you."

She jumped to her feet and raised her weapon.

J ackson bled. He grunted, the pain spreading through his ribs. His finger dangled by a thread inside the bandage. Better than losing a leg or an arm. If the disc wasn't here, what then?

He cleared rooms. Full auto. Semi-auto. One-shot kills into enemies along darkened corridors, an alarm piercing the black. His heart thumped steady, the rhythm pulsing in his wound.

Flynn has probably left with the disc. I should go back to Wren.

"Wren, respond." Silence. "Wren, come in." Her face appeared in his mind. Her hair. Her smile and sense of humor. "Wren, tu m'entends?"

Wait, I don't speak French. Don't think about her. Mission first, mission last. Go.

Jackson crept forward, listening to gunfire echoing in the tubes. He stayed far enough away from the main gun battles, skirting them rather than running directly into combat.

Swallowing, his mind more alert than ever before, he couldn't stop repeating what he'd said.

I don't speak French.

I don't speak French.

And with every passing moment and squeeze of the trigger, his focus increased. Was this what Alabama felt? This emptiness?

Up ahead, a ladder offered a way down, and Jackson dropped into a lower part of the facility. The space narrowed, only wide enough for two go-karts to travel side by side. Where were the emergency hatches in case of a flood?

Water reached as high as his boots. After a few steps, the lights died, amplifying the quiet.

One more time. "Wren, do you copy?"

Flashlight beams bore holes through the darkness, the light emerging from the north. Where was there to go? Jackson climbed up the ladder and waited.

Someone gave muffled commands. The man's voice held worry.

A soldier in a black beret and Russian camo sprinted ahead, wielding a rifle. Men and women in lab coats hurried after him. Keeping a good distance, Jackson followed them, descending a slanted ramp.

They lead him to a chamber filled with computer workstations and stacks of advanced military-grade electronic hardware, enough to launch one of Elon Musk's rockets.

Or a disc.

Scientists sat at a dozen stations, furiously typing and demanding answers from one another. A map of the world glowed on a paper-thin screen. A handful of engineers and scientists studied charts, confused. One of them pulled a 9mm from his waistband and set it next to a coffee mug. A few of the scientists became silent and stared at their screens.

The base shook.

"This place is going to explode," a woman said in desperation. "Do you want us to die?"

As more concussion blasts rocked the facility, Jackson put his back against the wall and stood akimbo. Inside their room, the power worked.

I can gun down one side of the room. But then, I'm trapped. The disc. It has to be close or controlled remotely from here. If I can get to a computer, I should be able to contact Wren. No, I must contact her. I'm not leaving without her.

Jackson peeked around the corner.

A man wearing body armor picked up a phone and dialed. He was built like a battleship, with arms twice the size of Jackson's thigh.

He hung up. "Your families will be taken care of, but we have been ordered to hold our positions. Spectra lockdown."

Loud gasps could be heard as the scientists stopped typing.

"That can't be right," a soldier with a Virginian accent said. He wiped the sweat off his brow, downed the rest of his coffee, and made a phone call. "Sir, Captain Parker here. I've received word we're to Spectra the station?" He lowered his voice to a whisper.

Take him out first. He's their commander. What am I going to do with the scientists?

"Yes, sir," Captain Parker said, "I understand, but we're preparing the disc. We're working to.... Sir, if we detonate now, we won't have time to evacuate." A pause. "Understood, sir. It has been a pleasure." The soldier closed his eyes and set the phone down. "Listen up!"

Heads turned.

"No one is coming to save us. Your duty to Eclipse is reaching its conclusion."

Desperate murmurs. Pleadings fell on deaf ears. Everyone looked at each other, but no one had an answer for what was yet to come.

Captain Parker raised his hand. "I want to thank you for your sacrifice to the cause. I know for many of you, this is not the end, but a new beginning, unlike anything you thought possible. Do not be alarmed when you wake up."

A woman with short bangs and thick glasses slammed her fist. "This isn't right! Our children!"

A scientist snatched the handgun. "I'm not dying here. You people are crazy!"

Jackson slid out his knife. *Here we go.*

"Put that down right now!" Captain Parker barked. "Professor, we have worked for many months together. You knew what could happen. Your work has been invaluable, and you and your family have been compensated."

The scientist thumbed off the safety. "You've kidnapped all of our families, and you expect us to go along with this? Let us out, you bastard!"

Every scientist in the room stood and shouted.

"Yeah, let us out!"

"You can't keep us locked up anymore!"

"I'm not going to let you kill my family!"

"We aren't going to listen to your orders."

A scientist raised his pistol. "We are done taking orders from you!"

Before Jackson would react, a guard downed the scientist in half a second.

Time for Jackson to earn his pay.

Across from Alabama, Hunter Flynn showed his teeth.

"I see you've found my office." He held up his empty hands. "I'm unarmed."

In her hand, she gripped her pistol, but it weighed as much as a house. "What have you done?"

"Aren't you going to shoot me, Alabama? That's what your name is now, isn't it? I barely recognized you. Hmm. I never believed perfection could be improved, but a little here and there and behold: a goddess."

Placing a hand behind her, she pulled the USB drive out of the computer and slid it into her back pocket. The pistol dropped to the ground. Her teeth ached, and pressure built under her eyes.

"What are you doing?" she asked, holding both sides of her head. "Where is Dubois? Is he alive?"

"Is that why you're here?"

A cold sensation flickered from her navel and crystalized over her body. She shivered as the hairs on her body stood.

Did he drug me; taint the air? "Where...is he? I know...he's alive."

Flynn pulled the chair away from the desk and told her to sit. When she did, he rubbed his jaw. "My, my. What love does to people."

The taste of copper and plastic coated her tongue. "You've drugged the air."

He gestured to a vent. "A precaution I added. Never assume the gates will be enough to bar the fortress, so they say. I'm surprised you didn't smell it."

The cigar smell.

Grimacing, he put his hands on his hips. "Dubois said you'd promised to not interfere."

She coughed and tried to wipe her eyes with her sleeves. But even that required too much strength. "You're going to start a world war."

"Yes. There is no other way." He pulled down the picture of Dubois and himself, smiled at it, and slid it into his pocket. "You're a beautiful woman. It's no wonder Dubois had feelings for you. I have always wondered what it's like to be in love." He stepped closer and sniffed her hair. "I have never told Director Hill or anyone else in Polaris about your relationship with Dubois. I would never betray my best friend, and it's the reason you're still alive."

As he moved away, he leaned against the door. She wheezed, her lungs begging for clean air. Why wasn't he affected?

"And Stone?" she asked.

"It never ceases to amaze me what my organization can accomplish. Answers aren't always pretty, Agent Wren. Sometimes, things get messy. Sometimes, people want things done behind the scenes, and they don't want to be implicated. The way of the world, I guess."

"You left Polaris and slaughtered dozens of our agents."

Flynn squared his shoulders and mulled over his answer. "I did what I had to do to make sure the human race survives. And that's what I will do now. If humanity unites, it won't be under the auspices of freedom, Alabama Wren. For far too long, Polaris has sat back and done nothing to stop the formation of a one-world government. Do you know why?"

Stone, I hope you've found the disc.

"You're insane."

"No, you've impeded progress. Do you know what they intended to do with the disc?"

"Who?" she asked.

"Polaris."

"We intend to destroy it."

Smiling, Flynn looked at her feet. "You intended to steal it and use it yourself."

She made a fist. The air was clearing. "We sought to study it."

"Director Hill is no better than anyone else. He would have used it for his own ends. People in power never change. You have been kept in the dark, agent. Why would Polaris tell you anything? You're a loose cannon, someone who can't be trusted with real intel."

Her toes were free, and she could flex her thighs. Any second.

"And the spheres?"

He frowned. "Well above your security clearance. I could tell you, but then I'd have to kill you, and I won't break that promise."

She launched herself from the chair, an ICBM aimed at Flynn's nose. Landing a hammer fist, she spun around and unholstered his sidearm. Firing blindly behind her back, the shots hit the wall behind him.

He grabbed her pistol arm, shoved it down, and brought his knee up into her elbow. She pulled away in time. The pistol dropped to his boots.

"I thought you were beginning to see reason." He belted her in the chin.

Her blood drooled from her lips as she clawed his face, her eye-hook missing and scratching a deep gouge in his cheek. He threw a jab, and she leaned into it, deadening its impact. Seeing an opening, she buried her teeth into his wounded cheek and pulled, tasting his blood.

Flailing backward, he touched his wound, gnashed his teeth, and growled.

She spat his flesh out and spied the pistol behind him. Her eyes met his, and he glanced down at the firearm. Throwing an elbow, she grazed him as he blocked.

He wagged a finger. "Agent Wren, you're starting to piss me off." He picked her up and threw her into the desk.

Her back slammed against the corner. White-hot pain blurred her vision.

By the time she recovered, he aimed his sidearm at her.

"As I said, I made a promise to Dubois not to kill you, but I have sent others to do what I will not. Perhaps I made a mistake. Perhaps I should have done the thing myself."

He's weak. He won't kill me. But the gun.... There's no way I can get past him to the door in time.

Flynn rested his hand on the doorknob. "I will leave you locked inside. The Americans will find you, and I will leave your fate to them. In which case, your employment at Polaris will come to an end." His expression changed, his eyes darkening. "Do you remember when you asked Dubois about the blue pills he was taking?"

Did he know about that? Rather than answer, she blanked her face, giving no reaction. This bastard didn't deserve the satisfaction.

"You shouldn't have done that." Flynn fired, blowing a hole in her kneecap, exploding the bone inside. Her leg wobbled to the side, supported only by her muscles.

The world went blank.

She screamed silently, the gunshot blast deafening her.

And the door closed behind him, locking her in as she bled to death.

J ackson fired off bursts, dropping three guards in a hail of gunfire. Captain Parker disappeared into the chaos. A scientist picked up the 9mm, aimed at a guard, and with three squeezes of a trigger, sent him into the afterlife. Flames rose from computers and electronic panels. Screens darkened. Sparks popped.

Seconds later, the scientists grabbed rifles from dead guards and shouted war cries.

Jackson squinted and took a knee. A guard began CPR on one of his men, only to be killed for trying.

"Wren," Jackson said into his mic. Nothing.

A guard stood at one of the computers, dead scientists at his feet, and typed like his life depended on it.

Bang!

Down went an enemy. Another.

Captain Parker popped off shots from behind a desk.

Bullets peppered hardware. Two more guards down.

Jackson shifted, incoming bullets missing by a breath. What remained of his ring finger thumped, and the bandage dripped with his blood.

His chest tingled, and an orange flood coated his tongue.

An orange Jello taste. Orange when he needed it the most.

Training inside Polaris. So many hours of repetition.

How many times did they make him eat the gelatin in training?

Then he gasped.

It's your adrenaline. Laisse moi aider.

What?

A thought raced across his mind, a phrase Wren used.

Mission d'abord, mission en dernier.

I don't speak French.

"That you, Stone?" Captain Parker asked.

Jackson rubbed the trigger housing. The air quieted.

"Let me evacuate the scientists," the captain said. "They had nothing to do with this."

Jackson's heart thumped steadily. "Show me your hands."

A woman spoke, her voice full of tears. "He's not going to let us go! Help us, please!" Then a pause. "Wait, wait, don't shoot me."

Boom!

Jackson balanced on his heels and peeked around the corner. Parker's men covered the scientists, and bullets zinged past him.

Unblinking.

Uncaring.

Two squeezes. Target down. Three shots. Two dead. Four shots. Target down. Target down. Another shot, to be sure. Every shot, a hit, every shot, a kill. Target down. Headshot.

Scientists huddled into the fetal position.

Captain Parker raised a .357 Magnum with a laser sight,

and Jackson dove headfirst into the room, a round blasting a light fixture.

A scientist with a knife rose behind Parker and plunged it into his back.

The surviving scientists pulled him to the floor and finished him off, Caeser-style. Parker stopped screaming.

A hunched-over man with liver spots on his face picked up Parker's Magnum.

Red lights flashed against the walls.

And the more they flashed, the more Jackson felt like someone spied on him through his eyes. Little embedded cameras taking in what he was seeing. His hearing, taking in sounds for someone else to hear.

And a taste of orange gelatin.

The tallest of the scientists pointed a boney finger at him. Jackson knew him the moment he saw the mole on his cheek and the upturn of his chin.

"Oscar Whiskey Tango Tango Alpha one," Jackson said.

Dr. Clive Bennett.

"Bravo Gold Lima Lima Charlie two. You.... You did it."

Jackson shook his head, and in the endless seconds that followed, he shook away the English and the baseball and the love for 80s music. The commune faded away. His father and mother, a distant memory.

Through the haze, a person who lied in wait began to emerge, Dubois Lavigne; a man who'd died in a freak plane crash along with Jackson Stone's wife. Polaris managed to save Dubois' heart, hoping to transfer his cells into a willing subject. Memories didn't live only in the brain.

The pills worked. Finally. They worked. And the gelatin.

Through cell memory and genetic augmentation, Dubois had lived in Jackson's body, unaware, asleep. Yet helping in reflex and pattern recognition.

All the details came into perfect focus, like pinpricks of light off the snow. The blood, bullets, and bodies. His hands, not his own. His flesh, younger, more vibrant. His muscles. His missing finger.

It worked.

"**M**on Dieu," Jackson said, his voice foreign.

"Are you aware of your surroundings?" Dr. Bennett asked in French.

"Yes."

Dr. Bennett gained a few pounds since the last time he'd seen him. Still the same Bennett, though. The same traitor as before.

Project Horizon had been a success. How much had Jackson Stone understood? Dubois had not only lived to see another day, but he'd also penetrated Hunter Flynn's nest. And now that he'd made it inside, his mission began.

But what about Alabama? Was she safe?

A few computers remained undamaged from the firefight, and when he looked at himself on the screen, he touched his face and stared into his American eyes. He picked up an MP5 submachine gun as those around him stared in disbelief.

"Is the disc here?" Dubois asked.

"Yes," Dr. Bennett said. "It's secured in on the other side

of this base. The Americans have surely recovered it by now."

"It must be destroyed."

The lights flickered intermittently.

Putting his hands in his pockets, the doctor shook his head. "It's not possible. The disc's electronic countermeasures will stop electronics and keep it hidden from radar, and with its SCAR technology, it confuses satellites."

"It can be shot down with gunfire."

"Not anymore. There's no way to destroy it other than a nuclear weapon, and it will remotely disable those as well."

Dubois grabbed the doctor's arm and eyed the gathered scientists. He switched to English. "Get out! All of you! Surrender to the Americans. No weapons."

As they scrambled to leave, Dr. Bennett's gaze wandered to the scattered firearms. "I wasn't given a choice. Flynn holds my two granddaughters."

Dubois pulled him close. "You helped Hunter understand how to operate the disc, and you understand the spheres. He's used it to slaughter innocent civilians and tested it near a military base. What did he promise you in exchange?"

"I....I told you. He's holding my two granddaughters hostage."

The same Dr. Bennett. Dubois laid his hands on him and pulled him dangerously close, where he could tear his throat out. "If you lie to me again, Dr. Bennett, I will hurt you. Do you understand?"

The doctor nodded and coughed.

"What did he promise you?"

"Power."

"Good. You may prove useful to me." Dubois let go and straightened the doctor's jacket.

The doctor wiped a bead of sweat from his lip. "You're letting me live?"

Dubois moved to Captain Parker's station. The comm had taken rounds but still functioned. "What does he plan to do with the disc?"

Dr. Bennett pursed his lips. "First, he will prove it cannot be destroyed. That will send a message, particularly to the United States."

"Doesn't it belong to them?"

He bought his hand up to his mouth. "That's a difficult question to answer. They didn't create it, but it belongs to them."

"Explain."

"DARPA and American intelligence agencies have used UFOs to spread panic or to hide other activities. They're often used in psychological operations, and they've been quite successful. But this craft was special. It wasn't until we retrieved it from the Americans we understood why."

"Space Force is more than capable of handling threats."

"We've used the spheres to modify it. Nothing on the planet can stop it. You don't understand. The ship is powered by a sphere. Anyone who comes within five hundred yards of the craft is affected by it."

Dubois remembered the times when Stone was hit by waves of psychic energy. "It controls their minds?"

"It creates a kind of negative emotion field as if the programmer built an invisible barrier around them. Our best instruments have been unable to detect the field, but it's there. If a person stays too long in the field, feelings of anger, nausea, confusion, frustration, violence will overcome them. The disc has been modified to amplify the signal."

"My body remembers seeing four of the spheres. Two in

a jungle, one in a forest, and one in an abbey, though. That one was shot and blew to pieces. Are they all the same?"

"No." Dr. Bennett opened a folder on the computer screen and clicked on a playlist of .jpgs. The black and white images showed bacteria-sized nano-machines in different shapes. "These are what we use in medicine and espionage. They enter through the nose, ear, mouth, or bloodstream, and attach themselves to an organ, usually the liver or the pancreas. We're designing ways to push them through the blood-brain barrier, as well."

"I've seen this technology before. Polaris uses it often."

The doctor zoomed in on a pixel and enlarged it to full screen, but it was too blurry to make sense of the image.

"These are what the spheres are made of." He circled a cluster of shapes. "Atomic-level engineering and it interacts in a type of quantum field, distorting perception, and by doing so, changing the fabric of reality. We think."

"You think?"

"We're not one-hundred percent sure what they are, but we're gaining more knowledge about them by the day."

The image sharpened, and now he could see it. A gorgeous machine, a twisting spiral that took on more texture as it captivated his attention. Tiny gears, woven and interlaced with organic structures, growing and dying in perfect harmony.

Dr. Bennett pointed. "Ah, you see that? See what it did? The image knows we are looking at it and changed. It corrected itself. Never fails to surprise me. We call them Fibonacci Engines. If I take a screenshot of this image, save it, close it, and open it again, it will be blurry."

"And these Fibonacci Engines are what the spheres are made of?"

"Yes. Yes, indeed." Dr. Bennett smiled from ear to ear.

"Can you believe it? We didn't create them. It seems like someone has put them here for us to find. Each one is unique."

"Where does Flynn keep them?"

Dr. Bennett opened a minimap. "Here. Separate from each other in a vault."

"Who has access?" Dubois asked.

"Now, wait a second. You can't ask me to release them. You don't understand. No, please. You don't know what you're asking."

Dubois dragged Dr. Bennett to the security station. "Do it."

He scoured. "You don't want to do this, Dubois!" Looking side to side, he chewed his lip. "He keeps them in a vault for a reason."

How far had Flynn's research progressed? Had he discovered their language or a way to communicate with the spheres? If so, no way would Flynn tell Dr. Bennett anything. But if Flynn found a method, it would change the world forever. That's all Flynn ever wanted; to know if alien life existed.

And he wanted to be the one to tell us what they said.

"We've been through a lot, Dr. Bennett." Dubois pressed the cold steel barrel of his pistol under the doctor's jaw. "Remember the 2016 Climate Accords? Tehran? The attack at Sudan? Do you recall me saving you in the fire?"

"All of them."

Dubois pulled the gun back. "The spheres will reveal a part of human history the world isn't ready to understand. Polaris has been compartmentalizing the information about them at the highest levels, and I know Eclipse has done the same."

Each Director received partial information sprinkled

with convincing lies and bleak half-truths in case of leaks. Dubois wrote the lies himself.

One man was on track to know the awful truth, and before he could brief Director Hill, he died in a fiery plane crash. According to the reports, much of his body burned. But had it? Polaris had no choice but to attempt Project Horizon and resurrect him. He wasn't sure what happened to his remains if they existed at all. Sometimes, he'd dream of being alive, catching glimpses of Flynn and Eclipse and plots as evil as the Holocaust.

Bowing his head, Dr. Bennett rolled his shoulders and ran his fingers through his thin, gray hair. "I don't even know who you truly are, Agent Lavigne. For all I know, you've been trained to say these things."

Dubois grimaced. "You're still alive, aren't you? We've had this discussion before."

"You said Project Horizon would work but be impossible to prove."

Project Horizon. The experiment to bring forth consciousness via cellular memories. It shouldn't have worked. Memories resided in the brain, not the heart. But with Flynn's help, what was impossible became possible.

Dubois had been preparing himself, waiting to die in service to Polaris. By taking a special concoction of pills, he'd have insurance once his body was found and recovered by a Scorpion team.

Too bad Alabama had found out about the drugs. She wasn't one to give up on a good mystery, and when he caught her probing his computer, he altered enough ingredient data to make the pills lethal to anyone who tried to replicate what he'd achieved.

After Dubois grinned, he gazed deeply into Dr. Bennet's

eyes. "You once asked me a question: When do I get to work for the good guys?"

"I remember. I've never worked for the good guys."

"Do you want to?"

Dr. Bennett lifted his chin.

Dubois opened his arms. "Continue to stay close to Flynn. Report everything he does to me."

"Then what?"

"Then we save the world."

The power flickered as another explosion rocked the underwater base. How long until all the pathways were flooded or depressurized?

Holding his hand over the main control panel, Dr. Bennett gave him a solemn expression, one mixed with trepidation and regret. "This is my last warning. If I release them, they cannot be controlled. They will find your empath. She will be a beacon to them."

"That's why she's here. Can you guide me out of this place using this?" He pulled off the exfiltration sticker Cormac gave Jackson.

"GPS?"

"Yes."

The doctor splashed through a pool of blood, tore off a scientist's jacket, and brought back a micro badge. "Carry this. It will get you through most doors. I'll make sure you avoid engagements." He shook his head. "I owe you many times over, Dubois. I wouldn't do this for anyone else."

"Good."

"When Flynn finds out you're alive inside of this body, he will try to reproduce the experiment."

"I wouldn't recommend it," Dubois said. "Didn't Captain Parker tell the scientists they'd wake up in new bodies?"

"He lied."

Alabama pulled the tourniquet knot tight, her knee nothing more than bone fragments and shredded tissue. A glistening pool of her blood coated the floor. She held a graphics card from the computer and a pen, the only makeshift weapons she could muster. The vent stopped working, and the air smelled like saltwater and gunpowder.

The DNA scanner was fried on the inside, the vent too small to squeeze into.

"Stone! Do you copy?" It was all she could do to speak through the blistering agony.

"Stone?"

I refuse to bleed out in Flynn's office. There must be something.

She pounded on the door, taking her chances someone would hear. When someone opened the door, she'd drive the circuit board through their neck and jam the pen in their eye.

"Stone?"

Still nothing.

By all that's scientific and good at Polaris laboratories, let's hope R&D came through.

She pressed the emergency locater and it warmed her skin.

Static crackled in her mic.

"Wren...to your location...interference. Repeat,...location, over."

"Cormac! Cormac, do you copy?"

"En route. Stand by, Wren."

She winked in and out of consciousness, each heartbeat a hope for Cormac to arrive. She'd never run again, not unless Polaris could create a miracle. Her last mission. Here, stuck in Flynn's office and bleeding like a stuck pig. Gross. Not the injured part; the stuck pig. Why does anyone eat meat?

"Agent Wren, come in," Jackson said.

"Stone! You're alive! Did you destroy the disc?"

"Negative. What is your location?"

Negative? Why did he sound strange? Was he under duress?

"Stone, you must destroy the disc." Every breath, searing pain flared from the remainder of her knee, and she bit her tongue. "Flynn...is on his way to the hanger. Hurry."

Bang! Bang!

Gunshots outside the hall.

Jackson roared. "What is your location, Agent Wren?"

"Where you last saw me," she said, not willing to give away her location over the comm.

A hail of M4 gunfire erupted outside.

"En route." Then his connection died.

Someone bashed a rifle on the door, and a drill fired up.

"Breaching!"

American Special Forces. They'd kidnap her.

Killing them would cause a ripple effect in the Department of Defense. They'd take her thumb drive.

She pulled the pen forward. Maybe play dead until one got close. She heard four men, but there might be a dozen. The pen is mightier than the sword, right?

"The drill bit is giving out," a man with a Brooklyn accent said.

"Use our last patch."

The doorknob jiggled.

"Set."

"Stand back."

Alabama threw herself flat, keeping her busted knee from touching the ground.

The lock exploded in a flash of light. The door flung open, guns sweeping the room. American camouflage. Kevlar. Helmets with visors. Their protection offered no avenue for an attack.

Damn.

"Hands up!"

She sighed, giving him a dumb expression.

Small office. Four men, but two of them would watch the hall. That left the two inside.

"Hands up!"

She let the pen slide down her wrist as she raised her hands, dropping the circuit board. One bent and snatched it, and another began patting her down.

Age wasn't always a sign of experience. If it was, the soldier who stood staring at her was a thousand years old, the type of man who kills with a glare.

And as he drilled his gaze into her, she steeled her expression.

In the narrow confines of the office, the other two couldn't get a bead on her with their weapons. She tried to hide the pen, flicking it up into her fingers, but it slipped, dropping into her shirt.

"Identify yourself."

She shook her head. "No English."

The man searching her found the thumb drive, showed it to the officer, and pocketed it. "Intel secure, sir."

Pointing to the PC on the other side of the desk, the officer nodded. "Get the hard drive." He showed her the video card. "What's this?"

She blinked.

One of his men examined what remained of Flynn's computer. "Sir, it's destroyed."

An M4 fired a burst from down the hall.

A soldier gasped. "I'm hit!"

The man behind the desk veered toward her, reaching for a grenade.

Another burst.

Bullets pinging metal. The officer bumped into the soldier behind him, and she yanked her shirt loose and grasped the pen. The video card fell from the officer's grip as he pulled one of his men inside. The other was dead.

Someone down the hall shouted in French, "Grenade out!"

The officer pulled himself inside and slammed the door.

The grenade clanked outside.

Boom!

The explosion blasted the door off its hinges, and it whacked the officer's head. He stumbled back.

Next to her, American Special Forces sent a barrage of death, scolding-hot shell casings bouncing off her.

"Captain!"

The walls and floor quaked like the eruption at Mount

Vesuvius. Her bones hurt, her ears ready to burst from the sonic pressure.

A familiar hum resounded through the ground.

The men inside held their heads, screaming.

"My head!"

"Get out of my mind!"

"I see them coming through reality!"

Someone had activated the disc.

Everything hummed and shook, and her earbuds warmed as they blocked the signal.

The officer held a knife to his throat, his eyes rolling in the back of his head.

Alabama grabbed an M4. A squad member prepped a grenade, opening his mouth wide, his sneer evolving into a demonic grin. She fired, the bullet piercing his wrist. The explosive rolled safely under the desk. He rolled back.

When she tried to reach the door to escape, bone fragments cut into her swollen knee. Swearing, she focused the pain away. Survival. Focus.

Sporadic gunfire. *Rat-tat-tat-tat-tat.* Silence.

The officer drooled, the knife still in his grip. The other soldier with the bullet hole through his wrist mumbled.

She grabbed the thumb drive.

"Wren, entering room," Stone said, storming in weapon first. Who was speaking French? He rushed inside and kicked the weapons that littered the floor. Falling to his knees beside her, he brushed her hair from her face. "Let's get you out of here."

Dubois grinned and flexed. Jackson Stone's muscles bulged and carrying Alabama proved easier than expected. With Dr. Bennett's help unlocking and locking doors, a path to safety was created that lead to the surface via a rarely used service elevator. He breathed all of her in, remembering her scent.

I'm sorry I've hurt you, but some things are greater than love.

The elevator groaned on its way up, and the inside hummed and buzzed.

Her eyes closed. She might lose her leg.

You shot her, Hunter, but I'm not going to shoot you. I'm going to feed you to the dogs.

"Stay with me, Agent Wren. Cormac, be ready."

"Hovering over your position," Cormac said, "but I can't hold for long. The Black Hawk is rattling apart."

The ascent slowed to a stop, and the power blinked off.

"The elevator is stuck. Can you see the opening from where you are?"

"No. All jungle. Impossible to land."

"Find a way, Cormac."

Alabama's blood covered him, and her skin turned whiter with each passing breath. He'd lost her when he died on the plane. His love. She was his soulmate, a thing he didn't believe until he met her. The more he loved her, the more he stayed away.

And until now, he didn't know if he'd ever lay eyes on her again. The love of his life, the only woman who ever understood him, and the only woman who he'd give everything to protect.

Alabama winced. "Stone? I can't see."

"The power is out. We're in the elevator. I'm here. Cormac is right above us. Hang on."

"Where's the disc?" she asked.

"Shh. It's going to be okay."

"I'm dizzy."

"You've lost a lot of blood. Stay with me. I know it hurts, but we're almost out of here." Dubois clicked his frequency to Cormac. "What's your status?"

He waited for a moment and asked again without receiving an answer. The hum ceased, and the world stopped vibrating.

"It's stopped," she said.

"Either everyone on the island is dead or it's run out of power. Probably both."

Dr. Bennett didn't respond to his calls either. His comm unit's battery read ten percent, the power drained from the disc's sound weapon.

"Do you think you can put weight on your good leg?"

"I can try." She grunted. "If I brace myself."

Dubois bashed the ceiling with the butt of his rifle. "Close your eyes." He fired, blasting open a locked emergency hatch, and climbed on top of the elevator.

A small blue emergency light glowed softly, and now he

could finally see. When he looked up, the shaft disappeared into the darkness. He unloaded the M4, smacked the magazine against a steel pipe, and listened for the echo. At least sixty feet up. Way too high.

He ripped off his shirt and tied it around her arms. "I'm going to lift you, okay? Grab the edge, and I'll pull you up."

Dubois tested the elevator cables. "Cormac, respond."

Without gloves, he wouldn't make it up.

"Pull me up," she said.

He bent, grabbed the shirt wrapped around her arms, and pulled. Screaming, she found purchase on the sides of the elevator opening, and he helped her climb inside.

He untied his shirt and tied it around her leg. "You weigh less than you look."

"It's dark in here."

"Your sense of humor will keep you alive."

A crackle came through Dubois' ear. "Can you hear me?" Dr. Bennett asked.

"I can hear you. We're stuck in the elevator shaft."

She asked who it was silently, and he turned his back to her.

The doctor didn't respond for a while. And when he did, he seemed giddy, like he'd figured out his secret present beneath a Christmas tree. "The power is out all over the base, but I managed to secure emergency power. I did as you asked. Just as you asked. I opened the vaults. I'm happy, happy. They're free, now. Free to roam the earth."

Alabama clawed the walls. "Stone.... Help me."

"Goodbye, Dubois Lavigne."

The connection died. Battery zero percent.

"Stone, there's someone else here. I can hear their thoughts," she said. "I feel something. Do you feel it?"

Dubois' skin crawled, the hair on his arms stood up.

Keeping his eyes peeled, he moved closer to her and kept his M4 aimed at the square emergency hatch. He nudged her, but she didn't move. He felt for her neck. Her pulse beat weakly.

In the elevator, a light oscillated a stark blue. An ultrasonic squeal emanated from below, and it rose in pitch until it hit a note that sung a thousand praises. Lively subsonic hums and organic machine vibrations not meant for the human ear. Sounds penetrating the third dimension.

Dubois pressed his palms against his ears.

Thrum.

Thrum.

"It's getting closer," she said. "Can barely think."

It smelled like rain; it smelled like sugar; it smelled like rubber.

A metallic sphere hovered gently through the opening, its surface smooth and polished. Waves of coruscating green energy sparked between sonic pulses. What appeared to be worms rode under its shell, driving in straight lines and merging at ninety-degree angles.

Feral growling came from deep within the sphere, and it spun on its axis.

Dubois froze.

"Stone, it's alive. I can hear it think."

She reached to touch it, but he held her back. "Don't."

A green aura surrounded the sphere, and a narrow beam of luminance shot from the top of it and highlighted the elevator shaft. A long series of metallic clanking sounds echoed inside the object.

Holding his arm, she shook. "It's speaking with me. Hard to understand. It speaks in pictures."

Thrum.

Thrum.

She nodded and rolled her neck.

Moving in front of her, he stuck out his arms. "Stay behind me."

A bright flash blinded him momentarily, and when he could see again, he stood on the other side of the shaft. The sphere drew a laser over Alabama's body, pausing on her belly.

"Get out of the way." He reached to put his arm between the laser and her, but a kinetic force pinned him against the wall and shoved his bones. He flexed his neck, his veins ready to burst. "Let me go!"

The M4 flew out of his hands. The sphere's worms grew on the side of the sphere, forming a shifting blister. A focused incandescent light moved to the M4 and vanished.

The weapon lifted in the air and aimed at Dubois' face.

Click.

The magazine slid out, hovering, and the weapon flew apart and hung like a diagram. Rifle rounds popped out of the magazine and then the rounds became disassembled.

"Wren?" he asked, hoping for an answer.

His earbuds floated from his ears and the small devices broke into pieces too small to see.

A red beam continued down Alabama's body and stopped at her knee.

"It remembers me. It remembers me from the other spheres. Even the one that shattered in your arms." She sobbed. Then a smile. A frown. She closed her eyes, shivering, and grunted. "It has emotions. Too fast. I'm trying to understand them. They are fast. Hard to comprehend. They don't want us to remember them. We're not ready to hear them."

Dubois strained. "Try to remember. Explain the disc."

She wrapped her arms around herself. "They know. But there is another."

Holding her palm out to it, she took a deep breath and held it. "It was birthed by a larger sphere. I don't know how. It's trying to show me. I don't understand. There are more spheres and few larger spheres. They're curious. It wants to know why it's here. Look."

Black hair-sized filaments grew from the sphere and reached toward her. Backing away, she cried in pain and held her knee. They crept closer and attached to her face, puncturing her skin.

Tears dripped from her eyes, and she writhed and fought against an invisible enemy. "I'm scared."

Dubois pushed against the wall, but his strength was met with equal force. "Stop!"

Alabama rose from her feet a yard off the ground, her damaged knee held in place by a soft pink glow. The sphere's hum changed pitch.

"It's inside of me. I hear them. Oh my God."

"Let her go!"

A knee bone bloomed from the light, and muscles grew. Tendons reattached. Veins appeared, and her neck went limp as she fainted. She floated to the platform.

Flashes of green. A red light scanned his head.

Something in the background buzzed faintly. Dubois smelled the color pink and violet and they were perfectly unique, like the Turkish kabobs near the Eiffel Tower. He felt the power of a square root equation. A perfect creation. The Great Plan. Songs of every human culture uniting as one, their bonfires and vanities.

The sphere is communicating. Inside my mind. What should I say to it?

Voices spoke all at once, too many to count—like the

entire universe wanted to have a conversation with him. Eyes fell upon him, but they didn't want him to look at them.

Voices talked about his plane crash.

Dubois sat in First Class, holding a vodka cranberry. Nice boring flight. He'd forgotten to bring a book. It was better to think this way. Make decisions about Polaris. Would he be voted in as a director? Director Hill made promises he didn't always keep.

But if he could become a director, it wouldn't be long until he'd meet the right people and convince them to do the right thing, really the only thing. If Polaris didn't recover the necessary artifacts, everything they've tried to stop would come to fruition.

And then goodbye human race.

An attractive couple on the opposite aisle spoke about moving to a small town. That would be nice. She wasn't into it. Her mannerisms pinned her as a city girl, 100%.

Jackson Stone and his wife.

Boom!

The explosion.

Dubois' thoughts wiped away like ink erased on a whiteboard.

Then wordless conversations evolved with blurry images, an alien, large, almond-shaped eyes, violet irises, then a surreal reply. The visuals smeared like oil paints across alluring landscapes of flowers, ebony machines, and an amber atmosphere.

Was that a city off in the distance? Look! It's an alien city. Thousands of craft zoomed in and out of the ivory structures. Great statues stood as tall as mountains, their elegant faces with stern expressions, oddly human but not quite.

Cheekbones. Thick lips. Handsome. Pretty. And those eyes. Those beautiful, almond-shaped eyes.

Who are you?

When Dubois asked, he wasn't sure if he was asking himself the question or if he interrogated someone else...or some*thing*. Where was he again? Who was he again?

The sound of jet engines roared faintly. The overhead air tube blew down on him. He raised the window shutter and sipped his vodka cranberry.

Long, boring flight. Why did she have to find out about the pills? She's so nosey. And then the computer? Bad move on her part.

But if I become a director....

Wait, I'm not on the jet again. Stop what you're doing to me.

Dubois' world went black, and a thick fog consumed him.

In the mist, he could feel them stare at him, invisible behind machine shadows.

Who are you?

A singular voice solidified from the swirling miasma of feelings and thoughts racing through him.

We will not be fully seen. Your governments aren't ready. Only glimpses.

Vivid colors spewed into view. A mountain range spanned around him like a jagged wall, and a white outline perched on it like a thin layer of static snow. Where was the city? The craft?

I need your help.

Thrum.

Thrum.

Dubois opened his eyes. The sphere's green glow began to fade.

"Wake up," he said to Alabama. "Come on! Wake up!"

How much time had elapsed? His pulse raced, and he dared not move.

The sphere had spoken to him, hadn't it? Was he asleep? Wait, that had to be real, didn't it?

His M4 rifle and earbuds were in pieces, and the power didn't work. He was here to stop Hunter Flynn. The disc. Or was this the real mission? Who is Jackson Stone?

What was that orange taste in his mouth?

A complex aquamarine geometric grid covered the sphere's surface like neon netting, and it cut grooves into the surface. Acrid smoke billowed from the cracks. Clouds of sickly fumes filled the shaft, stinking like burning tires.

His skin glistened with sweat as another sphere emerged from the elevator and maneuvered inside the shaft.

"Agent Wren!"

But she wouldn't gain consciousness.

The force pinning him against the wall let go, and Dubois blitzed to Alabama and put himself in front of her.

The other sphere's coppery hue reflected the world in reverse and upside down.

The coppery sphere pulsed. Lights dimmed dull. Hundreds of shadowy wisps flickered from its surface.

"Agent Wren...."

Thrum.

Thrum.

"Agent Wren, wake up!"

Schlack. Thrum.

Veils of thick darkness shrouded them and then a light burst forth brighter than Creation and blinded Dubois, sending him reeling into oblivion.

"Wren! I love you!"

Darkness overcame him.

His chest hurt.

Then his heart.

Beating slowly.

Slowing.

Concentrating with a singular focus, he could only muster one question: *Are you here to help us?*

Did it understand? Here, there was nothing but the void, and he sensed neither an entity nor distinct intelligence. Was he alive? He'd pinch himself if he could.

The return message arrived.

No.

He could feel himself clutch his chest, but it didn't feel like his body.

What if he was left here?

Why did his heart pump so slowly?

So, so slowly.

Oh no.

Wait. Wait. Don't fix my heart. I'm not hurt. This was done on purpose.

Pressure built in his arms; his legs. His chest beat in rhythm with the angelic sounds, far away, inside the alien sphere, a prison without walls.

He reached out for Alabama. One more touch before the long sleep. But he could feel his sense of touch disappear, too.

Where will I go?

Thrum.

Thrum.

I go alone.

A bright flash. An explosion cracked apart the ceiling. Rocks, grass, and dirt showered Jackson and Alabama. He glimpsed a man rappelling down the elevator shaft, the moonlight making him a silhouette.

How did he get here? Jackson recalled the control room and a doctor. Shooting. The rest was a crimson haze. Combat stress. That must have been it.

Where's Flynn?

Alabama shook her head, the lines on her mouth deepening. Like a viper, she sprang, grabbed an M4, and closed an eye. "Freeze!"

"It's me, your pilot," Cormac said, his voice booming down the narrow shaft. "You don't want to shoot the guy who's going to pull your ass out of this situation, do you?"

She stared at her knee and smiled. "My knee!"

Jackson got a better look. "What happened?"

Jumping on it, she grinned. "Incredible." She ran over to the rope. "Cormac, you're here!"

"Of course." He dropped down with a thud. "The whole

island has gone mental. Special Forces started shooting at each other a few minutes ago. Thank God they're not even coming close to hitting one another. My Black Hawk started malfunctioning, but I put her down safely. You won't believe the kind of radio traffic I'm getting."

Where did all the blood inside the elevator come from? Why was his earbud on the ground? His bandage still held what remained of his finger, but the pain had gone away. Until he tried to move it.

Jackson pointed to her knee. "You were hurt?"

She shrugged. "Not sure what to say."

"Ahhh. Damn." Jackson pulled his hand close to him.

"Lose a finger?" Cormac asked. "Damn thing looks like raw hamburger."

Jackson peeled back the bandage and regretted it. *Looks like a half-eaten chicken wing, actually.* "Thanks a lot. Hurts like hell, too. Are you going to get us out of here or chat my ear off?"

Cormac kicked aside rifle parts. "I won't ask. Ready?"

Soon, they stood above the elevator shaft and were surrounded by thick jungle. Clouds rolled in from the east, but for now, the moon gave them enough light to see. Thank God for fresh air.

"I landed the heli a hundred yards this way." Cormac led them onward, chopping through the foliage with a machete.

Lightning flashed, and the wind picked up, cooling his skin. Off in the distance...was that a jet engine?

Boom!

Cormac ducked, and everyone lifted their chin to the sky. A massive disc hovered over the horizon, and a fireball blazed toward the ocean, the remnants of a fighter. Missiles streaked, aimed at the ship, only to explode harmlessly. A second later, dozens of detonations as the craft swatted away missiles and drones.

Jackson panned as creatures ran for cover. "Maybe getting in your helicopter isn't such a good idea."

"You got a better idea how to get off this island? Better yet, you mind telling me what that UFO is up there?" Cormac picked up his pace, carving through the jungle. "Are we talking *Independence Day* or *E.T.*?"

"It's our problem child," Alabama said.

"Any little green men aboard it?"

She sighed. "Little green men. What *Twilight Zone* episodes have you been watching?"

"I think I'm starring in one right now." Cormac looked up. "So, is it real?"

Jackson stepped over a clump of green brush. "As real as a heart attack." A heart attack. Why did his chest feel differently? As he dashed, he felt ten years younger. Hell, he could run ten miles. Twenty, even. Refreshing. Maybe the transplant was finally working as intended.

Sonic booms could be heard in the air, and the disc continued to rise unharmed and unabated.

It's massive, and there's no way inside it.

They broke into a clearing and boarded the helicopter.

"Weapons are on the rack if we need them. This might get a little bumpy. Let's hope no one shoots us down," Cormac said.

Helmets on and buckling in, Jackson turned to Alabama. "How are we going to blow that up?"

She pulled the belt straps and locked herself in. She gave a look of defeat. His gut twisted. There had to be a way. Kinetic weapons weren't working. Would the U.S. drop tungsten rods from on high on it?

Alabama pointed to her ear. "Dr. Bennett? I can barely hear you. Yes, go ahead."

That name sounds familiar. I've seen him before, haven't I? How did he get her frequency?

The rotors started to spin.

"I can't hear you. You have what?" Her mouth fell open. "We're on the way." She changed frequencies. "Cormac, head back to the elevator shaft. We're picking someone up."

"Roger that."

Dozens of drones sought out the saucer. Attack aircraft banked and fired off a ripping salvo of rounds. Missiles blew to pieces. As the clouds swept across the sky and concealed the moon, rain gushed and splattered against the Black Hawk. A lightning bolt met the ocean.

"What's going on?" Jackson asked.

She beamed. "The doctor has one of the spheres."

"How's that going to help us?"

The stars flashed, and the sky exploded with enough force to vaporize the clouds. A shock wave rippled off the disc. Vibrations shook the glass.

Alabama passed him a Glock and armed herself. "Satellite weapons. They're getting desperate. Look, Flynn is moving east, toward China. He gets there, this starts a world war, or worse. Then everything we tried to stop... starts." The disc moved in the direction she pointed.

Streaks of smoke. Bright flashes and sonic booms. Jet fighters. Were they Americans? As a fighter leveled out of a climb, the canopy popped, and a man parachuted out.

Jackson found Dr. Bennett waving at them below, and he carried a box large enough for one of the spheres to fit inside. A harness was lowered to him, and he cinched himself in it and was brought aboard. He took off the harness and grabbed a seat, shoved on a helmet that

Alabama handed him, and gave a sideways glance at the weapons rack.

"Where'd you get this?" she asked.

He cast his wary eyes to Jackson and arched a brow. "In Flynn's vault."

Cormac reached over and pressed a button. A voice came over a pair of speakers near his seat.

The woman over the speakers sounded as though she read a script. "All units be advised. All units be advised. Dragonfly wind. Repeat. Dragonfly wind. All units be advised."

Cormac hit the switch. "That's an evacuation order. If we don't leave now, we're cooked."

"We're not going anywhere until I get aboard that craft and kill Flynn," Jackson said.

"Agent Stone," Cormac said, "I can't stay. They're calling in a low-yield nuclear strike."

Jackson took the box from Dr. Bennett and handed it to Alabama. "Good luck," he said to her.

She glided her hand across the top. "Understood." Cracking the vacuumed-sealed case, she lifted it out. The chrome sphere crackled with energy and surged with neon power.

Jackson dimly recalled a voice or an experience he couldn't define, and as he snapped out of his trance, he noticed Dr. Bennett and Alabama holding the same look.

He grabbed the doctor's collar. "What are you doing? What is this?"

Dr. Bennett considered him for a moment. "Stone?"

Thumbing off the safety, he jammed a pistol into Dr. Bennett's ribs. "How do you know my name?"

"There's no time to explain." Dr. Bennett and Alabama exchanged looks. "Are you the empath?"

He couldn't be serious.

"I am. Tell us what to do," Alabama said.

The Black Hawk slanted to the side, its tail rotor facing the incoming storm. Power blinked on and off, and the sphere began humming.

"All units be advised. All units be advised. Dragonfly wind minus five. Repeat. Dragonfly wind minus five."

Alarms blared. Cormac fought with the controls. "Wren?!"

Hate brewed in Jackson, bubbling lethal ink. Flynn had to be stopped. Flynn would falter. Flynn would suffer.

Alabama shivered. "The sphere is communicating. It's angry." Her eyes filled with tears. "It wants to help us destroy the disc." She cringed. "I can't.... It's too powerful. Taking over my mind."

"Fight it," Dr. Bennett said. "It can telepathically communicate with the sphere aboard the disc."

She raised a fist, clenching her teeth. "Can't keep up."

The Black Hawk's interior fluttered sea-foam green, the luster from the sphere like a globe of gold.

Holding his seat, the doctor glared at her. "You must resist!"

Alabama howled and popped open her eyes. Only her whites showed.

A warning sounded again. "All units be advised. All units be advised. Dragonfly wind minus four. Repeat. Dragonfly wind minus four."

"I am leaving!" Cormac punctuated every word like it was his last.

The craft floated at a whale's pace.

Dr. Bennett pointed out of the window. "The disc has not recharged fully, yet. It is weakened. We still have time."

The helicopter blades stopped spinning, and they locked in mid-air.

Cormac peered over his shoulder. "The controls won't respond!"

Lights sparkled inside the chopper. The air twinkled, the dust motes seemingly alive in the glow of the sphere. Outside, the blackest of clouds rolled in and lightning stabbed into the ocean below.

"My God, it's in control."

The instrument panel smoked from an electrical fire. Jackson held his breath.

"Help me get this damn fire out!" Cormac pointed to a fire extinguisher.

A hum smothered Jackson's thoughts, and the chopper rocketed up toward the disc. The sphere's hum grated and clanged and roared death. As they catapulted straight for the craft, the sphere hovered behind the cabin.

The craft grew larger and larger in the window.

Cormac took his safety belt off and held on. "We're going to ram it. Everyone, grab a vest and bailout!"

The disc pulled away, yanking a trail of clouds in its wake. Like a bullet, the Black Hawk gave chase, parts breaking away as the structure groaned under the sudden acceleration. Rain pelted the glass.

Green bolts of energy zapped the parts of the helicopter. Welds separated. Bolts shot out and floated in the air.

Shaking to pieces, the Black Hawk's twin General Electric T700 turboshaft engines burst into crackling flames. Cranking metal slammed the top of the helicopter, and the main rotor broke free, spinning like a top into the ocean.

Dr. Bennett held on to this seat. "Stone! Quick! Grab the sphere!"

Don't be afraid.

"Hurry!"

He opened his hands.

Reached to touch it.

Ready to do whatever had to be done.

He could see the bones through his hands, his missing finger mangled from the gunshot.

I'll miss you Alabama. You were right about everything.

The Black Hawk exploded.

J ackson stumbled in the darkness, hitting a honeycombed wall. A carpeted hallway was curved on each side of him. Haunting echoes and poisonous whispers permeated him and crawled on his face. He batted them away, his reflexes slow. It was as if he'd been slumbering for years, his body somehow still firm. His skin had wrinkles.

Where was this place? It seemed familiar. And his clothes?

He wore a skin-tight rubber suit with Fibonacci spirals covering every surface. His hands were free. His finger. Where was the bandage?

Was there an explosion a second ago?

Okay, how did I get here?

A man dressed in Russian camouflage pants and a black t-shirt ambled toward him, a six-inch knife on his hip. He carried a tablet, swiping the screen when he saw Jackson.

"Sir, are you okay?" he asked.

"Fine." That was *not* his voice.

What the hell?

"Flynn is in the bridge, sir. He wanted to know when you'll be ready."

This man was the same one in Guayabo, wasn't he? The one laughing as he shot those people in the trailers? When he showed his teeth, Jackson was certain.

"Tell him I'll be right there."

The man turned on a heel and started in the opposite direction.

Jackson patted himself down for weapons and discovered a sidearm and a long knife. Perfect. He slid the blade out and flung it, burying it through the man's neck. Before he hit the floor, Jackson caught up to him and cranked the handle, severing his spine.

As he died, Jackson wiped the man's blood off his black shirt. "I hope you didn't think I forgot about you."

Around the bend, two other men in camo talked to each other near a white sliding door. "You don't mind if I borrow your knife, do you?" Jackson asked, taking the dead man's knife. "I didn't think so."

The other voice inside him urged him to seek vengeance. But whose voice was that?

With two knives, Jackson approached them.

The urge to kill boiled in him, an irrational rage he needed to explore. Not his rage. Someone else's.

"Mr. Lavigne," one said, acknowledging him and then gazing at the knives. "Sir, are you bleeding?"

"No. You are." Jackson stabbed them at the same time. Death blows.

How many others were here?

Only Flynn.

But how would he know that?

A metallic stud was embedded behind their ears like a tick. A communication system? They didn't carry keys or keycards, and when he stood in front of the door, it opened into a storage room filled with weapons and ammunition. Grenades. Machine guns. Body armor.

His tight bodysuit wouldn't hide Kevlar or much else.

He felt behind his ear and felt a stud.

Okay, something is off. My finger is healed. My skin isn't the same, and my muscle memory is different. There was an explosion. I was in a Black Hawk with someone. These men called me Mr. Lavigne.

Jackson touched his face. Leathery skin, but tight. As if it healed from third-degree burns. And healed well. Wrinkles. Thick hair. His body wasn't his own, but everything seemed real. He'd been aboard the craft for quite some time in this body, but was this a dream? A fantasy? The afterlife?

I can't break apart. Focus. However I got here, I'm here now. I know the details of this ship.

The spheres were located in the center of the disc and incorporated into the defense matrix, rendering the ship invulnerable.

He'd helped steal the craft from the Americans. A tough mission but worth it. They'd lost a dozen of their best men and women in the ensuing raid. Flynn had sat next to him in the MRAP as he drove aboard the disc. They'd done the impossible, all thanks to his leadership.

But that wasn't right. Jackson was there, too, on the other side of that combat. And with his old heart inside of Jackson. Jackson infiltrated the warehouse. Shooting the MWRAP in desperation. Throwing a grenade. Watching Wren kill American military forces and being disgusted.

How could he remember being in two places at once?

I'm Jackson. Remember that. I'm Agent Stone.

The body he was in, Dubois', had a new heart. Dubois' body had been through many hearts? Many transplantations? Many experiments? He understood this as if Dubois' body, Dubois' mind, was his own.

Or this was a nightmare. No. He'd died and gone to Hell. Check that. Hell would be worse.

He nodded to himself. It couldn't be possible, but he was in Dubois' body. He had to be. The *how* would have to come later.

Wait. I'm not speaking English to myself. I'm speaking French.

"Dubois, I need you up here. The Americans are calling in a nuclear strike," Flynn said. The message transmitted in his mind. No sound.

Jackson shook his head. *Well, he can't read my mind because if he did, he'd know I'm coming to kill him.*

"On my way." He grabbed a fragmentation grenade and slid it behind him in his belt.

His instincts guided him onward, the thirst to crush his best friend sharpening his awareness. But he didn't know Hunter Flynn.

How did I get here, and why am I older?

In his thoughts, an outside entity spoke to him. What was that? None of this made sense. Only his mission; kill Hunter Flynn. The voice tried again. No time to listen.

The doors to the bridge slid apart. A curved panel bore a series of sensors and Smartware holograms. The bridge sat three, and on a holographic graph, Flynn's mental state appeared as a steady sine wave.

Flynn spoke French and sat facing away from him. "Our power is climbing slowly. When the missile is in range and I zero in on it, the military will panic. Help me with the defense systems. Something is trying to jam us."

Jackson held both knives, his hands dripping red. An

easy strike. He wouldn't see it coming, and he'd be dead. *So, kill him. Kill him. What are you waiting for?*

Flynn moved his hands over a screen and typed over an angular hologram. "You're not mad about Wren, are you?"

"Why?" As soon as he asked him, he winced and squeezed the knife handles.

"Just making sure. You seemed upset."

A hologram displayed a countdown.

1:58

"Hey Dubois, sit down. It's not going to be easy."

Jackson twitched. His arm wouldn't rise, and he strained, throwing his willpower into a final act of violence. Raise the blade. Kill.

Both daggers slipped from his grasp and clanked on the metallic, honeycomb floor.

Flynn turned and saw them. "What the...." He stood and faced him. "What's this?"

"I've come to kill you."

"Have you now?"

1:31

Flynn picked up both knives and gave him one. The two men stood inches apart, and a snarl crept over Flynn's lips. He sneered, twisting the blade handle.

I have a knife. He's right here. I can end this. Why can't I move?

The stud behind his ear warmed, and a stinging sensation raged under his skin.

"Your implant might make that a bit difficult. Who's in that skull of yours?"

"Jackson Stone."

Pain flared behind his ear, searing into his flesh.

"Killing me changes nothing, my friend. It will only

hasten the demise. I'm here to give us a chance. To unite against them."

His arm twitched, the knife creeping toward Flynn's gut. "You bastard. You're going to kill us all!"

"If a few billion die to save the rest of us, then so be it. Someone must make that decision. The New World Order will enslave humanity. We must stop that."

Knees quaking, the blade moved a half-inch closer to home. The stud burrowed in his neck. "And the spheres? You're using an alien entity to kill us."

Locked in place, Flynn's jaw set. "The spheres are *not* entities. They are *the future*."

The stud burned a hole through Jackson's skin, and it bounced, glowing hot. He gave a quick thrust. Flynn parried. But the tip of the blade managed to rip a laceration into his belly.

Flynn lunged, arching his back. "You're persistent. I'll give you that." He mashed a red button. "Security to bridge."

"I'm afraid they might be a little dead." Jackson smashed his dagger's pommel on top of Flynn's hand, meeting bone.

1:01

Pressing his position, Jackson drove a fist into Flynn's ribs and fought to plunge his weapon into Flynn's back. Expelling air, Flynn went in for a kill strike to his heart, only to be met with an elbow.

Jackson sliced, missing Flynn's fingers. But he landed a simultaneous palm strike into Flynn's solar plexus.

0:49

Flynn caught his breath and put a hand over his wound. "A nuclear weapon is going to hit us in less than a minute!"

Jackson smiled. "Good." He shifted the knife from hand-to-hand, Flynn off-balance.

The two glared, sought a better position, and prepared

for the precise strike to end the fight. But as precious seconds ticked, Jackson countered Flynn's maneuvers but couldn't gain a decent position from which to attack.

0:34

Flynn planted a foot. "Someone has to make that decision, Stone."

"The people of the world will decide on *their* terms, Flynn, *not* yours."

Pulse racing, Jackson feinted a stab to Flynn's groin, and when he parried, he grabbed Flynn's wrist. But his hands were slick. Flynn grunted and put all his weight behind him. Jackson's dagger fell away, but he maintained his grip on Flynn's knife wrist.

Flynn headbutted Jackson square.

White.

Little stars rotating.

But he held on like a python.

When his vision cleared the timer hologram blinked red.

Flynn sat at the station, his fingers racing across the controls in desperation.

Jackson reached behind him and prepared to pull the grenade pin.

0:15

"You're going to kill us!" Flynn planted his feet into the back of a chair and shoved Jackson away. As he bent to pick up Jackson's knife, the ship began to ascend. Higher, up through the clouds, rising to the stars. To freedom.

0:09

Hunter furrowed his brow. "The craft will protect itself. The spheres won't let themselves be destroyed, Agent Stone! If we don't control the disc, they will. Then we all die! It's not too late, Stone!"

0:05

A guttural roar rumbled through the vessel. A million scattered voices and memories of a lost civilization, of things which humanity may never discover screamed.

Jackson finally dropped the grenade pin he'd pulled moments ago. "Mission first, mission last."

A fireball washed away from them, the flames licking along the sides of the helicopter but never entering inside. The Black Hawk yawed, and Alabama pulled a handle, releasing a yellow emergency raft.

"Bailout!" Cormac said.

Dr. Bennett reached for a pistol.

She shoved him hard, and the handgun clattered, crashing into a wall. He lost his balance and slipped out of the aircraft, screaming.

The sphere's bright glow faded. Jackson pulled back.

She could smell the salt water.

Cormac dove out.

"Jump," she said to Jackson.

"Together." Jackson grabbed her hand, and they leaped to their fate. Tucking her legs and arms together, she pierced the ocean, expelling air. The warm water filled with bubbles. Kicking, she swam to the surface, the raft a few seconds away. Electronics don't appreciate water. There went the flash drive.

Pieces of the flaming Black Hawk rained like falling stars.

Jackson popped up and sucked in a breath.

"Nothing like a good swim to keep things interesting," she said.

"I prefer the Aegean to the Pacific."

"Since when have you been to the Aegean sea?"

"Oh. Some guy on YouTube talked about the water there."

Cormac paddled the raft over to them, leaned out, and offered her a hand. "Nice dive. 9.8." A disheveled Dr. Bennet was already inside, forehead in his palms.

She smiled. "9.8? That's generous. Would that qualify me for the gold or silver?"

"Silver," Jackson said.

Dr. Bennett ripped Cormac's Glock from his holster. He wore an expression of solitude and regret, and slowly, he raised the barrel to his head. "Some people don't deserve second chances."

Jackson held up a wet hand. "Wait! Don't!"

Dr. Bennett closed his eyes, pulled the hammer back, and squeezed the trigger. And pulled it again. He winced.

Cormac yanked it from the old man's hands. "You forgot to turn off the safety."

"No! Kill me!"

Alabama and Jackson climbed into the raft.

Cormac pursed his lips and wouldn't stop shaking his head in disgust. "There's nothing so bad you can't be forgiven." He holstered his Glock. "Well, maybe there is. Pineapples on pizzas. Only savages do that."

Jackson rubbed his foot against Alabama's foot. Maybe a mistake? She didn't pull away.

Dr. Bennett sulked like he'd lost a winning lottery ticket.

Patting the doctor on the shoulder, Cormac said, "Don't worry, old man. If Polaris interrogates you, just tell them the truth. They can get a little rough if you piss them off. Trust me on that one."

Checking his watch, Jackson lifted his head, let his shoulders fall, and gave Alabama the most serious expression she'd seen in her life.

He flashed two fingers on his left hand, tapped his thumb on his opposite wrist, and stretched his hand five times.

Who taught him the Dubois' code?

Using her hands casually, she asked, *Dubois?*

Jackson put his hand on her knee, his caress sending shivers up her spine. Only her lover touched her that way. Only one man. Him.

A grin. He smiled and sang in French. *Tu oublieras / Les sourires, les regards / Qui parlaient d'éternité.*

"You will forget the smiles, the looks that spoke of eternity."

"Teach me French," Jackson said in French.

Tears rolled down her eyes, and she fought them with every ounce of her diminishing will. *God, let it be him. Somehow, please.* "Dubois?"

A bright flash in the sky. Intense heat.

She put her head between her legs and covered her ears. A wave as tall as a skyscraper grew.

"Everyone! Hang on!" Cormac paddled, straining against the force of the nuclear blast.

Jackson pulled away and blinked. "Agent Wren?" He braced himself when they surfed the wave.

Cormac guided the raft up the crest and rode it like a surfboard. "Hold on tight!"

Knuckles white as porcelain, Dr. Bennett prayed in Latin.

Two massive metallic half-moons emerged from the clouds. Clouds of black dust swarmed the outside, ravaging it like greedy beetles. Slowly, it began to disintegrate from the bottom up.

"The disc," Cormac said. "It's still intact!"

But the swarming black cloud wanted more, and it ate and chewed it.

"There will be nothing left of it when it touches the water," Dr. Bennett whispered. "It's gone. They're gone. We'll never know."

"The spheres?" she asked.

"Everything."

The swarm enlarged as it chewed through the hull and then nothing remained of it. Zipping in chaotic rhythm, the cloud pulled itself apart and disappeared in the gloom.

Seconds later, a Black Hawk flew over them, and a Scorpion team lowered rescue harnesses to them. Dr. Bennett went first and then Cormac.

She inched toward Jackson, feeling his warmth against her skin. Her knees met his as her chest pressed against him. Expression blank, he didn't move. Placing her back to the light, she moved slowly, bringing her face close.

"Meet me at Holly's on 5th Street five days from now at ten o'clock."

"I know where it is. I'll be there."

59

On that night, he wore black slacks, a long-sleeved shirt, and wasn't sure what to expect. What would they talk about? She was so private. The world seemed empty since the mission, a big giant galactic void.

After debriefing Director Hill and writing reports until his fingertips bled, he'd kept a low profile, thinking of her touch when he should have been working, her gorgeous red hair when he should have been sleeping, her hard and sensuous eyes when he should have been training.

What did she want? Should he have brought something to give her?

Thankfully, the new orange gelatin and cyan pills helped with his nightmares. Director Hill asked him not to talk to Agent Wren about his psychological tests or the medical scans. Not that he would. The doctors checked his heart, and he'd answered their strange questions. Director Hill scheduled him for another medical exam in a few days.

Holly's was an upscale bar where the rich socialites plotted the takeover of the world. The new owners gave it a makeover—Cyber Roman. It was starting to become a thing in the posh parts of town. People with too much money on their hands, obviously.

"Hey."

He turned. She dressed conservatively; a navy blue skirt, a black blouse, and flats. Her spiraling tresses flowed over her shoulders, and her makeup made her look more like a goddess than a model. Men and women gave her sideways glances as they walked past her and then sized Jackson up.

"Nice place," he said.

"My treat. You look nice."

"Thank you. You, too."

Statues of Roman gods marked the entrance, and marble pillars helped delineate different areas of the bar. Braziers burned oils, and the staff dressed in sultry Roman garb. She ordered a glass of Domaine Weinbach Gewürztraminer wine and watched him closely as he asked for a beer.

The bar's three levels offered something for everyone, but they opted for the balcony. Twenty tables stood outside, and Jackson and Alabama took their place at the wall overlooking the twinkling city.

He glided his hand over the cold gray stone. "Beautiful view."

She paused. "I come here after every mission."

"Do you know people here?"

"A few."

"It's my first time here, but I feel at home for some reason. Holly's is an interesting name for a place like this."

She sniffed her wine. "The owner's wife won't let him change the name." She leaned back against the stone, keeping an eye on the door. "It's been a while since I've had a partner survive a mission."

"You think we'll work together again?"

She shrugged. "If the mission calls for it." Sighing, she set the glass down and took a deep breath. "I have to ask you something."

"You can ask me anything you want, Alabama."

"Okay. Why did you sing that song to me on the raft?"

"I sang? Some of the mission is hazy. Doctors say it's combat amnesia."

They watched the city together, sharing the moment in silence. He could have stayed there forever.

"There's something I want to know," she said.

"What's that?"

"Close your eyes."

He drank the rest of his beer and set it down. "Um. Okay."

Time trickled. Was she going to give him something? He could smell her hair. But it wasn't Nicki's smell. This wasn't right. No, what he felt was a betrayal. But he wanted her, maybe just to talk to for a while on a Saturday night. Or spend a day with her at the shooting range.

Would Nicki be okay with it? Would he have to be alone for the rest of his life?

Alabama must have felt the energy between them. Didn't she? Maybe he could move on. Maybe. And maybe be with her somehow.

What was she doing?

When he opened his eyes, she was gone.

In her place, she'd left a French dictionary.

GET THE NEXT BOOK IN THE SERIES

Dove Sequence: A Jackson Stone Thriller

At bookstores and on Amazon now.

Made in the USA
Las Vegas, NV
19 October 2021